THE AN

Muriel Gray was born in Glasgow in 1958, is a BA honours graduate in graphic design and illustration of the Glasgow School of Art, and worked as a professional illustrator before joining the National Museum of Antiquities in Edinburgh as assistant head of design.

She then moved into broadcasting starting as a presenter on Channel 4's seminal music programme *The Tube*, presenting all five series alongside Jools Holland and the late Paula Yates, whilst still retaining her post at the museum.

A full-time career spanning more than three decades in the media followed, presenting many diverse flagship network radio and television programmes, including: *The Media Show*, *Frocks on The Box*, *Ride On*, *The Booker Prize Live*, *Start The Week*, *The John Peel Show*, *Bliss*, *The Munro Show*, *Art is Dead*, *Walkie Talkie*, *The Snow Show* and many others, as well as producing, directing, and then founding her own award-winning production company which grew into the largest in Scotland.

She became a bestselling novelist with the publication of her debut horror novel, *The Trickster*, in 1995, and this was followed by *Furnace* in 1998 and *The Ancient* in 2001, which Stephen King hailed as being 'scary and unputdownable'.

She is also known as a political opinion writer for *Time Out* magazine, *The Sunday Correspondent*, *The Sunday Mirror*, *Scotland on Sunday*, *The Sunday Herald*, and continues to contribute regularly to *The Guardian* and other publications. She has won several prizes for journalism including columnist of the year at the Scottish press awards.

Muriel is a former rector of Edinburgh University, still the only woman to have held this post, and has been awarded honorary degrees from the University of Abertay and Glasgow School of Art via Glasgow University. She is currently chair of the board of governors at Glasgow School of Art, the only woman to have held this post.

She lives in Glasgow with her husband and three children. Her greatest disappointment is that she has not yet been abducted by aliens.

MURIEL GRAY

The Ancient

HARPER
Voyager

Harper*Voyager*
An imprint of HarperCollins*Publishers*
1 London Bridge Street,
London SE1 9GF

www.harpervoyagerbooks.co.uk

This paperback edition 2015
1

First published by HarperCollins*Publishers* 2001

A catalogue record for this book
is available from the British Library

ISBN: 978-0-00-815826-2

Set in Ehrhardt by Born Group using Atomik ePublisher from Easypress

Find out more about HarperCollins and the environment at
www.harpercollins.co.uk/green

For
Hamish, Hector, Rowan and
Angus James Barbour, with love

Acknowledgements

Thanks to Captain Robert Paje for access to the CSK *Tribute*,
Jim Shields of the Clyde Port Authority, Nick Nairn, Bruce
Hyman, Michael Fishwick, Jane Johnson,
and most of all, Hamish.

1

In other circumstances, Eugenio might have given the rat a name. Rats, and the bold rats of this sun-baked slum more than most, were hard to capture. He might have kept it under a crate and thrown it pieces of food, simply to be its master, to control it, to confine it, the way his own life was determined by pinched-faced adults.

But this rat was to die. It was their sacrifice, and as such, it needed no name.

The creature writhed and thrashed in the soiled canvas bag that Eugenio held out from his body. His two companions watched, eyes big in anticipation, waiting for their leader, their priest, to guide them.

As the oldest at nine years of age, Eugenio felt the weight of that responsibility: he moulded his face into an expression of suitable solemnity as he kicked at a piece of hardboard in the rubbish.

'Here.'

The two smaller boys glanced at him, then went to work, pulling the wood from the malodorous pile, farmers lifting a diseased crop from a toxic field. This slowly-shifting glacier of garbage was their home, their playground, their store cupboard. The fetor had long since ceased to make any impact on their senses, nor did the uniformity of its colour and texture, a mosaic of greys and primary hues, fill them with despair. They were the naturalized creatures of this place and the stained Nike T-shirts they wore ticked them with approval.

The board was extricated and positioned at the mute head-nodded directions of Eugenio the priest. He squinted at the sun to check its position and was satisfied.

Both boys knew what to do. The smaller took the awful thing, the thing none of them wanted to touch, from his plastic carrier bag and laid it carefully in the centre of this makeshift altar, while the other unsheathed the salvaged hunting knife.

Eugenio glanced at the doll, if anything so repugnant could be described as a doll. Its head was formed from the skull of rat, which had been stitched onto the leather body by means of a strap through the sockets, onto which two black orbs of cloudy stone had been glued to mimic eyes. Below it, tiny irregular tin teeth had been meticulously embedded into the yellowed bone, bestowing a manic grin upon the skull that was worse than the grimace of any corpse. It topped a grotesque torso, worn shiny leather that described a bulbous belly, gashed open and stitched back with the same loving craftsmanship as the head attachment. There was a cavity inside, open and ready to receive their sacrifice. It was ovoid like a recently-vacated womb, hardened and blackened from previous offerings, and the scabbed interior gave the slit womb an authenticity as though any baby's exit had been a bloody and fatal one. But if the figure was meant to be female, then the horrifically-oversized leather penis that hung obscenely between its legs was a strange contradiction. The arms and legs were thin, reptile-like, too long for the squat body; but the worse aspect of their fragility were the long, serrated shards of metal, like broken claws, that completed each limb.

Eugenio began to feel nervous. If his aunt discovered that he had taken this figure from her few possessions she would make him suffer. Her rage was always contained and deadly, and he swallowed at the idea of what she might do. But she would not know. The ceremony would be over in minutes and if successful, would grant him the power that would make even her spite mean-ingless. His greatest fear was that it wouldn't work. His knowledge was patchy, only a tiny portion of what his aunt and her clients discussed in their drugged ramblings. The rest he was going to invent. Somehow he felt sure that improvisation would suffice. The power of the ceremony after all, he had convinced himself, was in the intention, not the vocabulary.

Tiny as it was, it took all three of them to hold the rat down as Eugenio sliced through its filthy fur. It bared its teeth and piped its agony in a series of shrill screams that fascinated the boys as they worked. They heard rats fight all the time, but the piercing, high-pitched squeals that accompanied those scuffles, so high they operated on the very edge of human hearing, were quite unlike this. These protestations were guttural, having a power that defied the small lungs that expelled them, and secretly, Eugenio enjoyed the sound. He hated rats. They crawled on him at night, pissing on his blanket, boldly feeding on the scraps of food that were never cleaned from the hard-packed earthen floor of his family's shack. Now here was fitting revenge.

Delicately Eugenio sliced out the beating heart and pincered the ludicrously tiny organ between thumb and forefinger, quickly transferring it to the leather slit, poking it into place with a bloody finger and wiping his hand unconsciously on the side of his shorts.

Three pairs of eyes darted between each other's faces then closed in reverence.

Eugenio cleared his throat and began to speak with a curious mixture of the self-consciousness of a young boy, and the gravitas of a priest.

'Fallen One – whether male or female, at any rate commander of heat and reproduction, being one who even with his spittle can work sorcery – where art thou?'

He opened his eyes and looked at the now-still heart in its leather nest, but the figure's empty eye-sockets stared past him into space, oblivious to the gift in its belly. Eugenio closed his eyes again, this time screwing them tightly shut as though the effort would increase his potency.

'I shall be seen by thee, and thou wilt know me. Would that thou were not hidden from this son of thine. Eat of this sacrificed heart, and also of the one still beating in the body of thy servant.'

He stopped. This was as much as he had memorized from his aunt. From now on the quality of the prayer would plummet. He would have to make it up. His saliva dried, both from the tension of what he desired to happen, and the terror of looking a fool in front of his companions.

'I am ... no one. You ... thou ... are eternity. We want you to come to us ... and to give us power to ... do many things.'

One of the boys opened his eyes and looked across at his leader. The change in tone had not gone unnoticed. Eyes still closed tightly, Eugenio continued undaunted.

'Come to us now, as you have come to others before us. As you have come to the older ones before the Spanish came.'

He opened his eyes and saw that his entire congregation of two were now staring at him.

He stared back defiantly, then let his eyes drop to the useless, static doll, and the flat-furred husk of the rat, mottling the already-stained hardboard altar with its thick, poisonous blood.

A terrifying and powerful bellow broke the silence, and the three boys jumped in fright.

There was a brief moment of confusion, a moment in which they believed the Fallen One had answered them with that fearsome bestial noise, and then their inbred survival instincts processed the information and made them scatter like rats themselves. There was trouble approaching. But not of the supernatural kind. In seconds they had disappeared.

Their hurried departure knocked the altar at an angle, and the figure flopped over, slowly letting its tiny prize slither onto the wood and down into the trash.

The shout was repeated, but this time it was followed by a sharp laugh from another source. Scrabbling in the rubbish like a runner in sand dunes, a youth burst over the short horizon of plastic bottles, car tyres and old mattresses.

His face was contorted with fear, his mouth a black downward crescent of horror, as he stumbled across the unforgiving terrain like a drunk. Close behind came two men, running, but with less urgency, the broader of the two allowing a gun to dangle casually from his hand.

Anything could have tripped the runner; a piece of metal lying beneath the cartons and rotting vegetable matter; a rope tangled in the mesh of discarded chicken wire; a broken drawer from a chest protruding from the sea of trash like a dorsal fin. But it was actually the hardboard altar that snagged the pursued man's foot, and sent him slapping into the undulating mush with a soft, revolting thud.

His assailants slowed then approached him with party smiles, while the fallen youth stayed face-down in the trash, shoulders heaving, hands closing on discarded newspapers and coffee grounds.

There was no dialogue, no conferring or taunting. The man with the gun in his hand swivelled his limp wrist and shot the youth through the back of the head.

It was a gun without the benefit of a silencer. The sharp crack reverberated shamelessly through the still afternoon. Both men looked around like lions after a kill. Not afraid, nor guilty, but bored, indifferent, blank.

No resident of this filthy colony would come to investigate. No policemen would gallop to a chase. In this landscape they were the law. They had the gun. The smaller of the two men bent down and fumbled in the dead youth's jacket until he had retrieved the tightly-packed plastic envelope of white powder that had sentenced him to death.

Even then, there was no conversation, their companionship being the company of animals, dumb and cunning at the same time.

They turned to go, and as though some primitive electrical connection had been made in his brain to remind him of his last deed, the executioner turned back and spent one more bullet on the corpse.

This time the trajectory took it through the very top of the skull. He watched for a beat with satisfaction as the back of the head burst off and a dark black and grey mess oozed from the splintered head. Then he turned and followed his companion.

The leather doll lay on its side mere inches from the dead youth's head, its impassive features regarding the remains of the human like a satisfied lover. Eugenio's aunt would take her time in punishing the nephew who stole from her when she discovered that the doll had gone. It was old. Very old. She treasured it as nothing else, harbouring sick and atavistic fantasies about what it might do for her tragic life if she could unleash its rumoured power.

For Eugenio would not retrieve it.

Because as only the confused flies that had settled to sup on the viscous meal before them, and the blazing indifferent sun above witnessed, the impassive handstitched abomination began to shift slightly. Slowly and almost imperceptibly at first, its limbs began to be drawn down into the garbage. Not naturally, the way an object may shift and settle with gravity, but like prey caught by something unseen. In a matter of seconds the doll had drowned and was gone down into the trash – along with its still companion.

As the two figures, man and leather, sank beneath the fetid surface, it was only a matter of minutes before the burst video tapes and toilet paper, the mashed cloth and food remains, had joined once again to make a new skin over their secret and buried possession.

2

Just one short glimpse was all the dusty window afforded, but it was enough to confirm she was too late. Esther Mulholland wiped the glass with the flat of her hand, as if smearing more grime across the bus window would somehow make it not true. But it was true. The dock had revealed itself briefly between a low warehouse and some shanty huts and there, silhouetted against a glittering late-afternoon sea were four ships, none of them the one she had the ticket for.

She leant her head against the window and quickly removed it again as the bus dived into a pothole, shaking her bones and battering her forehead against the glass. The woman beside her, who had been nursing a fat, scabbed chicken on her lap for the entire journey, cackled and nodded a toothless grin at the bus in general as though it were somehow obeying her command. Esther had been watching her with fascination for the last five hours, amused as the wizened, squat old woman somehow anticipated the chicken before it shit, opening her legs at just the right time to let the startled beast squirt onto the floor beneath her.

The chicken, Esther reasoned in her most bored moments, must tense its muscles before taking a dump, allowing the woman who cupped it in her callused hands to feel its contortions and take action. But whereas this had been a charming diversion a hundred miles back in the stony monotony of the Peruvian countryside, now it was irritating her. The smell of the baking chicken shit on the floor and the musky reek of unwashed human flesh, which very much included her own, was making her stomach contents shift.

Unless that container ship was hiding, and it was unlikely that 150,000 tonnes of metal could achieve such a trick, then she was well and truly stranded.

It had sailed, and with it had gone her only means of getting home. It wasn't like Esther to be irresponsible. The diversion to the temple in Lacouz had cost her only five days, and she had calculated she would make it up on the journey back from Cuzco. And she would have done, had it not been for the curious, infuriating thing that had happened in the shanty town where she'd camped overnight to wait for the bus.

Esther had become aware, quite gradually, that a small Peruvian man, a peasant from the plateau, judging by his dress, had been following her all day, staring. He was there outside the tiny store where she bought mineral water and biscuits for the bus journey. He was there when she packed up her tent, standing a short distance away, his gaze unflinching. And he was there, gazing from the other side of the dirt road, when she sat in the shade at the side of the road, her back against a cool stone wall, waiting for the one and only weekly bus to Callao. She was used to being stared at by people the further she had strayed from the cities, but this was different. He was not looking at her with that naked and childlike curiosity natives have for foreigners. His was the stare of someone who was waiting for something. She'd tried waving, acknowledging his presence, but he'd merely continued to look. Esther had been getting freaked by it, and was glad to be leaving the town. But as she sat against that wall, she'd decided to meet his eyes and stare him out. All she remembered now was that his eyes had been slits as he screwed them up against the sun, and yet as she stared at him, she still felt the intensity of their scrutiny. She had felt her own eyes growing heavy, and that was simply all she could recall. When she'd woken up, her head slumped forward on her chest, her neck agonizingly cramped, the man was gone, and more importantly, so was the bus.

Her fury at her idiocy was incandescent, but pointless. There had been nothing for it but to wait it out for another week. And so here she was, seven days late, but at least she'd got here.

The optimistic part of her had thought that maybe the ship would be late leaving, that maybe the kind of luck a girl her age took for granted would hold out. But quite clearly it hadn't, and the truth was, she was stumped, stuck in the nightmarish industrial port of Callao with a non-refundable ticket for a ship that wouldn't be back this way for over a month.

Her fellow passenger opened her legs to let the chicken shit again, and Esther closed her eyes. Options. As long as you were alive, breathing, talking and walking, there were always options. She held that thought, but on her own chicken-free lap her hands made fists as if they knew better.

The bar didn't have a sign outside because it didn't have a name. It was housed in a metal shed that had once served as the offices of a coal-shipping merchant. Then it might have had desks, angle-poise lamps, piles of documents, calendars on the walls, fax machines and wastepaper bins. Now it was simply a shed. Running parallel to one wall was a long L-shaped wooden board nailed to metal trestle legs that created a crude barrier between the clients and a poverty-stricken gantry of a few greasy bottles of spirits and crates of unrefrigerated beer. On the wall a small portable TV was attached to a metal bracket. Its flickering images fought against the broad shafts of sunlight that filtered from high slits of windows, light that was made solid by the thick fog of cigarette smoke. A coat-hanger aerial stuck on with duct tape accounted for the snowy, hissing reception of the Brazilian game-show that was being watched by the occupants of the shed. Esther had time to take in these figures before they registered her quiet entrance, and it did nothing to lift her spirits.

About a dozen men slumped forward from the hip across the wooden bar, their positions so similar they could have been members of some obscure formation team. Each held a cigarette in one hand, the other cradling a drink, and their heads were uniformly tilted up to stare at the glow of the TV. The barman's position was in exactly the same aspect, but in mirror image. Even though his body was facing Esther, his head was twisted to watch the screen and he failed to notice her entering until the cheap double plywood door banged dramatically back on its hinges. But the pause had given her time to locate what she'd come in for, and without catching the man's eye Esther strode as purposefully across the room as her massive back-pack would allow to the wall-mounted telephone. There was only a one-hour time difference in Texas. She pictured exactly what Mort would be doing right now as she waited for the Lily Tomlin-impersonating AT&T woman to connect her.

Of course he would let the phone ring as long he could. His chair would be on its back two legs, leant against the wall of the trailer where he could monitor the residents of Selby Rise Park from the long window above his desk, and keep a doting eye on his ugly mutt tethered to a stake by the door as it barked at friend and foe alike. He would have a cheroot between his rough lips and a bottle of beer in his fist, and there was nothing on this earth that would make him take a call collect from Peru or anywhere else.

'No reply, caller.'

Esther scratched at the wall with a finger nail.

'He always takes a long time to answer. Can you give it a few more rings?'

The operator made no reply and Esther was about to hang up, assuming the call was terminated, but a few seconds later she heard the connection being made. It was weird hearing Mort's voice so far away, a voice that belonged in another world.

'Yeah?'

'AT&T. I have a call collect from Callao, Peru, from Esther Mulholland. Will you accept?'

'What?'

'I have a call collect ...'

'Yeah, yeah. I got the stingy bastard call collect bit, sweetheart. Where the fuck you say it's from again?'

There was a pause as the operator pondered whether to hang up on the profane recipient or not, and then she said curtly, 'Peru. South America.'

'No shit!'

Esther heard him chuckle.

'And it's Benny Mulholland's girl, you say? The one without the fuckin' dimes?'

'Will you accept the call?'

'Huh? Like all of a fuckin' sudden I'm an answerin' service for her old man? Tell her to send a fuckin' postcard.'

He hung up. The operator cleared her throat. 'I'm sorry, caller. The number will not accept.'

'I gathered. Thanks.'

Esther put the phone down gently. She had absolutely no idea why she'd made that call. Even if a miracle had happened and

Mort Lenholf had taken her call, what did she expect him to do? Benny would be blind drunk by now, asleep in the green armchair in front of a blaring TV. Mort could hammer on Benny's trailer door as long and hard as he liked but she knew it would take a sledge hammer to the kneecap even to make him stir. And the thought of her dad being able to help out in a situation like this was equally ludicrous. Benny Mulholland had probably just enough cash left from his welfare cheque to get ratted every night until the next one was due.

He wasn't exactly in a position to call American Express and have them wire his daughter a ticket home. She decided she had simply been homesick. Only for a moment, and only in a very abstract way, since home was ten types of shit and then ten more. But it had been an emotion profound enough to want to make contact, and now it left her feeling even more bereft than before. Despite having been to the most remote and inhospitable corners of Peru on everything from foot to mule, it was the first stirring of loneliness she'd felt in the whole three months of travelling.

Esther sighed and turned back into the room. The formation team of drinkers were now all looking her way. The men, although similar in posture, were varied in nationality. A handful were obviously Peruvian, their faces from the unchanged gene pool that could be seen quite clearly on thousand-year-old Inca, Aztec and Meso-American sculpture. Stevedores by the look of their coveralls, and not friendly.

There was a smattering of Filipinos and Chinese, some with epaulettes on stained nylon shirts that at least meant they were merchant crew and not dangerous. Only one face looked western, but it was such a familiar mess of mildly intoxicated self-pity mixed with latent anger that she looked away quickly in case she somehow ignited it. The barman was staring at her with naked hostility, but it was another kind of look in the assembled male company's eyes that was making her uncomfortable. Esther wished she wasn't wearing shorts. One of the Peruvians taking a very long look at her tanned, muscular legs said something that made his hunched companions snigger like schoolboys, and a flicker of indignant rage began to grow in Esther's belly. It was important to leave, so she lifted her pack and made for the door.

'He's pissed off on account you didn't buy a drink.'

It was an American voice coming from the western face. Esther stopped and faced him, but he had already turned to the TV again, his back to her.

'Who is?' asked Esther in a voice smaller than she would have liked.

'Prince Rameses the third. Who d'you figure?'

Esther stared at the back of his head until her silence made him turn again. He spoke without taking the cigarette from his mouth so that it swayed like a conductor's baton with every word.

'The barman, honey, that's who.'

'I guessed they don't serve women in here.'

He took the cigarette from his mouth, blew a cloud of smoke and squinted at her. 'They don't. Only liquor.'

Most of the men had joined this objectionable man in turning back to the TV, maybe thinking western man to western woman was a cultural bond too strong to break or maybe because they were simply bored with the task of making her uncomfortable.

Only a very drunk Filipino and a dull-eyed stevedore continued to stare. She was grateful for the shift in attention and it emboldened her.

'Uh-huh? Well maybe you can explain to him it's a shade up-market for me. Guess I'm not dressed smart enough.'

The man looked at her closely and this time it was with something approaching sympathy. Maybe he heard the slight break in her voice. Maybe he'd listened to her fruitless call home. Maybe neither of these. But it softened his face and the tiny glimmer of warmth in his bleary eyes relaxed a part of Esther that was gearing up for a fight.

'Shame. Looks like you could use a drink.'

He said it softly, almost as though he were talking to himself, and since the tone lacked any kind of lascivious or suggestive undercurrent, the words being nothing more than an acutely accurate observation, Esther inexplicably felt a lump of emotion welling at the back of her throat.

For no apparent reason, she wanted to cry, and at the same time, yes, her mouth was already moistening at the realization that a beer would be just about the most welcome thing in the world right now. She gulped back her curiously unwelcome emotion.

'They serve anything apart from paint stripper?'

The man smiled, then turned to the sullen barman and said something quietly. Reluctantly the man bent and Esther heard the unmistakable rubber thud of a concealed ice-box door being closed. A bottle of beer was placed on the wooden board, the cold glass misting in the heat.

Esther looked from the bottle to the American and back again, wrestling with the folly of continuing this uneasy relationship.

What was she afraid of? In the last three months she had travelled and slept under the stars with a band of near-silent alpaca shepherds, walked alone for weeks in the mountains, and resisted the advances of two nightmarish Australian archaeologists.

She had stood on the edge of the world, as awed and terrified by the green desert of jungle that stretched eastwards to seeming infinity as the Incas who had halted the progress of their empire at almost the same spot had been. A dipso American merchant seaman and a few ground-down working men were not going to cause her trouble, even if they wanted to, which judging by their renewed attention to the Brazilian game-show host now hooking his arm round what looked like a Vegas showgirl, was not high in their priorities.

She walked forward, touched the bottle lightly with her fingers and gave the barman a look that enquired how much she owed him.

'On me,' said her self-appointed host.

Before she could protest and pretend that she would consider it improper, the man behaved outstandingly properly and offered his right hand as though she were a visiting college inspector and he the principal.

'Matthew Cotton. Enriched to hear my native tongue.'

Esther studied him for a beat then took the hand. 'Esther Mulholland.' She removed her hand and touched the bottle again. 'Thanks.'

The beer was delicious. She took two long swallows, closing her eyes as the freezing, bitter liquid fizzed at the back of her dry throat.

'They write up Pedro's joint in some back-packers' guide, or did you just get lost?'

Esther wiped her mouth with the sleeve of her sweatshirt. 'The guys at the dock gate said this was the only phone.'

Matthew Cotton nodded through another cloud of smoke. 'Yeah. Guess it is.'

'Nice,' said Esther, gesturing to the room in general with her bottle.

'It's also the only bar.'

Esther took another swallow, watching him as he shrugged to qualify his statement. 'You off a boat?'

Matthew nodded. '*Lysicrates*. That pile of shit they're loading.'

'Just a long shot, but has the *Valiant Ellanda* been in?'

Matthew looked up at her with mild surprise. 'You some kind of cargo boat fanatic?'

'Cargo boat passenger whose boat looks like having sailed.'

Matthew raised an interested eyebrow, then turned his glass round in a big hand as he thought. '*Valiant Ellanda*. Container ship. Right? Big mother.'

Esther nodded, enthusiastically.

'Sailed last week.'

Esther nodded again weakly.

'Then guess you got a little time to kill.'

'I wish. Due back at college in ten days.'

'They'll live.'

Esther looked at the bar. 'I'm military. Scholarship.'

'Yeah?'

'Yeah.'

Matthew was looking at her more closely now, continuing to study her face as he drained the last of some yellowish spirit that had filled his glass. Without even looking at the barman, he gestured with the empty vessel and it was filled nearly to the brim. Esther looked away, reminded of Benny and the tiny, unpleasant ritualistic mannerisms that all alcoholics shared.

'What they do then, if you're late? Shoot you?'

'Put it this way: military students don't get a lot of slack to dress up in tie-dye vests and wave placards. And you sure as hell don't get to pick when you show up for semester.'

Matthew tipped the glass back and emptied half of it, baring his teeth in a snarl as the liquid drained down his throat.

'Bummer,' he croaked.

'You got that right.'

Matthew turned his head back up to the TV and leaned forward on his elbows. Esther waited to see if the conversation would be continued and when it was clear that it would not, she drained the rest of her beer and made ready to go. She picked up her pack.

'We sail for Texas. Two days' time.'

He spoke as though talking to the game-show host.

'Sorry?'

'Port Arthur.'

Esther's heart beat a little faster, then it slowed and sank.

'My ticket's non-refundable.'

'Aw, bullshit. Most companies say that stuff. They'll do a deal.'

Esther shook her head. 'Not with this ticket. Even the cheapest cargo ship ticket is way out of my reach. I'm only here 'cause a geek I dated at college has a dad who works for the shipping company. Man, to think I put up with that guy's bad breath and stinking taste in movies for at least two months to get that ticket.'

She paused and looked at the floor.

'And just on account of wanting to see some shitty old temple they've only just half dug out the grit, I've blown it. Big time.'

Matthew was still looking at the screen, but he was smiling. 'What'd he make you see?'

'*Waterworld*, for one.'

'Jesus.'

'Yeah.'

Matthew stared at the screen a little more, then looked at his wristwatch. 'Gimme an hour then come by the boat. Captain's pretty easy going.'

Esther put her pack down slowly. 'For real?'

'No risk to me, honey. He can only say no.'

'What rank are you?'

Matthew turned to her, a quite different look in his eye now, one that was difficult to read but undeniably harder than when he'd last looked at her. 'First officer.'

Esther cleared her throat, embarrassed, though not quite sure why. 'Right. Great.'

He looked back at the screen and Esther took the hint.

'An hour then.'

He made no reply.

She hooked the pack over her shoulder and made for the door. 'Thanks for the beer.'

'Sure.'

The plywood door banged shut again and although there was still an inch left in his glass, Matthew Cotton gestured to the barman. It was important to think ahead. After all, he would have drained that inch before the bottle was uncorked.

3

As the giant crane swung on its arc, the sun shining between the criss-crossed metal girders strobed across the deck of the MV *Lysicrates*, and bugged the tits off its first officer.

Matthew Cotton blinked against it as he leant heavily on the ship's taff rail and watched Esther's predicament with amusement. He was leaning heavily because he was only a few drinks away from the oblivion he'd been chasing since noon, and he watched with amusement because her ire was becoming comical.

'Give the greasy little sucker some cash,' he mouthed at her, then took another deep swallow from a can of thin South American beer.

As if she'd heard him from the unlikely distance of fifty yards, she turned her head and squinted up at the ship, gesturing violently again at the vessel to the undernourished harbour security guard, who was no longer even looking at her. The guard flicked his hand dismissively in her direction as though warding off a fly, and shifted his weight from one bony leg to the other. She towered above this little man, and perhaps if he hadn't sported an ancient gun in a battered leather holster by his hip, she would simply have elbowed him out of the way and walked on.

That option not open to a woman with an instinct for survival, she was vigorously pursuing the only other one, which was to shout.

In a moment Matthew would rescue her, but for now he was using the time just to look. There hadn't been the time or space to examine her properly in the smoky little bar, but now he was in a position to study her without fear of spiky feminine reprisal.

She was too far off for him to take in close detail, but already he liked the suggestion of athleticism in her angry body, the way she was practically stamping her foot, and when she mashed an exasperated hand into her hair he imagined he could register its shine.

He smiled and wiped his mouth clean of the acrid beer foam; shifted a drinker's phlegm from his throat.

'Hey! Hector!' His shout made the diminutive man look up lazily. Though he couldn't make out her words, Matthew assumed she had been braying at the guard in English that merely increased in volume as understanding diminished. No matter what her circumstances were, and if he were honest he was so loaded now he could barely remember their conversation, she was just your average American back-packing kid. Shout down what you can't control. He raked around for his best Spanish.

'Let her aboard. She's a passenger.' He hesitated, then added for no reason other than mischief, 'A little something for the crew.'

The guard scratched at his balls and did nothing. Matthew waited. He knew these people. To react to anything immediately was a sign of defeat. Esther waited too, her eyes narrowed to slits in Matthew's direction.

The weary Peruvian hand motioned again, this time obliquely directing her towards the gangway, then the man squatted down and got busy picking his teeth, as though all along his objection had been that she was preventing him from performing this important task.

She took her time coming aboard, pulling on that enormous back-pack complete with tent, hanging tin mugs and water bottles, then walked slowly forward with the gait of someone used to carrying a large burden.

As she came closer Matthew noted the deep tan on the thighs that protruded from her patterned shorts, and the incongruously masculine muscles that made them move with grace under such weight.

He stayed where he was, but lifted his head to greet her as she negotiated the skinny drawbridge of wood that was suspended over the moat of Pacific Ocean below. 'They don't speak English too good, those guys,' he said with what he imagined was a boyish grin.

She stopped and rubbed at her scalp again. 'You cleared it then?'

Matthew squinted, uncomprehending.

'With the captain?'

He grinned, swaying slightly. 'Aw, yeah. Sure. Sure I did.'

She looked doubtful, and the sudden childlike anxiety that crossed her face, the expression of a disappointed kid, touched a nerve in the deep drunken miasma that was enveloping Matthew Cotton. He breathed quickly and sharply through his nose and tried to focus, tried harder to clear his brain.

'Straight up. He's cool. You get the owner's cabin. It's cunningly marked "owner's cabin" on D-deck. Through there, two floors up. Third on the right. Not locked.'

Her face lit with relief, then a more unpleasant emotion betrayed itself as her eyes strayed to the beer can in Matthew's fist. Pity.

'Listen. Thanks. I owe you.'

Matthew nodded, looking away to avoid her pitying eyes, and she walked towards the passenger block, the cups and pan clanking on her pack.

'By the way.'

He didn't look round. He didn't want to hear any addendum right now. Nor look back into the eyes of an attractive young girl who was finding a drunken older man sad.

'Matthew?'

She spoke his name so gently it broke his resolve and he turned.

'Huh?'

'I think you'll find that grammatically, "little something" in Spanish, when you refer to an object with contempt, uses the diminutive to emphasize the colloquialism.'

The *Lysicrates'* only passenger scanned the accommodation block and disappeared through the door from the poop deck.

Matthew watched the heavy metal lozenge long after it swung shut, then drained his beer, crushed the can and threw it into the water below.

Esther Mulholland liked to pee in the shower. When the water was perfect, the hot stream of urine that spiralled from leg to leg was without temperature. Visible, but not tangible, it joined her with the needles of water in a way that made her sigh with satisfaction. It had been so long since she had revelled in this ritual that the developed world thought so important, this rinsing of the body that separated them from the savages.

It felt like a return. She let the hot water batter her for at least ten minutes, opening her mouth to let it run in and out, then stepped from the tiny plastic tray into the hot cabin.

Esther put her hands on either side of the porthole and leant her forehead against the glass. The circular window looked out onto a serpentine collection of pipes, their paint peeling like a disease, and beyond them the port of Callao clanked and whined with industry.

So what if the ship was shitty, this was luck beyond her dreams. She knew it was irregular, probably illegal. Bulk carriers didn't usually take paying passengers, only the bigger ships, the ones full of officers' bored wives slowly drinking themselves to death on bleak industrial decks, armed with the civilized pretence that somehow every hour was cocktail hour. But if the drunken first officer and his malleable captain were happy to take her, she was ecstatic to accept. If it was against the law then, hell, it would be their heads on the block not hers.

And look what she got for free. The owner's cabin, with shower. A seventies homage to Formica, flowered curtains and hairy carpet tiles, a cell of privacy that gave her a whole four days before they docked in Texas to make sense of the hundreds of pages of scribbles she'd made in her tattered red notebook, and more importantly, translate the pile of Dictaphone tapes. She grabbed a thin towel stamped with some other ship's name, rubbed at her hair and sat down heavily on the foam sofa. This was going to get her a first. A big fat, fuck-off-I-told-you-I-could-do-it degree, the kind that only the lucky rich kids walked away with, regardless of what was between their ears. Right now she felt luckier than hell. She laid the excuse for a towel over her face and lay back with a smile.

Hold number three was still dripping from the high-pressure hoses that had bombarded its sides. Now it was ready to receive its cargo. The two massive iron doors were rolled back on rails to either side, and the water that dripped from the lip echoed as it fell thirty feet into the dark pit below.

Two Filipino ABSs leaning on the edge of the hold regarded the black-red interior impassively.

It was nothing more than an iron box, featureless except for a rusty spiral staircase winding its way up one wall, and scaling the other, a straight Australian ladder leading to the manhole that emerged on the deck. Soon both would be smothered under the hundreds of tonnes of loose trash that the crane was already spewing into holds one and two.

'Fuck me, Efren. Where'd this shit come from?'

The smaller of the two sailors looked round lazily at the voice, with just enough animation in his body to avoid the accusation of insubordination. He grinned, and sniffed the air as if it was full of wind-blown blossom.

'Come from Lima. Big pile. People live on it.'

Matthew Cotton felt like puking, helped of course by four double rum and Cokes, six shots of grappa and five beers; but mainly because the smell from the holds was so terrible.

'Yeah? Well guess it ain't a whole lot different to living in Queens.'

Though he hadn't the remotest idea what his senior officer was referring to, Efren Ramos stood on one leg, smiled through gapped teeth and nodded. Matthew could have sworn they were going back to Port Arthur empty, but of course the suits at Sonstar would rather piss on their own grandmothers than have one of their ships burn fuel without earning cash. If they were struggling for a decent load of ore then he guessed the trash made sense.

Matthew didn't give a shit. He was on his way back to his cabin to sleep this one off. Then he would get up in time for dinner and start work on a whole new stretch of drunkenness. That was what mattered. Keeping it topped up. Keeping it all nice and numb.

He turned with a flick of the hand that meant 'carry on' and walked unsteadily back to the accommodation block. The sun was getting low, but even so its heat was bothering him.

He wanted the shade of a cabin with the drapes pulled and the darkness of sleep, where for a few short hours nothing and nobody could reach him.

Darkness brought a sour breeze to the dock, and to the ship it brought a nightly invasion of mosquitoes that could not only locate every inch of exposed human skin, but even the fleshy parts of the countless rats that ran the length of their metal sea-going home.

Of course there were no rats on the *Lysicrates*. Every official form and inspection sheet signed and dated testified to that, claiming proudly that the ship was free from infestation. Indeed, that was what the circular metal plates ringing the top of the ropes were for, to stop the vermin boarding ship.

But there were rats. And on a ship this size, that meant there was plenty of room for them to carry on their daily, and right now, nightly, business.

The MV *Lysicrates* was 280 metres long, weighed a dead tonnage of 158,537, had nine holds and a crew of twenty-eight, all Filipino except for two.

Even in this bleak industrial Peruvian port, the three other ships that lay alongside her were doing so with considerably more dignity, for the *Lysicrates* transmitted an air of decay that was hard to prove in detail, but impossible to ignore in essence.

It was the feeling that everything that was necessary to keeping her working had been done so only up to the legal limit and not an inch beyond.

The paint was peeling only in places that didn't matter, the deck was not littered with hazardous material that constituted an offence, but neither was it particularly clean, and the hull was dulled with variegated horizontal stripes of algae that clearly were not planned to be dealt with as a priority.

Its depreciating appearance was not unusual in a working merchant fleet, particularly in this part of the world, but it was nevertheless an unsightly tub.

She had been lying in Callao for twelve days, which pleased the lower-ranking crew who had been taking the train daily to Lima, returning with a variety of cheap and unpleasant purchases they imagined might curry favour with loved ones back home.

But the turnaround time was unusual. The *Lysicrates* worked hard for her living. Of a fleet of ten ships, she was the eldest, and sailing as she was under a Monrovian flag of convenience, she was hardly the most prestigious. The dubious registration meant that the company could avoid practically every shipping regulation in the book, and by and large, it did. While she was still afloat, the ship's task was to sail loaded, as often and as quickly as she could, so the fortnight's holiday in port was not normally on the agenda. But no one was complaining. And no one seemed to mind that the captain had spent an unusual length of the time ashore. All anyone cared about was that the holds were filling up and it was time to go.

Just as Leonardo Becko, the cook, was putting the last touches to a dinner of steak and fries, the door of the last hold of the *Lysicrates* was rolling closed with a rumble.

That would mean it was only a matter of hours, and the crew were already milling around above and below deck, making the comfortable and familiar preparations to ensure the constant uncertainty of the sea would once more be under their control.

As they did so, the cargo in hold two shifted its bulk as the strip of daylight that moulded its rotting undulations narrowed steadily with the closing door, and the two massive metal plates met, enfolding it in darkness.

What air remained in the three to four foot gap between trash and steel seemed to sigh as the finality of the doors being secured subtly shifted the pressure. And then the broth of waste that was as solid as it was liquid was alone in the dark. Locked in. Silent. Content with its own decay.

In the officers' messroom, Captain Lloyd Skinner was already at his table, pouring himself a glass of water, when he caught sight of his female passenger walking past the open door.

'Miss ... eh ...?'

Her figure moved backwards into the door frame. Esther had changed into a cotton shirt and jeans, and with her deeply tanned flesh scrubbed she radiated a health that was out of place in the atmosphere of mundane industrial toil.

'Hi? Mulholland. Esther Mulholland.'

The man cleared his throat, and smiled. 'This is where you eat.'

She looked down the corridor, to the open door of the crew's mess hall where she'd planned on eating, already accommodating five silent Filipinos, smoking and waiting patiently for their food. Esther returned the smile and walked into the room.

There were three round tables set for dinner, empty, their glasses and cutlery polished and waiting for diners. The Starsky-and-Hutch interior designer had been at work here too, adding plastic pot plants to the garish patterned fabrics, affording the room the atmosphere of a sad waiting area in a run-down clinic.

'Captain?' She held out her hand but didn't sit down, waiting to be asked. This was a different deal from the voyage out here. She had no passenger rights that normally elevated the ticket holder to the status of officers, only the good will of this man she'd never met, and Esther had an instinct for making herself worthy of good will when she needed to.

The man had an abstracted expression, his attention elsewhere. 'Eh, yes. Lloyd Skinner.'

He took her hand without rising, shook it limply, moved the book he had been reading to one side as though it were in her way, then motioned in general to the three ugly plastic padded chairs beside him like a reluctant furniture salesman.

Skinner, she reckoned, looked to be in his late forties, perhaps even early fifties, but in direct contrast to his soak of a first mate he was in such good shape it was hard to tell. Whereas Matthew Cotton was probably only scraping the ceiling of his thirties, his hair had greyed prematurely, and his face was lined, brutalized, the flesh sucked from the bones by abuse, leaving him with the mask of a much older man. Skinner glowed with health. Sandy hair topped an oval golden-brown face with distracted blue eyes and a mouth that was perhaps a little on the thin side. He was powerfully built, and the arms that emerged from his short-sleeved shirt indicated that his body hadn't always been behind a desk.

Esther gave an internal sigh of relief that at least the man in charge of this decidedly shabby tub seemed to be halfway human. She sat down happily.

'I really want to thank you, Captain Skinner. I mean, this is way past kindness and out the other side.'

The man coughed into his fist while looking beyond her at the open door, then at the plastic plants.

'No problem. These, eh, tickets, are pretty flexible.' He gestured vacantly into the air and continued. 'Merchant ships change their schedules all the time.'

Esther's heart started to barnacle with lead.

'Didn't your first officer mention mine was non-refundable?'

'Oh, we'll sort it.'

'No. I mean really. It's a grace-and-favour ticket.'

The captain looked at her properly for the first time, and there seemed to be something akin to alarm behind his eyes. 'You have family in the shipping line?'

Esther thought about Gerald McKenzie. Thought about his clammy hands on her breasts and his awful breath in her ear. Thought about him guffawing in the darkness of the theatre at the pathetic overwrought antics of Jim Carrey, his wet mouth full of popcorn. She gulped back a combination of revulsion and shame at how she'd used him, and like so many boys before, hadn't let him use her like he'd planned.

'No. No. It's a friend's father. He works for Croydelle.'

Skinner ran a hand over his jaw and neck and looked away again. 'Ah. Well ... whatever.'

There was an awkward silence, while Esther waited for some kind of confirmation that indeed everything would be all right, but was rewarded only by Captain Skinner looking down and touching his book absently as though he wished very badly to go back to it. She cleared her throat.

'So will that still be okay?'

'Mm? Oh yes. Yes. I'm sure. Your ticket. You can, eh, see the purser with it.'

He smiled weakly, then looked to a figure hovering by the door to the galley, more to avoid the awkwardness of this conversation, thought Esther, than out of an eagerness to be served. The glance, however, bore fruit.

A man in a stained white waiter's jacket approached the table, handed them both a menu encased in a thick red plastic folder like that of a cheap diner, then disappeared again. Skinner straightened his arms and regarded the menu as though it were the printed fare of a state banquet.

Esther looked at the intent on his face and quickly reviewed her first impression. She ought to have guessed that no ordinary captain would employ such a drunk for his first in command, but the level of this man's dismissive distraction seemed out of character for a man in charge of a large ship and sizeable crew.

The captain on the *Valiant Ellanda* had been a straightforward industrial boss, friendly, but very much in charge, his officers a reasonable selection of men doing their jobs and enjoying the limited social life at the end of their watches. That journey had been uneventful, the company boring, but the atmosphere comforting. This was disquieting. Esther glanced down at the paperback on the table, desperate to start a conversation that would at least engage him before he changed his mind about her free passage. She expected a Wilbur Smith or worse, the standard fodder of bored sailors, but what she saw shocked her, immediately halting the small-talk possibilities her brain was already preparing. He was reading an English translation of the Koran.

Esther looked from the book to the man and back again.

'Are you Muslim, Captain Skinner?'

He looked at her for a moment as though she were mad, then blinked down at the book placing the thick menu gently alongside it. 'Hmm? Ah. Ha ha. Good gracious no.' He lifted the volume and looked at it as if for the first time. 'Just working my way through the religions of the world.'

A small Filipino man entered the room, nodded to them both, showing no surprise at all at Esther's presence, then sat down at another table and took out a book of his own.

'Really? Some task,' said Esther, quite genuinely intrigued and not a little impressed. She tried to force his eye contact back to her again by touching the book lightly. 'You're interested in theology then?'

Captain Skinner looked over at the officer engrossed in his own less contentious volume, a Filipino translation of some ancient Tom Clancy, then gazed absently again at the plastic pot plant.

'Interested in the uniform stupidity of mankind.' He looked back round at Esther coolly. 'No offence of course, Miss Mulholland. If you're religious yourself.'

She shook her head slowly.

'Not at all.'

'Then you might take my point.'

'It's certainly one view of spirituality.'

He smiled benignly as though they had been discussing the weather, then folded his hands neatly on the menu in front of him.

As the three expectant diners sat in a tense silence the Filipino man at the next table was joined by one other, and as if on cue the waiter appeared again, handed them both menus and shuffled to the captain's table to take orders.

Esther endured the first course – some green wheatfloured soup – in miserable silence, listening to the two other men talking softly in their own language, occasionally laughing and nodding, enjoying an easy companionship. When the leathery steaks came and it became clear that her fellow diner had no intention of speaking, she decided it was too much. She was going to try again.

'So where you from then, Captain?'

Skinner looked up as if he'd just noticed her. 'Denver originally. Florida now.'

Esther beamed. 'Gee. That's a change and a half.'

He returned her smile without warmth, but the prompt seemed to work. 'And you?'

'Scranton PA, originally. Texas now. So guess I'm not one to talk.'

'Ah. Hence no southern drawl,' he said without interest through a mouth of fries.

'Why I do declare I can manage when I try,' said Esther in her best Pam Ewing.

Skinner ignored the burlesque but looked at her with renewed interest. 'And you do what exactly there?'

Esther moved her food around a little with the fork to mask embarrassment at her failed entertainment. 'College. Last year majoring in anthropology. This was my dissertation field trip.'

Genuine curiosity, the first she had noticed since their meeting, lit behind Skinner's eyes. 'Interesting. What do you hope to do with such a thing when you graduate?'

'Well it's a military scholarship. So I guess during the seven years of active service I'll owe them after I qualify, at least I'll understand people and their diversities of culture before I kill them.'

Skinner looked at her for a moment in stunned silence, then he put his big hands down on the table, threw his head back and laughed.

Surprised, but delighted at the reaction to such a feeble joke, Esther watched his face then joined in his mirth.

'I guess we're a lot alike, Miss Mulholland.'

And that was the last thing he said to her before he finished the remainder of his meal in cheerful silence, leaving her alone at the table to contemplate exactly how that similarity might manifest itself.

4

No matter what time of day or night it was, the accommodation block of the *Lysicrates* always housed someone asleep. Different shifts and watches meant the crew made their own day and night, and there was an understanding about noise and privacy that was delicately observed in the way that people living at such close quarters are forced to do. There were currently four bodies lying in their respective cabins.

The first officer was unconscious on his foam sofa, a crushed beer can held to his chest like a teddy bear. The second engineer was fast asleep in a neatly-made bed dreaming of his wife, and the sixteen-year-old deck cadet, the youngest of the crew, was snoring loudly on his back in a top bunk after having masturbated over a not-particularly-explicit porn magazine the cook had brought him back from Lima.

But although it was his turn to sleep, and with only another legitimate hour and a half in which to do so, Fen Sahg, a greaser and fireman, was wide awake. He had turned his back on the cabin in an attempt to avoid looking at the gaudy idols and 3-D posters his cabin mate Tenghis had fixed to every surface he could morally call his own. Even though he was staring fixedly at the white painted metal of the cabin wall, the image of Tenghis's plaster Virgin Mary, her head inclined in pity, her white arms outstretched as though for his soul alone, was burnt into the back of his eyes. He knew the man only did it to rile him. They were both Catholics by upbringing of course, but Tenghis had taken exception to what he called Fen's 'wicked pagan superstitions', and believed it was his duty as a good Christian to bring him back into the fold. It was true he was superstitious, but only with good cause.

Tenghis's fears were hypocritical, since Fen knew only too well that Tenghis himself could have his moments too. They had both worried when two voyages ago the chief engineer brought his wife on the ship. Surely every sailor knew it was unlucky to have a lone woman on board. Two or three officers' wives, well maybe that was okay. But one alone? No. And look what had happened. The cook had nearly sliced his little finger clean off during that storm south of Panama. There was no doubt amongst the lower-ranking crew who had been responsible for that. No, superstition was not always baloney and old women's fears. But as to his wicked paganism, Tenghis was wrong too. To amuse his fellow crew members, Fen often held Saanti readings in the mess hall or his cabin, the method of prediction and revelation being an obscure Asian mixture of Tarot and ouiji. The Saanti showed him the truth of things, and he would be a fool not to pay heed. That didn't mean he too couldn't be a good Christian, and Tenghis's sulk after such an evening, which would sometimes last for days, punishing his cabin mate by saying his rosary loudly in bed at random times, was a gross insult. But tonight it was not Tenghis's irritating piety that was making him wakeful. It was thinking about the Peruvian stevedores.

Gossip in any port spread quickly, and Fen usually liked to help it along if it was juicy enough. So when there was a rumour that the stevedores were unhappy about the cargo of trash being loaded onto the *Lysicrates*, Fen was the first to make himself amenable to the gang chief to try and find out why. The chief was a small suspicious man from the country and it took a lot to befriend him, but since the ship had been lying here for so long, longer than any other vessel usually did, Fen managed by persistence to make the man take him into his confidence.

It certainly was an unusual load. The *Lysicrates* normally carried coal, iron ore or gravel, and even on other bulk carriers he'd sailed with he had never come across the bulk shipping of uncompacted domestic waste before.

And apparently he was not the only one to find it irregular, since there had been some kind of negotiation being carried on between the company and the dock authorities, which had caused the trash to have been sitting in a vast rotting pile in the dock's loading area for nearly a week while Captain Skinner sorted out a bill of lading.

The rumours had started after two days. There were complaints about rats and roaches of course, but when a prostitute that visited the docks on a nightly basis had gone missing after servicing two of her regulars in her temporary boudoir inside an empty container, talk started that it had something to do with the trash. Fen couldn't quite get from the man what he thought the connection was, but some names had come up, curiously none of them Spanish, but of a tongue he didn't recognize, and there was a whispered uneasiness amongst the men about something one of them had seen in the great and stinking pile.

In itself this was merely the normal superstitious nonsense of simple under-educated working men, of which Fen was one, but he was more intuitive than most, and could usually distinguish the nonsense from the genuine mystery. What was bothering him now was that as he had watched the trash being loaded from the vantage point of the deck, Fen could have sworn he had seen something.

Rats probably, he reasoned, but then in fifteen years at sea, years when he'd seen just about every trick the repulsive vermin could perform in everything from grain to cocoa bags, he'd never seen rats undulate under a pile of anything in quite the way this grab-load of refuse had moved. If it had been rats, then there had been a lot of them, and working together. Because the surface of the junk had pulsated in a way that made him break out in a sweat. The thought of the rodents, however logical an explanation, was not in itself a particularly comfortable one.

Beasts that size that could move with such ordered intent were not beasts he looked forward to sharing a voyage with. But if the movement was not caused by rats, then Fen wasn't entirely sure how he felt. A hot sensation had overwhelmed him as he'd witnessed the swift but substantial movement, and the unpleasant notion had swept across him that it was moving, revealing itself, for his benefit only.

Fen's only consolation was that he had been so horror-struck by the sensation that he had made himself watch the grab drop the pile from a height into hold number two, monitoring it carefully as it fell, and could see all the individual pieces that made up the pile clearly revealed. Nothing alive and writhing had made itself visible against the bleached South American sky. No heavy rats tumbled and squirmed in the air, and neither did anything else.

Still staring at the wall, he turned over in his mind whether that was a comfort or not. Maybe the truth was that he never really saw the movement in the first place, that the talk of the stevedores had primed him with nervous expectations that his superstitious mind obligingly furnished.

Or maybe it was a simple trick of the sunlight and the unpredictable movements of the huge crane.

Fen sighed and turned back over in his bunk to look reluctantly at Mary.

This was not going to be a lucky voyage. First the girl passenger Cotton had brought aboard, and now the worry about what he thought he had seen. If sleep evaded him much longer he would get up and consult the Saanti. Then he would know.

The holy Virgin glared at him reproachfully. He would stare at her fixedly for the remainder of his rest period, because regardless of what his logic wanted him to believe, in his heart he knew there had been something moving in that trash. And whatever it was, it was now on board.

Adjusting the hard hat which was tipping over his eyes, Captain Skinner finished his leisurely perambulation of the long cargo deck, one hand in his pocket and the other holding the thin paper on which the details of the cargo were scrawled. He could see the second officer and the bosun leaning together on the rail, smoking and watching the dock hands mill about aimlessly on the harbour edge below them as they waited for the *Lysicrates* to go, and he detoured his route to join them. Instantly the bosun stamped out his cigarette and adopted a posture of readiness. The second officer made an upward nod of greeting and continued to stare down at the harbour. Skinner leant beside the officer and smiled past the two men at the lights of the port.

'Reckon that's us, Felix.'

The bosun smiled, nodded and left. Renato Lhoon, the second officer, tapped some ash overboard and looked up at his captain.

'Chief Officer Cotton?' enquired Skinner into the night air.

'In cabin.'

'Ah.'

The two men watched a cat dart surreptitiously along the edge of a wooden shed, spurred faster by a piece of coal thrown by the bored stevedore waiting to untie the ship. Skinner looked at his wristwatch.

'Fifteen minutes.'

He smiled again at nothing in particular then left Lhoon to figure out what was required. It didn't take much figuring. The second officer sighed, flicked his cigarette over the edge, tucked an errant shirt-tail into his neat pants, and walked toward the door of the accommodation block.

The door opened onto C-deck, the living quarters of the crew's lower rank, and to advertise the fact, the hand rail outside each cabin sported a motley selection of garments ranging from socks to grimy T-shirts airing in the hot corridor.

An elevator served the decks from the bridge down nine floors to the propeller shaft in the engine room, but Lhoon decided that to stand and wait for it to chug and shudder to his command from wherever it happened to be, would give every passing cadet and ABS the opportunity to bend his ear on some gripe or other, and frankly right now, with the task of waking Cotton before him, it was the last thing he needed. He climbed the metal stairs without enthusiasm two floors to the officers' accommodation deck and walked slowly to the door of Cotton's cabin. As usual he tried the handle first, and as usual it was locked.

He coughed into his fist, then used it to bang the door twice. There was no reply. He banged again.

'Matthew? Come on.'

A groan from within gave strength to the next bout of hammering, which Lhoon kept up relentlessly until he heard the groggy voice again.

'Fuck off.'

'We go now, Matthew. Your watch.'

'Sail the fucker yourself, Renato.'

Lhoon started to bang with both fists now, and kept it up until the metallic snick of the lock being thrown rewarded his efforts. The small man stopped his assault on the door, turned the handle and entered. The cabin was in darkness save for the orange-and-white light of the deck filtering through the thin porthole curtain, and he flicked the switch behind the cabin door.

The lights of Matthew Cotton's cabin revealed that at least tonight Lhoon would not have to dress him. He was lying back on the sofa again, fully clad, his arms across his face as a shield against the sudden glare. As far as the officers' cabins were concerned, Cotton's was no different in design. One room with a seating area and coffee table, a bed riveted to the wall and a half-open door leading to a shower room with WC.

What marked his out as unusual would not be immediately apparent to a casual observer, but to any sailor it was glaringly obvious. Unlike every other cabin on board the ship Matthew Cotton's was the only one that was completely devoid of family photos. Even the youngest cadets, barely out of school, and the filthy and objectionable donkeyman whose mother would find him hard to love, had photos, framed or otherwise, of sweethearts and family adorning every possible personal space of their quarters. Nothing in Cotton's cabin revealed anything about who might occupy his most intimate thoughts or longings. Apart from a few piles of clothes and shoes that cluttered the floor, more than a few empty beer cans that filled the wastepaper bin or sat redundantly on the table top, nothing suggested there was any sign of a man living here, that this was a private space in which a man could recreate part of his shore world on board.

Lhoon stood with his hands on his hips above the recumbent figure and waited. 'You want to puke first?'

Matthew's voice was muffled behind his arm. 'Yeah.'

Lhoon waited some more, knowing that even the suggestion would spur his senior officer's guts into action. A moment later Matthew raised himself up from the sofa, stumbled slowly through to the shower room and bent to his work over the sink. The noise made the second officer catch the back of his throat and he swallowed and looked away.

'I wait or you done?'

'Done.'

Matthew ran the tap and stuck his head under it, and after a moment of recovery walked through to join his colleague for the routine escort up to the bridge, and for the duration of the short walk Lhoon let Matthew walk in front, a guard escorting his prisoner to the gallows.

Apart from the fax machine behind Matthew, droning as the weather report rolled through, and the ghostly, muffled voices on the radio that he had turned down to a dream-like volume, the bridge of the ship was quiet.

Before him, the hold deck looked almost glamorous, illuminated as it was by pinpricks of white light, and framed by glimpses of the white ocean foam the stern was pushing aside.

Matthew ran a rough hand over his face and sat down heavily on a chrome stool that wouldn't have been out of place in a New York bar. They were well clear of port now, and there was nothing to do for the next four hours except stare at the darkness ahead, and drink neat vodka from a china mug that declared 'Swinging London' on the side beneath a garish Union Jack.

He'd planned to be asleep again before the end of the watch, but that didn't matter, since Renato would come and check on him every twenty minutes and do anything that needed doing. But nothing would. He'd pointed the tub for home and that was it.

This was the worst watch for him, the long hours of darkness, with nothing, no distractions, no human company, no chores or excuses to think, to keep him safe from his own black interior.

He'd tried reading at first, but his mind wandered after the first two paragraphs, his eyes scanning the meaningless words as other images replaced the ones conjured by the invariably bad authors, and with considerably more impact. So now he just sat and stared. And of course, drank.

Tonight the vodka bottle was behind the row of chilli pepper plants that Renato grew in plastic pots along the starboard bridge window. It was only habit that made him hide it. Skinner didn't care and there was little need for deception, but it was an important part of the alcoholic's ritual to conceal, and ritual was all he had left. He drained his mug, walked to the plants, retrieved the bottle and poured another big one.

Matthew fingered one of the swelling fruits and smiled at Renato's dedication. A storeroom below groaning with fruit and vegetables, and yet the man lavished attention on these scrappy plants as though all their lives depended on it. The nurturing instinct. As strong in some men as it is in women. With the thought, a black ulcer threatened to burst in his heart and he turned quickly from the fruits, swallowing his vodka as he walked quickly back to the desk.

With a shaking hand he fumbled through the folder of paperwork. Something to do was what he needed. He'd pretend to be a first officer. At least until the demons receded. Read about the cargo. That would work. The part of him that was still alive had been intrigued that loose trash was being loaded. It was a cargo he'd never come across. Compacted metal, industrial waste, sure. But domestic loose trash from some city site? Never. It would be interesting to see where it came from and more importantly where it was going.

Matthew skimmed through the piles of paper recording every on-board banality from crew lists to duplicate galley receipts, but there was nothing. No bill of lading, no sheaves of inspection certificates from the port authorities, no formal company documents with tedious instructions and warnings.

He found some dog-eared cost and revenue sheets that had been used practically unchanged on the last three trips. They told the company, the shipping federation, the world, that the *Lysicrates* was going home empty as planned. The ship contained nothing but ballast water. He blinked down at the paper and then stupidly out the window to the silent deck.

Presumably Skinner hadn't finished doing whatever he did so privately in his office with all that paper before entering it in the log and the document folder, but it was unusual, and unlike the captain's usual form, very sloppy.

You could load anything from custard to cows at Callao if you greased the right palms, and from the eleven voyages he'd made so far with this company, Matthew had decided they were perhaps not amongst the most honourable of traders. Forever trying to dodge regulations they'd even lost a vessel five years ago with all hands, and had despicably argued about compensation to the families of the deceased for as long as they could, even though the insurance company had paid up in full. Shysters and crooks, and naturally the only ones who would employ someone like Cotton after his fall from grace, although Skinner, he admitted reluctantly to himself, had had more to do with his second chance than the avaricious gangsters who owned the ship. But if the company was pulling some kind of a fast one, what in God's name were they planning to do with the trash when they got to Port Arthur? For a few moments the slow, drunken brain of Matthew Cotton thought about it. He let himself think like a captain again, think about the nature of loose trash, of how it would sit in the hold, how it might shift in weather. Gradually, as his brain cleared more thinking-space, he thought of methane gas building up like a bomb in the sealed holds, and the consequences of that when the hot South American sun hit the deck from dawn and started to bake it like a desert stone. A tiny sliver of rage started to build in his chest. Tiny but insistent. If he could die he'd be dead a thousand times by now. Dying was too desirable, too good for Matthew Cotton. It was a release he didn't deserve. It wasn't up to the slimy suited bastards in the Hong Kong offices of a shipping company to change that.

He glanced at the weather fax again, which he'd already registered indicated nothing but fine weather. Then he picked up the phone and called down to B-deck.

A deck cadet answered in Filipino.

'Rapadas. Open all the hatch covers fifteen feet.'

The man didn't even reply, but several minutes later two men walked lazily into the white light of the deck and started working the hydraulics that would wind open the huge metal doors, slapping each other on the shoulder and continuing some animated conversation as they worked their way along. For a moment Matthew almost felt like an officer in charge. Someone who'd taken a responsible and intelligent action to prevent disaster.

But the moment was brief. Reality hit him and reminded him he was nothing higher than pond scum. He sank down again and drained his mug. The holds wouldn't blow. The ship and the crew would be safer now than they were twenty minutes ago.

Big fucking deal.

The sun would come up and go down. The earth would turn. Stars in space would die and be born. And nothing he ever did, good or bad for the rest of his life would make him anything other than a piece of shit. Swinging London tipped up and Matthew Cotton's eyes closed. His free hand made a tight claw on his thigh.

5

The fantasies of most ancient cultures almost always included one of walking on water. From Christianity through Mayan domestic legend, even into modern obsessions with surface-bound sports, the defiant, burnished skin of the ocean presents a challenge to man that is considerably deeper than the mere domination of nature.

As the early morning sun gave the Pacific a pale cream solidity, Esther felt she could run straight off the deck and onto that glittering rugged surface without puncturing it. However, a dull but well-meaning officer on the journey down to Callao had regularly and unbidden furnished Esther with sea-going statistics, and the revelation that the sea along the coast of Peru concealed a trench that was over twenty thousand feet deep had induced in her an immediate vertigo as she thought of the blackness yawning beneath her feet. Gazing out now at the innocent shining surface, she felt that same mix of fear and thrill again at the ocean's secret.

Maybe, she reasoned, that was why mankind always felt impelled to make instant contact with water the moment it was anywhere in his vicinity. The child on the beach who runs without fail to the sea, the adults who pull off their socks and shoes to paddle in the shallows, the fisherman who catches nothing but is satisfied with the contact of weighted line and water; all are reassuring themselves that what excites them about what they see, that beckoning seductive sheet of light, is as flimsy as net and as dangerous as fire.

If she could, Esther, too, would have made contact with a cool sea.

A swim after the punishing circuit she was pounding would have been delicious, but even if the boat were a pleasure yacht that drifted to let her bathe, she wouldn't care to swim thinking of the sunless chasm that lay beneath her. A cramped, steamy shower would do and with only four more laps of the cargo deck to go, even that was pretty damned attractive.

She needed to get back in shape, and although the mountain treks had been hard, nothing in her field trip had left time for the kind of physical programme she liked to stick to back home. Fifty-one laps of the deck, twenty of them with a stitch ripping her side apart, only confirmed that she had serious work to do, and as she sprinted for the bow it was with a sinking heart that she realized she would have to stop and let the pain subside.

Her trainers squealed on the metal as she slowed down and jogged to the edge of the last hold, whose open hatch protruded about six or seven feet beyond the lip of its fixings. Esther put out a hand and leant heavily against the metal, her head bowed to her waist, sweat dripping onto the deck between her feet.

Less than a minute passed before her heart rate had slowed to near normal, and she straightened up rubbing at the side that was still tight and sore. Despite the eternal thrumming of the engine vibrating through her body that was so constant and rhythmic it ceased to exist for most sailors only hours into any new voyage, the serenity was exquisite. The breaking water around the hull swished erratically and the light wind that toyed in her hair was no more than a whisper.

She leaned back against the hatch and looked out over the sea. Although the route was hugging the west coast of Peru, Ecuador and Colombia, they were far too many miles from land to view it. The sun had an uncluttered stage upon which to rise and it was doing so with unparalleled magnificence.

This was a lucky time. Esther had always divided her days since childhood into lucky and unlucky times.

When things were bad, unlucky bad, she knew that by waiting, the lucky bits would present themselves, and however brief they might be, she had learned to grab them and hold them tight. She'd started it at the age of eight as she stood over her mother's grave, Benny's whisky breath filling her nostrils as he clung to her little shoulder as a means of steadying himself rather than of comforting her. Her grief had been too profound to articulate, but she had felt her father's confused adult despair being transmitted to her through his curled fingers the way a plant carries chlorophyll, and as she had shaken free of his grasp she had looked around in desperation to see something beautiful, something distracting, something lucky.

A heavy-set woman in a pink organza hat was tending a grave beyond the untidy scrub in that cheap little Pennsylvanian graveyard, and as she bent a gust of wind blew it from her head and made her stumble after it in a way that was both grotesque and funny. Esther had looked around and noted that no one else had seen it but her. So that, she'd decided, had made it lucky. She could think of that instead of her Mom lying in the ground, and that would help get by the unlucky bit. It became habit, and here she was at the age of twenty-three still doing it in the most mundane of moments.

And yes, at this moment away from the decidedly ragged collection of shipmates, with the sun and the sea as her only companions, her passage home assured and her dissertation shaping up in her head with every mile, she had the right to feel lucky. Lucky, even though the trash in the hold was tainting the perfect scene a little now that she'd stopped, by randomly releasing its foul odour in small nauseating gusts.

Esther waved a hand over her face.

'Shit.'

She turned and looked to the hatch as though a stern glance would halt its emissions, but since its metal surface was at least three or four feet above her head, the culprit – the mountain of waste – was impossible to see.

Esther inclined her head back out to sea, then looked slowly back again, curious. A sheen on the edge of the metal hatch had caught her eye, and she stepped back to examine it. There was a trail emanating from the lid of the hatch above her head, running over the edge and then continuing along the deck below, as though whatever had left it had dropped the seven or eight feet and continued its progress. She rubbed at it with a toe. It had been dried hard by the sun exactly like the trail of a slug, but with the marked difference of being at least three feet wide instead of the innocent half inch you would curse at in your glasshouse, and when her trainer made contact it broke off in wafer-thin flakes.

Esther bent and looked more closely at it. Under the hardened flakes of slime there were other things sticking to the deck, things that were still slightly moist, streaks of effluent maybe, a trace of oil or tar, but worst of all a brown-red smear that looked almost like blood. Still crouched, she followed the trail on the deck, her hand shading her eyes from the sun, until, squinting, she could just make it out disappearing over the edge of the deck about twenty feet short of the accommodation block.

Esther stood up and wiped her foot unconsciously on the edge of the metal hatch runner. She shook her head. The only explanation could be that someone had pulled an unpleasant portion of the trash from its pile, dragged it nearly seven holds further up the deck and then tipped it into the sea. She knew she shouldn't look a gift horse in the mouth, but everything about this ship was making her long for the dull, reliable neat container ship she'd arrived on.

Most likely the trail was the residue of drunken behaviour, a bet, a forfeit or a prank, and the worst of it was that discipline was obviously so lax no one had bothered to come out and scrub away the evidence. This was a crew that needed its ass kicked.

The stitch healed, she bent forward and took two deep breaths, ready to finish the circuit. She straightened. For no reason other than that the unscrubbed trail of goo had irritated her, she had an overwhelming desire to peer into the hold to see exactly what they had been up to.

A quick glance up to the far-off windows of the bridge suggested that she was not about to be observed, and so with her hands on the guide rail of the hatch cover she hauled herself up to the edge of hold number two. There was a moment of feeling precarious, the action putting her higher than the ship's taff rail, and she paused to steady herself. When she had adjusted to the height she walked carefully forward to the fifteen-foot slit between the open hatch doors and crouched down at the edge. The smell nearly knocked her backwards and she covered her nose and mouth with one hand, leaning heavily on the other.

Ten or twelve feet below her, the pile of irregular and unidentifiable waste was illuminated by a slim strip of daylight, while the rest of the load skulked in darkness beneath the ledges of drawn hatch covers. It was an ugly cargo, and looking down into it gave Esther the creeps. The sea breeze seemed chillier up here, and she hunched her shoulders against it as she scanned the top of the waste to try and understand what someone might have been pulling free from it.

From the dark starboard portion of the pile came a movement. Her eyes flicked to it immediately, her breath caught in readiness.

She focused hard on where she thought she saw the subtle peripheral shifting and waited for it to happen again.

Her leg was grabbed in a vice-like grip below the knee, and before she could cry out Esther was dragged backwards.

'What the fuck do you think you're at?' It was a male voice.

Esther found herself on her back, her fists clenched ready to strike, blinking up at the figure silhouetted against the sky. Her panting breath slowed and she untensed her body enough to sit semi-erect and recognize the figure of Matthew Cotton.

'My God. You near made me shit myself.'

'Yeah?' It was said with aggression, not apology.

He offered her a hand to get up. She ignored it and sat forward instead. Matthew pointed to the deck. 'Get down. Right now.'

Esther looked at him sulkily and slowly stood, walked forward and lowered herself to the deck. Cotton dropped after her, dusting off his pants and never taking his eyes from her sullen face.

'You any idea how stupid that was?'

'Aw, come on.'

Matthew nodded vigorously as though she'd offered to start an alley fight. 'Okay, smartass. Let's just say we hit a swell there and you tipped in. You think you'd just land on it and step right out? Huh?'

Esther said nothing, but put her hands on her hips and stared out to sea.

But Matthew had no intention of stopping the lecture. 'Year and a half back, an ABS who decided to take a jaywalk across an open hold full of grain while the hatches were still open in port, fell in. Okay? Crew thought he'd jumped ship, done a runner, when he didn't show up for his watch. So they sailed, they thought, without him. Found his body at the bottom of the grain at the next port. Care to think about what drowning in raw, unhusked wheat must feel like? No? Well try thinking about how drowning in a big pile of shit might be for laughs, because believe me, honey, that's what would have happened to you if you'd gone ass over tit.'

Esther looked at him. He was genuinely angry, breathing hard, his eyes lit with indignant fire. She held up restraining hands. 'Yeah. Okay. Sorry.'

Matthew turned and looked out to sea himself now, as though trying to calm himself. 'Man, you shouldn't even be out here without a hard hat. It's a bulk carrier, not the QE fuckin' 2.'

Esther was getting annoyed. This, after all, was the drunk who could barely stand upright yesterday, and even though she was grateful he got her on board, he was hardly Captain Kirk.

'Yeah, well it doesn't look like "shipshape" means much out here anyhows.'

He snapped his glance back to her. 'Meaning?'

She pointed down at the hardened slime trail beneath his feet. 'I got curious as to what that was.'

Matthew looked down, and followed the trail with his eyes from hatch cover to ship's rail.

She watched the slow wit of the perpetual drunk try to work it out and fail, and pity returned. 'But I guess I was out of line. Sorry.'

Matthew was still staring at the trail. 'Yeah.' He said it absently, obviously still perplexed.

'Can I finish my run?'

He turned back to her, his hand stroking the nape of his neck in thought. 'Huh? Yeah. Go on. You heard me out.'

She held his gaze for a beat then turned and sprinted for the bow.

Matthew watched her absently for a second then turned and walked along the trail to where it left the deck and slipped beneath the rail. He leant over and stared down at the stained hull of the ship. There was nothing to see except the oily blue-black of an insanely deep ocean and the virgin white of its foam.

By the time Esther had come around again, he was gone, but the third and last circuit saw her nearly run into two cadets wandering on deck with buckets and mops.

Although she didn't know why, Esther was pleased they were coming to clean it up. Very pleased.

The captain's door was closed, which Renato knew signalled he was either in the shower or asleep. But it was already gone eight-thirty and neither possibility was very likely for a man of such regular and early rising habits as Lloyd Skinner. As he paused by the closed door and pondered what to do, he was joined by Pasqual the radio officer, clutching a piece of paper and yawning.

'Taking a dump is he?' said Pasqual in their native tongue, secure in the knowledge that even if the captain was on the other side of the door, the words would be meaningless. That, of course, was the great advantage of sailing with American top brass. At least usually it was. Although the captain had picked up a word or two of Filipino, enough to say please and thanks, the crew could largely talk amongst themselves in front of Skinner without the threat of being pulled up for verbal insubordination. Unless, of course, you were a rating and second officer Renato Lhoon heard you. Then you were in big trouble. Cotton however, required more caution. His Filipino was pretty strong for an American, as was his Spanish. But since Cotton was mostly drunk the crew could afford to relax when discussing him in his earshot. Anyway Cotton wasn't here. They could say what they liked.

'Yeah, well we all got to go sometime, Pasqual.' Renato knocked lightly on the door.

'Come.'

The captain's voice revealed that he was indeed on the other side of the door, sounding, by Renato's familiarity with the master's quarters, as though he were merely seated at his couch and chart table.

The men entered, and Renato was rewarded by having his theory proved exactly right. The captain's quarters consisted of an office that was joined by a closed door to his personal suite of rooms, no more than a larger version of the officers' cabins with a slightly bigger shower room. In the office that the men entered, a large desk covered with papers was fronted by a seating arrangement of three cheap block-cushion sofas pushed together to make a C-shaped fortress of foam, surrounding a low table designed to be exactly the correct size to accommodate a standard navigational chart. Skinner was seated at the table, his hands cupping a knee, nothing on the table more sinister than a chart of the area they were currently sailing and a mug of coffee. He looked up at the men with the mild irritation of someone who has been disturbed.

'Gentlemen?' Skinner said shortly, as though they'd walked in on him naked.

The two men exchanged glances. 'Eight thirty-four, captain.'

Skinner blinked at Lhoon, then looked down at his watch. 'Ah. Right. Sit.'

The radio officer held out the paper. 'Just delivering this, sir. Two messages from company for you, and one for purser.'

Skinner took the paper, and Renato sat down on the ungiving couch opposite his captain.

'Thank you, Pasqual.'

Looking down at the paper without reading it, he spoke casually, absently avoiding eye contact with the man.

'Eh, yes. Make a reply in a couple of hours. You can let me know when will be convenient for me to use the radio room alone. Confidential ship-to-shore.' He scratched at his neck and added, 'Nothing urgent.'

Pasqual nodded. 'Sure. No problem.'

The radio officer left them, stifling a yawn again. He hadn't slept well last night as a result of eight hours of fierce half-waking dreams and half-conscious anxieties, an unusual occurrence for him, and now it was taking its toll. No matter. After he'd got his morning watch out of the way, maybe he would slip back to the cabin and catch up. After all, the sea couldn't be calmer and everything on board was normal to the point of tedium. He left the captain's door open as he exited, the way shipboard etiquette said it should have been when he'd entered.

Renato coughed into a fist, then clasped his hands in front of him ready to deliver his routine daily report. 'Quiet watch, captain. All's well. Only action, First Officer Cotton opened hatch doors round eleven-thirty. Thinks there might be risk of methane. Weather looks like being okay to leave them for now.'

Skinner raised an eyebrow, then nodded. 'Methane. Yes, well.'

'Third officer on duty now, and he knows to keep an eye on weather fax to close them if it blows above force four.'

'Good. Right.'

'Anything for today, sir?'

Skinner looked casually at the radio officer's communication again. 'Eh. Maybe some routine inspection. Down in the engine rooms and in the cofferdams.'

'I can organize that.' Renato held out his hand for the paper.

Skinner looked up at him, and there was nothing absent or distracted about the piercing gaze he fixed on the man. It took his second officer by surprise.

'That won't be necessary, Renato. This is my duty.'

The man nodded, withdrew his hand self-consciously, then waited. The captain continued. 'The bosun briefed for the day?'

'Sure.'

Skinner held his eye, then said quietly and with great finality, 'Thank you, Renato.'

Lhoon coughed again and stood up. 'Thank you, captain.'

He left quietly, and before he had got even halfway to the lift, he heard the quiet but unmistakable metallic sound of Skinner's door closing. Renato paused, thought, then dismissing the man's eccentricities of the day, went about his business.

Esther was enjoying her breakfast. The eggs and bacon were good, the coffee hot, she felt revitalized after her shower, and unlike the awkwardness of last night, her dining companion this morning was a jolly and talkative chief engineer called Sohn. Through broken English and equally broken teeth he was telling her about his family which consisted entirely of women: six daughters and what sounded like a formidable wife, and how even the nightmare of an overheating engine room was a blessed escape from the heat of their nagging when he was ashore.

He was candid and funny, and even Matthew Cotton entering the mess room, bringing a nauseating faint stale whiff of alcohol with him as he sat and joined them, couldn't dampen her high spirits.

Sohn nodded and grinned at Cotton as the lugubrious-looking first officer poured himself a coffee from the communal plastic flask on the table.

'Feel good this morning, Mattu?'

'Goddamn born again, Sohn,' he replied without warmth and took a long swallow of coffee.

The engineer laughed and nodded again. 'No one like night watch. Mattu get it every time. Ha ha.'

Esther smiled at the man's jollity in the face of the second officer's gloom. She crunched on some toast and smiled. 'So you do eat then?'

Matthew looked at her. 'The only damn thing Leonardo can cook.'

Given last night's dinner Esther had to admit he had a point. Sohn pointed at Esther as though Matthew had never seen her before.

'Esther army stoodent.'

'Yeah?'

The engineer cheerfully ignored Cotton's dismissive grunt and turned back to his considerably more charming companion.

'You shoot guns and all?'

Esther looked down at her plate as though she were talking about something dirty. 'Standard M16 A2. Nothing fancy. You get acquainted with your weapon at advance training camp.'

Sohn nodded enthusiastically, wanting more. Nothing came. Matthew sat back in his chair and looked at her.

'Guess you got on well with Lloyd last night then, huh?'

Esther narrowed her eyes. 'Why do you say that?'

'He's a Nam vet. Explosives. Used to defuse bombs, lay land mines.'

She was interested. 'Yeah? It didn't come up.'

Matthew drained his cup and poured another. 'Doesn't talk about it. You blame him?'

Esther shook her head at nothing in particular.

'Shit, it's crazy when you think about guys Lloyd's age, walking about looking like they spent a lifetime doing nothing more than mow a lawn and polish their Lincoln Continental, yet they've seen stuff that you and I only have nightmares about.'

Sohn tried to keep up with what she was saying, watching her with rapt attention now she was talking at regular speed to a fellow English speaker, instead of the slow deliberate words she'd been enunciating for him in the last half hour. He caught the gist.

'Yeah. He nearly go down on the *Eurydice* too. That really mess him about, I think.'

Sohn pointed to his head to illustrate where exactly he thought the captain had been messed about.

'What was that?' enquired Esther of Cotton, knowing that Sohn's explanation would be tortuous.

The same waiter as the previous night brought a plate across to Matthew and set it down. Obviously Cotton was a creature of habit. He picked up a fork and shovelled some scrambled egg into his mouth.

'Carrier Skinner sailed about five years ago. Got called ashore for some personal reason halfway through the voyage, and handed the command over to another captain at Lagos. Damn thing disappeared without trace a day later out of port. No survivors. No salvage.'

Esther was genuinely horrified. 'Jesus. That must have been rough. He would have known all those guys well?'

'Sailed with the same crew for nearly two–and–a–half years. Like family.'

'Did they find out what happened?'

Matthew shook his head. 'Lloyd had to give evidence at the enquiry. He'd kept his own log after they'd left Luanda and for some reason had taken his notes ashore when he left for Florida.

'Apparently he thought there'd been an irregularity he couldn't prove with cargo stowage by the African stevedores, and on account of everything he was able and obliged to check having been in order, they had forced him to sail.

'But he hadn't been happy, so guess that's why he took his copy of the log. Company loved him for that. With no wreck to examine, Lloyd's evidence was the only thing that counted. His log proved everything had been done just right by the captain and I guess by Sonstar too. Meant the insurance crooks had to pay up in full.'

Esther's estimation of the captain had risen again. No wonder the guy was reticent and distracted. It sounded like he'd had more than his share of shit. Sohn was nodding enthusiastically at this story.

'They make a lot of money when ship go down like that.'

Matthew looked sour. 'Yeah. They sure as hell ain't got the reputation for charity.'

Esther ate in silence, thinking of the horror of being sucked down on a ship this size into the blackness of that trench below them, and her food lost its taste.

Sohn pushed his chair back and bowed cheerfully to Esther. 'You want I show you my engine room later?'

Esther beamed. 'Aw, neat. I'd love that.'

'I on watch for four hours now. Any time.'

He bowed again and left. Esther was once again stranded with company she could well do without, and she watched Matthew eating in silence, much of her cheerfulness having exited the room with Sohn. Now might be a good time to set things straight, so she took the chance.

'Listen, I'm real sorry I made you mad on the cargo deck.'

Matthew shrugged as he ate, then mutely nodded his forgiveness.

She continued. 'Find out what that stuff was?'

He shook his head and shrugged again, completely uninterested, his mouth overful with hot food. Esther could see a repeat of last night's one-sided conversation looming, and she wiped the sides of her mouth in readiness to go. No one could say she hadn't given it her best shot.

Matthew looked up at her and intuitively caught the body language that meant she was getting ready to leave and, to Esther's surprise, did something to halt it. He waved a fork. 'So tell me. Why'd you choose the military?'

She looked at him to see if there was bitterness or sarcasm behind the question, and when she saw none, she answered. 'I wanted a degree. It was the only way I could afford one.'

Matthew looked genuinely interested. He swallowed what he'd been chewing and gesticulated at her again with his fork as though he needed it to talk. 'Yeah? What kinda service you need to put in for that? Three, four years?'

'Seven.'

Matthew raised both eyebrows. 'No shit? Hell, you must want that degree real bad.'

It was Esther's turn to shrug.

Matthew took another swig of coffee, watching her over the rim of the cup. 'Or maybe I'm getting it wrong here. Maybe you wanted to join up anyhow. Seen those commercials myself, the guys rappelling in California and cross-country skiing and shit? Makes me almost want to do it too.'

She scratched her neck and gave a light laugh. 'Well, since you ask, funny thing is, sure, I thought it was just a way to buy me some academic time. Stuff I thought my whole life I wanted to do. Kind of always dreamt that it was education could let me escape. Know what I mean? But when I went to advance training camp? You know, I found I had an aptitude for it I never knew I had. Surprised the living shit out of me.'

'Aptitude for what?'

She picked up her coffee cup and looked him square in the eye. 'Combat.'

Matthew looked at her, smiled weakly, then returned to his breakfast.

She knew he didn't believe her. He knew nothing about her, but she could practically read his thoughts.

He'd picture some white-collar home, see her playing at being a soldier, getting off on the masculinity of holding and firing a semi-automatic weapon. How could he know she'd been shooting guns since she was nine? Dogging off school with Henry-Adam Shenker to go to the wasteland of scrub willow a mile away from the trailer park, and shoot at everything that moved and everything that couldn't with his big brother's hand gun. The same gun that eventually helped put him and his other two drug-dealing, store-robbing siblings behind bars. And how could he know she'd spent her teens fighting with her fists and her teeth, against almost every kid at school that called her trailer-trash, or asked after her daddy with those shit-eating smug grins?

All that until the autumn term when Mr Sanderson took over as her grade teacher and discovered, like some lion tamer with the magic chair of academia and genuine concern for her, there was a brain in there, under that wild animal that tore and kicked and bit anything that got in her way.

Matthew Cotton couldn't know any of that, and frankly she didn't care. She was civilized now, a tamed creature that read philosophy and studied culture, and that was all that mattered. She would give her best to the US army, and then see what life held at the other end. But that was enough. It was Matthew's turn for spilling the beans, she decided.

'What about you?'

He stabbed some bacon. 'What about me?'

'Well where you from?'

'Nowhere special.'

Esther pursed her mouth. She was a private person by habit, and it annoyed her to have shared even a tiny part of her life with him when he was plainly so reticent to do the same.

'Oh pardon me. Did I say I came from anywhere special? Texas sure ain't frigging Arcadia.'

'You sail, you live on ships. There's nowhere else.'

'So I guess you were born and raised on a bulk carrier? Cool.'

He looked up and the pain behind his eyes made her regret her tone. He wiped his mouth. 'I was born and raised in New York. I lived for a time in Atlanta. Now I don't live any damn place. Okay?'

Esther held his gaze, embarrassed, then nodded.

'Sure.'

He got back to his meal.

Esther waited until a decent amount of time had passed to let the dust settle from his inexplicable ire, then pushed back her chair and stood. 'If I run tomorrow, I guess I'll wear the hard hat.'

Matthew nodded down into his eggs. 'You do that.'

She nodded back to the top of his head, cleared her throat and left. As she walked back up the corridor to her cabin, Esther let out the breath she'd been holding in for nearly a minute. A peal of laughter burst from the crew's mess hall, and she rubbed at her hair with an exasperated hand. Right now, Esther Mulholland wished she'd majored in languages. Namely, Filipino. Life ahead for the next five days would have promise to be a lot more entertaining if she had.

Fen had been keeping out of the bosun's way all morning, when he finally caught up with him on the main deck, crouching in front the accommodation block, staring at the long perspective of holds in front of him.

'What the hell are you up to?'

Fen looked up at Felix Chadin from the bucket of unused water he was squatting beside and blinked. 'Deck,' he said, standing and waving a hand weakly at the surface as if he had just named it. 'I was scrubbing the deck.'

'For the whole of your watch?'

'Eh, no. I was helping cook move some crates.'

Chadin crossed his arms. He was in a bad mood. Sleep had evaded him last night and he was grouchy.

'Well isn't it convenient that I find you just as your watch is over, particularly when the derrick cables need checking?'

'I can check them. I don't mind.'

Chadin looked at the man. It was not the answer he expected from a rating he suspected of skiving. It threw him.

'No. Go on.' He dismissed Fen with an imperial wave that was peculiarly Filipino, used liberally by foremen, mothers-in-law and dictators alike in their homeland.

'I want to know exactly where you are on the next watch though,' he called after the hastily-retreating figure. Fen disappeared into the block's door, and Chadin looked down at the bucket. It was clear that the man had not been scrubbing at all, yet the eagerness with which he'd offered to extend his watch was confusing. Chadin looked up along the open holds and squinted against the low sun, then went to find someone else he could make suffer for his poor night's rest.

Fen entered the crew's mess room, went to the coffee machine and punched in his command. The whining machine pissed a spiralling stream of brown liquid into a plastic cup that was too flimsy to prevent it burning any inexperienced hand that attempted to hold it. He waited until it had finished its business, grabbed the cup by its thick rim, and went to join the four men, three of whom sat smoking, one sulking, at the Formica-covered table nearest the serving hatch.

'Ah, now then, the very man,' exclaimed Parren the storekeeper, slapping the table top. He pointed at the surly sixteen-year-old cadet, Hal, and laughed. The other two men laughed in a snickering kind of way, childish, but entirely unkind.

'This little shit-eater wants to know if his girlfriend's being faithful.'

Fen looked from face to face, then sipped carefully at the nasty coffee. 'So?'

'So you're the guy to tell him.'

Fen scowled. 'Yeah, well not today. Okay?'

Hal emerged from his sulk. 'Aw come on, Fen. I'll pay you.'

'No.'

The boy snorted and picked up his own white plastic cup. 'Yeah, well it's a load of bullshit that stuff anyway. It doesn't tell you anything you don't know.'

Fen's face darkened and he lowered the cup. The three older men looked at each other with eyebrows raised gleefully in anticipation of an explosion.

'You want to be careful, kid. Stupider people than you have fallen foul of Saanti. The dumber you are the harder it is to take the truth.'

The boy made a face, pretending he was scared, then laughed. Parren leant forward, trying to break the iron rod of gaze that Fen had fixed on the boy. 'Do it for us then, Fen. Come on. I wouldn't mind asking a couple of things.'

Fen looked round slowly at the storekeeper and frowned.

'Yeah,' added the steward who sat slouched to Parren's right. 'Why not?'

Why not, indeed. Fen knew why not. Because when he had scattered the Saanti bone-dice last night and laid out the alphabet cards, reading them for himself instead of for someone else for the first time in fifteen years, they had terrified him. He would never normally cast those dice for himself. It had been the dream that had made him do it. The dream that had made him doubt what was real and what was not when he awoke in a sweat. But he had done it, and as it was with those he read for, he took what the dice told him very seriously. The reading always required the card-caster to read out the message that was being spelled for his eyes only, and sometimes Fen found that his voice adopted the tone of the person who was communicating, whether they were alive or dead. It had been uncanny at first, and almost everyone he read for imagined at first that he was faking it. Until, that is, someone they loved, or had lost forever, spoke through Fen's mouth. Then they believed. They had no choice.

But last night ... Fen shivered at the memory. Someone – no that wasn't quite right – some thing, had spoken to him, or rather made him speak, and done so in a voice and a language that was both unintelligible and indescribably horrible. He had broken off the reading even before it had completed its first communication, his mouth fouled by the noise that had come from it, and now he was afraid that if he read again, it would come back.

But that had been in the night. He had been too tormented by his dreams to sleep well, no doubt fuelled by the schoolboy superstitions of ridiculous peasant stevedores. Now it was day, and he was sitting in the brightly-lit mess room that was familiar as his own skin, the faces of his long-time shipmates looking at him expectantly, waiting for some fun. If ever there was a time to exorcise the demons of the night with a playful and harmless reading, telling these men of their loved ones at home, then perhaps it was now. Cowardice was not compatible with being a Saanti-master. Fen licked his lips and wiped the sides of his sweaty shirt with his palms.

'What kind of things?' he asked Parren.

The men smiled, sensing entertainment.

'Well, for one, I want to know if my boy working in Dubai will marry a good girl and give me grandsons.'

The man at the end of the table laughed and blew out a cloud of smoke. 'I can tell you that Parren. I have it on good authority he's choking on Arab cock right now.'

Parren made a mock-threatening swipe with the back of his hand, but he was smiling. He looked back at Fen. 'So?'

Fen toyed with his cup, his gaze fixed on the brown circle of liquid, then slowly put his hand in his trouser pocket and brought out the pack and dice. The four men shifted in their seats with delight and sat forward in anticipation.

Fen held the pack and looked from face to face, then slowly began to shuffle the cards. They watched closely as he laid out a semi-circle of ancient and bizarrely-marked cards, each with letters of the alphabet inscribed over a lurid illustration. The three bone dice had occult symbols burnt into them, two of them inlaid intricately around the symbols with tiny slivers of gold, one with silver.

Fen realized his hand was trembling. He stopped and took another swallow of coffee. This was ridiculous. All the more determined now to shake this night terror off, he sped up, concentrating hard as he laid and arranged the cards.

This task complete, he gathered two of the three dice together in his hand and looked up. 'Who's first?'

Parren wiped his mouth with a hand then looked to the cadet. 'Well I suppose it's Hal whose losing most sleep.'

'Yeah. Or his girlfriend,' sniggered the carpenter.

Fen looked to the boy. 'You answer only when I ask you a question. You touch none of the cards, but only this die when I tell you to. Understand?'

The boy smiled and nodded, looking round for approval. All eyes were on Fen, and the serving hatch filled as the two assistant cooks leaned forward happily on their elbows, well used to the show that the rating could put on.

Fen placed the single die in the centre of the semi-circle then shook the other two in his palm and cast them. They clattered onto the table top, rolled and came to rest in front of Parren.

'What's your name?'

Fen was looking at the cards, not the boy, but Hal knew to answer when he was poked in the ribs by a sharp finger.

'Hal Sanin.'

'What's your question?'

Hal licked his lips. It felt more tense now, less of a game. Fen's face was stern with concentration.

'Em, will my … no, sorry.' He took a breath and composed himself. 'Is my girlfriend, Phaara, being faithful to me?'

Fen looked at the two cast dice. 'And who do you ask? The wind, the sun, the water or the fire?'

Hal looked to the other men and gave a worried shrug. Parren shrugged back cheerfully and mouthed silently the word 'water,' for no other reason than to keep things going.

'Eh, water.'

Fen stretched forward and put his little finger on the die in the semicircle of cards. He breathed in hard, then waited. The men waited, Parren throwing Hal a fatherly wink. Slowly, Fen's finger began to move the die across the table top.

It bobbed and hesitated in front of the cards, then moved on, stopping and starting randomly before setting off again. And then his finger speeded up, sliding faster and faster until it was darting across the table top like some impossibly fleet insect captured between the laid-out cards. Most of the men had seen this many times, but they were still impressed. Even if it wasn't supernatural, just Fen doing some long-practised party trick, it was still damned dextrous. All the time, Fen's eyes darted with the die, reading the letters as it spelled them out, interpreting what the illustrated cards denoted, and waiting for the voice he had asked to come through.

Fen stopped. His eyes were closed but his head came up sharply. 'Hal?'

It was a woman's voice. No question. The stewards at the hatch nudged each other in glee. This was good.

Hal gulped. He looked around for support, but all eyes were fixed on Fen's face. 'Yes?' he replied weakly.

'You son of a sow.'

Hal gaped at Fen. There was no question it was his girlfriend's voice, and if he were honest, her language too.

'What?'

'You dare accuse me of infidelity, you bastard?'

The boy was silent, his mouth working without words.

'I'll tell you about infidelity. What about my cousin? Yeah? That bring back anything? Tasik and Carlo's wedding in Manila?'

Hal gawped stupidly at the cards then back up at Fen. He looked as though he might be sick.

'You tried to have her in my brother's car, didn't you? Go on deny it. Right there while the dancing was starting. Fumbling at her bra like a kid.'

'Stop. Stop it.' The boy was nearly crying.

'And you're asking if *I'm* being unfaithful? I bought that dress specially for you, not for the wedding. Blue, because I know you like blue. And what do you do? You take Deni out to my brother's car the moment I ...'

Fen stopped suddenly and opened his eyes. There was silence except for Hal's sharp hard breathing as he wrestled to compose himself like the man he wanted to be. Wrestled, in fact, to stop himself weeping with fear and shame.

Every face watched Fen intently, but his eyes, though open, were cloudy and unfocused. Then, slowly, Fen's mouth contorted, and from it came noises that chilled the blood of everyone present. Guttural, throaty noises that sounded almost like words ...

'*Caaahrdreeed. Cahrdreeed montwaandet.*'

On the table, Fen's finger started to move. It started slowly, then as before gathered speed, until it was flying from card to card. Sweat had started to bead on his temple.

The men watching stayed perfectly still, hardly breathing as though stalked by some invisible predator.

Spit started to foam at the corner of Fen's mouth, his eyes rolled in their sockets, and the finger on the die stopped abruptly. The next sounds from his mouth came from the same ugly contorted lips, but this time they were delivered in a low, almost inaudible whisper, as though something were experimenting with his tongue. The words started indistinctly, becoming more articulate, more formed, as the volume increased. It was as if someone were practising speaking in an unfamiliar language, growing bolder as they became more coherent.

'Yes. Yes. Scum. Scum. Oh filthy scum of scum. Listen, scum. Sons of scum. Fathers of scum. Husbands of shit. Brothers of barren spunk. Listen ... listen to me. To meeeee ...'

Parren broke his own spell of paralysis. This was too much. 'Fen. Fen stop it.'

Fen appeared completely unable to comply.

'Dung that drops from the dead. I am whole. You scum. Listen ... listen ...'

The die beneath Fen's finger started to tremble as though sitting on a vibrating surface, and it continued to do so, even when it shook loose from his grip. The men watched it with horror, then Parren leapt to his feet and slapped Fen hard across the face with a blow that knocked him back in his chair.

Fen let out a shriek, and raised his arms across his face, but not, thought Parren later, to protect himself from the blow. The die ceased its tremulous progress across the table top, once again becoming an innocent and inanimate object, and the men looked at Fen with horror.

The cadet and the steward had also leapt to their feet, and two of them grabbed Fen under the arms and brought him back upright.

'Get some water,' Parren barked to the two cooks standing dumb-struck in the hatch.

Water was fetched and duly administered, but even an hour later, the time when the men should have been laughing and reflecting on what must have been nothing more than a ugly prank, neither Fen nor his audience had recovered sufficiently to laugh at anything.

6

It was a matter of priorities. She'd washed all three of her T-shirts, her entire collection of underwear, which wasn't much and depressingly utilitarian, and even her trusty sandals, which had begun to smell like an old carcass. Now, they were all hanging like puritan bunting over the plastic frame of the shower cubicle, or on the rail that ran around the cabin, and it meant only one thing. It was time to do some work.

Esther sat down heavily on her sofa, crossed her bare legs beneath her and gathered the pile of paper, notepads, the Dictaphone and red, hardbound book that she'd carried halfway across Peru, onto her lap, sighing as she started to sift through the confused mess. She grazed until she found what she wanted, the cream of the crop, the thing that she believed was going to make this whole project.

She'd come up with the dissertation idea in a response to a particularly politically correct lecture from a lanky objectionable English professor on a book promotion tour, who had come all the way to their college to present his lecture, bearing the same title as his book: *Democracy: The Natural State of Man.* Esther didn't know why, but she'd hated him the moment he'd smoothed his sad academic beard with long fingers, smiled smugly at the audience, and said, 'What has politics got to do with anthropology, you must be asking yourselves?'

Esther was in fact sighing, asking herself why this man was patronizing them with his opening sentence.

By the time he got to, 'You know, you take it for granted that if I offend you, horrify you, or bore you, you have the power and the freedom to leave. Democracy, ladies and gentlemen. Voting with your feet. It is more natural, more immovably inbuilt into the fabric of humanity, from Piltdown man to a Wall Street broker, than any other form of known social behaviour,' she desperately wanted to prove him wrong merely for the sake of it.

He went on to argue that dictatorships, however benevolent, held back humanity and halted progress, and at question time Esther put up her hand.

'What about the Roman Empire?' she asked without aggression.

He smiled again, a father to a child. 'Ah yes, Fascism.'

Before he could begin a prepared response about that particularly abhorrent form of human politics, she interrupted. 'I mean, specifically, how did it hold back humanity and halt progress?'

He had raised his eyebrows. 'How about slavery, genocide and corruption?' He was looking forward to humiliating her. She could tell he made a living out of it.

'How about social order and justice for the majority, engineering and military advances of a type that have survived even until now, creativity in the arts equal if not superior to anything we enjoy today?'

'No, no, no ...' He tried to stop by her shaking his head with sympathy, but she was undeterred.

'Oh yeah. And ice cream.'

The class burst out laughing. He laughed with them, but only with his mouth. His eyes were pinning her down, marking her out.

'And Hitler? I trust you admired the fact the trains ran on time?'

'Hitler was voted into power.' She spoke the next word deliberately slowly to irritate him. 'Democratically.'

She was starting to irritate him as much he annoyed her. She could tell.

'I guess you must be a National Socialist, young lady.' He smiled at his own joke.

'I'm Jewish.'

His smile faded and he looked at her coldly, cleared his throat and gave his pat response to the rest of the class while Esther sat thinking. It wasn't important to prove the point here. Of course she believed in the might of democracy. It had simply become interesting to her as a student to see if what the English jerk was saying was true or not, and more importantly, in the true naive spirit of the young, to try and ruin his experienced certainty.

That night she sat in the library and after three long hours chose the most successful ancient civilization she could find that was comparable to her own, and one that was not based on any form of democracy whatsoever. The Incas.

They were perfect. Haughty dictators who were so successful in building their empire that their people always had huge surpluses of food. They had plumbing they would be proud of in Idaho, irrigation engineering over thousands of miles that still defies modern understanding, and a hierarchy that by and large only slaughtered each other, leaving the man and woman in the well-paved streets unharmed. There was social welfare, free education and health care, little or no crime, and all with not a sniff of anything remotely approaching democracy.

Unfortunately there was also human sacrifice, but since church was not separate from state in the way it must always be in modern democracies, this would only help to further prove her point. So it was just what she needed. An enviable civilization destroyed not by its lack of democracy, but by an equally undemocratic horde of avaricious religious hypocrites from Europe. Now, thousands of years later, under the democratic rule of a bastardized Spanish civilization, was Peru more successful? No sirree. She was off, and her dissertation was born.

The paper she had created from the dross of notes and photos of temples and dig sites she'd had developed in Cuzcou included sketched diagrams and twenty-nine full pages of her writing. Because unbelievably she had chanced upon something she wasn't expecting. Something that was so exciting she could hardly contain it. A three-week trip onto the high plateau with some shepherds she had befriended in a small village had led her to an extraordinary piece of living human archaeology, something she hoped she was the first to find, and when she wrote of it might just cause a stir.

The shepherds had told her of a small group of nomadic people, rarely seen, who moved and lived on the very edges of the eastern mountain range that divided the high Andean plateau from the Amazon jungle. What was remarkable about these people, apart from the fear they seemed to inspire in the otherwise hardy shepherds, was the fact that they were Incas. Esther had tried not to laugh. There were, of course, no Incas. All the research told her that in the days of the great empire there were in fact only forty thousand full-blooded nobles who called themselves by that name. The hundreds of thousands of people who lived peacefully under their rule were merely Inca subjects.

The pure-bred Incas were either slaughtered or interbred with the Spanish to create through countless generations the modern Peruvians. To suggest that some of the original royal Incas had survived thus far intact would be outrageous. But the normally reticent shepherds were adamant, insisting, as further proof, that these people were still sun-worshippers, that they had the power and dark practices of the ancient ones very much in their grasp. Not only that, but the shepherds spoke enigmatically, and Esther thought, somewhat fearfully, about the tribe being unusually active recently. One had said in a small anxious voice that some of them had been travelling to towns and cities, a thing previously unheard of.

She begged to know where they might be found and after days of pleading and haranguing, they had left her in a place where the tribe were sometimes seen. She was afraid at first, being left alone in such a desolate spot, but even more afraid when after three days she emerged from her tent in the early light of dawn to find a small group of men sitting silently outside, waiting for her to emerge.

She'd had an incredibly brief twelve days in their company, before they disappeared in the night, their tracks indicating they had moved off in a direction that was too obviously a route to the jungle for her taste. Everything she'd learned from them during their time together was from a peculiarly intense and very beautiful seventeen-year-boy in their midst who could speak a little halting Spanish. She had spent time cultivating him, flirting even, to make him sit with her and talk into her Dictaphone in very broken and difficult Spanish. But then Esther had a talent for making men want her without ever giving them what they expected might be theirs after time. He was no different. Just younger. He'd started haltingly, shyly, glancing at the older men who regarded him and Esther impassively as they sat together by her tent. But as the days progressed he began to take a great, almost obsessive interest in her, talking more animatedly and rapidly, leaving her confused and ignorant of the majority of what he was trying to tell her. He'd been so intense, sweating profusely as he spoke, even though they were camped on the freezing plateau. But at least she'd confirmed what the frightened shepherds had told her. The boy had been to

Lima, an incredible journey from here. But his eyes shone when he spoke of it, even though the elders lowered their eyes when they heard the name of the city. *Teenagers the world over*, thought Esther. Here she was wanting him to tell her about the traditions and rituals of his tribe, and probably all he wanted to talk about would be discos and girls. He certainly became even more flushed and excited when she made him understand she was heading for Lima on the way back, and indeed after that, he rarely left her alone. But his Spanish was too rapid for her. No matter. She checked the tapes each time he finished, and whatever he said was all there.

All she would have to do was to take the time later to decipher and translate, no doubt kicking herself for not asking the right things when she had the chance.

She had also written everything down that the elders had said, in exactly the words they'd used, unfamiliar or not. It was not for her to interpret it until she could think straight later.

The diagrams she had were of the makeshift altar they would build and destroy each morning and she sat examining it, looking forward to comparing it with the ancient lay-outs of the temples she had visited endlessly throughout the rest of the trip. When she awoke one morning to find they had gone in the night, there had been a particularly intricate pattern scratched in the hardened dust directly outside her tent, and what interested her when she'd made a careful sketch of it, was that unlike the altars they built, there was nothing even remotely familiar about its twisting lines. She treasured that one above all.

Esther blessed the dull English professor with the beard. Through a routine academic exercise to try and discuss the effects of democracy on civilization, she might, quite incredibly, have run into what she firmly believed was an almost completely unknown tribe of people.

She had no one yet to share the thrill with, particularly on this ship of fools, but even if it was laughed out of college when she got back, right now she was as excited as if she'd struck gold.

She lay back, and with some difficulty started the long task of deciphering her own appalling handwriting.

Sohn was trying not to laugh. Lloyd Skinner was a big, powerful man, and from the engine room, the only hatch into the cofferdams between the cargo holds and the outer hull was one that was considerably smaller than him. The fourth engineer and a cadet had unscrewed it laboriously to give him access, but he was struggling to get in, especially with the big industrial torch and ridiculously formal flightcase he was carrying. 'You need that in there?' Sohn asked, pointing to the aluminium case.

Skinner looked back. 'The only way to keep this damned paperwork together.'

The chief engineer grinned and shrugged. Skinner was a strange man. Anyone would have accompanied him if he'd ordered it, would have held the papers for him and offered their back as a makeshift table for any documents that needed ticked or filled in at site.

Indeed, Sohn would have been pleased to do it himself. He hadn't been inside the cofferdams on this ship before, and he was always delighted to acquaint himself with the concealed architecture of any vessel he powered through the water. But Skinner was a loner, a perfectionist, an utter stickler for duty, and if any inspection needed to be done, he always wanted to do it by himself.

The curious thing was not only why the company would want this done now, while at sea, but why they wanted it done at all.

There was nothing in there. Just a long dark space, at least eight feet wide and as tall as the entire hull, running the length of the ship, both to port and starboard. They were supposed to be checked and flushed regularly at port, so that any problem would become rapidly obvious on the loadicator. But that took time and manpower, and Sonstar were not a company to waste either if it got in the way of making money. Skinner was to be admired for pursuing the official line when his bosses would almost certainly have turned a blind eye to its omission. And if he wanted to go wandering in the dark, fumbling with plans and treading on rats, then that was his business. It was Lloyd Skinner's ship to command and he could do what he wanted.

The captain had already pushed through and was standing upright on the other side by the time Sohn formulated his last offer.

'You want to take walkie-talkie? In case you fall or something?'

Skinner shook his head, but smiled weakly. 'Thank you, Chief Engineer. No. I only need to check and see there's no leakage from the holds. The bosun reported there might be a small lesion near the bow. It'll only take half an hour at most. If I'm not back by Friday you can send in the dogs.'

He turned and walked away, his boots making a lonely echo on the virgin metal floor. As the circle of his torchlight retreated into the long dark tunnel of dripping metal, three heads peered after him, glad to be on the side of the hatch where the striplights burned bright and Radio Lima played Mariah Carey.

'Shit fuck bastard and double fuck!'

Leonardo Becko looked round quickly and tutted with exaspera-tion. The galley boy was hopping from foot to foot, his hand tucked protectively under his arm, his face contorted with pain. One glance down at the deep fat frier he'd been feeding told the cook all he needed to know.

'You stupid fucking idiot. You drop the potatoes from a height, ooh, surprise surprise, they're going to make a splash.'

The boy was hissing through bared teeth, immune for the moment to his boss's taunts. Leonardo wiped his flour-covered hands on a filthy apron and walked across the galley floor.

'Here. Let's see it, you moron.'

Salvo Acambra took his hand from his armpit and looked at it. It was burned only very superficially, a thin red weal rising from the wrist to the thumb. Leonardo tutted again, this time with heavy sarcasm, shaking his head like a vaudeville doctor making a fatal diagnosis. 'Have to come off, I think.'

Salvo scowled.

Leonardo gave him a harmless swipe over the head and turned away to get on with his pastry. 'Take ten minutes, and make sure it's only ten. You bloody moron.'

'Yes, Chef,' said the boy, brightening considerably. He moved quickly to the galley storeroom, and sat down on a crate. An examination of the weal told him it was indeed an injury of no consequence, and he smiled at the ten-minute break he'd earned as a bonus in the hot, busy hell that led up to lunch. He craned backwards and peered out into the galley to see where the cook was now. Becko's head was turned the other way, and the boy quickly shut the storeroom door a fraction more with his foot, reached into his back pocket under his apron ties and took out a packet of cigarettes.

He glanced up to the porthole, then stood on the crate and opened the window. Leonardo Becko hated smoking in the galley, so he would have to be extra careful. He pushed his body against the bulkhead, stuck his head as far out of the porthole as the limited hinge would allow, lit up a cigarette and took a long, delicious drag. The sun beat down on his hot face, but the breeze from the sea blew away both his smoke and his sweat in a way that made him close his eyes in pleasure, enjoying the rare moment of solitude.

Salvo loved the ozone smell of the sea, the fresh, salty tang that it left on your skin and in your hair. It was the one great consolation for working in this hole of a ship. He took another long suck of nicotine and let himself dream of home.

The breeze was souring. He opened his eyes and took a deeper sniff, curious as to where this new smell was coming from. Instantly, his senses were assaulted by an almost solid intake of air that was fetid and foul beyond reason. He coughed back a throatful of vomit, fighting to control it and sent it back below where it belonged.

Tears in his eyes from the effort of this, he stepped down from the crate and looked around to see if the cause was coming from within. The air he breathed freshened again, full of the hot comfortable smells of cooking, steam and condensation. The rotting had most definitely come from outside.

He looked quizzically up at the porthole, and this time stepped more gingerly up on the crate and put his head out. Only four or five inches of the window would open on account of the safety catch, but he forced his face out through it, trying not to breathe deeply this time. To his left, the limited space let him see along the outer hull of the ship as far as the bow. It was harder to see to the right, or above, but he could also look down and just see the foam breaking below at the waterline. He sniffed more gently this time, and the same reek attacked his nostrils like acid. He coughed, waited until his eyes cleared of the tears, then strained to see.

There was movement. It was above him, faint, only on the very edge of his vision, and he felt it rather than saw it. Salvo contorted his head to twist up and see what it might have been, but the movement was unfeasible. He flicked through some possibilities of what might have moved on a smooth metal hull of a ship doing twenty knots. A seagull, maybe, caught in some peculiar way on something sharp? Or maybe a rope or cable come loose, dangling and scraping on the side. But what was making the smell? He tried one more tortuous move then gave up. Who cared what it was?

He flicked his precious cigarette from the porthole and shut the glass tight. The air inside the storeroom was like nectar after the stench from outside, and he sat back on the crate, his back against the wall, to enjoy his last few minutes of freedom, gazing dreamily at the square of brilliant sunlight being projected onto a pile of potato sacks on the wall opposite him.

Not much would send a galley boy back to his work early from a break he had been gifted by the chef, but two things happened simultaneously that did just that.

Behind him, through the very hull of the ship itself, he felt a manic scraping, the vibration of some horrible metallic scuttling. The sound rats would make if they were ten feet long and made of something other than flesh. And the square of light that bathed the potato sacks blackened quickly into shadow and lit again. The boy leapt to his feet and whirled around to the porthole. It framed a perfect blue sky and bathed him in nothing more than benign sunshine.

Leonardo was surprised to see Salvo back so quickly, but he was pleased to have the help.

'Turn that bloody stock down. And get over here and finish these carrots.'

'Yes, Chef,' the boy said weakly and wiped his sweating upper lip with a burnt hand that he had quite forgotten.

Even the most expensive penthouse apartment in any of the world's greatest cities would have a hard time competing with the view from the bridge of the *Lysicrates*. Dilapidated and shabby though it was, when the ship was in sail and the cargo deck below stretched like a pointing finger into the dark blue Pacific, it would be hard to stare down from the bridge's angled windows with anything other than awe.

When Renato Lhoon entered, the third officer on watch was staring out ahead as one might expect, but not with awe at the might of the ocean and its domination by man. He had the look of a man who was half asleep.

'Wakey wakey, Ernesto.'

The man turned round quickly and tried to look alert. He nodded to Lhoon then looked down at the screen of the echo sounder as though he were interested. His senior officer stood at his side and glanced down at the array of flickering instrument screens between them and the ocean panorama.

'Set fair?'

Ernesto nodded and pointed to the curling weather fax on the console beside him, but Renato's eye had already drifted to the GPS.

'Have we altered course?'

'Eh, yeah. Just to the co-ordinates that Officer Cotton decided.' Ernesto gave an expansive sweep with one open hand over the instruments, imagining that might help explain things.

'Let me see the log.'

The third officer handed it to him and he scanned last night's entry. There was no mention of a navigational alteration. But then Cotton would forget to make an entry in his log if dinosaurs roamed onto the cargo deck and tore down the derricks with their teeth. Renato sighed with exasperation.

'What was the alteration?'

Ernesto fumbled for a moment then told him. The ship had been re-routed five degrees west, and their course was taking them directly up the middle of the Milne Edwards Trench, the one that had so freaked Esther. It was not the usual shipping lane and although it was only a small detour, its purpose, in fine and settled weather, seemed meaningless.

Renato was not going to challenge his senior officer's decision in front of a subordinate, and so he nodded as though he knew about it and had simply forgotten.

The man seemed relieved, took back the log, and turned again to feign interest in the echo sounder, which was presently showing a vertiginous depth of seventeen thousand feet.

Renato walked casually over to the starboard window and checked on his chilli pepper plants, then as quietly as he had entered, left to go and find Cotton.

'Recreation Room' was rather a grand term for a space that boasted only one bookcase with some dog-eared pot-boilers in various languages, and a pile of elderly magazines. But Matthew Cotton was not slumped back on one of the three foam sofas, a rum and Coke in his hand, because he was attracted by the possibilities of the reading material. The sideboard that ran the length of the wall was the officers' makeshift bar, a trusting affair run by the catering staff, from which imbibers took what they wanted from the generous gantry and filled in their intake for later payment on the personalized sheets left for the purpose.

Matthew had long since given up entering his drinks on his dog-eared piece of paper measure by measure, and it was understood now that he would simply purchase his ration by the bottle.

The dent he had made on his current bottle of Bacardi was not inconsiderable, and his eyes were closed, his head leant against the hard foam as the effects of it started to make their mark.

'Double watch again, Matthew. Eight till four.'

Cotton didn't open his eyes. 'Shit, have a drink, Renato. I know when my fuckin' watch is.'

Renato Lhoon left the doorway where he'd been standing for some time, looking at his senior officer with contempt, and entered the room. 'It's two-thirty. I don't need no drink.'

'We don't need no stinkin' badges,' sniggered Matthew in a mock-Mexican accent, enjoying the unfunnyness of his joke alone, in the way only drunks can. When there was silence in response he opened his eyes and blinked around him to see where Renato Lhoon might be. He was standing over him, and Matthew lifted his head to focus on his face.

'What?'

'Thought we had a deal, Matthew.'

'Huh?'

'You gonna drink all watch, then you tell me what happens. I fill the log. That's how it works. That's how I save your skin.'

'Yeah? What, you want me to thank you for it like every day?'

Renato crossed his arms. 'I want you to tell me what you do on duty.'

Matthew shrugged in agreement. 'So?'

'You changed course last night. I told the captain everything this morning, like you know you should do and not me, but I don't tell him that. Know why? 'Cause I don't know, that's why.'

Matthew sat up and blinked at Renato. The man was angry. Not like him. 'What's the big deal, Renato? So I forgot.'

'What the captain going to say?'

Matthew took a swig of his drink and exhaled his words on the resulting expellation of air that followed his swallow. 'Nothing, I shouldn't reckon.'

Renato snorted. 'Yeah? You alter course, don't log it and you think he don't mind?'

'I know he won't.'

'Yeah? How come?'

Matthew lay back again and looked at Renato as if he were dumb. 'Because the captain came to the bridge and changed it himself.'

A subtle alteration in Renato's face made Matthew sit up slightly, ashamed momentarily of his slovenly appearance. For no reason that Matthew could comprehend, the second officer looked as though he had been betrayed.

Matthew cleared his throat. 'Sorry, man. I just forgot to log it.'

Renato looked down at him for a moment, then walked across to the gantry and poured himself a Sprite. 'What time?'

Matthew was now uncomfortable, staring at the man's tense back as he drank his lemonade. 'What time what?'

Renato turned to face him, his face now inscrutable. 'What time did he come on the fucking bridge?'

This was not like Matthew's friend and partner in crime, Renato Lhoon. This was the man who kept him in a job, who kept him on the very edge of the legality of his post, who made sure he got up, made certain he fulfilled his duties, made absolutely sure that First Officer Matthew Cotton didn't plough the vessel into a tanker at three in the morning.

And in return Renato Lhoon got paid. He got paid well. Why now, was he getting so upset about such a tiny regular misdemeanour as forgetting to log? Matthew ran a hand over the back of his neck. 'Uh, let me see. I reckon around two, maybe half past. I dunno.'

If only Matthew knew it, there were in fact two reasons that Lhoon was getting upset.

But then there was no way that he could have known, since Lhoon spent a great deal of time and energy concealing them both, but they were nevertheless at the forefront of his ire right now as he stood regarding the hopeless drunk who was one rank higher than he was in the important chain of command.

The first reason was probably the most important: Renato Lhoon hated Matthew Cotton. Hated him with the kind of passion that was bordering on animal. He hated the fact that this man had been given a job he was incapable of doing, that he was given a second chance and employed again after throwing away ten years of being a captain because of his decline into alcoholism in the last two, and that he took the job and paid Renato to keep him there in the full knowledge that he should be ashore, ashore for good.

It made him sick, dressing Cotton when he was naked and ranting, fulfilling his mundane duties for him when he was on watch, keeping the gossip of the crew at bay to prevent the withdrawal of co-operation, and most of all taking his money.

But the second reason was the captain. Lloyd Skinner was a decent man. So decent he had deliberately chosen this wreck of a human being to be his first officer when he could have chosen anyone he wanted. Anyone, for instance, like Lhoon.

Renato knew something had happened to Cotton ashore that had made him the way he was. He didn't know what, but frankly, he didn't give a shit. He'd never asked, and he didn't care. Everyone had bad times, everyone had tragedies. This man had once been a respected captain and now he was a bum.

The sea demanded more of a man.

Lloyd Skinner should know that, and it irked him that if he did, in this case he turned an extremely blind eye. Renato's relationship with the captain had always been good. They had, he thought, an understanding, an empathy, a rapport. Now, just lately, he felt Skinner was excluding him, and to exclude him in favour of this useless baggage was too much. He couldn't give a flying fuck about a tiny change in course. What was upsetting him was that the captain had visited the bridge at a highly unusual time in the night, altered course for no reason that Lhoon could see, and most importantly, hadn't mentioned it to him during the report of the watch he always gave on Cotton's behalf in the morning.

Sure he was mad about it, but for now he would maintain his inscrutability. Because Renato Lhoon had plans.

He looked back at Matthew. 'Half-past two? He say why he changed course?'

'Search me. Maybe there was a tanker or shit. I didn't see anything on the radar.'

Renato nodded, as though satisfied, then placed his can on the sideboard and walked to the door. Matthew watched him go, expecting more, but he disappeared from view without a parting word.

'Hey!' shouted Cotton to an empty door frame. 'You forgot to write down your Sprite.'

The spaces between the cofferdams were open and stepping over them was possible with care and a little effort. The torchlight illuminated the long cathedral of buttressed iron that supported the main holds like some insane gothic fancy.

A lesser soul might have been tempted to turn and run with every creak and clank of shifting metal that reverberated along the endless corridor, but Lloyd Skinner was not a man to spook easily. He had been surprised, unpleasantly so, to discover that there were rats down here. He knew there were rats on board. He himself had falsified the inspection sheet to claim that there were not, but it was unsettling that they had penetrated into the part of the ship that should be sealed and secure. More than once, the beam had caught the ugly back of a scuttling grey beast, scrambling for safety over the iron spines of the tanks and splashing through the small puddles of sea water that still persisted even after flushing.

Skinner gave a moment's thought to wonder where there might be a breach that allowed them access to this area from the main holds where he knew they lived, foraged and bred, then as quickly dismissed it and carried on.

He had turned the corner, away from the square of light that came from the engine room, and now he was in a world of total black, with only a cavernous echo to remind him of the scale of his largely invisible surroundings.

Back there, he knew, the engineers would be gossiping, pouring mugs full of the repulsive Filipino coffee they drank in unhealthy quantities, and looking curiously from time to time at the hole through which their captain had gone to do his duty to the company and international safety regulations. But in here, well below the line of the sea that pushed against the iron skin, eager to enter and fill those gaps with its heavy, salty, irresistible body, he was alone, unobserved.

Skinner stopped and put down his heavy flight case.

He pointed the torch at the wall between the tank and the
hold and calculated where exactly he was standing. His progress
had taken him into the curve of the bow so this would make him
level with hold one or two. He swept the torch beam across the
ceiling of the tank and down the vast iron wall to his right. The
surface seemed dry. He put out a hand and touched it, paused
for a moment, enjoying the vibration that the engines sent
through the ship like a heartbeat, then ran his fingers across the
flaky, oxidized surface. There was a smell to the rusting metal
of the ship, and he breathed it in: a musky, sharp aroma of
minerals and water working together to break down the iron that
had come from the earth and wanted nothing more than to return
to there.

A glance back confirmed there was no glimpse of light, either
from door or rival torch, and he sighed and withdrew his hand.

Captain Lloyd Skinner knelt down and placed the torch on the
ground facing his flight case. In the concentrated beam of light
he turned the combination lock carefully to its four-digit sequence
and waited until he heard the satisfying click. For a moment he
placed his hands together, fingers making a steeple, and tapped
at his chin. He closed his eyes and just as quickly opened them,
as the visions he daily kept at bay with superhuman effort tried
to surface like black shapes from the deep.

From his right came a scuffling. A rat, mistaking the silence
for safety, emerged from its shadows and, panicking in the unexpected circle of spilled light, planned a route that would take it
across Lloyd Skinner's case. It was a youngster, no more than four
or five inches long. Skinner watched it with his eyes, without
turning his head. Watched it as it stopped and sniffed the air with
a pointed pink nose, and watched it as it moved quickly forward
and hopped onto the flight case.

His hand came down with such force that the rat's spine snapped
before the message had reached its brain. Its jaws wrenched open
in agony and fury, unable to exact any kind of revenge without
the co-operation of its body. It screamed and twitched, and Skinner
watched it impassively, doing nothing to end its pain. He watched
it for three minutes until the twitching became no more than a
slight tick, and the body, bent in a hideous upward crescent,
became still and stiff.

Lloyd Skinner picked up the rodent by its long worm-like tail and threw it into the darkness, then slowly, carefully, like a man uncovering buried treasure, opened the case and regarded the contents with the closest his hard blue eyes came to satisfaction.

Tenghis closed the cabin door, turned the light on, stripped off his shirt and hung it on the radiator where the sweat would evaporate and grant it another day's use. He ran a hand over his tired face and then moved to his altar and knelt before the Virgin and her imploring outstretched plaster arms. He bent his head and began his muttered gallop through the prayers that were so monotonous and familiar that he was three or four minutes into them before realizing his mind was occupied with anything but piety. Through all the Hail Marys he had merely been freewheeling over a variety of petty mundanities, from the unjust nature of some shift alterations, to the price of a Japanese car back in Manila. He took a deep breath and tried to concentrate. The love of Jesus and the purity of His mother on earth stayed with him for around thirty or forty seconds of chanting, until his concentration gave up in favour of whether he was eating too much dairy fat for his own good.

'She doesn't hear you.'

Tenghis jumped up and swung round in alarm. Fen was leaning against the wall at the end of his bunk, staring past his cabin mate at the statue.

He was naked, his arms crossed, not casually, but as though protecting himself from the cold.

'Fen. For Christ's sake.' Tenghis breathed his protest from a body that was fighting to make its heart beat normally again.

Fen slid down the wall and crouched, still staring at Mary. He smiled, then slowly began to laugh. Tenghis had recovered enough to become annoyed.

'What were you doing skulking in the dark? And put some clothes on.'

Fen stopped laughing. 'You like it that way, don't you?'

'Get dressed.'

'You like to think of her as soft and loving and forgiving.'

Fen took his eyes from the statue and looked at Tenghis. His pupils were large and unfocused, but there was no smell of drink from him. Tenghis stepped back without even realizing he had done so.

'But you see,' continued Fen, 'God isn't like that. God is brutal. Unforgiving. Demanding. He's the god of shit and death, of tears and torture.' He raised an arm and pointed at the statue. 'And that new-made thing is not even good enough to be his whore.'

Tenghis had had enough. He pulled his shirt from the radiator, opened the cabin door and left. He was going to see the bosun. Clearly, Fen was ill.

As the door closed behind him he paused, halted by the sound of Fen's low voice, still talking as though Tenghis was still there.

'So new, you see. So new the Lord the Sun has risen and set a thousand million times before you even cast your whore's shadow in his light.'

And then he laughed again.

Tenghis put his arms through his shirt sleeves and walked quickly away without stopping to button up the front.

He wanted to put a hand over his nose and mouth, but the rating standing over him with the mop was watching his every move. Instead, Bosun Felix Chadin attempted to look as calm as his awkward crouch would allow, tapping his knee with a finger as though what he was looking at was perfectly normal.

There must have been around twenty of them. All fully-grown rats, all dead and every one skinned, with its belly slit open. The bodies had been dropped down the back of a life-jacket fixed shelving unit on C-deck, and so recently that there was no smell. It had been the thin serpentine trickle of blood that had attracted the attention of the rating who had been mopping the floor and now, after extricating the bodies with a length of coat-hanger wire, Felix was trying to figure out what it meant.

'When did you last clean around this area?' he asked, still staring at the mess of shiny red skin and guts.

The rating shrugged. 'I dunno. I guess about noon yesterday. I didn't see no blood then.'

Felix stood, wiping his trouser legs as though there had been physical contact with the dead animals, though plainly there had been none.

'Go to the galley and get some refuse bags.'

The rating stared at him, expecting more, his impassive eyes demanding an explanation of the horror.

Felix stared back. 'Now.'

The man retreated sulkily, dragging his mop and leaving the bosun with the unsightly little pile of corpses and the blossoming horror of what the Christ this could possibly mean.

She rewound the tape and held her forehead in her hands as it whined backwards. Not Spanish. Definitely not Spanish. But neither did it sound like the other two commonly-used Peruvian languages, Quechua or Aymara. Esther stopped the tape and pressed play again. The boy's voice was soft but he was clearly enunciating, trying his best to be understood by this strange foreign woman he had so obviously wanted. On the page she had been writing on, she traced with her finger the words translated so far, listening as he spoke, matching the words with her English, ready to stop the tape when she came to the unidentifiable section again.

'... *so we come long time, long long time, to the mountains here ... far, now ... the sun tells us ... we come ... he is risen ... and when he is fully risen then we will be ...*'

She stopped it. It was the next garble of guttural language that had completely stumped her. She cleared her throat, got her pen ready and started the tape again.

'*Kuchitoowah ghukkewal ghukkenalla kareeh ...*'

She clicked it off and checked to see if what she'd written matched the phonetics of what she was hearing. There had been a phleghmy, back-of-the-throat quality to the words, like German or Gaelic, so unlike the lyrical sing-song of the boy's basic Spanish. It completely confounded Esther. Worse. If she were honest, there was something that spooked her about the sounds.

She sighed and closed her notebook. Doubtless there would be someone on the internet who could identify the dialect, but she was irritated. She had hoped to have the majority of it translated, even roughly, before she docked, and now it looked as though that wasn't going to be possible.

Maybe she could work out the context, and therefore its meaning, by labouring through the rest of his lengthy babblings, but judging by what she had already successfully deciphered, none of it seemed to be making much sense. Esther stood up and rubbed her back. She had been working for hours, oblivious to the time, and now she was surprised to find that it was dark outside and she was hungry. The thought of another stilted, tasteless dinner in the officers' mess filled her with gloom, but she had to eat. She pulled on a sweatshirt and left the cabin to see if there was any alternative.

The button on the lift glowed red as she passed, indicating that someone was using it, so she moved to the stairs that would take her from D-deck down to the upper deck and the galley. Not that she would have used it anyway. She thought of the tiny cramped box that shuddered up and down between floors, smelling of sweat and stopping at floors without warning, as a hellish device. The peephole on the outer doors told her all she needed to know about how often it might break down. Why else would you need to see into a lift? Presumably to check the occupants were still alive. She skipped down the metal stairs pausing only to look curiously at the small group of men on C-deck who were standing round the life-jacket shelves, and continuing quickly as the ratings on the periphery returned her inquisitive gaze with inscrutable stares that were not entirely without hostility.

Esther had learned the layout of the ship sufficiently to know that the entrance to the galley was a few doors down from the officers' mess, and so she passed along the corridor and halted in the open doorway. The galley was mayhem. Becko the cook was barking staccato orders to three young men, amidst a cauldron of steam and unpleasant cooking smells that seemed always to contain a hint of rotting cabbage. She waited patiently until his frantic gaze swept across the doorway and caught her in its beam.

She raised a hand. 'Hi!'

Becko stared back mutely then nodded almost imperceptibly and wiped his hands on the filthy cloth around his waist. She was intuitive enough to regard the slight change in his facial expression as a question.

'I'm working in my cabin right now. Is there any chance I could maybe take something back? A sandwich maybe? Anything really.'

Becko looked as if he hadn't heard her, turning back to the large aluminium pot on the stove, but as one of the young men passed behind him, Becko grabbed at him and pointed to the doorway with a terse order. The boy approached Esther and smiled. She hadn't noticed him before, either above or below deck, and was struck by how beautiful he was. Around sixteen, he was tall and slim with perfect skin and glittering black, almond-shaped eyes. But it was more than just his youthful perfection that made her feel peculiar in his presence. The boy was shining with a kind of inner glow, an almost manic enthusiasm and vigour that made her want to step away from its heat. Becko, she mused, must run a pretty thrilling galley if this was an example of how his staff reacted to his instruction. She fought back a blush she hoped could be attributed to the heat and rubbed at her hair.

'I was just wondering if I could maybe take away a sandwich or something ... you know ...'

The boy nodded furiously and waved his large hands. 'I bring you dinner. You say you want.' He turned around and scanned the galley. 'Tonight it fish or maybe a little pork.'

Esther shrugged. 'Fish, I guess. That would be great. Thanks.'

The boy nodded again, beaming at her with a row of gleaming white teeth. 'It good. Real good.'

She smiled back. 'Shall I wait?'

He gestured for her to go. 'I bring. I bring.'

'Sure. Thanks.'

She smiled again, then turned and left. Behind her, the boy watched the empty doorway until Becko kicked at him and called his mother a cock-sucker. The boy, beaming, went about his tasks, unaware that Leonardo Becko's narrowed eyes were following his every move, weighing up what drug his normally sullen surly trainee cook had taken that was making him float around like a girl on her first date, and had done for the last three or four hours.

'What do you reckon?'

Cotton held his hip-bones through his trousers and shook his head at the pile of corpses.

His captain tried again. 'Ever seen anything like it?'

'Nope.'

Lloyd Skinner sighed and gestured to the rating clutching the plastic bin bag that he could shovel away the rats.

Felix Chadin had waited long enough. He was bored with this group of silent men standing around the bloody mess as though examining a car at auction. 'What shall I do, Captain?'

Skinner looked up and regarded him with distaste, almost as though he found him responsible for the outrage. 'Find out who did it.'

The bosun returned the look and crossed his arms across his chest, biting back the sarcastic retort that had already formed itself in his native tongue. He looked to the first officer for something a little more expansive, but Cotton's attention had already moved from the pile of rats now being bundled into the bag, to the area of floor at the bottom of the stairs.

It was clear that the rating had started mopping there, working his way towards the life-jacket shelf and then stopped abruptly on finding the horror. What made Matthew so sure of this was the fact that a subtle residue of glistening, snail-like trail was still present on the stairs. If he were a betting man he would have laid money on the fact that there had been more of the stuff. More of it that would have led directly to the shelf, and had mercifully been wiped away.

Captain Lloyd Skinner let out a long sigh and looked around at the group of men. The flat look in his eyes betrayed that this bizarre event was no more or less than he expected from the complex and irritating species that was humanity, that somehow everybody present had let him down. He nodded curtly to the bosun and left them to their mystery and the mess. Cotton didn't join the other men in watching him go. He was at the bottom of the stairs, squinting up to where they turned on a landing.

'Felix.'

'Uh-huh,' the bosun replied with a dull tinge to his voice as he watched the unconcerned captain's back disappear around the corner.

'Come here a second.'

Felix motioned to the men with the bags to carry on and walked forward to join his first officer.

'What the fuck is that?'

The slime trail was so faint that at first Felix Chadin couldn't understand what Matthew was pointing at.

Then gradually he picked up the faint reflective sheen of the dried mess meandering up the stairs and at the point it turned the corner, climbing a little way up the wall. It was his turn to sigh. 'That, Matthew, is ... how you say it? ... ass needing kicked.'

Matthew looked at him uncomprehendingly.

The bosun indicated the men behind him with a slight incline of the head. 'Looks like a burst refuse bag been dragged instead of lifted.'

Of course it was. It was exactly the residue left on a kitchen floor when a plastic bin bag decides to leak its glutinous contents, except this time, as the man had pointed out, this one had been dragged. Cotton nodded. 'Yeah, well let's find the ass and kick it good.'

Matthew mulled for a second why he was more upset by this minor piece of insubordination than it merited, or was usual in his own slack command. He was irritable. That was all. His tank needed topping up.

His tone did not escape the bosun. Felix glared at him. Sure thing. He would find out who was killing, skinning and tearing the hearts out rats, then he would find out what slut of a deck hand was dragging leaky refuse around, and then maybe he'd have some spare time to find the cure for fucking cancer. Meanwhile he knew his captain would be helping out by pottering in his quarters and his first officer would be busy elsewhere drinking himself silly. He could use a little more support. 'I got a problem with a greaser right now.' He brought it up not because it was important, but merely to try to burden Cotton with any other difficulty he could think of.

'Yeah? What kind of problem?' asked Cotton without much conviction, his eyes back on the shiny trail.

'Fen Sahg. Cabin mate say he's acting real strange.'

Cotton looked at him. 'Strange enough to go cutting up rats?'

The bosun shook his head. 'Nah. I spoke to him. He sure is uptight, but he's not going as psycho as Tenghis had me believe. But I reckon I need to split them up.'

'Yeah. Okay.'

The men stayed silent for a moment, then Cotton spoke quietly, conspiratorially. 'Any theories? The rats, I mean.'

Felix studied Cotton's face and read his eyes. He felt anger rise in his throat again. 'Ah, you mean maybe the common Filipino custom? The one where the first-born must eat rat hearts to be a man?'

Cotton looked hopeful. Chadin sighed through his nose, held Matthew in his gaze inscrutably for a second then turned and walked away, leaving his first officer in no doubt whatsoever by the set of his shoulders, of the contempt in which he was held.

Cotton felt a fool. He closed his eyes for a second and pinched the bridge of his nose. He needed a drink, and in just a minute, when the shame had passed, he would go to his cabin and start working on the evening's oblivion. This weird shit was already too much for him. And what was worse was the question he couldn't get out of his mind. The bosun was comforted by the leaking-bag theory, and if Cotton hadn't known better, he would be too. But he did know better. Whoever did it needed more than just an official reprimand for sloppiness. They needed to explain why they would drag leaking refuse not just up and down the accommodation block stairwell, but more importantly, haul it out from hold two halfway up the ship and then drop it over the side?

He let the two men brush past him with the bag of rats, then decided to return to his cabin by lift.

The stairs suddenly seemed rather unappealing.

8

The cayenne pepper genus he had chosen was the F1 Apache. That did the best in such small pots, and produced a crop that was as useful as it was decorative. Renato Lhoon felt the soil with a finger to check it was moist, them wiped his hands on his trousers and put his hands in his pockets. He thought of his greenhouse back home in Iloilo and wondered if Mary was keeping the coriander going. The extra that Cotton was paying him would mean that maybe next year he could grow plants to look at and smell, instead of to eat, but the thought gave him little pleasure. After all, if he had Matthew Cotton's job and the extra salary and pension that went with it, he wouldn't even be weighing up the choice. And it should be his job. He did it, day in, day out, as well as his own. And he did it better than the captain would ever know. Except Renato was going to make sure that this voyage would be the one on which Skinner found out. Then he might change his mind about his precious first officer, and stop protecting him from the company and every international shipping regulation known to man that said that hopeless drunks shouldn't pilot ships.

He frowned and walked slowly back to the instruments in the middle of the bridge. The telephone was silent. Still no word from the captain as to when they should resume normal speed. Skinner had come on the bridge at the beginning of Renato's watch and made him hove to. They were doing no more than around seven knots, waiting, the captain said, to hear from the company about a possible back-track and change of route. That had been nearly three hours ago and the *Lysicrates* had barely moved.

The second officer was becoming increasingly curious about the nature of the captain's communications with the company.

Not only had they altered course to come farther out from the regular shipping channel, taking them up the middle of the Milne Edwards Trench, and not only was the cargo highly irregular, but now they were treading water, standing still while someone in Hong Kong decided where they should be heading. The *Lysicrates* had never had such a mess of a voyage. It was an ancient and unprestigious ship, but it was a creature of habit and had more or less run the same half dozen routes for its overlong life, and Lhoon had become used to the mundanity of it.

But in a way it was perfect. The very irregularity of the voyage gave him more opportunity to escape his ties to Cotton. It would have to be more than just Skinner finding him drunk and asleep on watch. That had happened once before, the time in fact when Cotton had decided it would be worthwhile paying Renato a substantial portion of his wages to ensure it didn't recur, and yet somehow it got forgiven and forgotten.

No. Renato longed for Cotton to be caught in some public and unforgivable dereliction of duty, one than even the *laissez faire* attitude of the captain couldn't find a way of overlooking. He hadn't thought of what it might be yet, but as the captain's orders became more peculiar, and this voyage looked like lasting longer than any of them anticipated, Renato Lhoon knew his opportunity to stop being Cotton's safety net would come.

He sniffed back some mucus and sat down on the chrome stool, with only the thrum of an idling engine through the floor and the hum of instrument panels as background noise, while he savoured, with all the time in the world before him, the delights of stepping over his drunken superior into a better future.

'*Lo tiraraon a los cerdos ... con la miedra humana ... pero el que constituye partes del hombre ... les cuales el hombre mismo evade ...*'

She stared at the Dictaphone with her mouth slightly open.

'What the fuck?'

Esther tutted and played it back again. This section of the tapes was driving her crazy. She remembered the chilly dawn when she recorded it, and remembered too that she had been paying the boy very little attention as he spoke, watching instead the elders of the tribe as they broke up their altar the moment the sun had risen safely over the barren line of mountains. The reason she recalled the recording so well was that the boy was more agitated than normal. He had sweated and shifted around, talking too fast for her, but had obviously wanted her full concentration. The irritation the boy had felt was quite plain here in his voice, a rising, darker quality in it indicating he was insisting on her attention and not receiving it.

But now she came to translate it, the stuff made no sense at all. She hadn't a clue what he was talking about. Was he referring in some way to the men taking down the altar? A legend? A tribal story? It made little sense, particularly when she hadn't taken the time to ascertain its context. She glanced at her translation so far.

'They threw him with the pigs ... with the human shit ... but he is made from the parts of man that man himself shuns ...'

There was a gap in the tape after this, presumably where the boy waited for a response and Esther provided nothing. The faint background noises of men talking, alpacas stirring the bells around their necks and the calling of alien birds was all that wall-papered behind the hissing silence. The boy spoke again.

'*Adoramas al sol, pero sabemos, asi como sabian nuestros antepasados, que adirar la oscuridad el sol vuelve a aparecer ...*'

She glanced down at the notebook again to check her own interpretation.

'We honour the sun, but we know as our forefathers did that only by also honouring the dark will the sun continue to return ...'

More silence. A sullen silence. She fast forwarded.

'*Esperamos ... y ilamara ...*'

It was here she must have given up watching the men and turned back to her indignant interviewee. She listened with mild embarrassment as her voice on the tape cleared its throat and asked in an indifferent, dreamy way, and in a very poor Spanish accent, 'Hmmm? Who? You wait for who?'

The boy's voice grew so soft she could hardly make out the words. She listened once more, rewound then turned it up as loud as it would go.

'*Aquel que camina con el sol pero comanada a las tineblas.*'

She scribbled, rewound, and scribbled again, then looked hopelessly at the phrase. 'He who walked in the sun but commands the shadows.'

And then soft, softer than even before: '*El* ... something ... *sin* ... something.'

Rewind. She concentrated hard, ear to the tiny speaker.

'*El ... cura ... sin ... iestrio.*'

Esther switched it off, put down the Dictaphone. She toyed with the pen and then in capital letters, though she was not sure why, she wrote the boy's words in English and sat forward looking at them.

'The dark priest.'

The hammering at the cabin door made Esther drop the notebook. It bounced from a rapidly jerked-up knee and landed spine-down on the sofa like a dancer doing the splits.

'Christ!'

The hammering came again.

She expelled a long breath, leapt up and hollered. 'Yeah?'

A muffled voice from the other side of the metal door. 'Dinner. Bring you dinner.'

Esther put a hand to her beating heart and slowly let a smile spread over her face. She had no idea she had been spooking herself so badly. It was her dinner. Of course it was her dinner. She smoothed down her sweatshirt, ran a hand through her hair and walked to open the cabin door.

The boy's smile had not become any less dazzling since the last time she saw him. He stood in the corridor brandishing a tray that boasted a glass of milk and a round steel lid covering a plate.

'Hey, thanks,' said Esther, returning the smile and stretching out her arms to receive the tray.

The assistant cook shook his head and gestured that he was going to bring it in, and she stood aside with a polite and grateful nod. He laid the tray down on the mean little fold-down shelf beneath the window, and as he did so Esther found herself unable to stop staring at the slim nape of his girlish neck and the sheen of sweat that moistened it.

'Thanks,' she said again as he turned.

The boy stood and beamed. 'Pork. Very good.'

The fact that she asked for fish seemed too ungrateful an observation to make. So she decided against it. After all, she was Jewish by birthright alone. Her maternal grandmother had been orthodox, but Esther's mother not only married a Gentile, but neither she nor Esther had ever crossed the threshold of a synagogue in their brief lives together. Pork would be fine.

'Great.'

He nodded, still standing, showing absolutely no sign of wishing to leave. Esther wrestled with this for a moment. Were you required to tip if the crew brought you food? If so, how much? It didn't seem right. She had felt from her encounter with the cook that her request was not all that unusual: it had the feel of a favour being granted rather than of ordering room service.

'And milk,' he added, increasing his smile.

'Milk. Yeah. Great.' She nodded back, and while smiling walked a few steps towards the door in rather an obvious movement that signalled she was going to see him out. It had little effect.

'You drink milk back in Texas?'

Esther looked at him, contemplating the level of gossip amongst the crew that would bring the information concerning her geographical origins to this boy she had never even noticed before. It annoyed her. She masked it.

'Uh, sure. Everyone kinda drinks milk. You know, from time to time.'

He nodded again. The sweat she had noticed on the nape of his neck was blooming on his face, neck and sharply-sculpted collarbones now. Becko's kitchen must be close to hell in the middle of the day, she mused, if this was the effect it had on his staff even at a distance and in a cool night.

'They got stores sell milk in that trailer park?'

The annoyance abated, and in its place something chilly ran over Esther's heart. How could he possibly know where she lived? She had told no one on the ship about her home. Her smile remained, but it wilted around the corners and her eyes narrowed. 'Sorry?'

'Mort sell it, maybe? You know when he come round for rent?'

'I don't ... I ...'

She was stuttering, but the boy threw his head back and laughed like a child. He pointed at her as though she were in on some great gag they shared.

'I bet that big dog he got not let anyone buy it, though. What he called again ... Tyson? ... you like see him try? Here Missy, you take milk ... good price ... woof woof ... Tyson grab milk with those big teeth ... ruff ruff, milk gone ... ha ha.'

He slapped his thigh in mirth as Esther's mouth dried of saliva. Her smile had faded completely now, and when she found the power to speak her voice had an edge to it that was a million light years away from friendly.

'What are you talking about?'

He wiped some more sweat from his brow, laughed some more and waved a big hand. 'Make joke, make joke.'

She watched him as he struggled to control his glee and let his eyes wander to the pile of work on her sofa.

'Going good?'

Esther made no response. She was on red alert, watching this boy in her room now with a feral caution that was increasing in intensity.

He, however, was unfazed by her silence, and his grin remained wide. 'You gonna have work hard get that by Professor Radcliffe, huh?'

She nodded, keeping her eyes on his face, her body tense. 'Yeah. Maybe.'

He beamed back at her. 'Yeah, 'cos he not like you much, huh?'

'I'd like you to leave.'

The assistant cook nodded again and shrugged, still smiling. He walked across the room to the door and Esther instinctively moved back into a defensive position. He halted in front of her.

'Not worry. Be okay,' he said with genuine friendliness.

'Sure,' she placated, eyes steely.

'We the same.' He patted his genitals.

Esther registered the action without taking her eyes from his, her muscles readying for action. 'Yeah?'

'Yeah.' He nodded vigorously, and turned to leave. He stopped in the door frame. 'Both virgins.'

Before she could draw breath he had left, leaving behind only a faint odour of Becko's stinking galley, the acidic metallic tang of sweat, and a pork dinner that was unlikely to be eaten.

Ronaldo Valdez glared at his new cabin mate as he unpacked his belongings on the bunk. As a humble wiper he wouldn't normally have enjoyed a cabin to himself, but since his usual constant companion, Benito, had been taken sick back in Port Arthur and stayed ashore, he'd been surprised how much he'd appreciated the solitude. Now this clown from the country, who did tricks in the mess with his cards and dice, was joining him. He wasn't pleased. The bosun stood over Fen like a gaoler, watching him as he unpacked.

Fen seemed perfectly normal to Felix, the usual mix of sullen subservience and disaffection most greasers adopted around their superior officers. It made him wonder if Tenghis's report of insanity hadn't merely been retaliation for some minor dispute, although Felix had heard the reports of Fen's over-zealous Saanti reading in the crew mess hall, and he didn't like the effect it had had amongst the men. But there was enough to worry about on board without the added complication of feuding ratings.

Felix was already composing the address he would make to the lower-ranking crew members in the morning to try and get to the bottom of the skinned-rat mystery.

'Don't put that there,' barked Ronaldo as Fen reached over to lay a shoebox of possessions on the Formica folding table.

Fen glared at him, and withdrew the box.

'This is a two-man cabin, Valdez,' said the bosun, and motioned that Fen could do as he pleased.

'I use that space every day,' whined the wiper.

'Tough. Benito'll be boarding again anyway at Port Arthur. You'd go blind with any more opportunity to pull your knob in private.'

'Yeah, well Benito knows how to behave,' muttered Ronaldo under his breath.

Felix glanced at Fen to see if a fight were brewing, but the man was oblivious to the unwelcoming demeanour of his new companion, squinting instead at the dark window and holding the box in his hands as though weighing up some problem.

Chadin sighed and left them to it, bestowing a patriarchal warning glare to both men as he exited that he trusted would be properly interpreted.

The wiper watched the cabin door close then turned and looked at Fen. 'You snore, I'll kick you right up your shit-hole.'

Fen continued to ignore him, putting a finger gently to his mouth, still staring at the square of black glass, tapping at his lips as he thought. Slowly a gentle smile spread across his face. 'East. Yes. East. Good. Very good.'

Ronaldo scowled at him, lay down on his bunk and turned his back.

* * *

He had no idea what he was looking for. Nor, for that matter, why. Matthew had given it his best shot in the privacy of his cabin, trying to put his uneasiness about the rats in the same numbed-down box as everything else, with the assistance of a bottle of export-strength gin. But even through the familiar padded cushion of quickly-consumed alcohol, the anxiety had niggled like a tooth-ache. Now, like a fool, he was walking unsteadily along the white-lit cargo deck, holding a powerful spot flashlight in his fist.

The figure of Renato Lhoon moved about through the glass of the bridge above him, but Cotton was undisturbed about being observed. In fact, for some curious reason, even on this bright familiar metal stage, he was rather glad of it.

It would be fair to say that Matthew Cotton's senses were not at their most finely tuned. He registered only very distantly the fact that the ship was barely moving, and it had taken him nearly three or four minutes of clumsy crashing around to find and fit the rechargeable batteries for the flashlight in the apparatus room at the end of the deck. But he had already made the decision to eschew the comfort of passing out on his sofa until Renato woke him, and here he was. Drink and its familiar befuddlement had mellowed only his co-ordination, not his curiosity.

He wove his way along the yellow-painted pathway that led across the deck to hold number nine, and stopped at the lip of the open hatch. The holds on bulk carriers were always numbered from the bow backwards. Hold number one was right at the bow and the last, number nine, sat beneath the bridge at the foot of the accommodation block. There was a strange silence when the ship was hove to. A melancholy lapping sound from the sea, instead of the busy swishing noise it made as the ship normally pushed it out of the way, was the only break in the monotony of a distant and stifled engine.

Matthew's ears were already muffled by the night's first stages of drunkenness but he felt the stillness as he walked, and found himself treading more lightly because of it.

He stopped at the first hold, and with the concentration that all drunks employ in performing simple tasks, placed the flashlight carefully on the hatch door above him and hauled himself up.

The fifteen-foot gap between hatch doors illuminated the refuse below, but Matthew knelt at the edge and probed under the iron lids with the spot. A rat scuttled from the intense beam, moving snake-like over the repulsive uneven surface until it disappeared, burying itself beneath some unidentifiable piece of human detritus. The smell was terrible. Matthew put a hand to his mouth and backed off before he puked.

He crouched on his haunches for a moment to try to think. If someone were merely dragging refuse from the hold along the deck, there was another question that needed to be answered. Now that it had settled, the top layer of waste was at least nine or ten feet below the hatch opening, which meant that no one could reach it to remove it without some form of grabbing device. Certainly no one could drop down there onto the surface and live to tell the tale. But surely a man with equipment to scoop and retrieve waste from the holds, however bizarre that might seem, would certainly be spotted by whoever was on watch? A hot flush of shame washed over him as he realized that his watch would almost certainly prove the exception to that assumption. But the ludicrousness of the whole imagined operation made him dismiss it as fancy. There had to be some other explanation.

He wiped at his nose in an unconscious and pointless effort to relieve his senses from the hot, thick reek, and stood up on the square metal hatch cover to continue his tour of the holds.

There was a distant sound. He looked round slowly, listening to identify its source, and as it came again he turned his head to locate it. It was a remote noise, as far away as holds one or two at the very bow of the ship, and it was peculiar.

He crouched down again and waited, holding his breath.

A combination of scraping and scrabbling, it was a noise that only avoided sounding like the magnification of a rat's progress behind a barrel because of a certain metallic quality.

It stopped abruptly, almost as if it knew it had been heard, and after less than thirty seconds Matthew let his breath go in a long exhalation. Keeping his eyes on the rough location he'd guessed it had come from, he gripped the flashlight and gently dropped down from the hatch cover. He glanced back and above him briefly to see if Renato was still at the bridge window, but the glass was dark and he could see no one.

Matthew Cotton ran his wrist over a dry mouth and weighed up his options. He could go back to his cabin where two-thirds of the gin bottle waited along with a bucket of ice and a carton of fresh orange. Or he could walk the length of the deck and find out what had made that noise.

For a moment he allowed himself to remember how it felt to be a captain, how the welfare of his ship and crew would never have allowed him to think twice about such obvious decisions, and the part of him that still cared started to grieve again for the man that was lost. But he was a master at subjugating such moments of emotional weakness, and he skilfully stamped out its weak flame before straightening up to face towards the bow.

For once, the gin could wait. He would go take a look.

The harshness of the tungsten lights cast hard but conflicting shadows across the deck, and as he walked, he was aware of his own dark shape crossing itself and multiplying in certain pools of light where the beams fought to illuminate the same patches of confusing metal shapes.

The cargo deck was over two hundred metres long, and the open hatch doors of the remaining eight holds that protruded over the walkway took on a formality in the light and shade, like the complex geometric topiary that might have lined some Boston colonial mansion's driveway.

He moved between them with a gingerness that was as much to do with his reluctance to trip drunkenly, as it was to be on alert should the noise recur.

It recurred as he reached hold six. But this time it had a shape.

From the corridor that separated holds two and three, running from port to starboard, something dark darted out, and vanished as quickly as it had appeared into the space between holds one and two. It happened so quickly that Cotton stopped and blinked, doubting his own vision, but the increased beating of his heart confirmed that even if his mind took its time to catch up, his eyes had already conveyed a primeval panic to his internal organs.

What was it? It had been big. At least as big as a small to medium man. But the residue of image it left on his retina had not been that of a man at all. In the fraction of the second he had had in which to register it, the shape had seemed more animal, but moving like an insect or a reptile, unnaturally quickly and with a gait that was unpleasantly unfamiliar.

Cotton blinked and tried to calm his heart. An animal on board, a big one. What sort of animal? But that was ridiculous. Of course, he might simply be more bombed than he realized, his suppressed senses merely witnessing a guilty deck hand up to no good, trying to hide from his first officer. The thought delivered a welcome injection of courage to his veins, and from his current advantageous position, placed as he still was at the end of the holds, Matthew could scan the surface of the hatch covers and the corridors that ran between them, deciding which way to proceed. If it was a deck hand, Cotton would make sure he was sorry for making him use up some extra heart beats on his behalf. And hopefully, the explanation of what the hell he was doing out here would be interesting to say the least.

There was no more movement, and Matthew decided to take a route that would double back, crossing to the port side of the deck and creeping up under the shadow of the hatch covers until he reached hold one.

Slowly and as silently as he could he dropped down, keeping his body low as he moved to the port side of hatch eight.

His plan was good. The bright illumination made the shadows dark by contrast, and there was at least a five- or six-foot-wide line of deep black under each hold's hatch cover that gave him almost complete concealment. The only place in which he could be seen would be when running across the mouth of each well-lit corridor that separated the holds. He scrambled from the cover of hold eight to hold seven, then paused in the black to listen again. Nothing.

Now that he had regained his nerve, his concern was that his quarry might escape back to the accommodation block by utilizing the same guerrilla tactic on the starboard side. He stopped to think about that, gazing out at the space between his dark hiding place and the taff rail.

The deck glistened in the light. He narrowed his eyes.

The trail of refuse slime was running parallel to his oblong of shadow, taking a bold path along the metal walkway mapped out for sailors between the yellow lines. Cotton glanced ahead at the empty starboard deck, licked his lips and, still keeping low, moved forward, out of the shadows. Here, the trail was not hardened and flaky. It was wet and sticky and he bent to touch it with his finger. A stench arose from it, and it was with some disgust he discovered that it had a viscosity to the touch that made him want it off his finger tip the moment it made contact. He wiped it hurriedly on his trouser leg and squinted at the line of mess. It was clear in patches, with a milky effluent marbling running through it, exactly, as Felix pointed out, like the run-out from a refuse bag.

But it had an under-layer of reddish brown, a tainting of its clarity with a cloudy darkness, that most definitely resembled watery blood. The dilute nature of it reminded Matthew of a discarded wound dressing, or the residue of butcher's-meat blood on the bottom of a supermarket carton of steak. His unease returned and he moved quickly back into the shadow.

The scuttling noise again. He snapped his head up and listened. It was brief, but it had almost certainly come from the bow.

Matthew caught his breath, clutched the spotlight and ran. He sprinted from hold to hold, glancing anxiously to his right each time he crossed a white-lit corridor, dreading and hoping in equal measures that he might glimpse his target doing the same.

He reached hold two, dived into the shadow of its hatch cover and panted against the cold metal. His head was spinning, and since the only organ that got any regular exercise was his liver, his heart was having to struggle to keep pace with its owner's unusual exertions. The only way to surprise his prey, he decided, was to move quickly. He regained his breath then scampered forward to the corridor between holds one and two and grabbed hold of the metal rail that guided the covers together. With one swift move-ment he pulled himself up onto the hatch cover and crouched low as he regained his balance, allowing himself a quick glance back up to the distant bridge to see if Renato was visible again yet.

He was not. But in that fraction of a moment, when Matthew Cotton turned his head back to face across the split hatch covers, something else was. It was crouched lower than him on the opposite cover, the fifteen-foot trench of opened doors between them, the figure hidden in the inky black shadow cast by a derrick. But it was watching him with an intensity that prickled his scalp.

In the time it took Matthew to open his mouth and attempt to draw breath, it had leapt from the shadow, scrambled across the metal surface and disappeared with a brief, obscene rustling and squelching, into the abyss of the hold.

Cotton stayed very still. His body was ice and the mouth he had just opened stayed that way. He tried to recapture what exactly he had just seen.

It was an impression. Just an impression. Blackness and decay. Bits of things that couldn't possibly be part of an organic creature. Shards of metal and patches of scabbed fur. Rotting flesh and melted plastic. Bone and fabric, and blood-matted hair.

Cotton swallowed back bile. If the contents of hold number two had really formed themselves into that hideous semblance of a man, he was unable to find the strength to move forward and confront it again. He crouched in the same position for a long, long time, and when the two deck hands sent by an exasperated Renato approached him with subservient offers of assistance, he climbed down silently and walked back to the accommodation block without acknowledging their existence.

Her hands were on either side of the window and her forehead touched the glass. Attempting to work had been pointless, and eating even more so. As proof, a pork chop lay with a solitary slice taken from it, in a congealed half-crescent of gravy, and Esther's notes and tapes lay scattered around the sofa and floor where they had been since the boy had left her cabin hours ago.

The worst of it was, she was a girl who could work out stuff. Esther had a velocity of thought that could either impress or intimidate, depending on who was witnessing the process. Perhaps it was a primitive skill, the very essence of survival, or the reverse, an example of a modern mental finesse that had taken millions of years to achieve. Either way, Esther had it, and knew she had it, which was why it had taken her a matter of seconds to realize there was no rational explanation for the boy's display whatsoever. The rest of the time, she had simply spent fretting.

She had been through everything. From the conversations at meals she had contributed to since boarding, right back to making the phone call home from the bar on the dock when she met Cotton. And there was nothing, not a single lapse in any of her social intercourse, that would have revealed a fraction of the information that the young Filipino boy had so cheerfully repeated.

She banged at the glass with a fist and turned back into the room. Was he a mind reader? A clairvoyant? And most importantly, did it matter? She remembered his patted groin and his parting words, and decided, that yes, a total stranger being privy to that kind of personal detail mattered very much indeed.

She looked down at the tray. The milk had been quickly consumed, but the food had stuck in her throat. Esther stared at the grey meat for a moment, then took a deep breath.

It was nearly midnight, but she needed to get out of the cabin. She would take the tray back to the galley and if the boy was still about, confront him. Or even better, maybe she would talk to Becko.

Esther rounded up the plate and cutlery with a clumsy clatter, grabbed the tray and left her room.

The well-lit corridors confirmed that it was late, humming with fluorescent light and an underlying silence that was not dissimilar to the eerie nocturnal stillness of a hospital. She crossed to the narrow stairs and descended carefully, trying not to let the plate slide from the cheap plywood tray.

The corridor that served the galley and mess rooms was more comforting in that it contained a low murmur of human conversation. On any ship with rotating shifts, there are always those whose day is night, and right now two of them were having a smoke and a coffee from the machine in the crew mess diagonally opposite the galley entrance.

Esther was surprised at the relief she felt on hearing the curious staccato of Filipino voices in the room, realizing now as she did that the galley was completely empty of its hard-working kitchen staff. She looked in and nodded to the two men as she passed, and they returned the gesture through a veil of smoke with minimum effort and inscrutable gazes.

All the lights were on in the deserted galley, the long, stainless steel surfaces scrubbed clean and shiny, and the thick-bottomed aluminium pots all stacked and ready for another day of mediocre institutional cooking.

It felt intrusive, being in this room when its master, the chef, was not, but Esther found it mildly thrilling. She had hoped that maybe at least one of the staff would be there, although thinking about it now, she had no idea why. Of course, they would be on duty very early in the morning, but for now they were in their cabins asleep and she had the opportunity to look around Becko's little kingdom at will. She placed the tray near the big sinks, and scanned the room.

Esther enjoyed detail. She'd waited plenty of tables in her time, shouted at her share of short-order cooks to get her three soup and crackers quickly, but it was interesting to her to note the differences between a ship's galley and the kitchens of the greasy diners she'd worked back in Texas.

Here, the stoves had rails around the hot-plates to stop the pots sliding off in a swell, and everything was on a smaller scale, being designed to fit into the space that the ship afforded it rather than demanding the room it needed. She walked along the line of stoves and ovens, running her hand over the scarred steel top, burnished by a thousand circular wire-wool marks, feeling the residual warmth beneath the metal as if it was skin.

There was always something comforting about a kitchen, no matter how municipal. She had always wanted one. A real one. Not the phoney walnut-veneered, swing-down cabinets of the trailer, the tiny aluminium sink with foot-pedal faucets, and the crappy little propane hob that Benny heated up his tins of beans and hash on. Something like the Waltons' kitchen was more what she had in mind. A football-pitch-sized room with gingham cotton and colonial pine dressers, and a table that was always groaning with food and ringed with laughing diners. Something, in other words, that she had never had, and probably would never have. The commercial kitchens of the diners had provided the next best thing. Big and noisy and hot, clanging with industry and profanities, but ultimately friendly.

She wondered if the same atmosphere prevailed in this floating version.

Undercutting the buzz of the lights was the buzz of insects, a few fat ugly blue-bottles darting in and out of the galley from the half-open door she assumed was the storeroom.

The trainers at base camp who had given Esther top marks for just about everything would have patted themselves on their backs at the unconscious physical nature of her response, although their pride in their training would have been misplaced. Esther had been born to the philosophy of survival, not taught it, and the scrublands of trailer park hell had made the military's simple obstacle courses seem laughable.

Because while her mind was still mulling over the kind of sloppiness that would have allowed rogue food to be left out in the storeroom, and contrasting it with the obsessive cleanliness of the galley, her body had already naturally assumed a position of defence.

She had rocked onto her toes, her hands were now above waist height, palms open, held a few inches from her body, her balance and posture perfect for either swift flight or sudden defence, and as she moved forward, which she did without having planned to, it was with impressive stealth and precision.

Two or three flies buzzed around her face, banging against her like drunks trying to pass through a late-night movie line, but without causing her to blink or alter her posture.

The storeroom was lit, and as she approached the half-open door she paused. Esther Mulholland had no idea why she was uneasy about the presence of a couple of flies in rooms dedicated to the preparation and storage of food, but there was no doubt whatsoever that she was.

With a caution that would have seemed misplaced and ludicrous to any casual observer, she slid her body round the frame of the metal doorway and entered the storeroom.

It was a space that had been divided meticulously into the perishable and the non-perishable.

Behind the sacks of potatoes and shelves of giant cans that could last a whole voyage without spoiling, the back wall housed the massive walk-in freezer, the room-within-a-room that contained everything from the catering packs of greens that Becko would systematically ruin by ruthless boiling, to great haunches of meat swinging from hooks.

The reason that Esther could know its secret contents so intimately was that the freezer door was hanging open, its icy atmosphere seeping onto the warmer floor in small puffs of vapour that spilled across the lip of the doorway onto the metal floor of the storeroom. To the side of the door a red light burned brightly.

This was where ship was no different from diner. Anyone who had worked near a walk-in freezer knew the rules. You turned the light on when you entered, and you turned it off when you left. That meant that even in the event of some moron closing the door on you, they would know you were still inside if that light still burned red. The light on the *Lysicrates*' freezer door was still red. She listened, trying to make out if the person responsible was moving around, and heard nothing.

Esther moved forward and slid cautiously along the edge of the storeroom shelves. She should have called 'hello,' should have coughed and made her presence known, but somehow she wanted to remain undetected until she had worked out what was wrong with this picture.

Quickly she gained the space behind the freezer door. Her gaze started at the top of the large cream door and dropped to the floor. There was a piece of meat lying half out of the door, red and shiny and skinned. It was on this portion of opportunity that the flies were busy. Whoever was in there was hardly being a model food hygienist. She put a hand up to the large chrome handle and pulled the door open all the way, stepping out from behind it as she swung back the weighty slab.

Blood is interesting when it freezes. Perhaps its most interesting aspect is its tendency to crystallize. All around the torso of the corpse that lay splayed like a crucified Christ on the freezer floor was a large pool of flaky, iced blood, jagged and whitened at the edges where the temperature was at its lowest.

Where the heat of the outer room had got to it, right here, at the leg hanging over the threshold that Esther now realized was human and not porcine, there was just regular thick, congealing liquid. She didn't scream. She didn't even step back. She crouched and turned, covering her back, flicking her eyes only briefly one more time to the unbearable horror in the freezer.

It resembled an anatomical drawing. The flesh was still intact, since only the skin had been removed. It was where the flesh had left the face that she saw the tell-tale sign of a task that had been done in a hurry. Eyes bulged from sockets, devoid of lids to give them expression, and one had been dislodged so that it hung precariously against a shining, bulbous cheek.

But despite the skill with which the body had been liberated from its skin, there was a glaring aesthetic atrocity. The torso was slit from collarbone to navel, and a gaping ovoid between the rib-cage grinned up at Esther.

She was out of the storeroom, through the galley and into the crew mess hall before the flies on the skinned leg could stir, orbit and settle again.

The two men who looked up at Esther's entrance needed no great command of the English language to understand that their presence was somewhat urgently required.

9

'Panic,' the captain had said quietly as he'd stood impassively over the boy's body '... is the enemy of survival.' But that had been three or four minutes ago. A lifetime away. Now, Matthew gripped the taff rail and bit the inside of his cheek in a vain attempt to stop a second stream of hot vomit from scouring up his throat. It was too late. He arched his back and threw up noisily over the rail.

Behind him, the door from the galley to the main deck constantly opened and closed as men spilled out, shouting and gesticulating, herded out by their bosun to await orders. But their rising staccato foreign exclamations were not providing the placebo of human companionship he so desperately needed right now to chase away the bitter chill of death. He hunched his shoulders against it, his hot head pressing much too hard into the unforgiving metal of the rail.

The door banged once more and with his head still bowed, Matthew felt a body position itself close to his. He wiped his mouth with his forearm and looked up. Esther was hugging herself against the cool night breeze, her back against the rail, eyes scanning the growing number of alarmed faces that were gathering on the deck.

'Why do they want us out here?'

Matthew blinked at her. The part of him that still retained a sliver of vanity was both embarrassed by being caught with the threads of mucus-bound vomit adhering to his shirt, and also curiously riled by her use of 'they' that excluded him as a senior officer.

He wasn't part of this herd.

A few minutes ago he'd been a constituent of that grim, superior delegation, standing over the skinned and eviscerated horror that spilled out of the freezer and into their nightmares, trying desperately to decide what to do.

They were merchant seamen, for Christ's sake. Not military. There simply wasn't anything in the handbook that prepared a crew like this for their junior cook being skinned alive and having his heart ripped out.

He'd only come outside to be sick, not through drink for a change, and for some reason he wanted her to know that. Matthew straightened up and looked at her anxious, frowning profile. 'We're searching the cabins,' he said, over-emphasizing the 'we'.

She nodded, not meeting his gaze. 'Uh-huh? For what exactly?'

Her tone was crisp, unfriendly, nervous. Despite knowing what this young girl had just gone through, Cotton found he had little compassion to spare, and that her clipped tone merely irritated him further.

'Someone didn't bring back their coffee mug.'

Esther turned to look at him, and her eyes froze him. They were as hard as coal, but somewhere deep behind their cool, contemptuous appraisal of him he could read a menu of sadness and fear. He wiped the sweat from his upper lip and softened his voice as he turned his gaze back out into the black ocean.

'Blood.'

Esther was silent for a moment, and then she began to speak quietly and steadily to herself as though she were a coroner dictating over an autopsy. Matthew wiped at some vomit stains as casually as he could manage, and watched her with caution. She was wired, it was plain, and he couldn't blame her.

'But there were no blood trails around the corpse at all. Nothing. The floor was clean. Completely clean. How could a murderer kill, skin and split apart a body without leaving a trail like an explosion in an abattoir? How? Unless the boy was killed elsewhere and deposited in the freezer. But even then, there would be trails, signs, some kinds of disturbance, and of course the actual site of the killing wouldn't take long to find on a vessel this size ...'

'Esther.' Matthew's voice was gentle now.

She kept going. '... but, importantly, how would it be possible to covertly move such an atrocity from one part of the ship to another when there are always other people around ...?'

'Esther!'

'… and even if you could, how could you …'

He put out a hand and laid it on her arm. It stopped the torrent of her talking abruptly. 'Enough.'

She surprised him and laid her own freezing hand on top of his, turning her face to him, the smooth skin contorted into lines of something approximating grief. 'He brought me my dinner.'

Matthew nodded. 'Yeah.'

Esther Mulholland scanned his face rapidly, aggressively, searching for a fight. She blinked twice, then bent her head to her chest and began to cry. As he ringed her shoulder with an awkward arm, Matthew Cotton wished he could join her in her weeping.

But now that his nausea had passed his attention was focused on only one thing. The long partially-lit corridor of metal that ran alongside holds one to nine.

The funny thing was, he could tell there was something wrong before he even opened the door. Maybe that was how mothers felt with a cot death. They knew the baby was there in the crib when they crept up in the morning, dressing-gown just tied, cup of coffee in fist, maternal smile twitching and ready to catch the returned gummy grin of their most beloved possession. But before they even looked in, they knew there was something missing. Something important. The breath. The life.

And that was exactly it. Pasqual knew before the door swung back that his baby, the radio room, the beating heart of the ship, was not breathing.

No lights spangled the grey metal panel fronts. No crackle or hum of electrical life came from the industrial punched-hole speakers. And the air that he took for granted was always full of a million potential voices, music, information, just waiting to be filtered through his radio, was as still as the grave.

Pasqual wiped his upper lip with a finger and put his hands on his hips. He had been the first one despatched by the captain after the discovery of the horror that they would not let him near enough to see, his duty to send out an immediate distress call, and it was partly a sense of that responsibility that stalled his panic.

If it was an electrical fault, which it most probably was, then there was back-up. And that was exactly what he was going to get on top of right now. Problem, action, problem solved. Nothing to worry about.

He walked more confidently into his little twelve-by-eighteen-foot world, rolled out his worn chair from under the console and sat down.

He flicked a couple of switches just to confirm there was no life in the equipment, and then pushed back to access the panel behind the main medium-wave radiotelephone containing the back-up controls.

His hand brushed the top of the scarred wooden desk and something tiny and metallic skittered to the floor.

Pasqual blinked down at a small screw that pirouetted on the linoleum like a child's top, then turned away to continue his task. He stopped, then slowly looked down again.

His gaze rested on the slowing screw then transferred itself to the panel above the desk. The main control panel had eight screws holding it in place. Now it had eight holes.

Pasqual put out his hands and rested his fingers on the grey metal. He pulled the panel gently and the large rectangle of steel shifted forward, catching slightly on the left side as it always did when he had to remove it for maintenance.

It took him a moment or two to register what he was looking at when the panel finally came away and rested face-down on the desk, but when it did, it was not quite so easy to stifle his previously-contained fear.

Whoever had opened Pasqual's precious equipment and removed its guts had done so with considerable skill and knowledge. There was barely anything left, and nothing that was usable. He knew before he checked that the rest of the room's equipment would be the same, and while he contemplated that, he placed the metal panel in front of him and rested his hands on the desk, wishing that he had heeded the captain's orders for everyone to move around the ship only in twos or more.

The thought of the journey back to his superior officers was not making his stomach churn because of what they might say about a ship stranded with no means of communication.

It was making his hair prickle and his sweat bead, because whoever had murdered the boy might also have murdered Pasqual's radio in order to stop anyone shouting for help; and unless the murderer had come like a spirit from the sea, he was still on board, and his job was not yet finished.

Felix Chadin stood at the door of the cabin while his two assistants entered. Ronaldo's living space had been largely unaffected by Fen's recent occupancy, its Spartan interior more or less the way it had been since Port Arthur, and it was clear the moment the bosun swung open the door that it was also not the scene of the great carnage for which they searched.

Chadin was weary of this task already, and nervous of its failure. The captain had been obliged to order it, but his logical mind told him that no murderer would leave a trail of gore where he slept, and Felix was already searching for alternative courses of action while he dutifully carried out this one.

'Clean,' shrugged the ABS scouring the outer cabin, while the one in the toilet shouted an echo from the tiny cubicle. The men were as perplexed as their bosun. They were frightened and confused and detective-work had most certainly not been part of their scanty training for life at sea.

Felix nodded and inclined his head to the next cabin down the alleyway, and they skulked past him to obey, casting anxious glances left and right as they went.

The bosun tightened his grip on the handle to shut the door and then stopped. On the fold-down table was the shoebox that Fen had so jealously guarded on arrival, and Felix's eye fell on it with interest.

True, no one had been guilty of bloodthirsty work in this room, and it was therefore not his place to use the search as an excuse to invade privacy, but the sight of the box pricked a compulsive curiosity in him.

He stepped into the cabin and with one quick backward glance lifted the tattered cardboard lid and looked inside.

It was empty. Guiltily, Felix Chadin replaced it and sighed.

He was tilting at windmills now. There were still eight more cabins to search, more corners and crannies of the ship to poke into until they could truly say that nothing had been found, and quite frankly in the dire circumstances he wasn't sure whether a find or a blank would be more comforting. Another look at the grey-green cardboard carton that proclaimed that it had once contained sandals from a factory outlet store in Galveston, made him embarrassed at his abuse of power. What had he imagined could possibly be in a shoebox that would help them understand the nightmare that had engulfed this ship? With his shoulders set in a position that would take a stress-managing masseur a couple of weeks to put right, he turned and left the room.

As he went, the usual contents of Fen's box lay sightlessly facing the bosun's retreating shoes, from the shadows beneath its owner's bunk.

Dawn was a long way off. Lloyd Skinner stroked a finger over the white, yellow and blue Admiralty chart, number 4608, Guayaquil to Valparaiso, and let his radio officer whine breathlessly about their perilous situation. From the other hard foam couch, Matthew Cotton and Renato Lhoon watched silently, Renato sitting forward, hands clasped over his knees, Cotton lying back, hands holding either side of his neck as though it were leaking.

'No back-up. Not even no back-up. They take everything. I don't know how we ...'

The captain interrupted this high-pitched monologue with a question to Lhoon: 'The body, Renato. Where is it now?'

Pasqual looked as though he might cry. Lhoon cleared his throat, embarrassed for his colleague. 'In the freezer. We shifted it back and closed the door.'

'And the crew?'

'Re-assembled in the crew mess hall. Waiting for Felix to brief them. Third mate Ernesto Sevilla is on watch on the bridge.'

'Alone?'

Renato shook his head.

'Got a greaser for company.'

Lloyd Skinner said nothing for a moment, then stood up and walked to a darkened port hole, hands in pockets as he stared out into the black night. Lhoon and Cotton bristled with tension while Pasqual made tiny involuntary noises from the back of his throat. They were men trying to keep it together, trying to stay professional and calm in the face of a situation that their deeper instincts suggested might be better served by running and screaming.

But if he was aware of these primed bombs of fear and uncertainty that were wrestling with their fight-or-flight instincts while perched on his unpleasant furniture, then the captain hid it well. When he spoke it was as though the other men were not present.

'Well, I guess we got two choices. We either run for port without a radio or we stay here and wait for the company's ship to reach us.'

Cotton spoke and the surprise of an interjection from him made the captain look round from his ruminations, which had been directed at the black glass.

'There's a company ship coming?'

Skinner regarded him with interest. 'Why do you imagine we're hove to … First Officer?'

Cotton sat forward, ignoring the barbed question and the over-long pause before his title, and responded only by wringing more blood from an already-white hand. Skinner continued, apparently unsatisfied by Cotton's lack of response.

'I assumed you realized that our straying from the usual shipping path had a point.'

'Point being?' said Matthew without any retaliation in his voice.

'Meeting them at the co-ordinates they requested.'

While the radio officer echoed Cotton's physical anxiety by nervously mashing a clump of trouser material in his fist, Renato looked from Cotton to Skinner, his feeling of exclusion overcoming his fear to prickle him like a nettle. He cleared his throat. 'When is the ship to make contact, Captain?'

Skinner looked pointlessly at his watch. The answer was in his head, not on his wrist. '0500. Just under five hours from now.'

Renato nodded. He wiped sweat from his upper lip and looked down at the chart on the low table. Then he pointed weakly to the coastline. 'We could head for Chicama?'

The captain raised an eyebrow. 'Without VHF? And what kind of assistance do you think we might get at an ass-end of nowhere port like that?'

Lhoon looked down.

He knew that if they met the sister company ship, a ship that unlike the *Lysicrates* had the lifelines of radio and satellite communications, plus a fellow crew that would be comforting in its sheer numbers, things would get a whole lot better. There would be a helicopter from the mainland before you could say boo, and the relief of having events handed over to the proper law enforcing authorities. But that would mean five hours. That was a long time.

Cotton was looking at the chart now. He waved at it vaguely. 'If we routed back into the shipping lane on the way to a port, we could use the Aldis lamp to signal another ship.' The captain raised an eyebrow again. It made Cotton frown as he continued. 'It's all we've got.'

Skinner looked a little more kindly at his first officer. 'You know as well as I do, Matthew, there's no guarantee there's anyone out there right now. We change course without a radio and the company ship'll never find us.'

When Matthew spoke, his voice had a direction, a resolve, that was clearly unfamiliar to the other occupants of the cabin, demonstrated by the way each one turned to look at him as he spoke. 'We should sail for shore.'

Skinner remained standing. 'You seem very sure.'

Cotton bent his head to the floor and clasped his hands over the back of his neck. 'The boy had his skin removed. Then he was gutted and there's no sign of his heart. You reckon whatever did that to a man is going to let the rest of us just go about our business for five hours?'

There was a glimmer of surprise on the captain's face. 'What ... ever?'

Cotton looked up. 'Huh?'

'You said *what*, rather than *who*.'

Matthew looked from the captain to the faces of the other two men who were studying him. His palms grew clammy and he licked dry lips that had been denied their usual lubrication for at least three or four hours. Although it was Skinner's last observation that had rekindled his sweat, he chose to ignore it. 'I'm just not sure how safe we are, that's all.'

Skinner's face hardened back into inscrutability. 'I think you'll find that's my responsibility.'

Matthew let out a short mirthless laugh. 'Jesus, Captain. You saw what was left of Salvo.'

The use of the boy's name made Renato swallow and look at the floor.

'Believe this, Matthew. All of you. We'll find and contain the killer in a matter of hours. This is a ship at sea. There is nowhere to hide.'

Matthew nodded, and kept nodding as he replied softly. 'Guess that goes for us too.'

10

The mess room was not large and there were too many people squeezed into it, so some of the men stood on chairs to see the bosun as he spoke. It had the effect of a raked football stadium, and it gave Esther the opportunity to study every face in detail as they listened intently to the man talking briskly to them in their native tongue.

One of these faces was the face of a psychotic murderer. That was important to keep at the forefront of her thoughts. Important, because reminding herself of it could keep her alive. She swept them with her gaze, stopping only when one of the rapt expressions twitched, or movement caught her eye as a hand was raised to a face or a head turned. Some of the faces being rubbed at by anxious hands were terribly young.

A whole line of gangly boys, ABSs she presumed, stood at the back, their brown eyes lit with terror. And some were much older; the engine-room men, whose faces were inexplicably lined with grime as though this were a steam-driven vessel instead of diesel.

But which amongst them could have taken a knife and sliced at that beautiful boy like a butcher? From where she sat, they were nothing more than a group of hard-working, under-educated, frightened men. But there was danger in the oversight of the obvious, and she narrowed her concentration as the bosun continued.

Felix Chadin sounded as though he were barking, but the men were hanging on every word, leaving Esther stranded in her linguistic ignorance. But as he spoke she realized her gaze had rested on one face.

It was a face of a man in his early thirties, and what had snagged her subconscious searchlight was not his expression, or the set of his features, but merely the focus of his attention.

All eyes were locked on Chadin's earnest face, but though the man's was turned to the bosun, his eyes were looking at something else. Only occasionally, and only for a fraction of a second, but Esther caught it once and watched for the shift of concentration again.

She waited for a beat or two, watching as he listened intently to the speaker, then was rewarded. The man's eyes flicked once more to the left, and this time she followed his gaze to see what was diverting him from the words of his superior officer.

He was looking along the line of young boys who were crushed up against the wall, pressing the sides of the coffee machine like book ends, their bony shoulders grazing each other in an attempt to get more space. It was impossible from her angle to tell which one was so diverting the man, but by watching the flicking of his eyes she narrowed it down to two. He was looking either at the small, slightly spotty youth who wore a cheap, soiled blue nylon shirt, or the taller boy with the grease-streaked face wearing the plain brown coveralls of the engine room. Both had the characteristic high cheekbones of their race and the suggestion of latent energy that only youth bestowed without demanding return, but there was no question that the engine-room boy was the better looking.

Esther's heart beat a little faster. Her eyes returned to the man and she studied him with a growing unease. Was he gay? Would he be capable of murder, perhaps in revenge for some sexual favours either refused or tantalizingly withheld? Blackmail? Obsession? What?

The man's gaze had innocently returned to the bosun and she glanced back at the young lad, trying desperately to rid her memory of the sight that had met her in the freezer only hours ago. The picture would not recede and she screwed shut her eyes against the abhorrence, willing it away.

She bent her head and ran a hand over her face, then sucked in a lungful of air, opened her eyes and snapped back to attention.

He was staring straight at her. It was not the stare of a bored listener, gratefully distracted by her slight movement. Nor was it even the simple stare of a hostile seaman regarding a foreign outsider with contempt.

The reason that it was chilling her blood was hard to define, but it was mainly due to a feeling that the eyes that regarded her so coldly did not seem to belong to the man in whose impassive face they were set.

They were older. And the age implied by them left Esther reeling, struggling uncomprehendingly against images of dust-blown bones and a rancour that would endure eternity. With an effort of will she broke the gaze and looked back across at Felix Chadin, her chest shuddering as she struggled to take the breath she had postponed for longer than was healthy.

Fen Sahg held his gaze on her face for another long minute, then slowly turned his attention back to the object of his more immediate interest.

In the dark, a raft of roosting gulls bobbed on the swell of the Pacific Ocean. The crests of the waves were occasionally lit by the deck lights of the *Lysicrates*, and although Lloyd Skinner, leaning on the rail of the poop deck, could not see them, they could see him.

His frame was considerably more hunched than normal, shoulders held low, head bowed, hands clasped in front in an attitude of prayer. But he was not praying. He was thinking.

The deck had never been better suited for such a purpose than now, being silent and still, devoid of a crew who were busy being briefed and further terrified by their bosun. But there was an uneasiness about the silence, and after only a few quiet moments, Lloyd Skinner drew himself up and softly left the deck to the stillness of the night.

Perhaps the static nature of air and ship played tricks with the night sounds. Perhaps not. But the fact remained that it was an unnaturally long time, in fact a good two minutes after Skinner had gone, and the door of the accommodation block swung shut with a barely audible thud, that the raft of gulls startled and dived.

No one had cleaned the blood off the tiled floor, and now that the freezer door was shut, it had melted. Matthew stood in the doorway of the storeroom and regarded the violent smears of red, holding the back of his hand to his mouth. It was hard to tell now if the abstract-art quality that the blood had bestowed on the floor had been caused by the struggle of the boy as he died, or had been spread around in angry crimson arcs by the seamen handling the body back into the freezer. Either way, it was lurid and gruesome, and it made Matthew question why he had come here. But he needed to see the body again. More importantly, he needed to see the area around the body.

Outside in the galley was his companion for the trip, a deck cadet named Jose, who refused to come into the storeroom.

Despite having protested about the two–person rule the captain had imposed on moving around the ship, Matthew was comforted by the sounds of Jose only a few metres away, swallowing back a throat full of snot, fiddling nervously with cooking utensils, and shuffling his feet.

Cotton took a breath and walked forward, stepping as best he could around the murderous red pattern.

Slowly and methodically he drove his gaze around the edges of the bloodstains, searching for any sign of the thing he dreaded seeing. But the tiled floor was pristine where the blood stopped, an antiseptic, polished surface unsullied by the shiny dried trail of slime he had been almost certain he would find. Cotton rubbed his brow with a finger and considered the room. Only one set of lights was on. Maybe he wasn't seeing properly.

'Jose?'

His voice sounded strained and unnatural in the room, and so did the voice that answered.

'Yeah?'

'Turn on the rest of the lights in here, would you?'

Cotton heard the man shuffle forward. Suddenly the room was plunged into black.

'Hey!'

Jose shouted back. 'Sorry. Sorry. Wrong switch. I got it.'

The striplights guttered, hummed and flickered back into life. It was this normal intermittent start-up that made Cotton glance gratefully at their position on the ceiling; but when he did, he felt his spine being slowly replaced by ice water.

Between the two lengths of tube lighting bolted firmly into their fixings, was an area of white painted metal, crossed by three pipes. Cotton stared up as though being addressed by a god.

Across the pipes and continuing along the ceiling all the way to the door into the galley, was a faint red-brown smear, varnished with the flaking, egg-white shine of a trail.

'Jose?'

Matthew's voice was soft, as if he were speaking in church.
'Huh?'

'Go tell the captain I say we need to close all the holds.'

Jose appeared in the doorway tentatively, trying not to look in.
'Go? With you?'

'No. Go now.'

Jose shook his head. 'Two people. Remember? He say ...'

'NOW!'

The bark made the deck cadet jump, and Cotton waited, his gaze still firmly fixed on the ceiling until he heard the man's steps retreat from the galley into the corridor. The fact that the trail ended in the middle of the ceiling, had an implication that Matthew was struggling not to visualize. Garbage bags being dragged had, he realized now, been a comfortable if bizarre theory. But now he knew for sure that it was wrong. Because garbage bags could not be dragged across ceilings. And garbage bags did not drop down from ceilings on top of victims. And garbage bags most certainly did not eviscerate and skin young boys.

He ground his back teeth together, clenched his fists and turned back to the freezer. He needed to see the boy's remains again, even more now than when he'd entered the room. But what was he looking for? A calling card? Matthew closed his eyes and tried to clear his head. The whole thing was as crazy as it was terrifying, but he needed to concentrate, to keep his head and think clearly for perhaps the first time in three years of anaesthetized hell.

He walked to the freezer.

Out of an unbreakable habit, he punched the red light before pulling on the massive metal handle, and stood back as the door swung open. As the mist of cold air meeting warm cleared, what was left of Salvo Acambra could be seen lying twisted and hard on the floor beside huge drums of frozen orange juice concentrate. Matthew stepped into the icy tomb and bent down beside the body. Gulping back his disgust, he pushed gently at the head to turn it face-up. It was no longer able to move independently to the body, the whole thing being frozen into an immovable block, and so with a force of will he was surprised still to possess, Matthew put his hands beneath the torso and rolled it over. The knees, bent in a spastic rigour, pointed almost comically into the air as the skinless body rocked on its back and came to rest in a tortuous position of unfathomable ugliness. Matthew let go his held breath in a thick cloud, and gazed at the frosted red mess, searching for something that might help him understand. It was useless. He was a seaman, the first officer of a beat-up bulk carrier, not a forensic expert. Gazing on the horror of this mutilated human being meant nothing to him, except that the theory that was building in the part of his brain he would not yet acknowledge suggested that Matthew Cotton, after all he had been through, was now finally losing his mind.

Salvo's frozen, raw death-grin snarled up at him. Matthew bent his head and dug his fingernails deep into the palms of his hand. The breath clouded from his panting nostrils, and he screwed his eyes shut against the pain of things that were threatening to surface in his normally well-guarded consciousness. They were still screwed shut when the muffled thud came, and by the time they opened in response to the noise and the immediate change in air pressure, it was too late.

The freezer door was closed.

The only makeshift weapons Thomas and Antonio could find were a short length of chain and a piece of aluminium tubing that had fallen off the back of a dining chair in the mess room. They held these armaments close to their bodies as they progressed slowly along the walkway between the holds, carrying out their orders to search the ship with maximum reluctance. The silence, teased by the sea's random breaking against a static hull, made the two men keep their own voices similarly low as they spoke.

'Why doesn't Chadin just lock him up?'

Thomas glanced across at Antonio and shook his head. 'You're fucking crazy.'

'Yeah? Well if it isn't Fen, then who is it?'

Thomas chose to remain silent, staring ahead and lifting his chin in a manner that stated the subject was not one for discussion. Such reticence, however, was not going to deter Antonio.

'You've seen him. You know the kind of stuff he's into. Ronaldo's shitting himself that he shares a cabin with him.'

Thomas kept his gaze forward and frowned as his companion's voice increased in volume and pitch, the flame of Antonio's indignation and nervousness fanned by the absence of a sympathetic ear.

'He says there must have been something going on between Salvo and him. I mean, I can't say I'm surprised, fact that he's not got a wife ashore, not even a girl or anything ...'

'Hey.'

Antonio looked surprised by the interruption of Thomas's softly-spoken single word.

'If you think he sliced up the boy, why don't you go lock him up?'

It was Antonio's turn to be quiet.

'Yeah,' said Thomas. 'Exactly. You've sailed with the guy for four years, just like I have, and you know it's not him. And like you just said, if it isn't him, then who is it?'

They considered the implication of that thought in silence for a few moments, long enough to bring them level with hold number five. The smell from the open holds increased the further from the accommodation block they walked, and by this mid-way point it was becoming unbearable.

'Jesus and the Holy Mother,' exhaled Antonio.

'That's getting serious in there.'

Thomas looked ahead then motioned to the open lip of the hatch. 'We should go up top. Get a view along the holds.'

Antonio held out his arm in theatrical protest. 'Oh, for Christ's sake. They can see that from the bridge.'

Thomas stopped walking, and looked at his companion as though he were a stupid child. 'You forgotten Chadin? When he said we should search every nook and cranny of the hold deck, he meant it. Now, just a wild guess, but I bet he's going to ask if we checked along the tops of the hatches, and if you want to look him in his ferret eyes and say "yes, bosun," when the answer is plainly "no, bosun," then go right ahead.

'Don't know about you, but I got at least five more voyages to make before I even make a dent on the payments on some shitty little Korean car my wife couldn't live without, and I'm not screwing it up just because of the stench from that garbage.'

Antonio looked up at the overhang of great metal shelf, and for a moment his eyes glittered with the flitting suggestion of anxiety. Thomas sighed, remembering the smaller man's aversion to heights, even this unchallenging one, and softened his voice. 'Besides, if we can view the whole lot of the hatches from here and say we've done it, which we will have quite truthfully, it'll save us climbing up onto the top of every fucking one. Okay?'

Antonio's expression returned to a sulk, then he glanced guiltily up to the distant blackened windows of the bridge. 'Well, you do it then.'

Thomas sighed, handed his companion his length of tubing, and silently clambered onto the metal winding gear that moved the great hatches back and forth. A hoist and a push-down like a free climber and he was on top of the hatch. He leant down and stretched his hand out for the weapon, which Antonio passed up with little grace before leaning against a metal support and crossing his arms.

The smell on top of the hatch was unbearable, and Thomas slapped his hand over his nose and mouth against the assault, but the urge to retch was hard to fight, and he felt the passage of hot bile rising. He knelt on the hard metal and concentrated, fought the vomit back to his stomach, and won.

'Christ,' he muttered, wiping the sweat from his face with the hand that had been protecting his nose.

Thomas breathed heavily, took a moment to recover, then gripping the aluminium tubing, stood up and ran a sleeve over his wet brow.

'Hey! Antonio!'

The man being hailed moved away from his metal support to the rail at the edge of the ship until he could see Thomas.

'What?'

'Don't ever let me moan about hauling coal again. This is the worst fucking cargo I ever sailed with.'

Antonio made an upward nod of the head, doing little to mask his lack of interest in his companion's opinion, then started to wander slowly down the deck towards the holds at the bow.

The illuminated deck seemed to float not in water, but in deep space, so dark was the night that surrounded it, and the absence of a white bow wave only bolstered the illusion. Thomas squinted along the row of hatch covers as he walked forward to the edge of the partially open hold. He didn't like the feeling of the ship being hove to.

Perhaps it was the instinctive unease a sailor has for being becalmed, or merely the frustration felt by any traveller by land or sea, when forward motion ceases. Whatever the reason, his unease was exacerbated by the view of the hold deck, so still and silent and white-lit in the inky black infinity that surrounded it.

On account of the ship's stillness, he was able to stand right on the edge of the great rectangular pit, the toes of his cheap Manila-bought shoes overhanging the metal lip of the hatch. The random nature of the normal swaying and pitching of a ship under sail automatically stopped any experienced seaman from such folly, but having wrestled his stomach under control he was curious about the nature of something that could produce such a violent, tangible stench, and he wanted to look at it in the same way that small boys want to prod road-kill with sticks.

There was, however, disappointingly little to see. A dark marsh of irregular shapes and viscous lumps lay still in its strip of illumination, the everyday objects like portions of bike wheel or springs from upholstery, taking on an organic appearance that was assisted by the occasional twitching of a rat concealed beneath smaller pieces of detritus. Thomas crouched down, arms on his knees, his weight on the balls of his feet, mesmerized by the repugnance of it, and glanced up to look for Antonio in order to express his disgust verbally.

His companion was now at least three holds away, still in view but out of earshot. Thomas blinked at the figure. Antonio's small frame was casting a sharp star shadow in the halogen lights that came from four sides, and as he walked, it undulated over the pipes and capstans like pieces of trailing black silk. What made Thomas stop thinking about the trash in the hold, and the comments he wanted to make about it to his colleague, was the fact that a larger, but similar shadow was being cast further ahead between holds eight and nine, out of Antonio's line of view, but moving quickly towards him. Thomas felt his pulse quicken and he stood up. With merely the benefit of the height difference between crouching and standing, part of the figure that was casting the shadow so far away up the deck came into view.

It was hard to make out, but for the brief moment during which Thomas squinted and glimpsed its upper body passing through the narrow alleyway between the holds, the impression was of a man dressed like a carnival animal. There seemed to be a great deal of fussy elements to the figure's attire, maybe even an elaborate head-dress. It was confusing and impossible to make out in detail. All the more so since the speed and gait it moved with was quite unlike a man. It had an animal swiftness of foot and purpose that made Thomas call out in alarm.

'Antonio!'

He yelled as hard as he could, but even in the silence of the calm night, his voice was incapable of rising above the idling thrum of the engines, or carrying the distance it required to be heard. Antonio strolled on oblivious, and cupping his hands to his mouth, Thomas made ready to shout again, when an unconscious halfstep forward in his alarm at not being heard the first time caused the man-made sole of his shoe to slip over the edge of the hatch. His leg buckled. His arms windmilled for a beat like a cartoon animal on the edge of the cliff, then the reality of gravity that was unfortunately only afforded to real living beings and not those rendered in two dimensions, took over and did the rest. It was only a fall of eight, maybe nine feet, but he landed awkwardly on one knee, and tipped forward onto a hard piece of wood that gouged and bloodied his cheek as his hands grabbed for something safe. As it would have been in quicksand, the best solution to Thomas's peril would have been to remain as flat and spread-eagled as he could manage, as well as keeping calm.

But both of these options were fast becoming academic, as he screamed and struggled in the foul viscous mess that was closing over him, with every thrashing movement he made in his panic. Already his torso, to the bottom of his rib-cage, was buried beneath the surface, pinned and pressed by sharp metal, hard-packed organic material, and long pieces of sewage-marinated rags. Thomas's screaming was silenced when more frenzied contortions pressed his face into a thick, poisonous pool of unidentified decomposition. One gasp, and fluid that was unspeakable in its consistency, stench and taste filled his lungs to the point at which no amount of hysterical, strangled coughing could ever empty them.

His eyes bulged and his mouth made a contorted arc of retching terror, and as his left arm and shoulder ground down below the surface as effectively as a screw, it left only half a face and a flailing right arm visible in the impassive and wretched casserole that engulfed him.

Two hundred metres away, Antonio stopped level with hold number eight and cocked his head. Had he heard a shout? He looked back towards the hatch cover that Thomas had been climbing on and found he could no longer see him. He hesitated for a moment, then turned back and walked out to the edge of the ship once again to get a clearer view of the holds.

'Thomas?'

His shout was loud, but the lack of reply made him sigh with the realization that he would have to walk all the way back to where they had parted.

Part of his weary reluctance to return to his companion was phoney. For the last few minutes his hand had been tightening unconsciously around the length of chain he held, and his footsteps had been getting slower and shorter as he approached the bow. He would scold Thomas for making him abandon his part of the search, but beneath the scorn would be gratitude that he need not continue alone to the end of those half dark, half brilliantly-lit metal tombs.

He expelled a lungful of air in irritation then started to walk back towards hold five.

As his shadow crossed the alley between holds seven and eight, the shape that had been perfectly still in the dark corridor beyond quivered for a moment, then darted away with a velocity that almost left its misshapen shadow behind.

As Leonardo Becko wept, the bosun and the second officer of the *Lysicrates* lowered their eyes. Lloyd Skinner did not. His gaze remained fixed firmly on the cook's contorted face, his posture as still as his stare.

A minute or so was granted to allow Becko to compose himself, then the other two pairs of eyes rose again to join Skinner in his forthright examination of the cook. No mention was made of his tears.

The captain continued as though the pause had been to pour coffee or light a cigarette. 'So what time, then, do you think you left him?'

Becko sniffed, his eyes still fixed on the cabin floor. One large hand gesticulated as he spoke, its fingers waving the memory away in an unconscious Filipino dismissal. 'I don't know. I say something to him around eleven. Something about cleaning the stock pot. Then I go. And then I remember I come back, just for a minute to remind him not to use cheap cream cleaner no more on my chopping board. Yeah. That was eleven. I'm sure.'

Skinner's face betrayed nothing, not even interest. 'Why are you sure?'

''Cos I angry I have to go back. That maybe I miss *Enzo! Enzo!*'

One eyebrow raised slightly in a questioning arch, as Skinner looked across at Chadin. The bosun answered as if the subtle query had been verbal.

'Game show on satellite. You can win a million dollars.'

For the first time Lloyd Skinner displayed a faint tick of irritation, though whether it was due to the seemingly pointless interrogation of a man who knew nothing about a murder, or the fact that America's great space programme had merely provided the hardware to bring such entertainments as *Enzo!* was unclear.

Enzo! to the stupid and the under-educated, was not clear. What was clear, however, was that in Skinner's opinion the interview was terminated. The other men read the captain's face, and Felix Chadin made restless movements to indicate he wished to be excused. Watching the cook cry had been unpleasant, and by the bosun's reckoning, unnecessary.

As Becko glanced up at his senior officers, realizing his testimony was no longer required, he seemed to grow calm, and unbidden this time, he began to speak.

'Salvo not like himself, though. Not yesterday. All day. All day. Crazy.'

Skinner, who had looked away, returned his focus to Becko. 'Crazy?'

Becko shifted in his seat, nervous again, and blinked in a startled way as though he'd said too much.

The captain sighed. 'Crazy how?'

The cook swallowed. What could Leonardo Becko tell them? That a kid from some provincial village hundreds of miles from Manila, who knew nothing about anything, save for chopping onions and avoiding work, suddenly knew everything? And when Becko thought of that 'everything', he felt the sweat bead around his neck once more. He closed his eyes, but it merely enhanced the memory of Salvo's face, grinning at him over the steaming pots as he happily congratulated the cook on the birth of a baby boy to Becko's secret mistress, commiserated with him on his wife's dependence on painkillers, and his teenage son's over-enthusiastic fondness for his six- and seven-year-old boy cousins.

What had made Becko's blood run cold was that Salvo had not delivered any of this terrifyingly intimate information with the tone of a blackmailer, but rather with a gusto and fevered excitement, like a born-again Christian revealing an encounter with Jesus. It had paralysed Becko with fear. How could he have known any of it? He couldn't. That was the worst thing. The sheer impossibility of it, the eerie and nightmarish implications of someone having access to such knowledge, had silenced him, preventing Becko from challenging the boy. Indeed, it had made the cook take two frightened steps back from his grinning assistant, and ensured that he avoided talking to him for the rest of the day except when absolutely necessary.

Now the boy was dead, he could make no sense of it at all. There was real grief. Becko had liked Salvo. The fact that he had been frightened by him before he died did not diminish the affection he had built up for the kindly, if work-shy, youngster over the seven months they had sailed together. But he was still frightened. Frightened of the murderer, frightened of whatever made Salvo know unknowable things, and now when it came to it, frightened to tell anyone else these secret horrors. He opened his eyes and looked as straight at the captain as he could manage.

'I don't know. Just crazy. Like young boys are crazy.' He hung his head and sobbed again.

Felix Chadin cleared his throat and looked at Skinner with a plea in his eyes. The captain nodded with barely disguised contempt, and Becko was escorted from the room by the bosun and first officer, leaving Lloyd Skinner alone again with his thoughts, a place it was becoming increasingly preferable to be.

The oiler who had been assigned to be Esther's companion seemed as disgruntled by the arrangement as she was. They sat silently in the crew mess, along with at least eight others, looking miserably down into greasy cups of coffee. Chadin hadn't made it clear in this pairing of people whose needs had priority. When Esther had indicated she wanted to go back to her cabin, assuming the man would accompany her, the surly oiler just shook his head once and indicated his wrist watch, meaning, she'd assumed, it was his shift and he would be staying on this deck awaiting instructions.

So here they were, sitting waiting for nothing, hoping they would be safe by huddling together in a pack.

Esther knew she had to get out of this room. It was not in her nature to sit and wait for things to happen. The man she had been watching in Chadin's briefing had gone, and there was a lot to do. She stood up. 'Got to go to the bathroom.'

The oiler looked confused, unsure of what to do. After all, it wasn't as though Esther were under guard. They were sticking together for security, nothing more. He couldn't care less if this girl passenger got cut up. In fact, like most of his superstitious crew members, part of him blamed her presence for the disasters that were crippling the voyage. He thought for a moment, a process that was as visible as a fairground grab machine picking up a prize, shrugged and looked back at his coffee.

She walked slowly from the room, then on gaining the corridor, moved quickly to the stairs that led to her deck. As she reached the top of the short flight, frantic footsteps came pounding up behind her. Without thinking, Esther swung round, knelt to a crouch, hands forward, and braced herself for whatever was in rapid pursuit. It may have been an instinctive precaution, but it was a wasted one. The only threat posed by Jose the deck cadet was one of collision, as he narrowly avoided tumbling over her as he rushed around the corner of the stairwell.

He stopped, startled, and glared at her as though she were mad.

Esther stood up slowly, as though it had been normal to find her here in this position. She put a smile in her voice. 'Sorry. I gave you a fright.'

The man scowled, recovering from this unexpected encounter.

She was still blocking the way, and she made no move to vacate the position. Not completely off guard, but no longer afraid, Esther wanted to know why the man had been running. 'What's the hurry?'

Jose considered using the worst Filipino word he could think of to tell her to mind her own American girl's business. Instead, he threw her one inscrutable glance, pushed past and hurried on his way like the white rabbit. She gave it a beat, then, like Alice, followed behind, out of sight. The sound of his footfall didn't lead her far. He was heading for the captain's cabin.

From the corner of the stairwell on the officer's deck, her back pressed against the cool painted metal, Esther could hear everything Jose said to the captain. Cotton wanted the holds closed. Unless he said it quietly, Skinner said nothing in reply, and she waited silently and expectantly until, with disappointment, she heard Jose moving off towards the direction of the bridge.

Esther thought about that order, then thought about what exactly Cotton might have found to make him send a messenger so urgently to relay it. In a minute she would search him out and ask him herself. But first, there was something she needed to remind herself of in her cabin. Something that had been nagging at her for a while. She slipped away with stealth, but more importantly, with purpose.

The two-person rule didn't apply to Fen Sahg. He was accompanied by three men. All four sat in Fen's and Ronaldo's tiny cabin, watching each other silently like participants in a kids' stare-out contest. It was no coincidence that Fen's three chaperones were the bulkiest of the crew. Chadin might have publicly dismissed his crews' superstitious fears that Fen was somehow behind the death, but his instinct nevertheless told him that all was not well with the oiler. Fen, however, seemed curiously cheerful about the company, and sat peacefully on his bunk looking from one face to another, like an eager interviewee expecting questions from a prospective employer. He settled on one face and smiled.

'This beats scrubbing decks, eh, Rapadas?'

The big deck cadet looked back at him sourly. 'Yeah? Maybe for you. This wasn't my shift. I should be asleep.'

'You can sleep if you want,' grinned Fen. 'We're here to keep each other safe after all.'

Rapadas snorted and crossed his arms.

Fen was undeterred. 'Anyone worked out what we're all supposed to be hiding from anyway?'

The ABS sitting on the floor by Ronaldo's bunk shifted uncomfortably and muttered under his breath. 'Maybe you should tell us.'

Fen turned his gaze to the man. He was still smiling, but his eyes were clouding. 'Huh?'

The ABS glanced at his two companions for moral support. None was forthcoming. The man looked away and stared at the wall.

Fen spoke again, friendly, uncomprehending. 'What do you mean?'

'Just what I said.'

The man shifted his eyes from the wall to the floor in sullen defiance. Fen was quiet for a moment then laughed, and three faces watched him anxiously. Fen Sahg had no reputation for violence. He wasn't a drinker, and his slight build never tempted stevedores or drunken sailors to single him out for a tussle. If anything, he was regarded as the ship gossip, a bit of an old woman, always trading tales with men from other ships, always the first to know when something bad or scandalous had happened.

No, he wasn't violent or volatile, and apart from the occasional unwelcome revelations of his Saanti readings, Fen Sahg scared no one. But the mirthless sound that was bubbling from his mouth, if not frightening, was certainly unsettling.

The larger of the deck hands frowned across at Fen. 'What's so fucking funny?'

Fen stopped laughing abruptly. He turned and looked at the man, who to his credit, held the gaze. If he had expected to see a lunacy in Fen's eyes that matched his cauterized laughter then he was mistaken. The man who looked back at him did not look like a lunatic at all, in fact he stared back with an intelligence that was far beyond an unschooled oiler from Manila.

'What's funny? *Homo sapiens*. Man. The canker that infects the planet. Always at his funniest when he's afraid.'

Rapadas was shaking his head, his face betraying sadness rather than horror. 'Man, you need help. You really do.'

Fen appeared to think about this for a moment, then a smile spread slowly across a face that was beginning to bloom with sweat.

'Yes. You're right. For the moment, I do.'

11

Sohn had no intention of waiting around in any mess room until the bosun decided things were safe. Even when it was idling, his engine needed constant supervision, and he was damned if it was going to be abandoned. Chelito Baylan, the young apprentice fourth engineer, had accompanied his chief after his defiant insistence that duties should resume as normal, and together they now moved happily around the huge cathedral engine, silently tweaking and prodding, checking and adjusting as they did every day of their working lives.

Sohn was not a man to be afraid of much, except perhaps an engine failure in a storm, and a poor navigator who couldn't buy him the time against the weather in which to fix whatever had ceased to function. His was a world of cause and effect, a world of moving parts that could break or be mended, and he had little time for the superstitious nonsense that was being chewed over by the crew still huddled in the mess room.

Of course an unthinkable thing had happened on this normally peaceful and unremarkable ship, and everyone had to have a theory. Sohn's was as pragmatic as the rest of his thinking. It was clear to him that there had been an unpleasant and secretive feud between Salvo Acambra and someone on board, his years at sea suggesting that it was most likely of a sexual nature. The murder had been grisly and revolting, but he doubted it would happen again, convinced that it was a matter confined to the victim and murderer, and more importantly he knew that the culprit would be discovered in the course of time.

In other words, for Sohn the whole affair was over, and he cared only that his engines would continue to give him no cause for concern while they idled at the command of the bridge.

For this reason, there was nothing in the chief engineer's physical vocabulary that indicated caution. This huge cavern of steel was where he was at peace, and despite the circumstances, this night was no different.

Sohn was standing at the fuel gauge, unconsciously running through mental calculations that his sea-going brain was quite unable to resist whenever confronted with an opportunity, when the figure of Chelito moved into his peripheral vision.

'Yeah?'

The chief engineer mumbled the word as a question, but when the moment that would normally be filled with a reply had passed, and there was still silence, Sohn looked round.

The boy was standing a few paces to his chief's left, smiling and staring at him expectantly. Sohn was not an irritable man, but it was unlike any of his crew to hang around waiting to be told what to do, and it irked him. He tried to keep the annoyance out of his voice and made the assumption that the boy was still there indicated that he wanted to ask a question.

'What's up then, Chelito?'

Chelito Baylan merely shrugged, wiped at the dampness from under his collar with a rag, and continued to smile.

Sohn narrowed his eyes, scanning the boy's face for a clue to his intention. His irritation grew to something more volatile at the lack of reply, but he kept the emotion in check as he tried again.

'The oil? Anything wrong?'

Chelito's smile widened. He shook his head. With an elegant brown hand, stained with the oil to which Sohn referred, he gestured at his chief's torso. 'I know you know it's in there. But do you know how big it is?'

Sohn's mouth dried. He tried to swallow and failed, instead a croak came from his mouth. 'What?'

'The tumour. Well, actually, tumours. It's going through you like wildfire, chief. It's this big now, the one in your colon.' Chelito made the shape of a small sphere with his cupped fingers.

Sohn took a small step back from the boy, and put his hand out to steady himself against the cold metal behind him. His voice was still small and hoarse when he spoke. 'Get back to work.'

Chelito made a shrugging motion again and continued to smile. 'I don't mean any trouble, chief. I sure won't tell anyone you sent your brother to the medical examination for the life insurance you took out last year. How will they ever know it wasn't you? They won't. They'll pay up, sure they will. But you know how you think your wife doesn't know you're dying? Yeah? Well, get this. She knows. She found the underpants you peed blood over. She's been watching you every time you've come home for the last eight months. She knows, chief.' He smiled some more, turned and walked away, wiping at his neck and still talking as though to himself. 'Yeah, she knows okay.'

Sohn was now leaning fully against the drive shaft casement, the sweat on his brow almost as profuse as his assistant's. As though it had been prompted by the horrific encounter, the familiar pain started to gnaw in his gut, and he ground his back teeth together, waiting for it to subside before he could even try to rationalize the horror of the last few moments.

The chief engineer had learned over the last few months, that if he concentrated hard, he could usually bear the secret agony that writhed into life in his lower abdomen at unexpected and increasingly frequent times, until it eased off. All he had to do was to focus and stay still. But right now, although he remained perfectly motionless in a semi-crouch trying hard to find that focus, all that Sohn could think of was the madness in his assistant's eyes, the impossibility of his knowledge, and much more importantly, the size of the circular shape that Chelito had made with his thin brown fingers.

'For Christ's sake calm down.'

Chadin was close to slapping the deck cadet, but the audience of half a dozen crew stopped him as much as his own professional self-control. Instead, he gripped the whimpering man firmly by the shoulders and tried again to get him to make sense.

'Listen to me, Antonio. This is really important. How can you be sure he fell in the hold?'

Antonio gripped one of his bosun's wrists like a baby wrapping a fist round a mother's finger, and waved at the hatch cover once more with his other hand. 'He was up there when I thought I heard him call. I know he was. I know. I know.'

'For the last time, is there any chance he could have gone overboard?'

Antonio shook his head, glancing feverishly from the bosun's face to those of his fellow crew. 'No. No. He couldn't have. He's in one of the holds. I'm telling you. We got to get him out.'

Chadin let his hands fall from the man's shoulders and looked round at the row of open hatch covers.

When he looked back again and met the terrified man's darting gaze, there was no mistaking the implication and weight in his next question. 'Which one, Antonio?'

The deck cadet shrank from those eyes and his panting turned to sobs. He shook his head violently and covered his eyes with a hand. 'Don't know. Five, six or seven maybe. I don't know. I don't know.'

Chadin looked at his feet and then turned to the waiting men. 'Unchain the derricks. And two of you start checking the surface right now.' He regarded Antonio as he continued.

'All nine holds.'

At least the light was still on. Matthew had allowed himself only one fleeting moment of hypothesis concerning how it would be in this frozen box if the light was not on, with only a skinned corpse for company, and then sensibly put the thought away. The rest of the time had been spent between the practicality of trying to figure a way out, and a disturbing speculation on who had closed the door.

The two were not unrelated, since given the circumstances, gaining a release might not necessarily result in his deliverance from danger. Whoever had closed the door had done it with intent, and who was to say they might not still be out there? His first and immediate option had been to bang and shout, but the silence that greeted his noise only confirmed the non-accidental nature of his captivity.

So now he paced back and forth between the skinned, frosted remains of the boy and the locked door while he thought, his breath blasting out in clouds around his face.

Unsurprisingly, the safety handle on the inside of the door had been rendered inoperative by whoever closed the door from the outside, simply by slipping the bolt. Matthew was faced with the reality that the steel door was not an object that could be persuaded to give way to force, and since there was no other portal to the outside from the refrigerator than that immovable metal lozenge, his options had come down to the only possible one left. Survive the biting cold, and wait for help.

It had only been around thirty minutes, but already he was chilled to the core in his thin tropical shirt, the back of his hair beginning to bead with tiny balls of ice.

It wouldn't be long before someone came back to the galley, surely. After all, the crew would have to eat sometime. He slapped at his bare arms and scratched the ice particles away from the back of his neck. If his skin was chilled, then it was matched by the cold band of fear that was tightening around his heart. Whoever, whatever, had closed the door on him was out there, freely roaming amongst the crew. And had Jose persuaded the captain to close the holds? Even if he had, what difference would it make? There was madness in Matthew Cotton's soul right now. It was a madness that was making him believe the unbelievable, and fear the unknowable, in a way he had never done in his entire life. He knew fear. He knew one particular version of it better than most. But not this kind. The half-glimpsed image he had witnessed on the hold deck had not only stayed with him, it had fleshed itself out in his imagination, and was haunting him here in this dimly-lit ice-box as he visualized what might be waiting on the other side of the door.

Salvo Acambra's deathly grin, leering up at Matthew from a face that was not so very different from the racks of frozen meat hanging on hooks above it, was almost comforting in comparison to the creature that Cotton's mind had constructed. Against his will, it forced him to contemplate the ugly death at his feet. But there was nothing to fear from the dead.

The dead didn't have the power to harm you. The dead didn't have the power to surprise you, or pursue you. Matthew stopped walking, stared at the boy's remains and slumped against a drum of frozen fries. But it wasn't the boy he was seeing any more. It was someone else entirely. The dead, above all, thought Matthew Cotton, didn't have the power to forgive you. He screwed his eyes shut and bit his cheek to lose the thought.

There was a noise. He opened his eyes. A small and hesitant noise, but he had heard it clearly. It had come from the storeroom on the other side of the door. Cotton stayed deathly still, frozen this time by instinct instead of temperature. He waited, his breath escaping in tiny bursts from his nostrils. There was silence, but there was a quality to the silence, perhaps its timing, perhaps simply the contrast to the initial noise which had given the impression of being a clumsy mistake instead of an unselfconscious announcement, that made him sure that someone or some*thing* was listening on the galley side of the door, as hard as he was on this side of it.

The temperature in the freezer was such that Matthew Cotton, dressed as he was, realistically had only a few hours left before parts of body and brain would start to shut down. But now there was someone out there. He should shout, bang on the door, scream at the top of his voice. Of course he should. But Matthew stayed quiet.

It seemed like an age, but in reality it was probably less than a minute. As he watched, the safety bolt was slipped back into its casing, and very slowly the big round wheel that accommodated the outside handle began to turn.

Matthew let go his breath, and looked around quickly for a weapon. His choices would have been comedic had it not been for the considerable lack of comedy that the situation presented. A tub of fries, a side of beef, cartons of frozen juice and a stack of frozen vegetables piled high in their plastic bags. Nothing came immediately to mind as having the efficacy of a gun. Matthew moved to the frozen meat and tore at a packet of ribs.

He grabbed the biggest he could he find, holding the bone like a caveman in a cartoon, and tried to ready himself for whatever came through the doorway. The metal wheel made the other half revolution it required to pull the handle fully down and break the seal on the door, and then stopped moving. Matthew licked at dry, frozen lips, waiting and watching as silently as his trembling body would allow.

The freezer door must have weighed at least four hundred pounds, so the pull that made it bang open was impressive. The sudden rush of warm air to cold made the atmosphere fog, and it was a second or two before Matthew made out the form that had ended his entombment so abruptly.

So youthful a female should have looked ridiculous, standing as she was with a large meat cleaver held at her shoulder, but Esther Mulholland did not look ridiculous. She looked dangerous.

If anyone looked foolish, it was Matthew, pale with cold, tight with fear, and clutching his barbecue rib. Very slowly she relaxed her position and lowered the weapon.

First officer and passenger looked at each other for what seemed like a long time and Matthew watched as conflicting emotions vied for dominance on Esther's face. Quickly, visible relief, and what looked just a little like pleasure in seeing him, gave way to naked contempt.

'One question. Were you locked in, or did ten stiff Jack Daniels make you think you were in a bar instead of an ice-box?'

Cotton, who had been on the verge of thanking her, scowled back. 'Never been more sober.'

She nodded. 'How long?'

'Sober, or locked in here?' He threw the rib to one side and walked out of the freezer, pushing past her without making eye contact.

Esther ignored the snub and repeated the question to his back. 'I said, how long?'

Cotton stopped in the door frame of the storeroom, shivering involuntarily as the delicious change in temperature played over his skin. His eyes flicked to the circuit breaker on the outside of the door that made the freezer stay on an emergency battery even if the power was cut. He put his hand out and cancelled it, then flicked the big black power switch to 'off'. Who gave a shit if the meat went off? Salvo wasn't exactly going to complain if it got hot in there. Help was on its way.

Until then, Matthew Cotton wanted to make certain that no one was going to get locked in that death trap again. He looked to Esther. 'What exactly brought you down here anyway?'

She held his contemptuous gaze. 'I needed to see the body again more closely.'

'Shouldn't you be back in the mess room with the crew instead of playing Kay Scarpetta?'

She looked back at him without emotion. 'Shouldn't you?'

Matthew leant against the door frame and allowed himself a sarcastic laugh. He gestured at the cleaver that now hung loosely at her side. 'Oh yeah, like that's going to keep you safe from whatever did that to Salvo.'

Esther glanced briefly into the freezer and then back at him, this time with a change of expression, although one equally as impenetrable as the last. 'Yeah, you're right. A bunch of unarmed deck cadets drinking coffee are going to do that job so much better.'

Matthew watched her face for a moment, then rubbed at his freezing arms and looked at the ground. 'About thirty minutes, I reckon. Maybe more. Only thought to look at my watch after I'd realized there was no way out.'

Esther nodded and they remained silent for a moment, until Cotton's gaze strayed to the slime trail that still glinted faintly on the ceiling. Esther watched him without following the path of his gaze, and when he looked back down at her and found her still staring at him, he intuitively knew why. She had seen it too. There was a curious kind of relief on First Officer Cotton's face as he nodded at her.

'I think we should talk.'

She nodded back and then indicated the open freezer door with a small shrug. 'I want to look at him one more time.'

If one went, then they all had to go. That was the rule. And the bosun needed Rapadas to help with the derricks. Fen had seemed nervous when he heard they were being called away from the cabin. His eyes darted shiftily around the room, coming to rest nearly always, the youngest of the ABSs noticed, on the edge of a shoebox that stuck out from under his bunk. His mood, however, picked up enormously when he found they were headed for the hold deck. The three men who had been keeping Fen such uncomfortable company in his cabin, were now completely absorbed in the new alarm that had gripped the ocean's unluckiest ship, and Fen's unwanted presence amongst them went largely ignored, free from the confines of the small, hot room.

Thomas had fallen into the holds of trash. None could articulate the horror that information held for them, and so their arrival and subsequent carrying out of instructions was silent to a man.

As they worked, all kept the same thought hidden in their hearts, a thought that was shared by those who had kicked the derricks into life, and were already swinging the first one over the hatch of hold five ready to claw uselessly at the surface of garbage. If Thomas had really fallen in there, it was already way too late.

They went about their tasks, and Fen Sahg watched them with gimlet eyes.

Lloyd Skinner and Renato Lhoon had joined Chadin on top of the hatch cover of hold five, and two of the men were staring into the dark pit that lay impassively below them. Only Skinner kept his gaze higher, looking out into the blackness of the ocean around them, not like an anxious seaman checking the seas, but with the air of a retired industrialist searching for the lights of land from a romantic cocktail cruise. Chadin ignored his superior officer's distracted demeanour.

'Like I say, Captain, it's different. If it was grain or salt, then we could dig and unload the surplus overboard. But in this ...' the bosun gestured with a limp hand '... we run the risk of not even seeing his body if we find him. We could lift him and drop him overboard without knowing it.'

Renato Lhoon ran a hand over the back of his hot neck and looked from Chadin's face to Skinner's. He had no solution. And more acutely than any time before, he desperately wanted his superior officer to offer one. This was the time when he needed Lloyd Skinner to sparkle with inspiration, to comfort their fears out of a well of experience and maturity of leadership. He ached for it, and he stared into the man's face, waiting to see if he would be rewarded.

Skinner tore his gaze from the invisible horizon for a moment, and glanced briefly down into the hold before looking up at the two men as if seeing them for the first time. He divided his attention equally between the two faces, before settling on Renato's. 'Did First Officer Cotton convey any order to you about closing the hatches with some urgency?'

Lhoon bristled. 'No.'

The reply was unnecessarily staccato, and it was intended to be so.

Skinner nodded, apparently indifferent to his tone. 'Where is he now, do we know?'

Neither man answered. The question seemed so rhetorical, the manner in which it was asked so casual. Skinner, unperturbed by their silence, looked back out to sea.

'So what do we do, Captain?' asked the bosun, voicing the helplessness than Renato was sharing but not revealing.

Skinner cleared his throat and put one hand in a trouser pocket. 'Carry on.'

Neither the bosun nor the second officer exchanged glances. To do so would have been a two-fold disaster. Firstly, it would have revealed that they were scared, and neither man would want that exposed. But secondly, it would have been nakedly obvious, one to the other, that their unshakeable belief in duty, rank and orders, the lifeblood of survival at sea, was at this moment hanging precariously in the balance.

Instead, both gazed across the tops of the hatches and considered a great many things in their private thoughts, only a very few of which concerned Thomas Inlatta and his fate.

The sensation was so powerful, so overwhelming, that any description of it stood outside the boundaries of language. But if he were forced to use the inadequate tool of his vocabulary, then the closest word Chelito could find was ecstasy. He could not even recall when this state of grace had begun, or indeed if he had always been part of it. It was timeless, rendering his own memory of self an irrelevance.

To know everything, to understand all from the complexity of the atoms that made the matter of the universe, the path of the planets, the feral thrust of life in every form, right down to the weak secrets held in the hearts of men, was intoxicating almost beyond what he could bear.

But his body was suffering. The effort of containing this new level of consciousness was already having a physical impact. Chelito sweated profusely as he moved around the engine room, seeing as much with his mind as with his watering eyes. Sohn was crouching where he'd left him, racked with a pain that Chelito knew had only a few minutes more of attack before it gave his chief some respite.

How he could know such things was the only knowledge gap in an understanding that seemed to have no limits. It was simply a fact to be known, just as he knew with equal certainty that his own body was under strain, that his heart was pounding to keep up with a metabolism that it would be impossible to sustain for much longer. And yet the ecstasy of knowing continued.

He wiped at his neck again with the cloth he clutched, and tried to catch a fleeting truth that had slowly begun to present itself as more prominent than the others.

It concerned the one who had granted him this state. Just glimpses to begin with, and then gradually, more. It nagged at him, prodding at him for attention in the cacophony of information that swamped him. And how well he understood it when he focused. It was so simple, so obvious.

Chelito was not repulsed in the way the others had been. He could smell their fear, even though he knew it was the fear of those who had lived many thousands of years in the past. They had been so very wrong. His crime was not a crime. Their punishment a folly. And the consequence ...?

He laughed out loud, a maniac's giggle.

He tried to speak the name of the knowledge-giver, and found that though it was huge in his mind, he could not form it on his lips. The boy frowned, tried again and failed. No matter. The beatific smile returned as he allowed himself to continue viewing the past, with a complete understanding of how his own destiny was a part. Soon he would fulfil it, and what was left of Chelito's simple human ego, the part that was not godlike, swelled with the pride of having been chosen. It was because he was beautiful. Because he was special. Because he was pure.

And then suddenly, there came more of the knowledge-giver. More than he wanted to see. There was no way to turn off this stream of enlightenment. It could not be ignored or filtered out. It was like blood through the veins.

Chelito could no longer be sure if it was the giver, or Chelito himself who was on the temple steps. But it was real. He, it, someone, was there, feeling it, seeing it, tasting and living it. The smell of spices and burning incense was overwhelming as he was dragged up the rough stone, his captors not caring if the skin ripped from his flesh. There was fear in the air. Fear of the sun that should rise in only a few moments. Fear of the figure whose being he seemed to be occupying, both felt by himself for the ordeal that was to come, and from the captors who held his manacled arms so tightly. But above all, there was the stench of human effluent from the settlement below the temple, the sewage and rotten food that he could smell so acutely through the incense, that he knew was nothing more than a familiar irritant to his captors.

But it was to be his power. They didn't know that. They hadn't known at what dark breast he had suckled in the dense, canopied rainforest: it had been beyond their understanding. If they had known, they would have taken more care. Chelito giggled again, hugging himself with delight, seeing with the giver's eyes, the delicious course and destination of the blood gutter, and knowing for certain, as he knew all things, that their error ensured that his death would be meaningless.

Chelito's hand went to his heart. It was racing now, bursting under a pressure that was becoming intolerable. He stumbled towards a metal bench screwed to the bulkhead, and sat down heavily. Sweat was pouring from him in a fever and he wiped at his brow to clear the salt sting from his eyes. The cavernous room was a blur, but as he scanned its familiar steel buttresses and painted pipe caryatids, his bleary gaze settled on an unfamiliar shape. He sat up and blinked.

In the dark space that divided two gleaming pistons was a ragged pile. His new knowingness scanned it, probing it to discover its physical truths, its detail, its substance. It was closed to him.

With an effort, seventeen-year-old Chelito Baylan got to his feet and walked carefully toward the heap. He peered at it, curious as to why nothing could be understood from this jumble of misshapen form, while all around him the rest of the physical and abstract world was explaining itself, turning itself inside-out to reveal secrets.

It was nothing special. Just a big pile of garbage. But its resistance to his understanding perplexed him, and Chelito took a fraction of a second to scan his chief engineer's mind to discern whether this trash pile was his. Sohn, the knowledge confirmed, knew nothing of it. His was a spotless engine room. He scanned the rest of the crew and finding no culprit who could have dumped such a pile in the heart of the ship, he turned back to the more conventional use of his human senses.

Its odour and decomposition was a plain fact that required no supernatural sense to experience. But to Chelito in his heightened sense of awareness, the smell was an unbearable assault. A thin, viscous slime oozed from its base, and he wiped at his eyes again to examine what was causing the discharge. There was a quantity of rotting vegetable matter, welded by decay to what looked like matted fur and twists of bloodied rag. Woven between the mash were shards of metal, glints of steel or tin, dulled and stained, but contrasting with the soft belly of the pile in their sharpness. A bone protruded here and there from the dark mass of discarded matter, and he found himself moving forward with a hand outstretched, wanting to touch it. With a delicacy that would not normally be employed in reaching towards something so repulsive, Chelito put his hand out and made light contact with the edge of what looked like a split and rotten gourd.

The matter beneath his fingers stirred, making him withdraw as though he'd been burnt. Chelito stared at the pile, then slowly touched it again. There was a shudder beneath the blackened surface, more powerful this time and Chelito giggled, sweat dripping from the end of his nose.

It was the kiss to the sleeping princess. He put out his other hand and laid them both on the top of the mound, level with his broad shoulders. It might have been only a fraction of a second, it might have been minutes, the boy's ability to mark time being so skewed, but however long it took, there was a balletic elegance to the way in which the pile of garbage unfolded itself. The matted fur pulled itself free from the body of wet material with a sucking sound to reveal something approximating an arm. It was an arm that terminated in long, ragged pieces of steel and tin, forming a macabre claw.

It was not animal, though there were clearly parts of several corpses of decayed beasts incorporated in the neck and head. But to describe it as part human would have been equally incorrect. There was a torso of sorts, where red glistening flesh mingled with the pulp of garbage, and the white glint of ribs remained visible under a thin wet skin. Chelito stared at this centre of the creature, fascinated by a collection of internal organs that appeared to be working despite their external location. He continued to stare at them for another reason. This was because he dared not look at the thing's face.

All he knew, all he felt, all he had ever cared about was now, this moment. And as the steel shards encircled and gathered Chelito Baylan close to the oozing body, the boy threw his head back and released a hiss of pleasure. It would have been hard to decide exactly when that hiss turned from ecstasy to agony, as his mouth was quickly filled with a thick, semi-solid knot of matter that stopped the sound forever. Nor would it be simple to discern whether the violent shuddering and writhing of Chelito's young frame was to do with his spiritual arrival at a place of enlightenment, or merely a mortal response to the bone and metal claws that were hungrily slicing and ripping through him. All that could be said for sure was that while his death was nowhere near as quick as Chelito might have elected, it was almost completely silent.

12

Matthew sighed and bent his head over his clasped hands.

'But these are not Peruvians. They're Filipino, for Christ's sake. Catholic Filipinos.'

Esther was still pacing the cabin, flushed with the lecture she'd just given him. She wasn't for backing down. 'Yeah, I know. But if I'm right, that doesn't matter. And how long did you say you were in dock at Callao?'

He shrugged and looked back up at her with something approaching disappointment. 'Nearly four weeks.'

She stopped walking and waved a hand at him. 'See? Enough time. Plenty.'

It was Matthew's turn to pace. He'd heard enough. He stood up, choreographed a walk that finished at the port-hole, and stared out into the black night. 'You don't know the crew of a merchant ship very well, do you? No reason you should.' He turned to face her again. 'But if you did, you'd know their interests lie a little more in shopping, gambling and drinking when they go ashore. Signing up to join murdering sects hasn't featured that large in my experience.'

Esther set her mouth into a tight line, then picked up her Dictaphone and shook it at him. 'The boy had been to Lima recently. Really recently. I'm sure of that now. Now that's utterly bizarre. This is a tribe that hardly ever show their faces on the high plateau, never mind catch the frigging bus to a city hundreds of miles away. Now even you have to admit that the stuff I translated so far is pretty weird considering what's gone on here.'

Matthew nodded. It was, as she said, pretty weird. But the thing he'd been hoping to discuss with her was much, much weirder. He hadn't expected to be taken back to her cabin and given a lecture on ancient Inca sun-worship. More importantly, it had been a revelation to him that of all the humans on board, many of whom had sailed with Cotton for a few years, the person he suddenly found himself most disposed to confide in was this complete stranger of a girl. It had made him realize how unutterably lonely he was, that his time on board had collected colleagues, but no friends. Now, for a reason that he could not entirely define, not even the obvious one of sexual attraction, he felt he had someone who was really looking at him when she spoke, really listening to him when he did. But the relief he felt was mostly short term and not entirely complete, since Matthew Cotton was not looking for a soul mate.

All he wanted right now was someone else who believed there was something not human, not animal, stalking the crew on this boat. Esther's theory merely concerned the religious folly and brutality of humans. His was insane, and she was giving him no opportunity to introduce it.

'Run it past me again.'

She looked at him sharply for a moment, then sighed. 'You think I'm crazy, don't you?'

He shook his head, and watched her soften.

'Okay.' She put the Dictaphone down and held her hand up to tick points off her fingers like a teacher. It was an attractive gesture, and for a brief moment he found himself examining the feminine architecture of Esther Mulholland in a way that was neither helpful nor relevant to their situation. The moment passed as quickly as it came, and he braced himself to hear her enthusiastic student bullshit one more time.

'The boy was killed precisely in the manner of an Inca sacrifice. I mean, to the absolute last detail. They used to take out the heart still beating, and the skin was removed carefully in one piece so it could be worn by the priest.'

She fumbled in her pile of books and thrust a picture of a squat stone statue in front of Matthew.

'There. You see? He's wearing the sacrificed victim's skin, tied at the back with leather strips. They believed it gave them great power.'

Matthew glanced briefly at the picture and back up at Esther. 'So guess we just need to find the guy on board who's swabbing the decks with Salvo's skin strapped on like a barbecue apron. Shouldn't take long.'

She ignored him, and looked down at the picture of the statue, stabbing at it as she continued. 'Know what bothers me? These were people who were a lot like us. Modern Americans, I mean. I'm not talking about a bunch of ancient savages who would run screaming from gunpowder. They were practical, inventive, resourceful, pragmatic. They had one of the wealthiest and most successful civilizations in world history. They were governed by a feudal system but the workers were never slave peasants. Work was conscripted from ablebodied young men in a thing called *Mit'a* service and that's how the rulers could build such incredible temples and irrigation systems and cities. These were intelligent people, who understood the movements of the planets and the stars, whose medicine was advanced, and whose social ideals and political templates are still systems we recognize today.'

Matthew was staring at her. 'What has this to do with anything?'

She stared back, then spoke hesitantly. 'I don't think people like that, a society like that, would continue to carry out something as barbaric as child human sacrifice for century upon century … unless …'

'Unless what?' Matthew was losing patience.

Esther lowered the book and looked straight at him. 'Unless it worked.'

Matthew said nothing. Esther looked down at the book again avoiding his eyes. 'The sacrifice could be male or female, but they were always young, beautiful virgins, chosen from a favoured family who considered it a great honour to have one of their children taken for the gods. It ensured a place in heaven for them all.'

'Aw, come on, Esther …'

'Salvo was a virgin.'

He looked at her quizzically. She held his gaze. Matthew Cotton put his hands on his hips and gave a low whistle. It was impossible to disguise the contempt in his voice.

'Well, well. You've been real busy for such a short voyage.'

Esther snapped the book shut. 'Don't be so fucking ridiculous.'

Matthew raised an eyebrow and waited. She hadn't answered the unspoken question. Esther looked bashful, but not for the reason Matthew thought.

'He told me, okay?'

'He told you?' Cotton snorted. 'So in between asking if you wanted tomato or spinach soup, the sixteen-year-old assistant cook just decided to tell you he was a virgin, the way he obviously would to a paying female passenger who has officer status in the junior crew's eyes.'

Esther stayed silent for a moment, then chewed at the corner of her lip before speaking. 'Can I tell you something crazy?' Esther looked pleading now.

'You'll have to work hard to make it crazier than that.'

She studied Matthew Cotton's face for a moment, trying to decide whether it was a face she could trust. The internal jury delivered their verdict and she sat down heavily and let her arms fall across her knees.

'One of the reasons the sacrifice victims didn't protest, resist, even run away – or at least this is what their families believed – was that when they were chosen they were delivered into a state of grace by the gods. A state of mind that made them all-knowing until the time of their death.'

Matthew absorbed this for a moment, unsure of where it was leading, then inclined his head cheerfully. 'Yeah, well guess it beats offering them a set of steakknives.'

She looked up at him, and the lost expression in her eyes made him regret his sarcasm.

'He came to my cabin with food. Probably only an hour or so before he died. He knew stuff, like really private stuff. Stuff that's impossible for anyone else in the world to know.'

'Like what?' To his surprise, Matthew found that he very much wanted to know those things too.

She waved the question away with a hand. 'That's not important. What's important was the fact that he couldn't possibly have known those things about me. Not now. Not ever.'

Cotton watched her eyes for a moment, trying to read them, then stepped forward and sat down beside her. She picked up the Dictaphone again as if it was a talisman, and asked the question to the tiny machine rather than to Matthew's face.

'So how do we explain it?'

Matthew shrugged, awkward now. 'Maybe you mistook what he said. His English wasn't great.'

She looked round at him, annoyed. 'Yeah, right.'

He looked away. 'I don't know what you're saying here, Esther.'

She lowered her eyes. 'Me neither.'

There was weariness in Matthew Cotton's voice when he finally replied. 'Someone skinned and eviscerated a sack-load of rats. Someone murdered a sixteen-year-old boy. Someone ripped the radio out, a crime that's almost worse than killing a human being when you're at sea. Someone tried to kill me by locking me in the freezer. On a ship where the main excitement usually amounts to seagulls mating on the derrick cables, those facts are plenty weird enough.'

Esther detected something strange in Matthew's delivery. She looked closely at him though he avoided her eyes. 'But that's not all, is it? Something else has happened. That's why you wanted to talk.'

Matthew clasped his hands in front of him. As a pair they looked like two baseball fans leaning forward in the cheap seats to view a home run.

They sat like that, in quiet, unhappy contemplation for a time, Esther waiting, sensing that to speak out of turn might dissuade him from whatever it was she instinctively knew he was aching to tell her, until Matthew broke the silence.

'I saw something.'

She looked at him and said nothing, sensing it had taken a measure of struggle for him to say it. So she waited some more. It took a while. He clasped and unclasped his hands until he felt like speaking again.

'Something strange. Hideous. Almost human, but not. I don't know. It moved real fast. Seemed to me it came out of the trash in the holds.'

Esther blinked at him.

Part of her wanted to laugh, but a close examination of that response would have revealed it could more correctly be attributed to controlled hysteria rather than comedy. Instead, she cleared her throat and slowly held up her Dictaphone. 'You speak Spanish, don't you? I think we gathered that.' He stared at her, and she nodded down at the slim black rectangle. 'I'm only halfway through. My Spanish is pretty basic, academic rather than colloquial. But if you can understand a rougher tongue than the plummy-mouthed guy on my home teaching cassette then you need to hear this. All of it.'

'Why?'

'I need to know exactly what he's saying.'

'What's this got to do with what I just told you?'

Esther blinked down at the Dictaphone. 'I reckon we might both be crazy.'

They hadn't noticed him going, and having witnessed the grim determination of their faces as they went to work on the holds, Fen knew they wouldn't notice his absence at all. That was good. So much to do. So little time.

The accommodation block was quiet now, the majority of the crew having joined the others on deck for the search. But there were still voices coming from the mess rooms when he passed the end of the corridor, and so caution had to be observed.

He moved quietly down the stairs to the sleeping quarters, checked there was silence from the two adjoining cabins, then quickly opened the door to his cabin and slipped in. Fen closed the door behind him and leant back against its cool surface with a sigh. He was alone again at last.

A smile played across Fen Sahg's lips as he thought about how well he was carrying out his tasks. He was so far along the enlightened path that he no longer had any need of the Saanti dice to speak with the one who came. He needed only to concentrate his mind on that portion of his heart that was already won, and the voice would speak to him, tell him the truth, instruct him on the necessary liturgy to bring about that which they both wanted so badly.

He longed for those moments when the voice kindled that ache of nameless pleasure, which he knew would be increased a thousandfold when all that had to be done had been completed. In fact it was tempting now he was alone again, after so many hours of enforced company, to call on that private voice and let himself slide into the oblivion and ecstasy of perfect truth. But there was no time. He had to collect, and he had to do it quickly before the men on the deck became alerted to what must surely by now lie below.

He pulled himself up, moved quickly to the bunk and pulled out the shoebox. He clutched it close to his breast and fingered the lid. It was tempting to open it and let his eyes feast on the contents, but he feared that too regular an audience, however appreciative, might be unwelcome. He would go and carry out his next task and then perhaps the one who came would talk with him again. He hurried from the cabin and took the stairs down to the engine room two at a time.

The body of Thomas Inlatta was not that far below the surface of the trash in hold five. But in terms of accessibility it might as well have been on the moon. The instability of the pile meant that any disturbance would bury it deeper, and the random nature of the shapes and textures that engulfed it would make identifying a human corpse amongst such visual confusion a most unlikely prospect.

But these difficulties were irrelevant at present, since the search for Thomas was taking place in a different hold. While the work went on elsewhere, his body lay still and undisturbed, bent and twisted like a broken doll, the fists still tight around tubes of unidentifiable spongy matter, the face an immobile mask of terror.

The derrick operator starting work on hold two was perspiring, trying to ensure that the claw on the end of the crane only lightly scoured the surface as he lifted what he could from the massive pile. Eighteen pairs of eyes watched the process, all concentrating hard, hoping to be the first to spot the shape of a living man hanging from the grab.

Captain Lloyd Skinner, however, was not watching the work in progress. He was watching his men, and considering all that had happened to his ship over the last twenty-four hours, he was doing so with remarkable composure.

His crew glanced at him occasionally from the corners of their eyes, admiring his collected demeanour, comforted by the fact that their master was still obviously so very much in control. But then even if Lloyd Skinner had been screaming inside with alarm, the men on board The MV *Lysicrates* would never be privy to a demonstration of that, or indeed, any other emotion.

He had been nineteen years old when he had first appreciated the merits of keeping calm, and ever since, he had worked harder than anyone could ever guess at maintaining it. But right now, as Skinner stood by the rail, hands on his hips, eyes closed as the smell from the disturbed hold corrupted the light salt breeze, the force of will that kept him so inscrutable was being tested. It was the earth smell from the hold that made his stomach churn. The odour of sour soil and decaying vegetation that was thankfully almost completely absent in a life at sea, an odour that he had spent over thirty years avoiding. He opened his eyes as his mind threatened to start rolling its own favourite movie, but it was too late. It was the smell.

The platoon leader had been only three years older than him. Ridiculous, of course, but then sanity had abandoned the entire war by the time he was forced to join it, and a twenty-one-year-old with the power over life and death seemed no wilder than anything else.

Maybe some other twenty-one-year-old would have handled it well, grown, matured, responded to the nightmare and conquered. Not Mendez. The wisdom and judgment of the heavy-browed sullen boy was so absent that emotionally, he could have passed for a toddler. In some respects they were all children then, but Skinner knew he was smarter than Mendez, and the indignation he felt at having to carry out orders of complete incompetence and retributive malice, grew to a fever that kept him awake at night more than the mosquitoes or the heat.

He had been anything but calm then. Lloyd Skinner was hot-headed and full of fury. He hated the war, he hated his part in it, laying mines in the red earth to kill and maim God knows who, and he hated Mendez for the simple but unforgivable crime of being stupid.

At the age of eighteen he had believed in a lot. He'd believed that men were fundamentally good, that people could make a difference, that there was a future. All those beliefs were dead before he saw twenty, and though he would never allow himself the indulgence to take the dark truth out and look at it in the light, the fact remained that he blamed not Mendez, but the evolutionary process itself, the one that could create the miracle that was the human body and mind, and then furnish it with the spiritual intel-ligence of bacteria. Mendez was, to him, not an individual to hate, but an example that accurately represented his species.

He had known what would happen. Despite his protests, Mendez made him do it anyway. Skinner knew, like the rest of the platoon, that the village housed no one but civilians. Irritating, unattractive, poverty-stricken civilians, who offered nothing of interest to homesick American teenagers, but civilians innocent of anything other than lack of education and silent resentment.

The skinny children spat at Skinner behind his back as they played in the dust round their huts. They would stare up at him with their dark, almond-shaped eyes when he looked back at them, leaving Skinner chilled by the unflinching alien scrutiny that is the speciality of the child.

Slow, shifty-eyed old men who shuffled from the fields with thin oxen on ropes, and women doubled over under the burden of sticks for the fire, or children strapped to their impossibly strong backs, were the only other inhabitants, and Skinner would watch them daily, aching to be elsewhere.

Nevertheless, Mendez's order was insane, and Skinner refused. But the eyes of his superior officer held nothing but dull, sullen incomprehension when he was challenged, and the order not only remained unchanged, but was enforced by the gun that he drew and held to Skinner's head. There was no law to help him. They were feral. Boys in the jungle who could do anything and go unpunished. He had looked deep into Mendez's eyes and knew that the crazy bastard was capable of pulling the trigger, and so he shut down another system of belief and survived.

Mendez stood and watched him as he buried the plate-mines, smoking and drumming the rhythm of an unidentifiable tune on his thigh. Skinner remembered the feel of the hot red earth beneath his fingers as he carefully smoothed the area around the trigger plate, remembered holding the soil in his fist and glancing up at the waving corn stalks that had sucked their life-force from it. From the closest hut he could smell that sour, rancid rotting. A mixture of sewage and plant life, of hot earth and animals, wood smoke and the thin, acrid tendrils of impoverished cooking.

Dawson had gathered the villagers, told them to leave. Told them that the enemy was coming, that the road north was mined and they would have to evacuate the village. That if they stayed, they stayed at their own risk. But Skinner knew they wouldn't go. Mendez knew they wouldn't go.

And then, less than a week later, there they were. Three of them. A tall, gangly girl, probably about ten or eleven, and two younger boys, maybe seven or eight. Siblings, obviously.

Skinner had been lying in the shade of a truck, watching the girl, idly examining the contours of the pitifully thin shift that covered her body to see if there was the swell of a breast yet and, finding none, transferred his gaze to the antics of the boys instead. The girl was in charge of the boys, an ox and a long, whippy strand of willow, but the stick was being used more on the two scampering brothers than the animal. They taunted her, laughing, running behind and in front of the ox to make her chase them, and although she used the sharp staccato bark of authority to bring them to heel, Skinner could see she was playing as much as they were. They wandered past him, the boys smiling and laughing, pointing at the ox, and darting into the corn as they headed into the fields, as the girl stared at him impassively flicking lazily at the ox's rump. Skinner fell asleep.

The sound of the mine, a dull sound, a deep-noted 'whumph', did not shake him roughly from his dreams, but brought him gently out of sleep. There was a moment as he blinked in the daylight, a coming-to, that timed itself precisely to coincide with the start of her screaming.

Skinner ran. He ran into the cornfield, thrashing at the dry stalks that barred his way to the road, and when he burst through on the other side, chaff from the corn was sticking to him like flakes of diseased skin. The mine had taken one side of the boy away, but the mess of material that was left was still alive.

The other two, the girl and the smaller boy, were frozen to the spot, the girl screaming, the boy shaking and panting.

Skinner stayed on the scrub at the edge of the road, safe enough, and three others, including Mendez, stood further back, safer still.

He had laid the mines. He knew where they were. The two surviving children were in the very heart of the minefield. He held up his hands to the girl. She turned to look at him, still screaming, spittle penduluming from her lower lip. His mind worked fast. He could run back to the camp and get the detector, but they would have to stay still and calm.

The war was already fucking crazy by the time he reluctantly joined it. There had been no tuition in anything, and so, at eighteen, Skinner was largely a self-trained explosives expert. He'd been interested in it. The physics of an incendiary device was easy to him. The procedure for dealing with the consequences was not. How did you make children stay absolutely motionless, absolutely calm, when the torn remains of their brother was oozing in the dust in front of them, his single existing arm twitching and flexing like a beached eel?

Skinner turned to Mendez, and his heart chilled. Mendez was grinning. He looked back at Skinner and there was a message in his eyes.

Mendez already had the gun in his hands, and he raised it as he held onto Skinner's gaze. There had been a moment, a response to Mendez's action that was so fast that memory had to be congratulated for logging something so swift. But Skinner could never forget it. For the mere fraction of a second as the gun came up to Mendez's shoulder, he was grateful that his platoon leader was going to do the decent thing, and finish the suffering of the dismembered boy. And then, almost before that hope had time to mature into action, the secret that Skinner had been silently semaphored by Mendez's eyes was made real.

The first two bullets that thudded into the ground, missed the mines. The third hit the target, and the world was filled with the controlled columnar fury of the exploding earth.

He shot three more, like a boy at a funfair trying to win the stuffed bear, and when it was over, Mendez spoke three words to Skinner before he lit a cigarette and walked away.

'Dumb little fucks.'

The earth. It was so red. So hot. Five months later, Skinner had lain down on the hot soil, and breathed in the smell of the rotting green jungle. The body of Mendez lay beside him, the hole in his forehead neat and black where Skinner's bullet had entered, the hole where it had left, not so. The dead Vietnamese soldier whose gun Skinner had used and replaced lay a short way off.

Lloyd Skinner had wanted the others to question him, to prove to him that men were not as stupid as he feared, to notice the obvious clues that would have pointed to his guilt. But of course they did not. The execution had been perfect.

He thought often about the last words he should have made Mendez hear as he'd held the gun to his head, and watched with a detached calm as the sullen face had melted into drooling, pleading primal fear. But it was too late to change that. What he'd said was written in stone.

'You dumb fuck.'

The man watching the operations from the hatch cover of hold five, shouted instructions that the first grab load was free of anything human, and the driver opened its claw and let the garbage tip slowly over the side of the ship. The smell of earth and rot was unbearable, the odour sticking to his soft palate, and the captain swallowed back bile. He put a fist to his mouth in a silent cough, and walked towards the accommodation block. It was a measure of his presence that not one seaman questioned whether, given the two-person rule, they should accompany him.

As second officer, never mind simply as a human being, Renato Lhoon's thoughts should have been with the murdered boy and the possible death of Thomas Inlatta. But Renato, as he patrolled the corridors of B-deck with a deck cadet one pace behind, scuffing his feet, was thinking of neither. He was thinking about the approaching company ship.

In all his time at sea, he had only ever once been on board a ship that was given an order to rendezvous during a voyage with another from the fleet, and the circumstances had been exceptional. A cargo had to be transferred at sea because of a paperwork emergency.

It had been irregular, and most likely illegal, but then the big shipping companies were not exactly renowned for being upright, honest citizens of the ocean.

What rankled Renato was that, in this case, he hadn't been informed what the circumstances were, not even by the usual conspiratorial nod and wink to senior officers that a loyal company captain might employ to prepare his crew for something irregular. He still fumed over that exclusion, even now in their perilous circumstances, when the meeting was clearly to be their lifeline. But Renato was more than angry and wounded. He was suspicious.

Cotton, of course, hadn't even noticed the irregularity of it all. But then Cotton wouldn't notice a hairy mammoth playing a trumpet beside his bed unless Renato woke him up and pointed it out.

But what if Matthew knew what the captain's orders were and simply didn't care? It was certainly a peculiar place to meet, in this odd spot out of the shipping lane, hove-to above one of the deepest parts of the Pacific Ocean where the currents were not exactly ideal. Renato could only assume that he did, and that he had probably been too drunk either to acknowledge them or to care. But Renato cared. He cared about having been excluded. He cared so much that he had made a decision. This extraordinary voyage was going to be the last he made as the crutch for Matthew Cotton.

When they next sailed, Renato Lhoon was going to be first officer and Cotton could panhandle for booze money in a doorway somewhere.

All he had to do was to prove to the captain that he was worth the promotion, that Cotton was unreliable and dangerous, and that Lhoon's loyalty was unshakeable. He must put aside his disappointment in Skinner's exclusion of him and work at becoming indispensable, and if this wasn't an opportunity, then what was? The other ship was coming, and when it came, there would be no doubt who was in charge, who had helped contain the horror, and who had been caught slacking on duty.

He frowned as his thoughts churned, hardly even seeing the interiors of the cabins he peered into as the deck cadet threw open each door for inspection. Pasqual's cabin door was opened and swung shut in seconds, and they moved on to the next.

Renato stopped so suddenly by the next cabin that the deck cadet nearly ran into his back. It belonged to the irritating American girl passenger and there were voices coming from inside. Renato listened for a moment, then looked back at his companion.

'It's okay. This deck is clear. Go back to the mess and wait for me.'

The small man started to protest and was silenced by a sharp look. He scowled and walked away, making a great show to his officer of checking round the corner of the corridor as though waiting to be ambushed by snipers. Renato watched him go with contempt and then walked cautiously to the cabin door, and pressed his face close against the metal.

He listened for the voices again, but this time there was silence. He knew the girl was not alone, and he could have sworn there had been a deeper male voice in there. He waited a moment more and then was rewarded. The male voice spoke. It was Cotton.

Renato stopped breathing to hear better, and was met only by Cotton's muffled exclamations.

The girl was speaking very quietly, but although he could hardly make out what they were saying, nor make sense of those words he did hear, the aspect of their conversation that interested Renato was the tone of it. It did not sound as though a senior officer was briefing a passenger in his professional capacity.

Renato Lhoon allowed a contemptuous smile to curl his lips. Loyalty. Unswerving loyalty to his captain, come what may. It was to be his future.

He walked on to join the cadet, putting a hand to his mouth to cough at the stench of the garbage in the holds which had quite suddenly entered the block, presumably, he reasoned subconsciously, with the opening of a door to the hold deck.

His step was light, and his mind fully occupied, which was why he failed to register the ticking noise the soles of his shoes made, as they dealt with the resistant friction of red-brown stickiness that trailed along the corridor from the stairs.

The engine room of the *Lysicrates* was never silent. Even at its most idle, as now, with the great turbines at rest, the ambient noise filled the senses with a low thrumming and a subtle, soft rushing.

Sohn Haro's senses, however, were only just beginning to return from the journey of pain they had been on for the last twenty-five minutes. His eyes were filled with tears, and his face was still contorted by the effort of remaining sane under such duress. But even though the pain was subsiding, he was far from sane. How could he be? His fourth engineer had just performed a conjuring trick, a mind-reading illusion of impossible accuracy that had left him reeling in a state of confusion and terror. Until this moment, Sohn's fears had been very simple.

He knew he was going to die, and only two things worried him. The first was what was to become of his family. He'd sorted that. Illegally, yes, just as the boy had so chillingly pointed out. But it was sorted. The other worry had been how bad the pain was going to get at the end. It was only because of his unique position on board, the fact that he could hide away in the depths of this huge steel cathedral, that he had been able to hide the attacks from the rest of the crew. But the agonies were becoming more frequent, and almost intolerable. He blinked away the tears and tried the first tentative movements of straightening up. It was getting better.

He blew sharply out between his teeth, and raised himself from the doubled crouch to a sitting position against the bulkhead.

Now, at least, he could think. Chelito would be back at his duties checking the oil, and in a minute Sohn would be forced to go and face him again. What could he say? He needed to know where the boy got his information, but it had been so personal and impossible for anyone else to know, that Sohn already knew he didn't want the answer.

He tried standing. It was possible.

Sohn Haro would never have classed himself as a brave man, but any independent observer would have certainly awarded him the title. He treated the management of his impending death as a duty, and likewise, he was about to go in search of the boy, to confront his worst fears and dark unspoken horrors, merely because he felt he had no choice.

The chief engineer wiped his damp face with the back of his sleeve and, stepping out into the cavernous room, cast his gaze around the hanging walkways and main deck. Chelito was not in sight. He walked down the central aisle, his footsteps clanking on the metal grid, to where he could see behind the turbines, then stopped, took a breath, and called out.

'Chelito!'

There was no answer above the familiar mechanical heartbeat that filled the room. Sohn walked on, more cautiously now, unsure as to why his apprentice wouldn't answer when called.

'Hey! Chelito!'

There was a small noise, a scuffling and the clang of metal. Sohn turned his head quickly in its direction. It came from behind the turbine closest to the propeller drive shaft. He opened his mouth to call again, and then closed it. If he could hear that sound, then whoever made it could almost certainly hear him.

Sohn was old enough and wise enough to guess there might be danger behind that massive metal tower, but he was standing doing something few other men would have done in similar peril.

He was weighing up the relative merits of dying in agony at home, or being dispatched quickly by a murderer.

The decision took no time.

'Chelito,' he said, very loudly and without fear. 'Come out. I can hear you.'

There was a studied silence, and then another scuffle, more urgent this time, as though something was being hurried.

Sohn tightened his fingers into fists and walked forward. There was a wrench lying on the edge of the upper walkway. He glanced at it for a moment and instinctively his hand uncurled and reached for it. The fingers froze a few inches away. No need. He walked on.

The space behind the turbine comprised a small corner that he knew well. It was one of the untidy areas that he disliked, a perfect den to host a work-shy apprentice or accommodate the detritus of engineering that the lazy couldn't be bothered putting in order.

This time, however, as he slowly turned the corner to face whatever might be present in its arc of shadow, it was shielding an altogether different tableau.

Since his life had started to be ruled by pain and certain death, many responses had died prematurely in Sohn, fear of personal injury being one of them. But there was still a little part of him that wanted to step back immediately, to run, to scream, even to fall to his knees at the sight before him. Instead, he merely stood and looked, his mouth a tight line.

Chelito's blood had coated every surface for at least a four-foot radius. It had clotted and darkened near the edges of the mess, but the thick pool around the remains was still arterial red and oozing. Sohn, staring, was rooted to the spot. He was not staring at the blood. Nor at the skinned nightmare that used to be his boy, or the gaping hole in Chelito's chest where the blackened tatters of ripped organs glistened. Instead, he was staring into the face of a fellow crew member who knelt in the gore and stared back at him.

If this was the moment that Sohn had hoped for, when swift violence would end his suffering, then he was disappointed. The figure's eye's stayed fixed on Sohn's for a long time, until the lips began to grow a slow smile that widened to a grin.

Then as Sohn watched, Fen Sahg calmly finished what he was doing, stood up and walked away, leaving bloody footprints as he disappeared from the engine room into the night.

*　　*　　*

'Stop!'

The derrick swung on.

'Stop the fucking crane! Jesus! stop!'

Three men waved their arms wildly at the crane operator, and the arm halted abruptly, sending the grab into a wild pendulous arc that would take minutes to calm. As the huge metal bucket swung lazily through the night air above hold number two, the assembled crew of the *Lysicrates* stared up at it, and even given the difficulty of examining a moving object from a distance with any accuracy, there was no mistaking what hung from the lip of the grab.

A human leg, flayed of its skin, which had consequently covered its previously sticky shiny surface with a fur of detritus, dangled casually from the edge of the bucket, as though its unseen owner was lying by a river bank and the watching crew below on the river bed, watching the dipping foot toy with the current.

There was silence as the cable steadied and came to rest, and the operator slowly lowered the grab down onto the main deck. The silence remained as the body that was attached to the leg slithered into view from the casserole of trash that surrounded it. No one could have mistaken it for Thomas Inlatta.

Despite the fact that the chest had been opened crudely, and judging by the ragged and splintered ribs, very quickly, it was still recognizably the body of a woman, naked, not only of clothes, but of skin. Large breasts, fatty and glistening and flayed, hung from the split torso, the unnatural divide between them making the picture even more grotesque.

Several crew members, in the crescent of watchers that surrounded the mess, crossed themselves, but no one moved forward to retrieve the body from its ignoble and shallow grave. Perhaps they would have stood in that silent semi-circle all night, staring and immobile, if the uncharacteristically authoritative voice of Matthew Cotton hadn't cut into the thick silence.

'It's going to take time to find out who she is. What matters here is that it's not Thomas.'

The men looked across at him. Cotton was standing with Esther at the edge of the derrick, his face a puffy and crumpled mask.

'If he's in there, he can't possibly have survived this long. We need to close the hold hatches.'

Felix Chadin scanned his men's faces and then turned back to his first officer. If Cotton's voice had contained an authority that was normally absent, then Chadin's contained an insolence that was equally rare.

'Are you crazy? We find an unidentified woman's murdered body in the holds, and you say we should stop searching and close them?'

Cotton held the smaller man's gaze. 'That's exactly what I'm saying.'

'Are those the captain's orders?'

'Mine.'

Chadin let a beat of silence stand between them for a moment, before he inclined his head slowly up to the crane operator, and motioned for him to carry on. Cotton took a step forward, then stopped and looked down at the hand that was gripping his arm in restraint. Esther looked up at him, feeling the muscles of his forearm tense as he clenched and unclenched his fist.

'He's right. You need to talk to the captain.'

There was sense in that. These frightened men were on his side. The side that wanted to stay alive. Why antagonize them? But as Cotton watched the grab begin to swing slowly over the top of hold two, leaving behind its grisly catch on the deck like an angler dumping his fish, the urgency of his mission pressed him. He did need to talk to the captain. He also needed a drink.

But then even men who had been abstainers all their lives would have been tempted to the bottle when, just as the crane got back to work, the stone-faced, blood-soaked figure of Sohn Haro appeared through the door of the accommodation block, and walked slowly towards the numbed watchers. He was a small man, but a lifetime of engineering had made him strong, and the burden he carried in his arms was presenting him with few difficulties. The difficulty lay entirely with the waiting group, whose instinct was to run from the sight of the thing that used to be Chelito Baylan, being cradled in the arms of his boss like a bride carried over the threshold.

13

The coffee had long gone sour, but with no galley crew to service the machine in the mess hall, the three men who remained there had no choice but to keep drinking it. Edgar Pasco, an oiler, was being the most vocal about its nauseating properties, and although his repetitive complaining was irritating his companions, they shared his view sufficiently to overlook it. Besides, they had other things on their minds. There had been no news from the main hold deck, where the search for Thomas Inlatta had been underway for over an hour, and the cadets Raul and Erol were deciding whether their growing discomfort was anxiety or boredom.

As Edgar lifted his coffee to his lips and prepared to make yet another comedy face of disgust, Erol took the cue to speak, simply to prevent the inevitable complaint.

'Isn't someone supposed to come and tell us what's happening?'

Raul Nestor flicked a coin through his knuckles and shrugged. 'Guess if they find him alive we'll know all about it.'

'Yeah, well you'd think Chadin would want all hands to help out,' Erol replied sulkily. 'Don't see the point of us being down here when almost everyone else is up on deck.'

Edgar put down the coffee cup and wiped his mouth. 'Think yourself lucky. Have you smelt that trash? Almost as bad as this coffee.'

Raul crumpled his empty Styrofoam cup into a ball and threw it at the oiler's head.

Erol was sniffing the air. There had been a faintly bad odour since they were posted down here, but it was as well that they stayed ignorant of its source, namely the powerless freezer in which

Salvo Acambra's corpse, unrefrigerated, was succumbing quickly to the heat of the galley. It was mild enough to get used to. But now, there was a stronger smell. Something much worse.

'Talking of which, can you guys smell that stuff in here?'

With nothing else to do they afforded the question a moment's attention, and Raul shrugged again. 'The smell's going to get in every time they open the goddamn doors.'

Erol screwed up his face. 'Pretty strong for that.'

The other two looked at each other. Erol was right. The smell was bad and getting worse.

'Yeah. Like that's all we need,' sighed Raul. He shifted in his chair and ran an exasperated hand over the back of his neck. Raul was more agitated than his companions might have imagined. The initial fear that Chadin had ignited in them after Salvo's murder had dissipated. Raul Nestor was not convinced they were in any danger at all. Sure, someone had done what they had done, but it wasn't likely to happen again with the whole crew on the alert.

The murderer, Raul surmised, rather than planning his next victim, must be shitting his pants. And anyway the company sister-ship would be here in only a few hours and they would be able to radio for help and let someone else find the killer. Raul wanted to get out of this mess hall and get on with his free time, which had been eaten into by this emergency. He knew exactly what would happen. His watch would roll back round in only five hours and he'd have wasted all his own time by sitting here with these two dolts instead of lying back on his bunk with a beer and some motocross magazines. Raul made up his mind. He stood, and walked to the door.

Edgar raised an eyebrow. 'What are you doing?'

'I'm going to find which door's letting in that cargo stench, and shut the damn thing.'

Before either of others could protest, he was out of the door and into the corridor. Erol watched him go, then looked to Edgar. 'Shouldn't one of us go with him?'

'That'd leave one of us alone.'

'So we should both go.'

Edgar inclined his head. 'We're posted in here. Remember the last time you crossed Chadin by disobeying an order?'

Erol did. They exchanged a look and then got back to the business of sitting and waiting.

The smell in the corridor was fearsome, so much so that Raul was forced to put a hand to his mouth as he walked towards the elevator and stairs. When he turned the corner into the corridor that housed the junior crew cabins, it was even worse, but at least the problem presented a solution.

At the end of the corridor the starboard window was wide open, the screw-down bolts on the hinged side having been turned fully and then lifted out. The corridor was open to the night air, or in this case, the fetid stench of rot.

Raul wondered for a moment why the window had been opened like that, and why it had been left so. It was bad seamanship to leave any windows or portholes open, and securing them was second nature to most sailors. He walked to the offending square of glass, his cheap plastic trainers making a tacky noise as they passed over something sticky, and put his head through the opening. A mixture of relief and puzzlement came over him, as the act brought him not the stench he had expected to be wafting from the hold deck, but a sweet reward of salty night air. The window was on the outer hull of the accommodation tower, and he peered down the edge of the metal cliff to the sea sixty or seventy feet away and enjoyed lungfuls of delicious air.

Raul allowed himself a minute more and then stood up again to close the window, reeling from the smell that was still as strong inside the corridor.

Reason suggested to him that perhaps a window or door on the port side might be responsible if the wind was in the right direction, and that would go a little way to explaining the mystery of the smell's origin seemingly being inside rather than out, although he still wondered about why the window was open. He would close it, and then go and search on the other side of the ship for the offending source.

As Raul bent down to search for the winged screw that had fallen from the bolt hole, a noise made him look up sharply. He stopped, held his breath and listened. There was a voice coming from one of the cabins. He stood up slowly and narrowed his eyes, listening more closely. It was coming from Ronaldo Valdez's cabin. Actually it was technically Valdez's and Fen Sahg's cabin, since the crazy guy had been moved in to invade Ronaldo's famous privacy, but whoever you attributed the ownership of the cabin to, there was definitely a voice coming from within it. A low voice.

Slowly, Raul crept forward to the cabin door, kept his back close to the wall, and stopped to listen.

The smell here was so bad that he covered his nose and mouth again and kept his breathing shallow. There was silence from the cabin for a few moments and then the voice again. Raul relaxed. It was Fen. He would go in and find out what the crazy oiler was doing, but as he put his hand on the door handle and pressed it down, the wicked part of Raul Nestor paused for a moment before going in to hear what Fen was saying and to whom. It was curious. It sounded as though Fen were talking to an animal, or a small child. His voice was cooing, soothing, if a little deferential.

'There. Look, there. How does that feel? Yes? Yes you can feel that now can't you?'

Then a high laugh from Fen and he resumed his fussing.

'Can I tighten it? Must I ...?'

If Raul had been about to laugh the next sound stopped him. It wasn't a voice, and yet it was. It made sounds like words, but no words that Raul had ever heard, or indeed would ever care to hear again. A low guttural rasp replied to Fen's womanly attentions, but one that held so much power behind it, it seemed underlain by thunder. And even though Raul could not understand the strange language the voice spoke, its meaning was quite clear. It was telling Fen to be quiet.

Before he had time to think, Raul let go of the door-handle quickly. It sprang back up to its horizontal plane with a click, and as if the metal of the handle had been a switch, the rumble of thunder that was the voice stopped.

There was a fraction of a second when the stillness of the night was unbroken even by Raul Nestor's breathing, and then three things happened very fast.

The first was that Fen Sahg's cabin door slammed open. The second was that Raul Nestor saw what was inside. The third was that Raul Nestor screamed, only just managing to contain the vomit that was rising in his throat, then turned and ran.

'Well now we know who it is, it shouldn't be too hard to apprehend him.'

Skinner was on the bridge, doing his duty as captain by dispatching his bosun to the cargo deck and taking the watch the moment he'd heard the news about Chelito Baylan. Now he was leaning against the bank of machines rendered useless without their radio, regarding Esther and Matthew with the same calm demeanour as if they were discussing the menu for tomorrow's lunch.

Esther found her eyes were narrowing, and she opened them wider in a conscious move to avoid the too-obvious display of disapproval. She nodded at the captain and kept her voice soft. 'Do we think that Fen's responsible for the other body in the hold?'

The captain didn't honour the question with a shrug, but the tone of his reply implied it. 'I imagine if one is capable of eviscerating a colleague and ripping out the ship's radio then one is capable of anything. Who knows how Mr. Sahg chose to spend his shore leave.'

Esther thought she detected a undercurrent of amusement in Skinner's words and she didn't like it. She got to the point. 'There must be a gun on board for emergencies. We'll need weapons.'

Lloyd Skinner maintained a steady, unwavering gaze, but one eyebrow rose in an arc of amusement. 'We, Miss Mulholland?'

'I can help. I can handle a gun.'

He smiled this time and looked out to the hold deck to the bizarre and grisly scene that stretched in front of them. In the halogen lights the cranes were still, and Sohn Haro sat in a crumpled heap being comforted by a group of men only a few feet away from the twisted and bloody mess of Chelito Baylan's corpse. But if such a nightmarish tableau was registering on the consciousness of the captain, who, after all, was responsible for ship and crew, both of which were clearly in unthinkable disarray, he didn't show it.

'Can you indeed?'

His light tone grated. Her voice hardened.

'Yeah. Can you?'

Skinner didn't take his eyes from the deck, but both Esther and Matthew noted that his jawline tensed as his back teeth ground together for a beat. The silence that the captain left hanging was uncomfortable, and Esther believed he meant it to be so.

She was determined not to be the one to break it. Cotton obviously was not so attuned to the tension, and after wiping at a dry mouth he spoke as though Esther's question had been rhetorical.

'Before we even try and track down Fen, we have to close the holds.'

Skinner turned to him and examined his face with an uncharacteristic curiosity. 'What is this about, Cotton? This obsession with the holds?'

Matthew looked at Esther for support but her eyes told him she was as stranded as he was. 'For safety. It's important.'

Skinner sighed and looked at his watch, and unlike Esther, made little attempt to mask his irritation in the presence of what he now clearly regarded were two fools. 'Several things are going to happen in the next three hours in the name of safety, First Officer Cotton. The first is that I am going to allow the crew, who you may have noticed are now almost paralysed by fear, a little more time to debate amongst themselves whether they will pursue their fruitless task of trying to find a dead man in an impenetrable cargo, and then I will ask Chadin to gather the entire crew in the engine room. The next will be that a selected band will hunt down Fen Sahg, restrain him and bring him to the engine room to join us, where we will handcuff the psychotic animal safely to a rail, and wait there until our sister-ship arrives to put us out of the misery of this mess of a voyage. Since I'm about to put this plan into action for the safety of everyone on board, and since the weather is set fair, with little chance of the holds flooding, don't you think a delay in keeping at least four men up on deck to close all the hatches would be rather a waste of everyone's time?'

Matthew saw his chance.

'We don't know the weather will stay fine. The weather fax is non-operational.'

Skinner looked at Matthew with rising irritation, but still, Esther noted, laced with an undercurrent of interest in his motives. 'How long have you been at sea?'

'Long enough to know it's insane to take risks with the ocean.'

The captain put a finger to his mouth and tapped thoughtfully at the pink skin of his lower lip. 'You never fail to surprise me, Matthew.'

He looked at Cotton for what seemed an unnaturally long time, examining him with as little self-consciousness as though he were a witness eyeballing a police lineup from behind the safe invisibility of a two-way mirror.

'Perhaps,' he continued with no recognizable emotion in either his face or voice that Esther could place, 'you could do with a stiff drink.'

Esther glanced at Matthew, who remained staring at the captain, his countenance unchanged. The captain returned the gaze until he broke the connection out of what looked like boredom. As if waking from a reverie, Skinner glanced back down to the deck, then briefly at his watch again.

'Put it like this. I'm getting everyone off that deck and down below in the next half hour. If you want to personally go along nine hatches and close them, be my guest, but I must insist you join us in the engine room immediately you finish. I need to know where everybody on this ship is. Everybody.'

Esther was looking at the captain with impassive eyes, but her body language was displaying impatience. 'The guns?'

He looked back at her as if she had just entered the room and he was seeing her for the first time. 'I hardly think guns will be necessary in apprehending a five-foot-four, slightly-built man, when we have twenty-seven other men available for that purpose.'

'Twenty-six,' said Esther quietly but forcefully. She nodded in the direction of the deck.

'Salvo.'

Skinner ignored her corrective accountancy and his voice took on that patronizing lecturing quality that never failed to make Esther Mulholland clench a fist.

'Anyone can carry out acts of great brutality on an unsuspecting victim. When the pursuers are forewarned and outnumber the murderer, one tends to find that the individual who was previously thought to be dangerous is rendered nothing more than a frightened, scuttling beast.'

Esther was as unimpressed as she was riled. 'There's nothing more dangerous than something cornered and frightened.'

Lloyd Skinner pressed his lips together, took a long look at Esther then drew a lungful of air in through his nose and sighed.

Esther watched his eyes as he regarded her, and she found the subtle change that flitted across them as he spoke uncomfortably enigmatic. She didn't like not being able to read people, and there was no doubt that Lloyd Skinner's internal code was hard to break.

'You imagine that as captain of this ship, I'm going to break open the weapon locker and hand a gun to a hysterical teenage girl passenger? You think that would indicate sound judgement?'

Esther kept her eyes on his, and worked hard to make sure her gaze didn't falter. 'In six months' time, Captain Skinner, I'll be a fully enlisted member of the US military. My job will be to be fight for my country.'

Something twitched at the edge of Lloyd Skinner's mouth and for one crazy moment Esther thought he was about to cry. Instead, his mouth cracked into an involuntary smile that split his craggy face in two. But it was a mirthless smile.

'I'm sure we'll all sleep safer in our beds.'

He turned away from them to look out of the bridge window, leaning forward on the sill as if his annoying visitors had departed, and for what seemed like an age, no one said anything.

'Captain?' ventured Esther with as gentle a tone as she could manage.

'Miss Mulholland,' he said, facing away from her.

Esther waited. It had not been a reply, she sensed, but the start of a sentence. Lloyd Skinner turned around, and unless she was very much mistaken, the impassive, distracted, distant man she had been observing over the last two days had been replaced with somebody quite different. Just how different she wasn't sure, although the parts of her that automatically calculated risk and acted accordingly were already taking readings and sending them off to the lab. All she could say for sure was that she didn't like the look that was gathering in the man's eyes.

It was anything but distracted, a million miles away from being indifferent. In fact Lloyd Skinner had the distinct look of a predator.

'You ...' he continued in a low and controlled voice that was silky and smooth but contained an aftertaste of something exceedingly bitter, '... are starting to get on my tits.'

Raul Nestor's body and mind had returned to a close approximation of the animal it had evolved from nearly three million years ago. There was no higher thought going on, no mature and civilized responses to the immediate threat. Instead, his entire being was running on the thin, primeval fuel of adrenalin that controlled his flesh and its flight.

He had half-stumbled, half-sprinted along the metal-floored corridor that led away from Fen's cabin, gasping for breath as the spit dried in his mouth.

But even before he reached the elevator at the end, his peripheral vision had informed him that something was pursuing him along the pitted and pipe-veined corridor of E-deck. Something that stank. Something that moved in a horribly fast and agile way. The same something, he knew, he'd just seen in Fen's cabin in a scene that defied explanation to the sane mind.

Raul's darting eyes scanned the only possible escape route ahead, the end of the corridor that led to the stairs and the elevator. The outer door of the elevator was shut as always, but the thin rectangular glass window of the inner door that revealed itself to those who were familiar with the appliance informed him that the car was on this floor. In the fractions of seconds that all this information was being absorbed and processed, the boy's instincts rather than his reasoning powers weighed up his options, and decided that a pursuit either up or down the narrow metal staircase between decks would not be a chase in his favour. The elevator. He would make a dash for it. Whether the two metal doors that were between the empty car and the rest of the world would offer any kind of sanctuary was still to be tested, but at the moment it was the only bolt-hole Raul could see. He lunged the last fifteen feet and grabbed onto the brass handle of the outer door. Behind him came the noise of his hunter, a noise that was a baffling combination of scrabbling claws, the slurping of mud and the rustle of something hideous.

Its proximity made him haul desperately at the handle, trying to foil the spring that was trying to do what it was designed to, namely slowing and controlling the speed at which the door opened and closed.

Raul Nestor was panting and crying like a child as the barrier to his imagined safety swung back, and let him tear at the lever that operated the side-opening concertina gate of the inner door. His fingers groped and clawed, until the handle gave way and granted him the ability to pull the sliding barrier back.

He was inside with the concertina gate slammed closed, before the full horror of elevator design became apparent. Through the small rectangle of cloudy wire-chequered glass set into the centre of the metal gate, he could for the first time see his foe full on.

It was only eight or nine feet away, seemingly unhurried and slowing up as it approached, almost as if it knew its prey was already caught, and the reason that Raul could see it so well was that the outer door was still open. He whimpered, a string of drool hanging from the corner of his down-turned mouth, and stabbed at the buttons on the wall panel. The elevator remained static. Without the hand of a human to force its painfully slow passage from the outside, the outer door would take its time to shut, swinging lethargically on its tight spring until the metal plate at the bottom made contact with the corresponding one of the inner door. The passenger inside the car was powerless to hurry the process, since as in most double-doored elevators, opening the inner gate with the outer still ajar interrupted the safety sequence. Faced with what was outside, Raul's intellectual decisions would never have over-ruled his primeval responses and allowed him to do anything that would remove a barrier, however flimsy, between himself and the bad, bad thing that was now unfolding itself in the corridor. Instead, he pinned himself to the back of the tiny box, and screamed, as he waited for the destiny that only the hinges and springs of the outer door would determine.

With the unhurried pace of a ballet dancer lowering a raised arm to bow, the door followed its excruciating arc towards the metal contacts that would make the elevator move. And within that arc there came two different opportunities to observe what stood outside in the corridor. The first was, as Raul had already witnessed, the view from the dirty window in the gate. It had afforded him the muddied but distinct picture of a thing that was the size of a man, but enlarged in volume by being encrusted and seemingly encased in a confusion of matter that was disgusting beyond the obscene. Although he saw it for only seconds, Raul took in details of mottled, purple dead flesh pulled tight around a misshapen framework of bloodied bone, of rusty tin, of matted fur, yellowed teeth and an unidentifiable black, dripping mash. But as the door closed, the horror was momentarily obscured from view as it swung through the part of the curve that blocked the window. Raul's screams were still pumping from his throat as he waited for the last ten inches of open door to be closed. It slowed even further as it neared its terminus, then with a tiny noise that was nevertheless sufficiently significant to make itself heard to

Raul above his own screaming, it shut with a click. He pounded at the panel of buttons on the wall with a fist, and the car lurched as it started to move. His screams now mutated into a whimpering from the back of his throat as he turned his head back to the yellowed grime of the window, now double-glazed with the matching glass rectangle of the outer door. Two eyes were staring at him. The face, if the obscene mosaic of matter could be called a face, was pressed up against the glass, looking in. In the seconds in which Raul looked into those glittering black orbs, he read an intelligent malice, depthless cruelty and contempt, and worse still, an ancient knowingness that atrophied his heart and stilled the whimper in his throat. And then, like a miracle, the elevator slowly slid the hellish picture downwards into the darkness, and replaced it with the bland moving image of the elevator shaft's metal wall.

Felix Chadin rose from the kneeling position he had been adopting for the last ten minutes, and winced at the cramp that it had inflicted on his legs. He stretched his calf muscles and glanced down at the chief engineer. When Sohn had first stumbled onto the deck under his hellish burden he had been as far from okay as it was possible to get. Chadin looked at him now and was relieved to see he had recovered. Chadin shot a look across at Renato, and signalled that he wanted to talk to him away from the frightened huddle. They walked to the bottom of the silent derrick.

'We should sail for port.'

Renato Lhoon looked away from Chadin's earnest insistent face and directed his eyes at his shoes. 'The captain's made his decision, Felix. The company ship's only hours away.'

'How do we know that? We don't have a fucking radio.'

'I'm sure he knows what he's doing.'

Chadin indicated the heap further up the deck, where Chelito Baylan and the body of the unknown girl lay together under a tarpaulin that had been hastily thrown over their remains.

'Yeah? Like this is part of knowing what you're doing?'

Renato said nothing. He knew there was no port near enough to bolt to, but he too had been unconsciously calculating how long it would take them to sail back to Callao and how they would attract attention with only an Aldis lamp and hollering, to get a pilot boat to guide them safely in. But loyalty was to be the thing.

Loyalty was the thing that would make the difference to his less than satisfactory life. Loyalty would win him promotion by the next voyage. He'd sworn to himself that it would. Renato set his face into a mask of impassive authority and looked at the bosun.

'He's got it under control. I'm going to check on the rest of the crew, then talk to the captain. Best thing you can do is keep these men calm.'

Both Renato and Chadin looked across the deck at the nervous huddle of shocked humanity, and instinctively knew that when they recovered their senses from the latest atrocity that it would take some considerable effort to keep these men from doing whatever they believed individually would save their own skins. Chadin had never witnessed a mutiny before, even when he'd sailed with a drunken captain who'd smashed a tanker into an East African pier, killing two luckless fishermen in a tethered boat. That had been bad, but this time he felt the undercurrent of something worse than the mere rising insubordination of the lower ranks challenging the authority of the higher. He felt the feral tang of self-preservation. And not just from his men. Felix Chadin knew somewhere deep inside, that if it came to the point at which he might never see his wife and children again, he himself would abandon any formality of rank, duty or service and do anything it took to make sure he stepped off this ship alive.

Chadin looked back at his first officer and Renato read the thought that had flitted so briefly behind the man's dark eyes.

'It's what you're paid for, bosun.'

Chadin nodded. 'And the captain is paid to bring back the same number of men he sailed with.'

Renato Lhoon wiped a hand over his hot brow, wishing the warm night breeze was a little cooler. 'I'll be back. Tell the men we're gathering together with the captain in the engine room.'

He walked away towards the accommodation block and didn't even stop when Chadin called out.

'And if the ship doesn't come?'

The bosun watched his superior officer's impassive back retreat and then slowly turned towards the men. Every eye was on him, because every ear had heard the question, and almost every heart was wondering the same.

*   *   *

'What the fuck?'

Edgar's hand, which had been in the process of carrying more coffee to his lips, halted in mid-air at his companion's half-whispered question. The scream that had pierced the silence of E-deck had been of a quality that neither Erol nor Edgar had ever heard, nor would care to again. It was definitely human, but it conveyed a terror that ripped the soul and froze the heart.

Edgar Pasco looked with wide, frightened eyes across at his friend and slowly lowered the cup to the table.

'Shit.'

Neither man moved. They knew to whom the screams must have belonged. It was an unspoken understanding that they communicated with their eyes, but fear rooted them to their seats until it started again, more distant this time, but if anything even fiercer in its intensity. It continued unabated as the sound moved away from them, until it became muted but still audible.

'What'll we do?'

Erol's voice had a tremor in it that indicated he was not far from tears. Edgar stood up, his eyes wide and fixed on the open doorway that had brought the nightmare sound to them.

'We'll have to go to him.'

Erol looked up at him helplessly, then scanned the room as though searching for a rack of grenades in a mess room containing nothing more than trestle tables and coffee machines.

'And do what?'

'I don't fucking know.'

Erol glanced across at the open serving hatch that joined the room to the galley. He pointed weakly. 'We could get knives?'

Edgar regarded his companion with contempt, annoyed at how quickly he had become a snivelling girl, then walked to the hatch and climbed through. He re-emerged a moment later, and clambered back through the hatch clutching a cleaver. It did not escape Erol's notice that he had chosen to climb through the serving hatch instead of walking out of the door and into the galley the conventional way, and the demonstration of Edgar's fear gave him a boost that at least allowed him to stand up on shaking legs.

They moved cautiously towards the door and peered out into the corridor. It was silent now, but the smell that had caused Raul to leave to investigate it was overpowering.

'Jesus,' coughed Edgar. He slammed a sweating palm over his nose and mouth.

Erol gagged back a rising knot of vomit and steadied himself against the wall, and both men stayed still for a moment until Edgar pulled at his reluctant companion's shirt and moved towards the T-junction at the end of the corridor. There was no more screaming, but somehow its absence made the tension worse. Senses that both men wished could be dulled against the onslaught of vile stench were heightened in anticipation of the dreadful noise starting again, and they held their breath against both violations as they approached the corner of the mess room's corridor. Edgar stopped abruptly, as from his right a soft noise broke the silence. Erol hung back as the cleaver in Edgar's hand rose to his shoulder.

Neither spoke, and it seemed to each of them that the blood beating in their veins was louder than the undercurrent of diesel engine beneath the floor. The noise came again. It sounded like shuffling. At almost the same time as a timorous moan started to be emitted unconsciously from the back of Erol's throat, the source of the shuffling noise revealed itself as it appeared around the harshly lit corner of E-deck.

Edgar Pasco did not lower his meat cleaver, because even though the figure that moved before them was pathetic in its countenance, it was sufficiently horrific to make him catch his breath in fright.

Fen Sahg was naked to the waist, his thin body smeared with blood, a shoebox clutched to his breast as though it were an infant as he shuffled down the corridor in the direction of the elevator. He turned his head to look at the two men, stopped and blinked at them as though they had materialized by enchantment. Edgar opened his mouth to say something, but found that words would not come. His mind was still frantically piecing together the combination of what they believed to have been Raul's screams, the cessation of those screams, and the horrific appearance of the MV *Lysicrates'* oiler Sahg.

Fen saved him the trouble of speech. Slowly he raised one thin, bloodied finger and pointed it at the huddling men. His lip trembled and in his eyes shone a fury that was as terrifying as the state of his body.

'He interrupted.'

His voice was low but it held enough spite to fuel a war. Edgar's fist tightened around his weapon and Erol pressed himself against the wall.

'He interrupted and it made him go.' Fen's finger remained pointing at them for a moment, then he lowered it as lethargically as he raised it, held his box tighter, turned from them and continued on his shuffled journey.

Neither man moved as Fen disappeared from view. Only Erol made a sound, and it was difficult to tell whether it was indeed a word or yet another involuntary expression of fear when he whispered, 'Raul.'

14

'He was right about one thing.'

Esther, the small of her back against the cool metal of the taff rail, looked across at Cotton, her troubled expression broken momentarily by curiosity.

'Yeah?'

'I could do with a stiff drink.'

Esther watched Matthew's face as he wrestled with the truth of that for a moment, then turned her gaze to the huddle of men further up the cargo deck being addressed in urgent terms by Chadin. She was glad he'd broken the silence, and particularly with that subject. Something big was on her mind.

'How long have you known Skinner?'

He leant forward on the rail, gazing out at the invisible black sea. 'Two years, four months.'

Matthew had answered too quickly and too accurately for the casualness of the question, indicating that the time had already been significant to him for a reason unimparted to her. She left it.

'How well do you know him?'

Matthew thought about it, bent his head and shrugged. 'As well as anyone you sail with.'

'Do you like him?'

Matthew continued to look out to sea, shifting his position in a way that told her he was uncomfortable with the topic. 'I guess he saved my life.'

Esther turned back and faced him, though the action merely afforded her access to the side of his face. 'Can I hear about it?'

Cotton shrugged again, then spat into the ocean. 'It's not that interesting.'

'I'm interested.'

He glanced up at her, then back at the sea. She waited.

'I was a captain. Lost my master's licence for drinking on watch. Couldn't sail again as an officer with any of the reputable companies. He persuaded Sonstar, not the most rigorous of companies when it comes to regulations, to bend the rules. Employed me when no one else would.'

Esther nodded, though not necessarily out of understanding. 'And you couldn't live if you didn't sail?'

'That's right.'

Esther was quiet for a moment, knowing that everything about his attitude to being here on this ship since they had first met suggested that this last answer was a lie.

'Why do you suppose he did that, Matthew?'

'Who knows? Maybe someone did him a favour in the past. Felt he should pass it on.'

Esther cleared her throat. She wanted her next question to be delicate, but she knew it wasn't a skill that the good fairies had given her over her crib. 'Isn't a first officer kind of important to a captain?'

Matthew looked up at her. 'Yeah.'

She'd started. She'd better finish. 'So wouldn't taking on a drunk then, even as a favour, be absolute folly?'

Matthew stayed leaning, but his hands wrung together. 'You got a point?'

'In the last two years has he ever tried to help you stop drinking?'

Matthew snorted in derision. 'What?'

'I'm serious. If he wanted to give you another chance, then presumably he'd want to stop you drinking. Get you sober, maybe even get back your master's ticket.'

Matthew was looking at her with a hint of anger in his eye. 'I'm not getting this.'

'What I'm saying is, if his plan clearly wasn't to rehabilitate you, then what was it?'

'Fuck knows, Esther. Maybe he's just a nice guy.'

'And is he?'

Matthew looked away for a moment, composed himself, then looked back again. 'I guess I hardly know him.'

Esther nodded again. Cotton stood straight.

'Don't you think with the kind of shit we're having to deal with right now, a character assessment of our captain is a little misplaced?'

Esther was still nodding to herself, sorting through stuff she couldn't quite figure out yet. 'Maybe. Maybe not.'

They were quiet for a moment until a clamour broke out from the men up the deck. Voices were raised and Chadin was waving his arms.

Matthew wiped his mouth. 'I should sort that out.'

Esther grabbed his arm. 'I didn't mean to hurt you there.'

'You didn't,' he lied.

'Matthew. Where does Skinner keep the gun?'

'He won't let you have it, Esther. He's right. There are regulations about these kind of things. Forget it.'

'I wasn't planning on asking again.'

Matthew Cotton looked at her closely. From a distance the voices clamoured, shouting each other down. 'You don't trust him, do you?'

'There's three bodies on board. We can't call for help. I'll start trusting people when I've got some steel in my hand.'

He blinked at her for a moment. For the last few moments Matthew Cotton had been feeling something he hadn't expected to feel again in this life. He knew why she was asking these questions. They were about Skinner, not really about him. But something in her voice, the way she looked at him alerted him to an undercurrent of emotion that he had found comforting. Her voice had not contained pity or contempt. It had contained sympathy, concern, maybe even a tiny glimpse of something else. Cotton couldn't afford to give it head-time, but there was no denying that a part of him had been touched by her, by a kindness he hadn't seen coming. Then his hand went to the pocket of his trousers where her Dictaphone and its garbled tape still waited to be translated. The memory of that thing between the holds flitted momentarily across his inner vision, and Matthew Cotton weighed his options.

'There's a hand gun in the metal locker in most captains' cabins. In the passageway between his bathroom and main office. It'll be locked.'

She gently squeezed the arm she still held. They both knew where she was headed next.

'And you?'

'I'm going to dig out my best Filipino for "pull yourselves together," then I'm going to close these fucking holds.'

'And the tape?'

'It's here. What about it?'

Esther removed her hand. 'It might not be important, but I need to know what that boy is saying.'

He glanced at her, and despite himself, sighed. 'So what if it's a cult? We know it's Fen. Sohn saw him.'

'And the thing you saw? The reason you want those holds closed?'

'I don't get the connection.'

She looked at him with an expression that made Cotton melt. It held trust, understanding, complicity and a fierce youthful intelligence. 'Humour me.'

He nodded. At that moment he would have done just about anything for her. No one had looked at Matthew Cotton like that for a very long time indeed. He cleared his throat. 'Maybe you should wait for me. You shouldn't move about this ship alone.'

She smiled. 'Funny. I was going to say the same to you.'

She slipped away leaving Matthew Cotton with the urgent and very real hope that she was a little more than just a bullshitting kid.

Renato looked at his feet.

'I think that might make matters worse.'

Skinner kept looking at his second officer with a gaze that forced the man to look away. 'In what respect?'

'Because they'll want to keep looking for Thomas Inlatta.'

Skinner looked down at the angry gathering of men on the deck below the bridge. He tapped lightly on the glass. 'I think, Renato, that if you asked them right now whether their priority was searching for an almost-certainly-dead colleague, or saving their skins until the sister-ship joins us, you might find they change their tune.'

Lhoon looked back up. 'You think we're all in danger?'

'Why do you think I'm going to confine the whole crew to the safety of the engine room until we catch Sahg?'

The first officer nodded, relieved that the captain was displaying some patriarchal authority at last. 'I think you should know that Chadin wants us to sail for port. That's what they're discussing.'

Skinner's finger stopped tapping the glass. 'What?'

Renato scratched nervously at the back of his neck. 'He thinks we should head back to Callao. Just in case the company ship doesn't come.'

Skinner turned around slowly, and in place of the mildly distracted expression that Renato was used to confronting, and tired of trying to penetrate, there was something else there. Lloyd Skinner looked focused and dangerously angry. Something in Renato's face must have alerted Skinner to the fact he was betraying an emotion that he had intended to remain private, for while he watched, Lhoon saw the captain's features settle themselves, with a little difficulty, back into the repose of an uninterested man.

'Really? And you?'

'I'm here to follow your orders.'

Skinner nodded, searching the man's eyes with a laser of scrutiny Renato didn't know he possessed.

'Good. Then gather the remaining crew members that are still below, take them to the engine room and wait for the rest.'

Renato nodded in compliance, but didn't go. Skinner raised an eyebrow.

'Captain?'

Skinner didn't reply, but his face told Renato he was waiting and it had better be good.

'You're absolutely sure about the sister-ship?'

'I'm interested why you would ask me that.'

'It's the company. Even if they gave you a time and co-ordinates and a reason, they're not, you know, the most reliable people. They change their plans at a moment's notice if there's money to be made, and right now they don't even know we're in trouble.'

Skinner considered this for a moment with, to Renato's relief, a peaceful expression. 'So you're with Chadin?'

Renato flushed. 'No, no. It's just that, as your officer, it helps me to understand when I know what you know.'

Lloyd Skinner crossed his arms over his chest and looked down at the ground. 'Renato, do I look like someone who wants to risk not only the lives of all my crew, but my own too?'

The second officer kept his eyes on Skinner until the captain looked up and met his gaze. 'No,' Renato Lhoon said.

'Then that's all you need to know.'

'I just want to be of more help in persuading the men.'

Skinner sighed. He sounded weary. 'You know as much as I do. They haven't told me why we're meeting, but shall we say they were sufficiently insistent that I have no shadow of a doubt whatsoever that in exactly three and half hours from now, the MV *Elysium* will be docking alongside us. I have, as I explained before, weighed up all the best options, and believe me, Renato, this is the best.'

Renato Lhoon glowed with pleasure. Included at last in his captain's confidence, he smiled a smile that he hoped conveyed a shared wisdom and adult sense of responsibility, though the truth was that it did little more than reveal triumph. Second Officer Lhoon nodded once and left.

On the cargo deck below Skinner could see Cotton joining the throng, and watched as the faces of the men turned towards him to listen. Lloyd Skinner allowed himself a moment to ponder once again on how simple it was to manipulate the stupid, before he finished the small chore he had to do on the bridge and left.

It was spoiled. The ceremony, the ecstasy of divine service, the being at one with his master. All spoiled because of the scum that he sailed with. Fen wiped at his sweating mouth with the back of a hand, leaving a smear of blood like badly-applied lipstick. It changed nothing, of course. Everything was going to plan. Everything was so nearly in place. But it was only he, Fen Sahg, who had been thwarted by the foolish interruption to his sacred liturgy. And now he would have to wait until the real coming, the final and conclusive part of his duties, before he could bask in the physical joy that serving afforded him. There was murder in Fen's heart. When this was done, he would make them pay for the loss of that moment. Surely he would be allowed that. Surely.

For now though, he had work to do. The time was nearing and he knew that the old engineer would already be spreading the news of Fen's last chore. But although he didn't want to acknowledge it, Fen was growing tired. His ecstasy had a physical price and he could feel his heart beating too loudly and too quickly under his thin frame.

If only he could join again, feel that energy surge through him, the energy that came from so long ago, from so much past pain and long-lost knowledge, then he would be capable of anything.

He hugged himself when he called back the image of his master's briefly shared memory, the way he had seen so clearly why mankind casts away its waste in disgust, its unwanted things, its dead, its effluent, its sins and its shames, without understanding the dazzling truth only Fen and his master knew. The truth that everything is everything else, and that the things that have been cast away must come back.

He sniffed back a block of rancid mucus, an unpleasant but unavoidable side-effect of his contact, and shuffled along the engine-room floor towards the small hatch to the cofferdams. It was already open a fraction, and his bare feet clicked on the sticky trail that led up to it and through it.

Holding his box carefully, Fen Sahg crouched down and crawled through the hatch. He had no need of a torch. He knew where he would find him, and anyway, the route was already so familiar to him that he knew where to watch for obstacles, where to crouch low and where he could stand tall. There was safety in all that darkness. It was not a darkness he need fear. And as if to prove it, the carelessness with which he left the hatch door open was not only an indication of how tired he was, but of how little it mattered if they found him this time. It was all so near, there was nothing they could do to stop it. Nothing.

Skinner's cabin was on D-deck, one floor below the bridge, and as Esther loped quietly up the metal staircase, the foul odour that had greeted her on entering the accommodation block grew fainter. It bothered her.

The smell was bad on the cargo deck, particularly since the derrick's grab had stirred the trash around, but out there the breeze carried it in wafts and made it bearable. Why would it be so strong inside?

However, the ventilation and air-flow of cargo smells was low on her list of problems to solve, so she filed it under 'odd', and kept her wits on the jobs in hand.

The first was to check that Skinner was still on the bridge. The second was to get into his cabin and somehow force the lock on the weapon cabinet. Though her trailer park buddies had given her plenty of opportunity to watch and learn, cat-burglary and lock-picking were not her best subjects, nor, come to that, was subtlety, which was why Esther Mulholland was carrying a fire-axe to do the job instead.

As she tiptoed past the captain's deck towards the bridge, she slid the tool behind her back and moved closer to the wall. The door to the bridge, as always, was wedged open, and the black windows reflected the room back at her through the gap. She could see no one. Mindful of the fact that if she could see a figure in the reflection, then they would see her too, Esther bent low and ducked down below the height of the instrument panels. She moved cautiously forward and craned her neck. There was definitely no one on the bridge. If the captain was there, he must be out on one of the wings. This was annoying. She had assumed that she would merely check Skinner was still at his post, then retreat quickly to his cabin and get on with it. The fact she couldn't see him from here meant she was going to have to enter the bridge on some pretext and risk making him suspicious. For a moment she contemplated returning to Cotton and making him come up here to keep Skinner busy, but time was running out. Esther slid the axe beneath a pipe on the wall, stood up and walked into the bridge.

It was empty. A quick glance to both port and starboard wings told her they too were very much devoid of Captain Lloyd Skinner.

'Shit.'

She ran to the door again and picked up the axe, but as she started to descend the stairs a noise stopped her. Someone was closing a cabin door on D-deck. Esther crept quietly to the corner of the stair well and peered round. Lloyd Skinner was leaving his cabin. She ducked her head back behind the metal wall and waited for the sounds of his footfall, getting ready to move fast if they indicated he was about to return to the bridge by the stairs. But he wasn't walking. He must still be standing by the door of his cabin. She waited some more, and then cautiously inched her head to the edge and looked around. Skinner was busy. He was checking the bullet chamber of a small handgun. Finishing the job, he clicked it shut, looked quickly at his watch like a clerk checking his lunch-break, then slid the weapon into the pocket of his trousers as though it were nothing more than a pair of shades. He looked up as she dived behind her cover again, and she readied herself for a sprint. But his footfall told her that the bridge was not his destination. She listened as his footsteps clanged down the stairwell, and she mused firstly at how fearless he was alone in the face of such carnage, and secondly how bad her timing was. She was disappointed that he had retrieved the gun; but at least he had taken her warning that it might be needed to hunt down Sahg. Why that bothered her Esther couldn't quite say, except that for a girl who had rarely been without a weapon since she was twelve, it troubled her it was him and not her. The times that her own stolen cache of cheap weaponry had saved her from serious damage through her rough teenage years, merely by the fact that she had them and didn't have to use them, had made her respect rather than fear the gun. But she'd seen what they could do in the wrong hands, and Matthew was right. She didn't trust Skinner.

Not trusting a man who sailed a ship and made poor dinner conversation was one thing. Not trusting a man who had the only gun on that ship was quite another. She cursed inwardly and waited until she heard his footsteps die in the echoing stairwell, then slid round the corner and approached his cabin door.

She was an optimist. Maybe there was more than one weapon. Esther knew that was almost certainly not the case, but she was using it as an excuse to enter his cabin. As of this moment, she had suddenly become rather curious to know as much as she could about the master of the *Lysicrates*.

She pulled the handle down, looked left and right, entered and shut the door quickly behind her. Inside, the lights were on.

Esther looked round the mundane and tidy public living quarters of a man at sea. On his meeting table between the hard, unpleasant sofas, a chart was laid out. A few books had been abandoned on a variety of surfaces and his desk was an undulating landscape of papers and binders. She moved towards the more interesting of the suite's three rooms. His sleeping quarters. The adjoining door was closed and she opened it cautiously through force of habit. Sonstar's gift of luxury to its captains was not only a private bedroom off the living area, but a real single bed, instead of the bolted-on bunk the majority of the lower-ranking crew had to contend with. The room was identical to the one she enjoyed as the honoured passenger, but her eye for observation picked out a few differences, the main one being that her bed had a gap beneath it, a space she had immediately utilized by storing in it her pack and any dirty laundry she couldn't face. Skinner's bed was boxed in with a plank, considerably reducing his storage space. But at least they shared a bed-making obsession. His, like hers, was made up in military fashion, the sheets tight enough to bounce a dime on. A quick scan located the cabinet that Matthew had described, but before she was going to explore that barren possibility, she wanted to see something, anything that would tell her more about one of the two most dangerous men on board. Fen was the more dangerous, sure, but she wanted to make sure that the gun that could stop him was in the hands of someone who would use it for that purpose, and only that purpose. Who was Skinner? Why did he make her uneasy? Why, more importantly, was she not chasing after him offering to help?

There was certainly nothing she could see right away that suggested any answers. The bedroom was as officiously tidy as the office.

Two small, framed photos on a bureau beneath the porthole were the only apparent personal touch, and she stepped forward to look at them. The first was of Skinner himself. He looked younger and fitter, and he was standing on the top of a mountain somewhere, a snow-covered landscape stretching out forever at his back. He wasn't smiling, but there was a curious satisfaction in his expression that was not particularly pleasant, and though she wouldn't have risked the trailer on it, Esther guessed that the photo had been taken with a self-timer. The clues were there. One set of footprints leading to where he stood, one rucksack on the ground, a single flask and an apple sitting forlornly in the snow beside the pack.

The other was more the stuff of lonely men at sea. It was a poor-quality colour picture, an interior. A small boy on a tricycle grinned triumphantly from in front of a Christmas tree, as his new wheels tore at the rug. His face was an oval of pure joy, as he beamed up into the camera, his starfish hands held out from the handlebars imploring to be picked up by the beloved photographer. Esther sat down and held the picture. He was beautiful. Something in her softened as she recognized Lloyd Skinner's striking features in the boy. So he had a son. He loved someone. That made her feel a whole lot better, though she didn't know why. She sighed and looked around. There was so little else to see.

A large clothes locker with louvered doors was built into the wall. Replacing the photo on the bureau, Esther opened it and revealed a neat line of shirts, and a small half-open case containing some folded underwear and T-shirts. A glance back at the photo of the boy made a pang of guilt rise in her gullet. This was intrusion. Lloyd Skinner had done nothing wrong except express his irritation at her. An irritation that if you looked at it in the cold light of day, was not only sensible and proper, but understandable, given their situation. The distant siren of warning that had been sounding in her head when she'd been around him lately was obviously more to do with her than him. She rubbed a hand over tired eyes. Picking up the photo of the little boy again, she held it closer to her face to have one last look before she left this poor man's privacy intact. She smiled at the boy. It was hard not to. He had such crazy big shorts on that his legs looked scrawny, and his cardigan was so old-fashioned it was outrageously cute. On the mantelpiece behind the tree she could even make out a row of Christmas cards.

Esther stopped smiling. In the middle was a card with four big numbers. Four big silver numbers celebrating the year 1953. She put the picture back on the bureau beside the other one.

It was not Lloyd Skinner's son. It was another picture of Lloyd Skinner.

She felt a chill that was out of proportion to the discovery that a man at sea should sport only two photos, both of himself, checked the feeling and walked slowly to the gun cabinet. It was, as she suspected, no longer locked. Inside was a weapon's log-book, a small brown folder that required the user to register the time and date, and explanation of circumstances regarding the removal of the weapon. Skinner hadn't got around to fulfilling this part of his duty, but she read with mild interest that the last time it had been employed had been a mere caution when a suspicious pirate vessel had come alongside six years ago.

Perhaps explaining what had happened on the *Lysicrates* this time would take more than just a few minutes of form-filling. She threw it back with contempt.

Esther walked to the middle of the cabin and eyed the bed again. The guilt had gone, and in its place were wheels that turned in her head and wouldn't stop turning until she found out what was bugging her. Right now, it was the bed that was bugging her. Why would the ship's designers have provided a normal single bed and then screwed a piece of cheap plywood over the legs? Ships were like trailers. You used every bit of space you could find to fold things away, tuck things under and slide things back. It was how she had grown up. She dropped to her knees and had a better look.

It hadn't even been done well.

The wood was held in place by two fat screws at the top corners, and by the look of them the carpenter had had more than a couple of goes at getting them into the drill-holes. She looked at it for a moment, then her hand beat her head to the conclusion they were both coming to: her fingers reached out and twisted the first screw. It turned easily – it was a screw that was used to being taken out and replaced. Esther bit her lip and glanced back at the open door to Skinner's office. She'd come this far. She might as well continue. She twisted the screw out, then loosened and removed the next one. The wood immediately shifted forward, and it took no effort to slide her fingers under it and pull it away from the bed. She smiled when she saw what was there, although not with satisfaction. Her expression was bitter: she would rather have been wrong. There was a case in the void beneath Skinner's bed, a large red Samsonite case. Esther rubbed her hands together then grabbed the handle and attempted to pull it out. It was heavy, and although it was an ordinary-looking suitcase, with a combination lock at the handle, a few airline transit stickers adhering to its battered exterior, unless he wore lead diving boots to bed, this sure wasn't where the good captain stored his pyjamas.

'What you got in here then, mister?' she breathed.

The case resisted its full exposure from the safe haven beneath the bed, but one tug with her feet on the edge of the bed pulled it free and she pushed back her hair to look at it. She closed her eyes for a moment, wrestling with her conscience. This was not right. So what if he'd hidden a heavy case beneath his bed? It could be spare parts for his pick-up truck for all she knew. She had no business being here, no business invading his privacy. Esther opened her eyes and looked at it again. Instinct. She had lived her life on it. It had told her to move quickly, told her to run fast, that time when the gang of guys from Mottlefield had started congregating around Sal Norton's mom's trailer. It had told her that the guy from the store who had driven her out to the coast in his dad's car hadn't been planning to show her the waves. It had told her lots of stuff that had kept her in one piece. Right now it was telling her that this was a case she needed to see inside. If she was wrong she would do the decent thing. She'd explain. She'd apologize. She'd make it up to him. She was going to open it.

She tried the lock. The combination was set. Barely missing a beat, Esther picked up the fire-axe and smashed it down on the battered red handle. It gave way in the most satisfactory way and with one twist of the mangled plastic she felt the internal metal hinge snick open.

She lifted the lid like an archaeologist opening a tomb. The contents made her mouth open and her tongue travel slowly from one side of her lower lip to the other.

Whatever she had been expecting, it had not been this. The case had been skilfully divided into two compartments, The right-hand side, the bigger of the two, was still covered over with a thin, carefully-fashioned, wooden lid. In the open left-hand compartment, however, a shaped bed of foam cradled its treasure.

Esther Mulholland knew a VHF radio when she saw it, and she was looking at one. It was hooked up to a rechargeable battery, and nestling alongside in their own neat compartment were two spares. She found the on-switch and threw it. The radio crackled into life.

'You son of a bitch,' she breathed, more baffled than angry.

Esther switched it off, and frowned down at the treachery in the case, trying to make sense of it. Then, with the cautious delicacy of a surgeon opening a wound, she slid her fingers under the internal wooden lid of the case and opened it.

She blinked. The same cut-and-shaped foam held another secret, but this time, before her reasoning powers could kick in, Esther's mind was already automatically running through the specification of what she was looking at. Five-point-four-five calibre, sighting range of a thousand metres, magazine capacity of thirty rounds. Even though the Kalashnikov AK47 assault rifle was disassembled, it would be a poor military student who couldn't recognize the most popular fighting weapon in the world. She stretched out a hand and touched the dull metal of the muzzle, and her eyes narrowed.

This was a serious army weapon, not the stuff of fucked-up red-neck NRA members, and the chill she'd felt a moment ago returned, right along with its big brother.

The question was not what in God's name a captain of a beat-up cargo boat was doing with this kind of military hardware, nor even where he got it, or how he smuggled it on board. The big question was what the fuck was he planning to do with it?

Esther caught her breath, then dug out the component parts of the Kalashnikov and quickly assembled it, fighting back the respect she felt for how beautifully maintained the weapon was. There were four clips of ammo, and she snapped in one magazine, then took off her sweatshirt, tied it into a sling, stuffed the others into the home-made pouch formed by her hood and tied it round her waist. She dug the radio from its foam, closed the red case and with an effort pushed it back beneath the bed. Then she replaced the wooden panel, returned the screws to their holes and sealed it back up. Slinging the gun over her shoulder with an easy familiarity, she stood up and lifted the VHF.

Esther Mulholland had no idea yet why Skinner was keeping a working radio secret from his crew, nor what he was going to do with a weapon that could take out the patrons in the first five rows of a theatre without much more effort than a squeeze of a finger. But until she found out, she sure as hell could find a use for them. She had a quick look around the cabin to check her visit would remain secret for as long as possible, then left quickly and quietly.

Behind her, the room returned to silence. The man and boy stared from their photos, the neat bed remained tight and unruffled, and in the louvered clothes locker on the shelf above the shirt rail, an undisturbed aluminium flight case sat awaiting the return of its owner.

The rust in the cofferdams of the *Lysicrates* gave the stale air that was trapped there a sharp metallic tang. As a matter of course it boasted a hint of rancid sea water, a variety of sour smells of dribbled effluent from a hundred different cargoes, and an underlying odour of rat piss and decay. Right now, however, the air was so foul it would have made breathing difficult. Water dripped from the height of the void to puddles on the floor fifty feet below, and each falling drop was celebrated with an echo that kept the memory of its descent alive for many seconds after the event.

But in the inky black darkness of the narrow steel cloister, an organic shape that adhered to the bulkhead at least twenty feet up was interrupting the line of fall for some of those drips. Tiny globules of brine splashed silently onto matter that was almost blacker than the night that surrounded it, yet the shape was immobile, unmoved by the wetness. But although it was still, the thing that was the shape was thinking, scanning, processing.

There was a man coming. It knew who he was. It could smell him, smell his flesh, a smell that was easily distinguishable from the dead and decaying, since that undiseased living tissue was an affront to the thing's senses. It could feel him approaching through the engine room. There were men above. It could feel their fear. It knew where the woman was, and it followed the sensation of her for a moment, feeding on her passion and fear.

It hung from the bulkhead with its strong grip; sticky, mutated chemicals that seeped from its foul limbs holding it securely against the smooth surface. Since the woman's new emotions had stirred something in it again, it let the part of its mind that was not on watch sink into a reverie.

Fingers. It remembered fingers. Possibly the most underestimated part of the body, they received pleasure, or warned of pain. They implored for mercy, or pointed with finality at those who would die. The entity that did not yet have a name, but knew that soon it would have one that would be etched on the dark half of all men's hearts, stirred slightly in the blackness. A pool of water that had gathered in a hollow of its form spilled suddenly to the soaking floor.

When the echoing splash of it subsided there was no sound but the distant drip of water falling all along the black corridor to the bow, and the low thrum of the ship's engines.

What fingers the entity had reached slowly down to below its torso and searched out what was forming. A satisfaction effused its consciousness and at last it allowed memory to stir. The memory of a man.

The little bitches. Daughters of the Sun. So pious and haughty in the presence of the high priest. So dirty and scheming in his. Dark, heavily-lashed eyes flashed. Small, white, even teeth were cleaned by pointed pink tongues. Firm, rounded breasts moved beneath woven gold thread, and slim hips that no birthing child would ever push apart made jutting invitations below silken robes. Daughters of God. Inviolable high priestesses of the Golden One. Virgin handmaidens of the life-giver, the Lord Sun. Bitches as it rose. Whores as it set.

What arts he had learned in the dark forest: how their black-almond eyes lost their innocence and shone with hungry malice when they begged him to speak the unspeakable, to do the unthinkable. How their ignorant, insatiable mouths opened to hear of the squat tribal scum he had been among, the scum who'd thought they'd commanded those dark forces, but whose purpose they merely served. It was he who had mastered them and won. A shiver of gratification rippled through the entity as it called up slow tortures and creative deaths. *How easily they buckled, the rabble of the forest with their thick brows, gold-pierced flesh and slack-breasted women. They died like animals.* The entity held the time-locked pleasure of their screams for a moment like a favoured trinket.

And now time was of no consequence, neither what had been nor what was to come. Only hate survived the desert of time.

Everything mankind hated it always cast from itself, little knowing that it was the very act of trying to cleanse itself of the hated, the decaying, the diseased and the toxic, that made humanity so vulnerable to those who embraced these fruits and found succour amongst them. But to be in flesh again, to suck on the juices of the dead, and ferment a hatred that had for so long been without substance, was to be savoured.

It ran a finger over the bloody organ that hung from a knot of cartilage and macerated skin, and if it had had the use of eyelids, they would have closed in ecstasy.

15

'So it's going to be like this.'

Another voice started to protest. Cotton silenced it with a shout. 'Listen, damn you!'

The man held his tongue, but there was a muttering in Filipino that told him he would not enjoy this level of attention for very much longer.

'We close the holds, and then we stick together and make our way to the engine room for safety, like the captain has ordered.'

The clamour began again and he held up a hand.

'Think about it. Thomas can't have survived. You must know that by now. But the company ship will be here in less than three hours, and if you still feel the same when it arrives, then we can start searching again when the situation we have here is under control. Do you understand?'

Chadin scrutinized Cotton's face. 'No. They don't understand why you want to close the holds while there's a man still down there. Neither do I.'

Matthew considered for a moment as he looked from face to face, then put his hands on his hips and took a deep breath. 'Because I think the ... murderer is using them somehow.'

Chadin wrinkled a normally inscrutable brow. 'What do you mean?'

Matthew thought on his feet. Maybe it was the unusual clarity of sobriety, or maybe he just got lucky. But whatever the reason, in the dry place where he usually scrabbled around just to remember what he'd done the night before, an inspiration suddenly blossomed like a desert flower. It almost made him smile. He nipped that bud before he spoke, and when he did, it was with heavy, conspiratorial confidence. 'I don't think Thomas fell in by accident.'

Chadin looked at the first officer, then round at his men. He processed the information for a beat, then nodded, slowly at first, then more decisively. 'Okay. Okay. But I still say that we should sail, not wait. It may only be three hours. But look what's happened in the last three.'

Cotton nodded in return. 'Sure. Let's discuss that. Soon as we get these hatches shut.'

Chadin barked at the men in Filipino, holding up his own hands this time to quell their new protests and answer their questions, and within minutes the hatch covers were being rolled back on holds nine through to six. Cotton watched with a relief that had no founding in logic, and rubbed at his temples.

The job was going to take at least another fifteen or twenty minutes. He walked to a quiet corner behind hold nine, and took out Esther's tape. He'd promised, and now was as good a time as any. Besides, he admitted to himself, he was as curious as she was.

The cathedral engine was well named. Lloyd Skinner always felt an inexplicable reverence when he entered the engine room of any ship. It was the scale of the machine, the ecclesiastical architecture echoed in the huge turbines, and the fact that, like the human heart, it never stopped, even when idling. He stepped through the door onto the walkway that ran along the top level of the vast space, from where he could look down and survey the whole room, and coughed at the thick stench of garbage that hung in the air. Skinner closed the door behind him, and walked slowly along the metal gangway. There were three doors in total to the engine room, and the only other exit or entry was by the elevator. The unique feature of the engine room, unlike almost every other large space in the ship, was that for reasons of safety in the event of fire, all the doors could be secured.

Captain Skinner was checking them all. He climbed down the ladder to the next level, ensured no one had unchained the safety bolts on the door to the staircase outside, repeated it with the final door at the very bottom of the ship, and then turned and walked towards the hatch that led to the cofferdams. He stopped.

It was open.

So that, he thought, *was how the stench of their cargo was permeating the engine room.* But this was not a question to which Skinner particularly needed the answer. The more immediate one was who had opened the hatch.

He put his hand into the pocket of his trousers and brought out the handgun. Sohn's rechargeable flashlight hung on its mounting on the bulkhead, and Skinner unclipped it, turned it on and pulled the door fully open with his foot.

The smell was most definitely coming from the cofferdams, and he mentally calculated that on a ship that was so poorly maintained it was highly probable that there might be a lesion in the metal skin between cargo holds and the hull that was letting in not only the odour, but very possibly physical leakage from the cargo itself. Of course dangerous deteriorations of that nature were exactly what he'd entered the cofferdams only thirty-six hours ago to check. At least as far as Sohn Haro was concerned he had.

In truth, to Skinner, cargo-leak was of very little importance right now.

He flicked on the flashlight and stepped into the dark void, his gun held before him. The echoing drips glittered in his beam as he scoured the darkness with a rod of light that showed him nothing but empty space. Skinner moved forward cautiously. He knew he had sealed the hatch after his inspection. Perhaps Sohn had opened it again for some reason, but since that reason did not instantly present itself as logical to the logic-obsessed mind of Lloyd Skinner, then circumstances would suggest that someone else had been involved.

Moving as silently as he could, Skinner progressed along the narrow passage, mentally counting the iron buttresses that ran like ribs from the base to the ceiling of the cofferdams. He stopped when he came to the fifth, and swung the torch beam to the hull.

He had been breathing though his mouth to avoid gagging on the stench in this hellish and claustrophobic space, but on seeing what the beam illuminated, he allowed himself the luxury of a sigh through his nostrils. His work was still there, undisturbed. A finger run beneath the smooth metal of the mine told him the tiny switch was still in the correct position. He moved the beam to the last twenty feet ahead of him, where another hatch led to the bow cofferdams, and the corresponding space that ran all the way back to the engines on the starboard side. It was closed.

Skinner sighed again, irritated at having wasted valuable time, turned around and walked quickly, and less stealthily, back to the open hatch.

On the other side of the bow hatch Fen Sahg listened to him go, then turned his eyes upwards into the blackness that revealed nothing visually, but where he knew the split in the skin of hold number two was being used again, as a tiny avalanche of garbage tumbled from on high and scattered on the floor ahead of him. Fen smiled and pulled his knees closer to his face, glad to be alone in the dark again until his master returned next time, for good.

It had been more than just his job. It had been his pride and joy. Which was why Pasqual Sanquiloa would never forgive whoever had stripped his radio room of its guts and left him with the husk. When Chadin had assigned everyone in twos to various parts of the ship, there had been no question of where he wanted to be, although he could have done without the company of the gum-chewing cadet who sat silently in the corner picking his fingernails. Pasqual had spent the last two hours trying desperately to find something, anything, that was left of his equipment that he could build into some kind of transmitter. But the job of silencing the *Lysicrates* had been done so skilfully there was nothing he could do.

Instead he had fiddled with components, and in the absence of the intelligence reports from the cargo deck that would at least have allowed him to focus his hatred on Fen Sahg, sat brooding on who had done this to his precious domain and why.

Perhaps on account of the private torpors in which both men were wallowing, neither cadet nor radio officer were prepared for Esther Mulholland's entrance, and had she stopped to think how a female passenger with an AK47 across her shoulder might appear to two already-nervous men, she might have modified it. However, Esther had no time to apologize for the fright she induced in them, as she burst through the cabin door and deposited the radio on Pasqual's table with a heavy thud.

The cadet, Gaspar Libuano, leapt to his feet and backed towards the wall. Pasqual merely stood up and opened his mouth in a silent exclamation.

Esther looked at the two men and suddenly understood. She held up her palms in the universal attitude of placation. 'It's okay. Everything's fine. Everything's cool.'

Pasqual had now shifted his gaze from her gun to the present she'd brought.

Esther smiled and patted it like a puppy. 'Reckon this'll come in handy?'

Pasqual ran forward. 'Where did you get this?'

Esther shook her head. 'You so don't want to know. Let's just say it was an oversight that it wasn't found sooner.'

Pasqual had already switched it on, had the handset in his fist and was adjusting the tuner.

'It's only short range though isn't it?' she asked as he got busy.

He didn't look up, but he nodded. 'Line of sight. But we can send out an SOS, and if there are any ships out there, then we'll know.'

Esther nodded. 'Well if the sister-ship is near it should definitely hear us, huh?'

'For sure. For sure.'

Pasqual was grinning. He put the handset to his mouth and started to make the calls. Esther smiled across at Gaspar who still looked unsure, his eyes on the gun. She touched it lightly. It made her feel good. Safe. In control.

'Would telling you that I know how to use it make you feel better or worse?'

Gaspar, whose English was not great, nodded at her, his eyes still wide. Esther shrugged, nodded back and made for the door. Halfway out she paused, and bit at her lip. 'Listen, don't go to the engine room if anyone tries to make you. You should stay here and just concentrate on this for a while.'

Pasqual looked up even though he was talking to the handset. He nodded quickly, but more in gesture that said he wanted her to be quiet and go away, than to let her know he'd heard or understood.

Esther glanced at them both with concern, and left. She walked quickly but quietly along the corridor of C-deck towards the stairs. She had to get back to Matthew and the rest of the crew. They had some big decisions to make.

It was the stealth of her progress that enabled her to hear the tiny noise. She stopped dead, her hand automatically swinging the

Kalashnikov round to her hip. The noise came again and she snapped her head round to catch the direction.

It was coming from the elevator, and it sounded like a whimper.

Esther walked forward as though on hot coals, stopped at the edge of the elevator door, and listened again. Someone inside the elevator car was crying, but it sounded as though they were trying very hard to do it quietly. She could hear the shuddering intakes of breath, then the high-pitched whine of a suppressed sob.

Esther thought quickly, assessed the risk, then flicked off the safety catch of the Kalashnikov and turned to face the elevator door full on. From this position she could see through the murky glass. There was no one there. At least not standing. A beat of three seconds, then she pulled open the door and slammed back the inner gate.

Raul Nestor screamed, pushing himself even further back into the urine-soaked corner of the elevator car. He wrapped his arms across his head as though to ward off blows and continued to scream through the strings of saliva that hung from his lip.

Esther gaped at him. As a portrayal of undiluted terror, nothing could have bettered the boy's performance. Cautiously, and with the gun's safety-catch still off, Esther checked behind her in the corridor, then entered the car, her glance darting around to catch sight of anything in this confined space that could have rendered an adult insensible with fear. There was nothing in there except the boy. She clicked the safety back on, swung the gun to her back and crouched down in front of him. As her hand gently touched his arm, he screamed again and writhed as though she'd burnt him.

'Shhh. Hey, it's okay. Come on. It's okay.'

One eye stared at her from under the protective arc of his arm, and his screaming lowered to a pant. He had been doubly incontinent in the tiny box: the smell was overwhelming. She had to get him up and out of his own filth. She put her hands gently under his arms and pulled. Raul Nestor panted like a dog, but this time, staring at the open door behind her with eyes that couldn't open any wider, he allowed her firm and steady grip to get him to his feet.

'Come on. Let's get out of here,' she said softly.

Although it was like dragging a bull into a slaughterhouse, Esther somehow managed to guide the trembling boy from the elevator car to the stairs, and down to the door that would offer the release of the deck's warm, briny air.

Contrary to the supposed sea-going experience of Captain Lloyd Skinner, Esther Mulholland's instinct was not to gather the crew below. She wanted them on deck, where the bright lights shone and the only place someone could come at you without you seeing them first would be if they came from the blackness of the ocean itself. Esther very much looked forward to being in that place, because when he did come, she would be ready.

The trash in hold number two stirred as the thing that moved within its depths shifted like a nesting bird. A black oozing tar of rotting vegetable matter trickled over what was nearly a face, and the mouth opened to receive it. The fire of life ran through the dead skin that covered bone and the pounded flesh that stuck to it, and a scimitar of a tin claw that had been hinged to a framework of tiny rat bones loosened and fell away.

Like a serpent shedding its skin, the thing that was now nearly able to think as though it were flesh again breathed with pleasure at the sensation of change. It listened as it turned through an arc in the mire, but could no longer feel the noise of the metal covers grinding over their guides as the hatches had been closed. The thick protrusion of skin and matted hair that was serving as a tongue, poked at an ulcerous hole in the face, then moved aside again to let the worms that moved through the cleft go undisturbed about their work.

Such strength in diseased excrement. Such purity in filth. Soon, it would be able to enjoy the slow destruction of the scum that ran over this vessel like lice. Time meant nothing to that which was not physical, but nevertheless it toyed with how the men in this time would die.

Would they differ in their agonies from those whose screams it had left hanging in another age? And now that its cowering human priest, that pathetic reader of cards and dice, had helped bring about the final ritual, it was all so close. It was irritated that human help had been necessary at all, but it had needed the grovelling shit to gather the fleshly tokens from the sacrifices, to make incantations and worship over them as it grew in strength. *It would not need him forever. It would need no one. There were many more human scum*

*ashore who were waiting, already alive to the fact that their God was
being reborn. They were the ones in need. They needed the dark fire
it would bring, the power of filth and the unchallenged might of malice.
And they would not have long to wait. Soon, if not already, the final
human forfeit, the honoured gift to the dark nature of the Sun, would
find itself prepared for violation. Soon it would rejoice in the coming
of its agonizing sacrifice.*

It sighed deeply, and a bubble of methane zigzagged its way to
the surface of the hold, and gently puffed foul gas into the dark
space between the ragged surface of the trash and the sealed ceiling
of metal that enclosed it once again.

Renato had never been quite so pleased to see his captain as now.
Erol Gonzales and Edgar Pasco looked round in fright as Skinner
entered the mess hall, and Renato waved a hand to Edgar to lower
the cleaver he was so impotently brandishing.

'Fen Sahg,' said Renato quickly to Skinner. 'We think he may
have taken Raul.'

Skinner licked at his lips and looked at them all in turn without
emotion.

Renato went on. 'He left the room to check out the smell from
the holds about half an hour ago. They heard him scream, went
to find him, Sahg was there, covered in blood.'

'And the body?'

Renato was taken back by the brutal pragmatism of the question. His reply had a harder edge to it than he'd planned. 'We
haven't searched.'

Skinner closed his eyes and held the bridge of his nose between
a finger and thumb. Fen Sahg was proving to be more than just a
pain in the ass. He was a problem that needed dealing with urgently.
With eyes still shut, he contained his fury and spoke as quietly and
reassuringly as he could. 'How many more are below, second officer?'

'Just Pasqual and a cadet. Libuano, I think. In the radio room.'

Skinner opened his eyes. 'Then get those men down to the
engine room now, and I'll fetch the other two.'

Edgar looked from face to face, then lifted his cleaver again as
he looked back at the captain. 'Raul. What about Raul?'

Skinner turned to face him, and his gaze travelled slowly to
the cleaver and stayed there until the man let it drop slowly to his

hip again. Skinner's eyes rose to meet Edgar's, and though he spoke very slowly and quietly, the tone was so full of inexplicable menace that the three men in front of him would have preferred it if he'd shouted.

'The screams you heard. Did they sound like there was much left to rescue?'

No one spoke. Renato bowed his head, then gently touched Erol on the arm and guided him towards the door. Edgar followed, his knuckles white around the wooden handle of the cleaver. Skinner watched them go, waited for a moment to compose himself, then left the mess room and headed for the stairs that led two flights up to the radio room on C-deck.

They were gone. The stupid bastards had finished closing the holds and gone. Esther looked along the empty deck in despair, then led Raul to the edge of the massive pipe that ran the length of the hold deck, made him comfortable against it, and crouched down in front of him.

The boy stared up at her with terrified eyes, then glanced around and behind her like a startled woodland animal.

'Can you talk? What happened to you down there?'

She was gentle, calming, reassuring, but the terror that was still gripping Raul Nestor had almost completely erased the scanty grasp of English he possessed. He stared back at her, uncomprehending. The sea breeze ruffled their hair and Esther pushed hers from her eyes with an impatient hand. She breathed in a deep lungful of sweet ocean air, relieved that the closed holds seemed to be trapping the stink that she had been enduring in the accommodation block, and tried again.

'What ... did ... you ... see?' She pointed at her eyes, then at him.

The international language of mime seemed to get through this time. Raul's mouth turned down into a tight half-crescent as he pressed back against the pipe, hugging himself. He began to babble in Filipino, whimpering and crying, his hands shooting out occasionally to sketch something incomprehensible in the air.

She watched with narrowed eyes, but could make little sense of anything he was trying to convey, and as Raul continued his hysterical charade, he became so increasingly distressed that Esther put out a hand to his arm, patted it and hushed him into repose again.

Her head was aching. It must have been the foul air she had been breathing below, but a pain that had its roots in the base of her skull was growing from being dull and background to something sharper and more insistent. She put a hand to the back of her neck and rubbed.

Esther looked out to sea and sighed, thinking about what to do next, and then glanced back at Raul. *Raul Nestor. Raul Nestor from Batangas, a town south of Manila. Raul Nestor who wanted to own a motocross bike and win competitions. Who fantasized about Cameron Diaz and the slightly plump daughter of the sugar factory foreman where his father worked. Who had a genetic liver disease he didn't yet know about, that wouldn't make itself felt until he was in his thirties.*

Esther Mulholland blinked at him and knew all this. She caught her breath and looked away again, feeling her heart beating at twice its normal rate. It was an illusion, of course. For some peculiar reason, her head was making stuff up. How could she know things like that simply by looking at the boy? She breathed deeper, calmed herself and looked back. It was just a boy huddled on a deck, trying to tell her what had frightened him. For a moment or two, she joined him in his anxiety. Esther didn't like being out of control, and whatever made her temporarily hallucinate about the boy's private life was most definitely not being driven by her. But there was an explanation for everything. She was tired. The last six hours had been tough.

She rubbed her eyes and scrutinized the boy's face. This wasn't getting her anywhere. But it was essential she found out who or what had frightened him, and how long ago. *After all, it must have been something pretty bad to shake up a cool nineteen-year-old like Raul.* She stood up, walked a few paces to the rail, and ran through her options. And while Esther Mulholland's mind laid them out before her, it was probably too busy to make her ask herself how she knew that Raul Nestor was nineteen.

Renato Lhoon had not been pleased when his first officer entered the engine room leading the crew who had been deployed to the holds. Matthew Cotton was looking uncharacteristically in charge when he arrived, and that was not what Renato had expected or indeed desired. However, it was a look that seemed fuelled by some inner turmoil rather than by maturity or a renewed sense of responsibility. He watched Cotton carefully as he stormed in and started glancing about quickly. There were now twenty men in the room, and they milled around the vast metal gallery looking for places to sit, or stood in small groups smoking and talking in low voices. Cotton, however, was counting heads, ticking off crew members on his fingers as he mouthed their names silently. Renato walked slowly over to join him.

'Counting crew present, or just remembering who owes you a drink?'

Cotton kept his eyes forward, ignoring the barb, and continued calculating for a moment. He stopped, his brow furrowed and then spoke much too quickly, Renato's theory about this being a man who was far from being at peace starting to seem self-evident.

'Who are we missing?'

Renato scanned the room but made no reply.

Cotton turned to look at him. 'I said, who are we missing, Second Officer Lhoon?'

There was no mistaking the deliberate authority in Matthew Cotton's voice, or the emphasis he gave to the word 'second'. An internal spring in the dark portion of Renato Lhoon's heart wound a notch tighter. He returned Cotton's stare with a placid and inscrutable face. 'Radio Officer and Cadet Libuano. Fen Sahg, somewhat obviously, Raul Nestor, who if Pasco and Gonzales' story is to believed, may not be joining us at all. That just leaves the captain and ... your lady passenger.'

Matthew glanced over at the oiler and the OS, once again ignoring the jagged emphasis on Renato's last two words. 'What happened?' His voice held dread.

Renato gestured over at the two men. 'Nestor went out alone. They heard screams. Then Sahg appears from the direction of the screaming, covered in blood and crazy as a coot.'

Cotton mashed his mouth with a hand. 'Fuck.'

Now that Cotton was deep in thought, Renato took the opportunity to examine his face. He wanted to watch how it changed as he spoke. 'The captain's rounding up Pasqual and Libuano. Where's the girl?'

Cotton's face did not change. His brow remained furrowed, his hand remained over his mouth. 'I don't know,' he replied distractedly and completely truthfully.

Renato clucked in annoyance, though it was unclear whether it was because Cotton had been irresponsible again, or because the theory he'd been hatching about an unprofessional romance between his drunken superior and the passenger seemed to be wrong. He turned away in irritation. 'Everyone in twos, remember?'

'Yeah.'

'So who let her slip away?'

Matthew shrugged, still deep in thought.

Renato sighed and tucked a loose corner of his shirt into his pants with the pompous manner of a petty official dressing for office. 'Then let's hope she joins us soon.'

Matthew was thinking the same. And more besides. She would have finished her dubious chore by now, for sure. So where was she? He needed to talk to her about the tape, more to stop himself going mad than because he believed what he'd heard on it. A momentary flitting of fright passed over him as he suddenly feared for her safety, rather than for her discovery in an act of theft. The same feeling of dread he'd felt when he'd listened to the muffled recording of the words the Inca boy had been saying to an oblivious Esther.

He took in air sharply through his nostrils for a second, trying to compose himself, but the words came back as clearly as though the tape were being played right now in public.

'*I know who you are … I know all things … I have been chosen … you live in a shiny box … a trailer. Your father drinks too much. You broke a bone in your foot when you were six. Fell over a trailer gas canister running from men who were going to do something bad to your friend's mother. Your father was too drunk to notice you were in pain and you limped for weeks, the foot crippling, your blood growing septic. The trailer owner's wife saved you … took you to hospital. It made you take care of your body after that. You love your body now … you treat it like a gift … But it will be our gift. Our gift to him.*'

Matthew wiped at his brow.

'Then we need to find her. We'll both go.'

Renato raised an eyebrow, crossed his arms and shook his head, daring Cotton to contradict him. 'No way. We're in an emergency situation here. I'm not leaving the men short of officers just to find one crazy passenger.'

Cotton nodded slowly, scrutinizing Renato for the first time. 'Fine. If she turns up, don't let her go again.' He walked to the engine room door.

'Never sail with women,' spat Lhoon as Cotton passed him. 'Pain in the ass.'

It was a good impression of someone who was merely irritated by the inconvenience of the task that Cotton was carrying out, but it was far from true. Even though Reno Lhoon found his superior officer's company repugnant, given the circumstances, it was not for that reason at all that he was very glad not to be accompanying him.

Skinner's wristwatch told him the inescapable truth, the same way it had less than five minutes ago, when he'd looked at it last. Time was not on his side. The fact that Fen Sahg had become psychotic did not surprise Skinner, but then the capacity for man to turn to beast had never surprised him.

What had taken him aback was that he hadn't spotted it coming, and that oversight, more than the deeds the man had committed, was eating away at Skinner as he walked towards the door of the radio room. He should have contained the problem himself, dealt with it when he'd had the chance. Now things were almost out of control, and Lloyd Skinner didn't like anything being out of his control. Despite his ire, Skinner's face was a mask of composure when he opened the cabin door and entered, and only the most intimate observer would have argued that it failed to remain so when his gaze fell immediately on a familiar piece of equipment. Pasqual Sanquiloa looked up excitedly from his task and waved the handset at him as Captain Skinner closed the door behind him quietly.

'Saved, captain. A portable VHF!' he laughed delightedly.

Skinner nodded, flicking his eyes quickly to the deck cadet as he surveyed the rest of the cabin. 'And where did this appear from?' he asked casually as though loss of radio contact at sea had been nothing more than a minor inconvenience.

'The girl passenger. She found it.' He turned to the sullen cadet and threw him a question in Filipino. 'Where'd she say she found it?'

Gaspar Libuano shrugged back. He didn't speak much English and hadn't understood anything the American girl had said at all. He looked from the radio officer to the captain and repeated the shrug.

Skinner rubbed his chin then casually put his hands in his pockets. 'Any contact yet?'

Pasqual shook his head. 'Nothing yet.' He looked up at the captain with a huge grin. 'I've only just started. Give me time.'

Lloyd Skinner made an upward nod and returned a wide grin as he pulled the handgun from his pocket, turned his head towards the cadet and shot him through the head. Before Gaspar Libuano's legs had time to buckle beneath his body, Skinner turned the gun on a wide-eyed Pasqual, and put the second bullet between his eyes. Captain Skinner watched the lifeless body of his radio officer fall backwards against the radio bench, his hips catching the edge of the metal, making Pasqual Sanquiloa's torso fold neatly over his thighs before slithering to the floor. The fixed grin left Skinner's face as he replaced the gun in his pocket, picked up the VHF, and left.

16

The bolts on the manhole cover were stiff, but a tap from the monkey wrench loosened them sufficiently to let them turn the rest of the way by hand. Esther unscrewed the last one, then stopped and stood back a step.

There was no point in asking herself *what* she was doing. That was self-evident. But *why* she was doing it was a question that was suspended in dark syrup, somewhere in her head that was temporarily unavailable for examination. She wiped the sweat from her brow and lifted the top off the cover. The smell from the hold below hit her hard, making her reel back in disgust.

But there was a feeling of a job completed, and she knelt down for a moment to let her racing heart calm. She closed her eyes, and with reluctance was forced to admit to herself that she was not well. She could hardly breathe and her temperature was soaring. She concentrated for a moment, clenching her fists, and to her relief the moment passed. The ocean breeze played at her brow and cooled the sweat, and she sucked in a lungful of air and stood up.

Esther blinked into the halogen lights of the deck, trying to remember what she had been about to do. Cotton. That was it. She had to go to Cotton and tell him what she knew about the captain. The gun. Where was the gun? She stared around desperately. There it was, where she had put it, on the edge of hold number two where she stood. She snatched it up, horrified that she had let it part from her company.

She swung the gun over her shoulder and felt her heart start to race again. *Three and a half miles beneath her feet, at the bottom of the Milne Edward Trench, she could feel the immensity of the water pressure, sense the movement of the strange sea creatures that lived there in the inky dark, unseen, and as yet undiscovered by man.*

Esther groaned and put a hand to her brow again. What was happening to her? She was hallucinating. She must be. How could she feel the sea bed below her, and know what lay concealed there? She crouched down, closed her eyes and pressed knuckles to her temples, concentrating hard to empty her mind of these bizarre delusions, but the world was still light beneath her tightly-screwed eyelids. Not light in the way that closed eyes lifted to the sun will still admit some opaque pink illumination. It was lit with a conflagration of random, unstoppable knowledge, a visual and mental cacophony of images and senses that blinded her yet made her see at the same time. Esther crumpled, falling forward, forehead to the deck, her palms splayed out before her as though praying to Mecca. And as she remained panting for breath in that position, the intimate knowledge of the unholy thing that was moving stealthily on the ship, was of no more importance in her white-hot mind than any of the million other things she was being forced to know.

In his whole time at sea, Matthew had only ever been on a completely empty ship once, a tub he had captained that was about to be broken for scrap. Even then, there had probably been workmen on the hull he'd been unaware of. But like now, the effect of walking through an entirely deserted accommodation block had been the same. It was unsettling. The high metal tower that housed the crew was large, but its vertical configuration meant that corridors were short, the staircase was tight, and the cabins barnacled together. On a busy ship this arrangement was comforting. On top of the constant engine thrum, this huddled-together warren of humanity meant that there were nearly always the sounds of footsteps or voices drifting from around a corner.

The air was full of cooking smells from the galley, and the incessant ambient noise of radios being played in cabins or muffled laughter from a card game, made the ship live and breathe.

But when the *Lysicrates* was devoid of its inhabitants, this cosy ergonomic architecture became labyrinthine. For Matthew Cotton, as he walked quietly and slowly along the brightly-lit corridor of B-deck, the anticipation of encountering a colleague around a blind corner had been replaced by something considerably less pleasant. It was the deep, gnawing fear of encountering something inhuman, something indescribable that he had ached to consign only to his nightmares ever since he had glimpsed its swift and baffling outline. But Esther was not in the engine room, and while he still believed that the thing he had seen was not the stuff of dreams, Esther had to be found. It made sense that if the captain had gone to collect Pasqual and his cadet then they would be in the radio room, and that was where Matthew was headed. The line of cabins before the radio room were quiet, and he listened as he approached for the comfort of voices from within. It was silent. Matthew sighed, already running through his next course of action as he pushed open Pasqual's familiar door.

The measurement of time and its passing may be regarded as an exact science, but to the human mind it is entirely subjective. Matthew looked at, and tried to make sense of, the scene in the cabin for what seemed to him like an age. He would have sworn it was a slow motion turn of the head that guided his gaze away from the violently-twisted face of Gaspar Libuano, the black-red hole in the dead man's forehead resembling a henna decoration on an Indian wedding guest, to take in the equally awkward posture of Pasqual's corpse folded on the floor. All Matthew Cotton could hear was the beat of his heart and the rushing passage of his own blood in his ears, a noise more invasive and insistent than the idling turbines that throbbed below the floor.

Slowly, he stepped back in horror, and even more slowly, carefully and methodically scanned the room for the source of the slaughter before turning, leaving the cabin, and falling back against the corridor wall to regain his breath.

At least that was how Matthew Cotton perceived it. In reality the *Lysicrates'* first officer was in the cabin for no more than a few seconds before he stumbled out, his hand clamped to his mouth. But time caught up with Matthew as he leant panting against the metal wall. He had barely blinked away his tears of shock before his mind had compared and contrasted the dead men in the radio room with those who had been eviscerated, to wonder why they had not died by the same method, and whether they had died by the same hand.

A gun. Who had a gun?

Matthew Cotton took his hand from his face and looked both ways along the corridor. 'Esther,' he breathed.

He stepped forward, glanced once into the oblong frame of the door that housed this new nightmare, and ran for the stairs.

Resting his hands on top of the shoebox, his fingers toyed with dice he could feel but not see, pushing them between his knuckles and catching them in his palm. The men's voices, far away on the other side of the door, were distant and muffled, but amplified by the chamber of metal that towered above him. Occasionally Fen would glance up blindly in the blackness towards the source of the noise and frown. Then he would bend his head further towards his knees like a sulking child and ruminate on how much he hated the men who were talking and moving about in the warmth and light of the engine room. As he blinked in the inky black, for just a moment part of him wondered why.

They were his colleagues. He laughed with them, ate with them, drank with them, shared stories and experiences, and he had never, until now, been excluded or shunned by them. But as fast as the thought began to sow regret in his heart, the emotion was overwhelmed by the delicious knowledge of the master he now served. The one who demanded his complete loyalty, and in return gave Fen glimpses of the passion and ecstasy that the dark powers were capable of bestowing on the faithful.

The crew of the *Lysicrates* and their pathetic mortal pursuits were of little consequence in comparison. No matter. Soon every last one of them would be dead, and only Fen would be alive, and alive in a way that although he could barely comprehend it intellectually, he understood fully with his heart.

There was only one more sacrifice to make. The most important one. The girl. Another cloud passed over Fen. He was jealous. She had been chosen so long ago compared to the brevity of his service. If only he could have been chosen, but then Fen was no virgin. Fen had no claim to the kind of purity either of body and soul that the girl seemingly had. Inherent goodness. That was what the darkness needed as fuel for its fire, and Fen was flawed too deeply to be absorbed into that divine entity as the final, vital part of its new self. It had been in the midst of one of his too-rarely-granted moments of knowingness, that Fen had unwillingly seen into the girl. Her purity was not one of conventional religious piety. It was a deeper, less superficial good, a simplicity of spirit that would be

overlooked by any human eye searching for an incorruptible goodness. She was moulded so irreversibly with a desire to do the right
thing, to help and heal, to defend and protect, and above all, to
love and forgive. It was that which must be adulterated to finish
this, but Fen longed for it to be him.

To be utterly contaminated, destroyed and consumed by that
which was all-powerful, all-knowing, was a desire that burned in
his veins like an advanced addiction. He breathed sharply through
his nostrils, mulling on the perversity of his longing, and was
rewarded by a familiar stench. Fen's head swung round quickly
to face the deeper darkness of the cofferdams. He wasn't expecting
his master to stir yet. There were still things to do. He had expected
to wait where he was until it was time to help prepare the girl,
and that meant sitting here, patiently hidden until he was called.
But now the stench told him that he was no longer alone in the
darkness. Fen stood up, confused, feeling the bulkhead behind
him in the darkness for support.

He waited, his mouth drying as it hung open, his breath stilled
to hear the approach of the thing he both dreaded and adored. He
wanted to call out his master's name, but that name was not available
to him when they were not joined in thought, and since the approach
seemed stealthy, not pre-arranged, Fen knew in his heart they were
not about to be joined now. He tried to contain a rising fear, and
scoured his memory for even a syllable of the name, but none came.
If he could just talk to his master, then his fear would melt. But why
was he not being spoken to? He was always summoned, called by
that voice that lived inside Fen's skin. But this time, there was silence.
Silence, that was, except for a slick ticking noise and faint rustle that
Fen recognized with a sinking heart.

His fingers closed around the shoe box. Fen cleared his throat.
'Hello? Here. I'm here.'

The echo of dripping water far along the cofferdams was the
only reply.

Fen swallowed and fumbled at the lid of the box. 'It's here. Ready.
I have it safe.' He waited for a moment, his breathing momentarily
stilled to listen more acutely, and this time was rewarded with a
sound.

Its base suggested a hissing escape of gas from something wet,
but the main thrust of the noise was a rasping, staccato retch.

Something was laughing. As Fen Sahg turned his head towards the source of the noise, his eyes still blinking blindly in the impenetrable black, that mysterious branch-line of the senses that man calls instinct informed him of something he would rather have not known. The inhuman laughter was to be the last sound he would ever hear.

Death came not from his side, but from above. It came in the shape of bone and talon, of teeth and metal, and of a stomach-turning, putrid mesh of matter. There was no time to run, not even to fall and beg mercy. But as he screamed, the force of the scream making his nose bleed and his eyes protrude, Fen Sahg was at least rewarded with the memory of the creature's chosen name.

But what use was it now, as his heart was ripped from his chest and his face devoured, to know that He Who Remakes The World, was no longer in need of a priest? That the leather doll, blackened by the blood of the body parts that Fen had been storing so carefully in its grotesque open belly, was not now an essential part of the glorious dark coming, and had always in fact been nothing more than a pagan symbol of devotion?

Such knowledge was of no use at all. All that mattered was that the thing that sat on top of the writhing Fen Sahg, in the inky black that echoed with the oiler's screams, was nearly complete, and was very, very hungry.

He sat perfectly still, handset clutched in his fist, staring at the radio. The distorted hissing was still unbroken by communication, but Lloyd Skinner was not a man to make hasty judgments until all avenues had been explored. He looked at his watch and tried again.

'*Lucky Lad, Lucky Lad, Lucky Lad*, this is *Fishing Fancy*.'

His eyes never left the VHF as he released his thumb from the handset. Captain Skinner was not nervous. He could not be betrayed. The company might think itself more powerful, but they should know that he was the dangerous one, the one who called the shots. If there was any emotion that was currently overriding his inner calm, then it was one of irritation that everything was still not quite in place, that there were still crew members loose on board who had not been dealt with or secured. And the biggest irritation of all was the fact that the girl had his gun.

His jaw moved almost imperceptibly at the thought as his back teeth ground together. Other than that he was still and watchful, and when a voice mumbled through the fuzzy crackle from the speaker, Skinner's eyes betrayed nothing at all. He pressed the handset once more.

'*Lucky Lad*, *Lucky Lad*, this is *Fishing Fancy*, go again, please.'

The voice on the radio was indistinct, but even through the aural mire it was with some interest that Skinner discerned that it was American. So there was a company man on board amongst the South American peasant fishermen. Why? To stop them getting big ideas later? Perhaps, but Skinner didn't think that was the only reason. His mind, tuned for survival, quickly adjusted its plans accordingly.

'*Fishing Fancy*, this is *Lucky Lad*. Go to channel 23,' Skinner returned and waited.

'*Fishing Fancy*, we have you in sight. Are you finished fishing? Ready to come aboard? Over.'

With his mouth a thin, tight line, Skinner breathed in through his nostrils, the only physical concession to relief that any observer might note. 'Catch not quite complete. I'll contact you again in thirty minutes. Over.'

Skinner waited a long time for the reply. He didn't like that. The delay suggested someone formulating another plan of action, changing their minds. He was about to press 'talk' again when the radio crackled up at him.

'We'll wait. Over.'

Skinner put the handset back and stared ahead into space for a moment, making plans of his own. He picked up the gun from the table in front of him, opened the chamber and slotted in the two bullets that would render it full again. There were still four people who were not in the engine room. Six bullets. Four people. It was more than enough. He snapped the gun shut, stood up and went to finish his business.

The molecular structure of the metal handrail opposite derrick number four was weakening. It would last another six months and then a small hairline crack would appear. Black, black stench. Power in fear. The smell of young girls' sex. Pain. That stain on the main deck, the one that was two inches in circumference, was blood that had been spilled by a deck hand ten weeks ago when he snagged his arm on the untwined metal shard of a cable. There were three whales a mile and a quarter away. One had an ulcerous hole in its side. It was dying. Ripping flesh and snapping ribs. Their faces as they pulled the heart out. Smiling, smug, triumphant faces. Efren the electrician used to catch bats as a boy by stringing a net across his open window. Chelito Baylan had locked Cotton in the freezer. He'd wanted to stop Cotton from finding out anything that would spoil his own sacrifice, end his state of grace. Their eyes, the young virgin's eyes, now that they realize what lies on top of them, they brim with a mixture of fear and pleasure. Tenghis Maholes has a faulty heart valve. Skinner is near. The paint below her feet was stolen and sold to a company man in Hong Kong called Ingles. The remains of a Spanish ship lie crushed at the bottom of the trench beneath the Lysicrates. *The water pressure has crushed the soft gold of a cross on its deck into an unrecognizable shape. Rough stone steps scraping the skin from his face. Feces, sour vomit, the mix of effluent and cooking.*

'Stop ... Oh God, please stop!'

Esther fell forward, her head cradled in her arms. She was soaked with sweat, and she wiped furiously at her face to clear the salt from her eyes as she tried to breathe air that was too hot and thin with lungs that were working too hard. She had only made it as far as the crew cabins on B–deck before this new attack of madness had felled her, rendering her helpless as she struggled to cope with the mental and physical assault. But holding her head was not blocking the relentlessness of the unwanted visions. Nor was crouching in a fetal position helping to slow her heart or improve her breathing. She was fighting panic, fumbling desperately for some control of her mind, when suddenly in all the mess of information a tiny memory flitted by like a petal on the wind. Esther's mind reached up and grabbed at it. Bad dreams. Real bad fucking dreams. Apart from the gift of life and an unsupervised childhood in which she could pretty much do what she pleased, Benny Mulholland hadn't given his daughter much. But one thing he had given her was a trick to stop those night demons, and after a couple of successful attempts of employing his advice she had always used it, both sleeping and waking. It worked just as well, she'd discovered, to shut out other stuff. The pain of schoolyard humiliation, the agony of a stitch during a twenty-mile run, or just getting through a young girl's broken heart. And so Esther had used the trick all her life. Now, it had come back to her in the mire, and she could hear Benny's voice, thick with a drunk's whisper, telling her how to make the bad things go away. *Imagine a snowplough*, he'd said that night in the trailer, when she lay sobbing after dreaming her recurring nightmare of the dark man in a cloak who was trying to eat her soul. *Remember*, he'd said, *those big mothers of snowploughs we used to see up in Pennsylvania before we moved south? Remember, honey? Big yellow and black stripes on them. Huge throbbing engines behind that snout of steel. Remember how they used to drive through any old shit like it wasn't there? Well, just imagine you got one of those can do your bidding, and when you say the word, it drives on up to all that crap that's in your head and just pushes it clean out of the way.*

Esther was concentrating hard, her eyes tight, wrinkled slits. The plough in her head revved and coughed, and slowly started to move forward and push.

The coffee machine in the crew mess was burning the bottom of the empty jug ... push ... *a percentage of the plankton beneath the hull was contaminated by radioactive waste that had been dumped at sea six hundred miles west* ... push ... *Thomas Inlatta's body lying in the hold already had maggots in the mouth and eyes* ... push ... *Matthew Cotton had switched* ... no, she didn't want to see that one any more ... push push push ...

Esther sat up with a gasp. Her head had cleared momentarily. The feeling was like having something that had been stuck in your throat suddenly dislodge. She could breathe again.

A tear-drop of sweat fell from Esther's chin onto the floor, and she wiped her eyes as she slumped back against the wall. It was nearly gone. All the hallucinations. All the madness. All the impenetrable fog of knowledge that her sick mind was making up. Nearly gone. Nearly. But not completely.

Esther moved the gun off her knee, and pushed it away from her. Sitting with her back against the bulkhead like a resting border guard, and staring forward into space, she let her mind cautiously examine the thing that was still there. It was a memory. Was it hers? It was dark, but now that the rest of the stuff was temporarily held at bay there was something delicious about it, tempting, familiar but forbidden. It was hard to resist. Too hard. With the delicious abandon of falling asleep, Esther Mulholland, very much awake, started to allow the thought to drift into the forefront of the consciousness she was holding hostage.

Hot sun touched her face. The breeze carried village smells. Dogs barked. There was pain and humiliation. She clenched her fists, pushed the plough forward again. *The pain stopped.* For the first time in years, Esther allowed a large, salty tear to spill from her eye and roll down her cheek. What was happening to her? The two things she valued most in life were her health and sanity. Now she seemed to be losing both. She had work to do. The people on this ship were in big shit, and yet here she was, sitting on the floor of an empty corridor fighting with the urge to let some fever-induced piece of madness take hold of her. And, Jesus, it was insistent. She could still feel the effort of holding all the other stuff back, but the dreamthing, the imagined memory was beckoning like a release. She knew that if she just gave in to it, she could stop listening to everything else. Everything else would be as nothing compared to this. She was a curious person and all curiosity would be satisfied if she could just let it in. Esther had fought long enough. She was exhausted. Her mortal mind registered with dissatisfaction that her weapon was lying feet away from her grasp, but then her mortal mind was not in charge here any more. The immortal one was so much more appealing. She let her arms go limp, and her eyes stared forward into the middle distance, glazed like a drug addict being administered morphine. Slowly, the pupils rolled back in her head, leaving her open eyes white and sightless.

How beautiful he is. How the half-light of dawn catches the contours of his young, toned body. The other priests watch him enviously as he prepares, dark hatred in their hearts that he is almost more beautiful than the sacrifice they are about to make. Tikhua, the apprentice, ties the skin of a former sacrifice around his master's body, his trembling hands trying not to touch the firm brown flesh lest his excitement show. But with a smile that is lewd, suggestive, dark and irresistible, the master allows his own excitement to be visible. It's impossible not to when the skin of someone so exquisite as the boy they had offered is being fastened tightly around your own living body. Cuzna, the head priest, looks across with disgust at his assistant's erection, but talking is not permitted at this stage. From the time of the vows being spoken, when the priests crossed the threshold of their robing room, silence must be observed until the heart is removed.

The screams and pleading of the boy will be the only sound on the air in Chanquillo this day. The villagers know that death and a shamed family await anyone who will not silence their dogs and their children as the chosen one is dragged up the stone steps of the great temple. So there can be no speaking, even here in the privacy of this small, square room. He will keep the rebuke for later.

Now the sun has dimmed. But it's hot. Fiercely hot. A rainforest. Raucous birds scream murder in the canopy. A million insects chirrup under their green cloak of invisibility. The smell of cloying green life assaults the senses of the civilized priest, but makes little impact on the bestial humans who live amongst it. There's advantage in that awareness. Those ugly, squat savages don't recognize the power of their own rituals until he comes. If Cuzna had known where he had been for two years, they would have taken his life the moment he had returned. But they will not know. His lie will be that he had journeyed to the temples in the far north provinces to complete his service to the Sun God. But why would he go to such a mundane place when he has heard from a traveller that the true God was here, deep in the forest, amongst the decay and the green diseased growth, that strangled the life out of everything in its path on its way up to the sun? Here is where his destiny lies, amongst the ignorant savages who show him where the dark power is before they die screaming, as he sacrifices their useless carcasses to that deity that pulsates in the earth, under the feces and blood that squirts from the death he makes in its honour.

A hot, dry afternoon. The boy to be sacrificed, an elfin, honey-skinned fourteen-year-old from the southern province, is in the Sun God's final knowing state of grace. He babbles and sweats. His rant is disjointed, feverish, but Tikhua who guards him, now himself a fully-ordained priest, sits patiently listening in reverent awe to the Chosen One who knows all things.

The secrets and truths are beyond the young priest's imaginings and his mouth is open as he drinks in all the child has to say. It is Tikhua's job to listen, remember and relate the wonders that will be spoken until the final hour. He enters the stone room. Tikhua looks up in greeting, then quickly back at the boy. The ranting increases and they listen together. The llamas belonging to the high priest are loose. The plants growing on the stone below the temple can cure blindness. The marks on the moon are great holes the size of villages. They are made when rocks from the void of space hit them. An eagle two villages distant is carrying a serpent in its talons. The ocean that breaks on our land's shore is deeper that the mountains are high. The priest in this room is a priest of the darkest, most vile arts. He has magic far beyond the power of the Sun God's priests. He is in love with the blackness in men's hearts, with filth and depravity, with everything man despises. He hides from the Sun. The widow of Metikua is going to die of brain fever. There is a way to move blocks of stone the size of temples and marry them so that the hair of an infant cannot be passed between the joints.

Tikhua is already looking up at him in horror when he strikes. The blade cuts through his throat with little effort, and then for the sake of mild curiosity he pierces the young priest's eye to see what the viscous burst orb will look like on his cheek as he dies. The boy stares at them both, his uncontrollable stream of consciousness silenced for a moment by the murderous act, and utters only a tiny strangled cry as he is held down and has his tongue cut from his mouth.

Later, still hot in the room. Cuzna stands over Tikhua's body and clenches his fists, angry and confused at the betrayal. A little behind the high priest, he, the happy murderer, stands nursing the self-inflicted chest-wound that is proof of the struggle he had with the mad young priest who had tried to silence and kill their sacrifice.

He enjoys the feeling of blood on his own taut brown breast and rubs it in around his nipple with a sensuous rotation when the high priest is looking elsewhere. His story is being believed. He's safe. The boy cannot now betray him on the way up the steps to the temple. Without a tongue to tell it, all the knowingness in the universe is of little value.

The cool of the evening now. The warm air drifting in through the stone aperture of the window. The smell of these forbidden quarters is overpowering. Is it the smell of sex or death? To him it is life. Cloying, perfumed, dangerous, charged like the air before thunder.

No Handmaiden of the Sun can be looked at by any human, not even the high priest. Their extraordinary, childlike beauty can only be held as distant memory by the families who had been so honoured to have their daughters chosen, since these most highly-respected fifteen-year-old virgins now belong solely to the Sun God. Their quarters are nothing less than a fortification, though in truth such precautions are unnecessary. No man would dare try and pass through their door. Such violation would incur a penalty too terrible to contemplate.

But then since his return, he is no ordinary man. What ordinary man would have these girls licking at him like dogs as he lies on their finely-woven woollen mats and chews on the dream-making root he took from the jungle? What ordinary man would have these spoiled, bored bitches writhing and begging beneath his body, unsure whether they want more pleasure or pain? The rules of this Sun God are not for a man who has no need of gods. There are, after all, no rules for a man who is a god.

A cold dawn. So very cold. They believe that the sight of the handmaidens' torture and death will be a fitting appetizer to the pain he is to endure. His head is bound fast to a pole, his eyelids propped open with splinters, but it takes at least a thousand beats of the heart before his body and his smile betray that he is not experiencing distress and remorse, but excitement.

They rip his genitals from their root with the hot pliers that work gold. The gaping red-black hole between his legs oozes a thick trail of gore as he is dragged up the stone of the temple steps. The task is to stay conscious, to try and call what he can from the dark to save himself. But the pain is too much. His skin is flayed on the granite as they pull him slowly up towards the altar, and as he falls in and out of consciousness the part of his mind that needs to be clear is occupied with the agony of his body.

Dogs are barking. People are roaring and shouting abuse. Children scream and bawl. The silence that would normally surround the dawn of a sacrifice is rent by the fury of the crowd, but as his body is pulled up the last step to the altar an inner quiet takes hold of him. The pain has passed that line of intensity where the mind can no longer register it. There is a numbness, a stillness, an acceptance of death that is curiously soothing to his torn flesh. And with it comes a clarity of understanding that is born directly from the disciplines of both his old religion and his new. As the blade pierces the skin of his abdomen, he turns his head to catch the smells that waft up the heights of the temple from the squalid village that huddles in its shadow.

There is no ceremony in his execution. It is revenge, hatred and jealously that makes the Sun God's priests tear at his body, makes them hungry to pull out his heart. And since there is no magic in it, he is not granted the knowing state of grace that their younger, purer sacrifices enjoy in their last hours. The state that makes the young and the beautiful long to be chosen. But while his heart still beats there is a secret, more powerful ceremony taking place in his soul. His incantations are silent but spoken with the mind. How can they know that his liturgy is already taking place, since the blood and the pain, the hatred and the pleasure of killing are already present? All he needs is the filth to mix with his blood.

The dark tendrils of thought he sends out see what is to happen and he hisses with pleasure, even as the blade opens his torso to the first rays of the rising sun. The gutters are already trickling with his blood.

All he must do is stay alive long enough until his precious body fluids mix with the shit and the piss, with the decomposing stew of dead rats and rotting vegetables, with the babies' vomit and the women's stinking menstrual rags, discarded as they are in the sewers that swallow up the blood from the temple. He makes silent incantations as the waste products of these scum that call themselves human await the first touch of his blood. The blade is under his ribcage now. They snap the bones off, making him jerk with a new agony, but the trickle of blood is gathering momentum and he is still alive. It is only yards from the first pool of decay and effluent that lies in the sewer at the base of the temple's blood gutter.

It happens at the same time, as though his ritual decreed it. Cuzna inserts his thin brown fingers beneath the heart and as slowly as he can, to maximize the suffering, rips it from the ragged, gory chest cavity. And as the last artery tears, the first trickle of blood joins with the stagnant grey pool of sewage, marbling its oily surface with a roseate vein. His back arches, and he lets out a cry that thunders in the air and fills the hearts of those who hear it with an unnameable terror. It is not the agonizing cry of a frightened, dying man. It is the triumphant bellow of a warrior, and it hisses to a silence as his body, minus its heart, collapses lifeless back onto the cold stone.

Esther let out a wailing cry as her body slammed back against the wall, her hands groping at the air as she tried to recover her senses. Her body was slick with sweat, her heart pounded in her ears, and her temperature raged. She whimpered, panting, as she tried to calm herself, staring around desperately to assure herself she was really here, on this ship, in a real place, a real situation, a place where things made sense. Except they didn't. She was soaked with sweat and terrified of her own visions.

She leant forward and let the contents of her stomach spew out. The floor beside the pool of hot vomit felt cool against her forehead, and she stayed there, pressing the skin against the white painted metal for a long time.

It was strange that the time passed in that position was not calculable to someone who knew everything, but it was true. After the violence of her sickness, it could have been minutes, hours or days to her, but when Esther finally raised her hot head slowly and carefully from the floor, she was faced with two unpleasant facts. The first was that her body was not just soaking with sweat, but that the heat between her legs was due to a wetness she had only ever experienced in the fevered fantasies of adolescent desire. What kind of sickness had gripped her that would make her so aroused by visions of death and torture? But that was far from the worst of it. The other rude awakening was standing only a few feet away from her, and even without the unwanted power of an all-seeing eye, Esther would have taken little time to know that it meant trouble.

'You look a little worse for wear Miss Mulholland,' said Lloyd Skinner quietly, the gun in his hand trained steadily and confidently at its target.

17

'Jesus and all the fucking saints.'

After Felix Chadin's whimpered profanity, there was nothing but a profound silence. All the men were still looking towards the metal door that led to the cofferdams. They waited, breath withheld, and then it came again. The scream was bestial in its intensity, in the way it conveyed a wordless horror of being trapped, terrified, and insane with agony. But what made it unbearable to the assembled group of men being forced to listen, was not just the way the echo of the metal cathedral that contained the horror was magnifying the volume, but the fact that the scream was most definitely human.

Renato Lhoon had moved a step closer to the closed door. He stood poised on one foot like a dancer, his body frozen with horror and indecision.

'Do something, for fuck's sake.' It was a thought spoken out loud by a lowly deck cadet to the second officer of the ship, but the men were agitated, their fear cancelling out their hierarchical reticence to challenge an officer's decision-making. Lhoon looked at their faces, clenched and unclenched his fists, then moved to the door.

The catches that held the metal barrier in place were loose enough to be unbolted by hand, and he managed two until a new and more desperate series of screams stopped him momentarily. The noise stopped and then a moment later resumed, this time as barely audible groans. Whatever was happening to the suffering creature beyond the door was either ceasing or the perpetrator of its pain had succeeded in its task.

It took Renato only a few more seconds to open the rest of the catches, and he stood up straight to face the frightened men at his back.

'Gonzales. Get the flashlight.'

He paused as the man ran to comply with the order, looking around with a poorly-masked air of helplessness that did not suit a man in charge. Sohn Haro, who had already anticipated what that searching gaze was hoping to find, stepped forward and put a heavy long-handled spanner into Renato's hand.

'This is all we've got.'

Renato looked down at the inadequate weapon and then back up at his men. 'Felix, you stay with the men and get ready for anything. Jose, Vincent and Roberto: you come with me. Stay at my back.'

The three young men exchanged glances, then moved forward reluctantly as Gonzales returned and handed the flashlight to Lhoon.

The silent, dark cave of the cofferdams offered no clue as to the origin of the screams as the four men entered the blackness, and the overpowering stench of the trash in the holds made two of the four retch immediately they crossed the threshold.

Hand over his nose and shining the beam of light forward, Renato called out. 'Hello!'

His voice echoed and returned to him without answer. The light revealed nothing but diamonds of water glinting in the beam as they fell from the high ceiling, and the low metal ribs that crossed the floor every twenty feet prevented a clear view of what might be lying ahead of them. They had no choice but to move further into the blackness. Slowly they walked along the wet floor, stepping carefully over the first rib, the cadets glancing nervously back at the rectangle of light they left. Far down the darkened cloisters of steel, a distant sound made them stop. It was a rustling noise, the noise a big animal might make behind a barrel in a barn.

Renato held up his hand as though preventing a rush forward, though in truth it was a rush backwards that was more likely. They listened, but no sound came. The second officer stepped forward a few paces, gingerly lifting his leg over the next metal rib, and since his gaze was directed forward into the blackness, eyes wide and unseeing, it took a moment to comprehend what his shoe was making contact with when he placed his foot down on the other side.

There was not much left of Fen Sahg. The flashlight picked out the few bones that could be seen, split and broken into shards, and what flesh had been left in the pile adhered to those pitiful remains.

Two blood-soaked strips of rag were the only reminders of the humanity of the gory pile that lay tucked up behind the metal girder. Renato drew his breath in quickly and leapt back. 'Get back to the engine room.'

The men behind, confused by his action, his order and the thin, reedy quality to his voice, didn't move.

Renato turned. The beam of light turned with him, sweeping the floor and illuminating for a second a foot that was clogged with blood and cartilage all the way to the ankle.

'Now!'

They ran, stumbling, gasping and falling in the wet.

It took so little time to reach the light and heat of the engine room, yet to all four men it seemed like running a marathon. Renato could feel the weight of the darkness between his shoulderblades as he scrambled back along the narrow metal corridor, and as he gained the safety of the light he turned quickly and glanced back into its depths before falling out into the room full of waiting men. The darkness looked back at him from its charged rectangle of black and he slammed the door shut on it with a grunt.

Renato Lhoon slumped down against the wall and lowered his head to his knees, fighting for both breath and calm. The semi-circle of faces that surrounded him waited until he regained enough of both to look up and address them. Lhoon wiped his mouth and blinked up at them. 'There's nothing we could do. We need to go and get the captain.'

There was silence, but Becko glanced across at Felix Chadin and Sohn. It was a strange response to his suggestion.

'What?' asked Renato, looking at the men's faces.

Sohn Haro spoke quietly and without panic, but Renato knew the engineer well enough to know that furrow of the brow. 'All the doors are locked. The elevator's switched off.'

Renato clenched his fists in suppressed rage. 'Well, fucking unlock them then.'

Sohn kept his gaze on his first officer's face. 'From the outside.'

'Where did she go?'

Matthew Cotton's Filipino was good but Raul Nestor was still staring at him as though he were talking Chinese Mandarin. Matthew bit back his impatience and resolved to try again with a little more tact. The boy was clearly traumatized and he wasn't helping by barking questions at him. He leant forward to put a hand on Raul's arm. The boy's body jerked away from the intended touch and he whimpered.

'Okay, okay.' Matthew held up his hands in placatory surrender. He glanced around the deserted deck as the boy hugged himself, still analysing the horror he'd uncovered in the radio room. The same thought kept coming back to him, regardless of how ludicrous the implication was that accompanied it. The men had been shot. Esther went to get the only gun on the ship.

'It's made from garbage.'

Matthew turned back to the boy who had spoken the words in a whisper.

'What?'

Raul was looking up at him with wide conspiratorial eyes. 'From garbage. It's only half a man. No. No that's not right. No, it's not even half a man. It's ...'

Matthew looked at him closely, holding his gaze encouragingly, but the corners of Raul's mouth were already starting to turn down, his eyes beginning to dart from side to side as if searching for the monster, and worse, his precious words were drying up. Matthew put a gentle hand beneath the boy's chin to lift his face, and this time his touch wasn't resisted. 'It's okay, Raul. You're safe now. You can tell me. Listen: it's safe.'

Raul gulped back a sob and looked back at Matthew. 'It's not half a man because ... because ...'

'Shhh. It's okay. Slowly now. You can tell me.'

'It's made from garbage and ... people.'

Matthew blinked. 'People?'

Raul nodded fiercely. 'Bits. All stuck together. Bits of garbage and bits of people.'

Cotton nodded sagely as if he knew exactly what Raul meant. 'And Esther. Sorry. The girl passenger. Did she see it too?'

Raul shook his head. He looked scared and angry at the same time. 'She's with it. She let it out.'

'What do you mean?'

Raul beckoned for Matthew to come closer as if the huge empty deck was full of listening ears.

'I heard her talking. I understand a little English. She passed out. Right here. Was lying on the deck saying all kinds of stuff. Even about my mother.'

Raul was obviously pretty far gone. His eyes were bulging and his words were spoken breathily, but Matthew listened patiently hoping this stream of nonsense would stop long enough for the boy to tell him where Esther had gone.

'Yeah?'

Raul nodded rapidly. 'And she called it a name. Said it was in the hold. Hold number two.' He giggled, a horrible sniggering sound that was made worse as he put his hand to his mouth like a child. 'She was rubbing her own tits when she spoke about it. Got them out of her T-shirt and everything.'

Matthew had had enough. He nodded politely then slowly stood up. Raul grabbed his hand and pulled at him, the giggles abruptly silenced and replaced by the down-turned mouth again.

'Don't leave me. Where can I go? It's out.'

Matthew adopted a calm and fatherly voice. He had no time to deal with this deck cadet's mental condition. Raul was alive. That was good enough for now. They could get him help for his shock when the other ship arrived, but right now he had to get away and find Esther. Taking the boy down to the safety of the engine room would also take time he didn't have.

'Everything will be okay now, Raul. I'm going to help, do you understand me? You just stay right here and don't move.'

The boy was starting to sob again. 'But it's out. I smelled it go. I smelled it.' He pointed vaguely to hold number two.

Matthew sighed despite himself. 'The hatches are closed, Raul. Nothing can get out.'

Raul was shaking his head and crying. 'She opened the manhole.'

Matthew looked at the boy and then across at the hold. Leaving Raul sobbing into his chest, he turned and walked slowly across the deck to the edge of the hatch. The cover of the manhole was lying at an angle against the edge of a metal pipe, rendering the circular black hole open to the night air, emitting a stench that was almost unbearable. The rim of the hole was sticky and red-brown, and leading from it a familiar trail ran behind the holds behind

Raul, glinting in the lights until it disappeared in the shadows of
the derricks.

Raul Nestor sobbed for a few more minutes, hugging himself
as tight as he could against a breeze that chilled him, then wiped
his eyes and looked up. Matthew Cotton was not standing over
the manhole any more. The first officer had gone. It was the second
time that night he'd been left alone by someone he'd thought
could help him out of this nightmare. With a numb but insistent
realization, Raul Nestor accepted that no one would help him now.
No one, in fact, could help any of them. The thing he'd run from
was coming for them all. Raul stood up on shaky legs. He thought
of its smell, the way the poorly-joined pieces of flesh had glistened
with blood and sticky, clear fluid. He thought of how powerful it
had looked, how quickly and easily it had moved under its frame
of muscle, metal and bone. And he thought about how it would
feel when the substance that made up its vile body would touch
him, how it would crush him and tear him and bring about the
inevitable death he had only escaped so temporarily.

Raul Nestor walked to the edge of the deck and looked out into
the night. He gripped the taff rail with both hands and with one
smooth, athletic movement hauled himself up and over it. The
Pacific Ocean below registered nothing more than a small and
insignificant splash, before the freezing currents that swirled up
from three and a half miles beneath the *Lysicrates* curled around
the nineteen-year-old boy's thrashing body and silenced the panic
of his grunts.

If only she could stop sweating. If only she could reach the AK47.
The captain couldn't either. It was too near her hand. He would
pick it up once he'd killed her. That was the safe thing to do. The
pragmatic thought squeezed itself in between the knowledge that
there were weevils in the sack of grain in the galley that Becko
had bought cheap in Callao and that eight tiny adjustments would
make Rudolph Diesel's famous engine one hundred percent efficient. Esther struggled with the snowplough but the load was too
much to push away. Skinner was talking, but the concentration it
took to hear his words, to clear her head to all but the immediate
danger, was immense.

'... were you doing in my cabin?'

Esther gasped for breath, the sting of vomit still burning her mouth. 'I went to get the gun.'

Skinner's eyes did not leave his target once, even though the gun that could do considerably more damage than the one he held in his hand was still feet away from them both and very prominent in his peripheral vision.

'And Cotton?'

Cotton. His wife was called Heather. His daughter was called Molly. The AK47 is exactly four feet six and quarter inches from her grasp. The floor it's resting on has a screw lodged between the supporting girders that is weakening the structure. A man called Ho Lung dropped it when it was being built.

'I don't know where Cotton is.' She wiped uselessly at her soaking face.

'But he knows what you found.'

If you can't fight this, thought Esther in a tiny space her sane mind found for a fraction of a second, *then use it*. She looked up at Skinner and focused on him. 'You killed a man. A man called Mendez. Shot him at point-blank range.'

Skinner's face remained impassive but his eyes shone with something feral and dangerous. It was working.

Esther's mind filled with images of Skinner. The difficulty now was controlling them, sifting them for knowledge that was useful. She spoke in grunts and gasps, her eyes closed. 'You had a dog when you were seven called Ernie. You're mildly allergic to dark chocolate. It gives you migraines. You planted bombs on the *Eurydice* to sink it at sea. It was all planned from Hong Kong. The company gave you a quarter of the insurance money. Three million dollars. You've spent some on a ranch in Mexico. But you think you need more. You never understood why Proust's *In Search of Lost Time* is a classic. You think it's the self-indulgent ramblings of a pathetic mummy's boy. It's bothered you all your adult life. The ranch has windchimes on the back porch. They make you think of your childhood. You think you're getting seven million for this job, for sinking the *Lysicrates*, since you'll be officially dead. But the man from the company on the fishing boat a mile away is called Charles Lee. He's planning to kill you when the *Lysicrates* goes down and you try to climb aboard. He's going to shoot you while you're in the life raft. There's a can floating off the side of the fishing boat with some tomato puree in it. The incendiary devices for sinking this ship are on the wall of the cofferdams. The radio detonator is in an aluminium attaché case. Charles Lee likes British football and has a tiny fracture in his pelvis. His wife is the daughter of a Chinese judge ... no stop. Stop.' She gasped, concentrating again. 'The company are paying him a million dollars for the job. We're above the Milne Edwards Trench because no one will be able to investigate the wreck at that depth. Kelly, the woman you have sex with in Mexico, has aborted the baby you made. It was a boy.' Esther groaned with the strain.

Skinner's voice was hushed, reverent with a terrified awe. 'Who the fuck are you?'

Esther blinked through screwed up eyes, gasping for breath after her effort. 'The Chosen One. First handmaiden to be consumed by the Dark Sun.' She spoke the words without thinking them first, and when they left her mouth she looked up at Skinner with almost as much fear as he was regarding her.

They regarded each other in silent horror, each privately digesting the impact of the words she'd been spewing out. If evidence was necessary to reveal how deeply Skinner was disturbed by Esther's soliloquy, then he provided it at that moment. In an uncharacteristic moment of unguardedness, Lloyd Skinner looked away.

With an effort that she dug from the very depth of her strength Esther leapt forward, lashed out, caught his leg and brought the captain down. He made no noise except a gasp, but his strength was daunting while they wrestled for control of the gun that was still loosely in his hand, though the fact that his wrist was held by Esther's sweaty grasp made it impossible to use.

'Drop it. Both of you.'

The struggling couple looked up though Esther already knew who was holding the AK47 in his inexpert hands, had known he was approaching, knew what was in his pockets and in his heart. From his undignified position on the corridor floor, Skinner quickly assessed the threat from First Officer Matthew Cotton. The safety-catch was off the gun. One stupid tug on that sensitive trigger and Cotton would blow them away without even having to try. Skinner let go the handgun and sat up. Esther put out her hand to retrieve it but Matthew barked at her.

'Leave it.'

'Matthew ...'

'Leave it and stand up, both of you.'

The gun stayed on the floor. Skinner and his troublesome passenger stood up slowly, both of them fixing Cotton with glares, but for very different reasons.

'Matthew, be careful. You don't know how to use that. The safety-catch is off.' Esther struggled to stop saying all the things she knew about the gun, about Matthew, about the Peruvian fishermen on the nearby boat who were planning what they would spend their share of the company money on, but in fact were also going to be killed by Charles Lee. She struggled some more, pushing the crap from her mind.

Matthew looked from face to face. His voice was broken with emotion. 'They're dead. Shot. Through the fucking head. Now why would anyone shoot two innocent men? Huh? Why would anyone do a fucking insane, evil piece of shit like that?'

Skinner's eyes were steady, fixed on Cotton. 'Look at her, Matthew. She's gone crazy. I found her running from the radio room. It's drugs. She didn't tell you, did she? That's what she's been doing in South America. Look at her. Look at her, for Christ's sake.'

Esther was shaking and sweating with the effort of trying to keep the wall of excess information at bay.

She opened her mouth to warn Cotton, but the only thought that came to mind concerned the body of Raul Nestor which had been carried nearly seven miles away already by the strong undercurrents. A shoal of fish were cautiously investigating it as it tumbled slowly in the cold water. She closed her mouth and eyes and tried again.

Skinner put out pleading hands. 'She's carrying a load of heroin for the Mafia. It's seriously organized. I caught her using a VHF radio she had hidden along with that weapon. There's a fishing boat a mile away that's due to pick her and the stuff up. Pasqual must have got in the way of their plan. But we're in luck. I reckon she's been sampling the produce. Overdosed and gone crazy. Give me the gun. I know how to use it.'

Esther's eyes snapped open. Suddenly her mind was very clear indeed. 'He's coming,' she breathed, looking around with an expression of love and wonder. *He's coming*, she thought. *He can smell me. He can hear me thinking.* Another thought nudged her from the place that was still Esther and only Esther. *She knew how to turn off those thoughts that he could hear so clearly. She was special. Not like the others. More like him. But why would she want to do that? She wanted him. She wanted him very badly.* She kept her thoughts open and loud.

Skinner's eyes remained fixed on Cotton, never wavering, even as the smell in the corridor increased. Matthew was staring at Esther, the barrel of the AK47 waving around erratically as he shifted the weight from one foot to another.

'Who's coming?' His voice was still emotional, but there was a knowing fear in it that Skinner picked up on and didn't like.

Esther looked across at Matthew, her face in repose for the first time since she had been discovered on the floor by Skinner. 'He Who Remakes The World.'

A tick at the side of Skinner's eye twitched into life, and in the face of this madness he licked at dry lips and concentrated on keeping his voice low and calm. 'She's out of it, Matthew. Give me the gun and let's deal with her before she goes crazy again. Enough people have died.'

Matthew Cotton ignored his captain. He stared in despair at Esther's peaceful face. 'Esther. Who killed those two men?'

Esther's hands had gone to her breasts. She began to stroke herself with subtle but slow sensuous movements. 'Am I beautiful enough, do you think?'

Matthew Cotton groaned at the profound insanity that had overwhelmed the determined, decent and practical features of the friend he had parted from less than an hour ago. His face contorted with grief and he wrestled his emotions to stop tears from welling.

But even had he given free rein to those tears, they could have easily been interpreted as a response to the stench that was now filling the corridor so thickly it was making it hard to breathe.

Matthew's eyes darted around in search of the invisible threat, but this brief inattention to his targets was not sufficiently total to make Skinner think of tackling something as volatile as the Russian semi-automatic. The captain made no move. He would wait. Timing was everything in the fine art of staying alive.

Matthew looked quickly to both ends of the corridor, deciding that the stairwell and elevator offered a better escape than the route to the other cabins. He gestured with the gun, a motion that made Skinner draw in a sharp breath.

'Move. To the stairs. Quickly.'

The captain, eyeing the handgun still lying on the floor, turned and did as he was told, Esther doing so equally obediently but with considerably less purpose in her step.

It was only a few yards to the end of the corridor where the ceiling opened up from the claustrophobia of the line of cabins. Skinner reached the landing first and halted to await instructions.

Matthew Cotton had no idea what he was planning to do. His captain was no murderer. Lloyd Skinner had been his saviour. Despite the malaise that was affecting her it was hard to believe that Esther Mulholland could really have taken that gun and felled his two crewmates with such cold-blooded intent. But people were still dying on this ship. Raul's equally mad testimony had frightened him, and finding the manhole opened as the deck hand had said had dented his trust in Esther. Something he couldn't explain made his flesh creep and his heart fall when he gave it head-time, and here he was training a lethal weapon on his companions' backs as he marched them away in search of an escape from nothing worse than a bad smell from the holds. He stopped when they all reached the door of the elevator and tried to gather his fevered thoughts.

He'd felt Esther and Skinner watching him as he bit a lip and thought about the next move. If he had been Esther, trained to watch and wait, trained her whole life to notice the small things people did that spoke of the bigger things they were about to do, then perhaps he would have been quicker to act. He would have noticed that two of the four eyes that regarded him were gradually drifting from his face to look at something else.

But by the time Matthew Cotton had noticed that Esther was looking at the ceiling above their heads, and that a drip of something sticky and red-brown was trickling down the white-painted wall of the stairwell it was almost too late.

It dropped like a stone onto the floor between him and his prisoners, and although there was no more than a split second, a fraction of a heartbeat, in which to look into its face, Matthew felt that he had gazed on that horror for most of his life. Black eyes that seemed like the eyes of a bloodthirsty crowd rather than an individual bored into his soul. A patchwork of a face, hideous in its mess of flesh and seeping putrescent sores, housed a grin that was too wide, had too many sharpened teeth, shattered bone-pieces and metallic glints in it to be considered being called part of a mouth.

The pressure required to pull the trigger of the AK47 was infinitesimal. Even as the gun exploded into its maniacal, juddering delivery of bullets, Matthew was already regretting having trained such a monstrously violent and efficient weapon at two of his friends. The stinking, diseased blood that splattered from so close a target blinded him for a moment, but even in those unseeing, gasping, gagging moments, he found his way somehow to Esther's hand, grabbed her reluctant body to him and was pushing her through the open door to the main deck, the gun still firing behind him as he ran forward.

He ran and pushed as far as he could go, stumbling along the sides of the deck until he reached the last hold before the bow. Only then, in the shadow of the hatch cover, did he stop and look at the woman he had propelled from death to the night air. Like him, she was covered in a cocktail of sticky brown blood, effluent and bullet-torn bits of long-dead flesh. But unlike him, Esther Mulholland was crying. He put out a shaking arm to comfort her.

She pushed it away angrily, gasping in a sob. 'You bastard.'

Still mad, he wanted to believe. *Still sweating. Still shaking. Still no idea what was going on.* But Matthew Cotton knew he was mistaken. Of the two of them it was he who was the more ignorant, and as he looked at her contorted face the part of him that housed his intuition and instinct nudged him to pay attention to that fact that when she spoke to him it was with a malice he had not imagined her capable of.

'You fucking stupid prick.'

Matthew opened his mouth to reply but there was nothing to say. Esther looked away from him with contempt, her eyes softening when they were no longer focused on her human saviour's face.

'He needs me.'

18

Skinner held the small gun to his chest. His nails dug into the palms of the other hand as hard as he could push them. It wasn't enough. He wanted to feel something physical, something to ground him in reality, but it would take more than an insignificant, self-inflicted pain to clear his head of the things he had just witnessed. With his back firmly against the locked door of his cabin, he panted through gritted teeth and struggled to regain the composure he prided himself on mastering, no matter what the circumstances.

Everything in Lloyd Skinner's world had just changed. He was a man who fed hungrily on information, who acted on knowledge he gathered secretly and constantly when the attention of others around him was elsewhere. It had kept him alive, but more than that, the power it gave him by always being alert, always watching and planning, always being quietly in control of every situation, was what he lived for. There was nothing else. There was no love in Lloyd Skinner's life. People could not be sufficiently trusted to love. Nor was there anything material he desired. The girl was only half right: he had plenty of money. The seven million this job was to have paid was important merely because he could get it rather than because he needed it.

But the memory of all those impossible revelations the girl had unveiled and the nightmarish sight of that monstrous creature were the two things that could not be logically stored, processed or understood by any of the many mental mechanisms Skinner had at his disposal. Unless he could come to terms with them both, they threatened to unhinge him.

He let his tense body slide down the door until he was on his haunches, and with an effort closed his eyes and forced himself to see the thing again. He had only seen its back as it had dropped from God knows where in between them. But even that had been bad enough. The matted hair or fur or whatever it was that covered its patchwork skull had been moving with parasites. But the worst thing, the thing that had made him want to scream even now, was that the skin that was tied around its uneven torso, skin that was bruised and purple, looked as though it had been recently flayed from a human body. He had been staring in horror at the neat knots that held the hellish apparel in place when Cotton had let the AK47 go. Skinner was no stranger to what his beautifully-maintained and cherished weapon could do to solid flesh and bone, in fact he had never stopped being fascinated by it. But the eruption of rotten material, stinking flesh and pus that had exploded over him from the beast, was too much to bear. It was still covering the front of his shirt and the tops of his trousers, and although its stench was urging him to vomit with every intake of breath, he was still too shaken to touch it as he would have to in order to remove his clothes.

The single factor that was keeping him sane was that Skinner's instinct for survival had not deserted him when he'd needed it. Despite the bewildering horror of the situation by the stairs, the animal in him had seen the moment of escape and taken it. Instinct had made him run back up the corridor, grab the forgotten handgun on the floor and run. And here he was. Alive. What else mattered?

His eyes opened and a new sense of resolve started to form. So, as Shakespeare had suggested, there were indeed more things in heaven and on earth than were dreamt of in Lloyd Skinner's philosophy, but that didn't mean they couldn't be put to work on his behalf. The girl had frightened him with her supernatural knowledge, but now he was regaining his calm he realized that having heard it was nothing short of a miracle. He now knew things that could not have been known by any mortal man. He was in control again. But he had to get off this ship. Everything had gone wrong, and there was nothing left of the previous plan that made sense.

Now, there simply had to be a new one. He knew, of course, that the company would try and have him killed. How could someone with as much dangerous knowledge be allowed to live?

He had, of course, planned to clear the fishing boat of all its occupants and contact the company later from a safe and secret location when it was time to transfer the money. He had expected resistance, but now he knew the specifics and that knowledge was outstandingly powerful. If she was right about everything else then she was right about this too. But Skinner had only the pathetically inadequate handgun at his disposal. It would be hard to win against the opposition he suspected the fishing boat contained. That had to be rectified. He was, of course, going ahead with the sinking of the *Lysicrates*, but even when he got his AK47 back, how could he survive going aboard the fishing boat when there was a marksman waiting for him with the advantage of height and cover?

Skinner thought of the *Lysicrates*' life raft, how part of it could be covered with canvas stretched over metal hoops. The company assassin would not know what Skinner looked like. It would be dark. It was simple. There needed to be two of them in the life raft. One, a decoy sacrifice out on view; and him, hiding, alive and waiting for his chance to board unseen and pay back the compliment.

All he needed, apart from the weapon he was looking forward to retrieving, was the willing and unknowing stooge. Someone who trusted him, believed whatever he said, who would do anything for him.

Skinner smiled. He stood up slowly, cautiously, unbuttoned his shirt and slid his soiled trousers to the floor. It would take him only minutes to change. Then he would calmly pick up the attaché case, leave the cabin quietly and go and fetch Renato Lhoon. His second officer was about to get the promotion he desired.

'Look at me!'

Cotton's thumb and forefinger were digging into the flesh of Esther's jaw as he held her reluctant, sulking face a couple of inches away from his desperate one. Her skin was slick with sweat and he could hear by her shallow breathing just how fast her heart was beating. Matthew was frantic.

Esther, when she spoke, revealed she was not. 'He's still alive, you know. So is Skinner.'

Matthew wanted to sob. He controlled his voice and kept a hold of her face as he brought his even closer. 'You have to listen to me now. Really carefully. I know a bit of you can still hear me. So, concentrate. Concentrate really hard.'

Esther replied by talking softly, almost in a dream. 'Heather, your wife. Her father was Scottish. She liked to wear men's woollen kilt-socks in bed in winter.'

Cotton held her face fast, though his heart had leapt with a pain that threatened to topple him.

Esther smiled, not unkindly. 'You're not really a very good alcoholic, are you? You don't even like drinking. You just do it to forget the accident. Molly already had a tooth when she was born. You called her Popeye because of it.'

'Stop it,' said Matthew weakly.

Esther, though her head couldn't turn, swivelled her eyes away from his to look beyond his shoulders. 'There's a mineral deep under the sea-bed off the coast of Greenland that we haven't discovered yet. It's going to change everything when we do.' She laughed. 'Wow. Big time.'

Matthew wrestled back control of his senses and talked over her as she tried to continue. It silenced her. 'I listened to the tape, Esther. They wanted you as soon as they saw you. They made all this happen. That thing. It wants to rape you, kill you, take your heart and your skin. The boy was talking obscenities in Spanish that would have him jailed in any civilized country. He was telling you they're a sect of pure Incas that believe in the return of some disgraced occult priest who'll make them powerful again.'

He felt a sob at the back of his throat well up again.

'And it's true. Can you hear me? It's fucking true!'

She blinked at him, and for a moment he saw her behind those opaque eyes. Her voice was tiny. 'Help me.'

Matthew let go of her face. The marks where he'd held her were red and angry. His voice was not much stronger than hers, and the night breeze nearly carried it away. 'I don't know what to do.'

Esther looked at him. His kind, battered face was contorted with pain, and it was a pain she now understood completely. Panic rose in her throat and she used it to get busy. Her snowplough was revving up and she was pushing as hard as she could to clear the debris of thought, trying to clear a space where she could be Esther Mulholland and not just a receptacle for the white noise of facts. But harder than silencing the knowing was the insistence of her desire. She was awash with it. Aching to be touched, to be consumed and defiled. Aching for something that her conscious mind knew was beyond obscenity, but had drilled itself into her soul. Her eyes screwed shut in concentration. 'Matthew,' she gasped.

He held her hands.

'It's coming again.'

Cotton whirled his head round, searching for the imminent danger. 'Where? Where the hell is it?'

Esther shook her head, sweat spraying from her as she did. She had no strength to search in her mind for its location. All she knew was that it was getting near and that the part of her that thrilled to its approach was the part that was taking all the energy to resist. *Push, push.* The plough shoved at the blackness, making a tiny white space where she could think, remember, be herself.

'You can ... stop this.'

Matthew turned to her again, his hands tightening on hers. He spoke rapidly, panic-stricken. 'How? Quickly. Tell me how.'

Her eyes opened and as she gazed earnestly up at him he knew he was looking at her when she spoke, and not at the mad person who had spat at him for shooting a monster. It was as well he did know, because if he hadn't recognized Esther in that soft, pleading face, then the words she spoke so gently would have been taken as nothing more than another gross obscenity. But they were not meant to be obscene. They were merely an order from someone who was temporarily very sane indeed.

'Fuck me, Matthew.'

Every face in the engine room turned to watch the door as it opened slowly, and as Captain Lloyd Skinner appeared from behind it, every face registered visible relief. The captain was calm, unruffled, with the familiar, quiet self-assurance that sent a warm wave of comfort through his crew that was almost palpable. The fact that Skinner was far from calm, that on discovering that the body of the thing Cotton had blasted apart less than ten minutes ago was no longer lying at the top of the stairs, that he had felt a fear unlike any other he had known, was not something that Renato or his men would suspect. The captain had regained his skill of in-scrutability, but in the face of the problems that lay ahead its maintenance was taking its toll.

Skinner walked toward the group of men, looking around until he caught sight of Renato Lhoon. 'Is everyone safe?'

Lhoon stepped up to meet him, and the men, having been silenced by fear when the door had started to open, started talking amongst themselves again.

Renato looked grim. 'We were locked in, Captain. Every door.'

Skinner nodded. He moved closer to the second officer to ensure they were not overheard. 'There's been trouble out there, Renato. It's under control but I'm going to need you firstly to keep the men calm, then come with me to help contain it.'

Renato raised an eyebrow but it was impossible to mask the small glow of pleasure he was experiencing in being so needed and valued. He kept his voice as conspiratorially low as the captain's. 'A man is dead in the cofferdams. We think it may be Fen. There's not much left to be able to tell.'

Skinner felt his mouth drying. *The mines. Was someone messing with his mines? Shit.* An anger and uncharacteristic panic rose in his throat again that he quickly contained. 'What happened in there?'

Renato shrugged. 'We don't know. We heard screams. Terrible screams. I went in with three of the men. We only found ... remains.'

'How long ago were the screams?'

'About twenty minutes.'

Skinner nodded. So that's where the thing had been before they'd been attacked. He allowed himself the weakness of fear again to wonder where it was right now, then suppressed the terror with the pragmatic thought of the job in hand. The rest of them could worry about its location when he was safely off this tub, and that was what mattered now. The important factor was that it didn't sound as though his explosives had been discovered in that search for the screaming man.

Men afraid of the unknown would be unlikely to notice or question the innocent-looking circular steel objects stuck to the hull. The captain cleared his throat and adjusted his body language to alert Renato to the fact that the next exchange was delicate, and must be received calmly to avoid any panic. Renato's eyes registered understanding, and he responded in kind, walking a few paces away with Skinner as casually as he could.

'The strain got to Cotton.' Skinner looked saddened. 'I can only imagine he's been drinking for hours, but the girl made it worse.

I didn't check her before she came aboard. This is partly my fault. But it seems she's a drug addict, obviously a courier. I should have guessed as much. They've been doing some drug together, God knows what, but the outcome is they've both gone apeshit, and somehow they're armed.' He shook his head. 'Don't ask me how.'

Renato's eyes were wide with horror. 'Shit.'

'Shit is right, Renato. Now here's the good news. She had a short-wave VHF radio with her, obviously there was going to be some pick-up of the stuff she's delivering. I've managed to get it from her and hailed a fishing boat that's less than a mile away. You and I need to launch the life raft and get to the captain of that boat. I'll explain why when we're aboard. But the important thing is to get that gun off Cotton and the girl. I can't stress enough how dangerous they've become. I'm going to need your help.'

'They locked us in?'

Skinner nodded. He looked at the floor and then back at Renato as if weighing up whether to tell him something or not. It was a brilliantly subtle performance.

'They did worse than that, Renato.'

Renato Lhoon stared at him.

Skinner continued his acting masterclass by allowing a tiny flit of emotion to cross his face – just enough to indicate a controlled grief, but not enough to undermine the calm, reassuring authority he was displaying. 'They shot Pasqual and Libuano.'

Renato put his hand to his brow and looked round quickly to the men to check that no one was looking at them. His pulse was quickening as he absorbed this fresh batch of unspeakable news. 'My God. My God.'

'Let's stay calm. You come with me and we'll hunt them down. Make sure the men stay here for their safety, and this whole thing will be sorted out as quickly as you and I, as the senior officers, can manage.'

Renato looked at his captain and nodded.

Skinner held his gaze. 'I'm making you officially first officer of this ship from now. Tell me now if that's a problem for you.'

Skinner enjoyed watching Renato trying to mask his glee and assume an air of a man accepting a heavy burden, marvelling at how easily stupid men could be manipulated, but he kept his face impassive as the new first officer shook his head sagely and replied, 'No, Captain. I'll accept that duty and do the best I can.'

'Good. If you start by addressing the men for me, I'll just check the cofferdams.'

Renato put an unwelcome hand on his arm. 'Be careful in there, Captain.'

Skinner looked at him and for a fraction of a moment his mask slipped before he could repair it. Renato had a brief glimpse of a face filled with contempt. He withdrew his hand.

It took only a few minutes with the flashlight to ensure that the mines were still in place and then Skinner hurriedly and gratefully closed the metal door for the last time.

Renato was finishing his talk to the crew: '... and that's why we must stay here until it's safe to leave. Felix and Sohn are in charge until we get back. Keep the doors closed. No one leaves. You hear me? No one.'

The men shifted about uncomfortably until the captain spoke.

'We're nearly out of this mess. Thanks for your support and for keeping so calm in the face of all this horror ... Renato and I won't be gone for long and when we come back, this thing will finally be over.'

Lloyd Skinner had a soothing and mature timbre to his voice and the men nodded and settled.

The captain let Renato go first. It seemed polite. In reality it was simply a precaution. That way if the thing was still at large it would have something to work on before it got to him, and secondly it meant that his new first officer didn't notice his captain slipping the bolt back on the engine-room door as he closed it behind him.

The seagull on the roof of the bridge was asleep when its head was pulled from its body. Even if it had been awake, its reaction time would have been no match for the claw-like hand that tore it apart and crammed it into a gaping, hungry mouth. The ripping of this new flesh was nothing more than a delay, but it had its penalties. Repair needed sustenance. The bones of the gull crunched between sharp teeth, and the thing that moved the jawbone to pulverize it looked down with an unfathomable hatred in its narrowed black eyes, and the stench of clean living humans in its wide nostrils, on the place where its destiny was being withheld.

'Matthew. Please.'

Matthew still had his back to her, the gun in his arms like a baby, his head bowed. 'Don't talk to me. Just leave it.'

Esther was groaning with the effort of keeping her mind intact. 'I can't ... it's the only way. I'm still a virgin. He ... needs it to be a virgin. Please. This madness in my head will stop when you ... please.'

Matthew Cotton turned and looked at her, his face a stony oval of misery. 'How can I, Esther? How can I do that?'

She groaned again. 'I don't know. You have to ... you have to try.' It was getting too hard to push the mental mess back. She closed her eyes again and grunted.

Matthew looked at her sweating, contorted face and closed his own eyes. He had to do something. Was she right? Was this all he could do? He walked a few paces out from the shadow of the crane and breathed hard in the night air. It was sweet. The ocean breaking against the hull of the ship was as delicious as the breeze, and he listened to its frothy sound as though it were music.

He stared out to sea, searching his heart for a solution, trying to shut his ears and his heart to the sounds of the suffering girl behind him. Then he saw it. A light. There was a ship out there. Matthew's heart stopped.

'Esther. There's a ship.'

She groaned again. 'I know.'

'It's the company ship. We're going to be saved.'

'It's not. It's ... it's a fishing boat. It's here for Skinner.'

'What?'

'He's going to sink the *Lysicrates*. Sonstar are splitting the insurance money with him ... oh God, I can't keep this up.'

Matthew was breathing quickly, his brain filling in blanks, questions he hadn't asked but that had been there all along being answered faster than he could collate them.

'Esther. Try. Tell me.'

'The boat's for him. He killed Pasqual and the cadet because I gave them his radio.' She groaned and held her head.

Matthew turned back to the dark sea and scanned along the invisible horizon until his gaze swept past the accommodation block. There, it halted. A tiny movement in his peripheral vision made him swing his eyes back to the bridge. Something had moved up there. Something on the roof. As if it was his ally, the breeze immediately brought a whiff of rot. Faint, but enough to remind Matthew Cotton that he had a decision to make.

The boy on the tape that Esther had given him had been young. She had said so. But the things he had described, the importance of the virgin in their vile ceremony was something he could hardly bring himself to think of. He stood, heart in mouth for a beat waiting to catch another glimpse of movement. None came. He fought back nausea and won, but whether he was imagining things or not, it had been enough to rekindle his terror.

Matthew gulped in some more air, rubbed his face and turned back to the trembling girl in the shadows. He stood over her for a second, then knelt and touched her face lightly. 'This is madness. It's not the way I'd hoped this would go, Esther.' He bowed his head, shame and fear in his eyes. 'I'll try,' he said softly. 'You have to help me.'

She opened her eyes and looked up at him with a mixture of gratitude and affection that started to melt something in Matthew Cotton that had been cold for a very long time.

'We haven't much time.'

She sat up with an effort, and still looking at him unflinchingly, took his hand, placed it on her firm breast, then lifted her face to his and kissed him. Matthew closed his eyes and felt the softness of her lips as her tongue prized his tight lips gently apart. His head was reeling. Part of him stood apart from his body laughing at him. *Look at you*, it roared. *In fear of your life and yet a young girl kisses you and death seems less important than the stuff that's already happening in your pants.* His heart had increased its beat again but this time it was not from fear.

Esther withdrew her mouth and he opened his eyes to look at her. She was struggling now, desperate to say something.

'I ... want to tell you something. Need to tell you. Before I lose this gift ... this curse ... whatever the fuck this madness is. I ... don't know if you get to remember this stuff or not ... so in case it all goes when I'm ... well you know, there's something you have to know.'

Matthew blinked at her. His desire had been aroused embarrassingly quickly. What was the delay?

She wiped at her face and looked at him.

'Molly.'

Matthew's desire melted. He clenched his back teeth.

Esther continued. 'You never knew if she would have recovered or not … when you … when you gave them permission to turn off the life-support machine. You never knew if she could hear you, if she knew you were there but couldn't speak. You've never been able to live with that, have you? You've been wanting to die too.'

Matthew stared at her. Molly. His darling baby Molly. He saw her again, was powerless to stop the picture coming back into his mind again after all these years of keeping it out. He saw her four-year-old body twisted and stiff from the brain damage the lack of oxygen from the fire had inflicted on her, as it raged through their modest but much-loved house and took the life of her darling mother. He could see Molly's lifeless eyes staring grotesquely in opposite directions as the ventilator breathed for her, and a glucose drip kept her flesh alive. Molly. Molly McKenzie Cotton. The girl that could sing all the verses of 'New York, New York' and not know why it was funny to hear it sung in such a little helium voice. The girl who didn't like to wear shoes in the yard in case she stepped on a bug and killed it. The girl who wanted her daddy to get a job on shore because she and Mom missed him so much. Molly. The most beautiful girl that had ever lived. Before he could even open his mouth to speak, great hot tears began rolling down his cheeks. They were tears that had not fallen for five years, and as they fell it felt as though his soul was being skinned.

Esther was gritting her teeth again. She groaned and then drew in a deep breath. 'You need to know this … she wouldn't have recovered, Matthew. She was gone. She was gone before they got her in the ambulance. The bit that was Molly died as a fireman called William Legget passed her body to the paramedic. She died then … at that precise moment, 2.34 a.m. and she was happy in the last few seconds of her life. Her feet and legs had burned, but there was no pain at the time she died. The burns had gone too deep. She was thinking about a plastic paddling pool you used to blow up for her in the back yard, of how much she liked the fish design on it and how cool the water felt on her hot feet. She died believing that you and Heather were holding her hands, dangling her legs into the cold clear water. All those weeks in the hospital. Those long twelve weeks. She wasn't there ... just her body. You ... you did the right thing. She loved you. They both did. Molly's at peace now.'

Matthew Cotton opened his lips a little then closed them again, and then from nowhere that he recognized a wail erupted in him that tore his mouth open and threatened to burst his heart. And although the noise was like that of an animal in agony, it was a noise that was long overdue.

Esther's mouth turned down as she watched the man's pain, and tears fell down her own cheeks. She lay back and groaned. Why had she done it? The Dark One was so near. Matthew's arousal was her last chance and she had thrown it away for no other reason than because she had the chance to help heal his broken heart.

She had no more strength. Esther gave up her fight and immediately the hot lava of knowledge flooded her head and made her gasp with the combined pain and ecstasy of it. The snowplough had run out of gas. She was his again, he was coming to claim her, and there was nothing she could do.

There were too many things to think about at once without panic drying his saliva, and so Renato Lhoon tried to focus on them one at a time. He had barely recovered from the shock of what the flashlight beam had picked out in the cofferdams, when Skinner hit him with this. Renato was struggling. They had reached the bridge safely, and Renato stood quietly in tortured thought as Skinner trained binoculars on the pin-prick lights of the fishing boat less than a mile away.

Cotton a murderer? Renato rewound the memories he had of Cotton at his best and worse. There hadn't been a single incidence of Cotton getting loaded that Renato hadn't been party to, usually since it was Renato's paid duty to scoop him up and get him to bed. There had been plenty of shore incidents too, but without exception Matthew Cotton's drinking bouts resulted in nothing more than some routine melancholy philosophizing before he quietly passed out. In all the time he'd known him, Renato had never seen one single display of violence or aggression from the sad drunk, even in the face of extreme provocation. But drugs.

Everyone knew they made you crazy. The difficulty was that Cotton never took them. He'd been offered plenty, particularly when they were ashore in some of the seedy drinking dens Cotton ended up dragging them to.

But unless Matthew had the supernatural power of deception to hide such a habit from him, even when the power of speech and standing up had deserted him, Renato had only ever observed a sad loser of a man who drank until his tank was full and then slept. Cotton wasn't looking to alter his mind. He just wanted to be unconscious. Why would he change the habit of the last few years and take something that made him go mad? Was the girl a factor? Perhaps, but that seemed as crazy as the idea of Matthew Cotton messing with mind-altering chemicals. Like most seamen, Renato had seen plenty of drug couriers. The good ones, the ones who didn't use, were harder to spot.

But the low-life ones, the junkies paying for their habit by risking their freedom, often tried to use merchant ships and were usually foiled by their gaunt, dull-haired appearance and shifty, rodent-like behaviour that was a give-away to all but the most unobservant of crew members. They rarely got passage unless the captain was taking a cut. Esther Mulholland, in stark contrast, glowed with health. He thought of her taut, muscular body jogging around the deck, of the way her thick hair shone and how the whites of her eyes were almost blue with the clarity that sleeping soundly brings. You didn't get to look like that by injecting smack. Even if she was a courier she most certainly wasn't a user. So what the hell had happened? It didn't make sense. How could two such unlikely people get out of their heads enough to commit a pointless, motiveless double-murder? But then, if he stopped for a moment to think about the other things that he'd witnessed on this ship in the last twenty-four hours, Renato realized that virtually nothing made sense any more. He rubbed a little too hard at the back of his neck, trying to find something in all this confusion and horror that could make him feel safe again.

'Captain.'

'Mmm?' replied Skinner, refocusing his binoculars.

'Is the company ship near?'

'Yes. I guess it's very near.'

'Can I know now why we were asked to meet it here?'

Skinner kept looking through the binoculars, his face stony, his hands steady. 'To be honest, Renato, I have no idea. I simply do as I'm instructed. Given our stricken circumstances let's just be grateful we were.'

Skinner was not particularly cautious in his reply and didn't even cast a glance to his companion to see how it had been received.

This unusual oversight was because his attention was elsewhere. The binoculars were no longer trained on the fishing boat, but on the shadows of two figures that he could just make out behind hold four. Slowly Skinner lowered the binoculars from his face and turned to face Renato. 'They're on the deck.'

Renato's eyes widened but he said nothing. He didn't need to ask who.

'Now listen. This is going to take guts, and if you aren't up to it just say.'

'I'm cool.'

Skinner nodded in approval, a duplicitous and double-edged nod since what was receiving the captain's approval was that Renato was as far away from cool as it was possible to get. That was just fine. 'We need to go down there. It's our last chance. I firmly believe they might run amok in the engine room where the men are unless we can stop them. Have you any idea what a Russian AK47 can do to a group of human beings in a confined space?' Skinner let himself think about that for a moment with longing, then continued. 'Here's what to do: I think I can approach unseen from behind using the starboard side of the holds while you walk right on up and confront them. They'll be distracted. They're not expecting to see you. If you think you have the balls you can keep them busy, reason with them while I come up behind and get the gun away from them.'

Renato listened solemnly. None of that made him nervous. Far from inspiring fear in him, he was actually fighting to make himself afraid of two people he didn't believe were any threat at all. He nodded, glad that the plan was so straightforward.

Skinner held his gaze as though summing him up.

Renato waited. There was clearly more.

'There's something I think you should know before you talk to them.'

'Yeah?'

'When I found them in the radio room, just after they'd killed Pasqual, they claimed they didn't do it. They were wired but they both claimed innocence.'

Hope started to grow in Renato's heart. No matter how hard he tried to imagine Cotton as a drug-crazed, cold-blooded killer, it still wasn't working. Maybe he wasn't. That would be good. He hated Matthew for being Matthew, for keeping him back, for treating him like a lackey, hated him enough to want to do him down, to take his job. But the kind of hate he would have to kindle for the person who killed his two crewmates would be quite a different thing. Renato cheered considerably and visibly. 'Well, maybe they were telling the truth. I mean, did you actually hear the shots, did you actually see ...'

Skinner interrupted. 'They said ... it was you.'

The captain's slight hesitancy was perfect. Renato's mouth opened a little.

'What?'

'Cotton said they'd caught you. That you had a gun. That you'd shot them both because they knew it was you who'd been behind all the killings.'

'But that's insane.'

'Yes. It's insane. But it's best you realize how completely out of it they are, that they'll say anything, the first thing that comes into their spaced-out heads, before you go down there and deal personally with that insanity.'

Renato took a moment to work out a way over this new mental obstacle course. He expelled a mouthful of air and put his hands on his hips.

Skinner turned his attention back to the deck.

'Captain?'

'Yes?'

'When they said that stuff. About me being a killer. Did you believe them?'

Skinner smiled an internal smile, the secret smile of a tiger gazing through long grass at an innocent and trapped animal. *Good question, Renato. Fucking great question.* Renato was proving to be the perfect patsy. It was almost too easy. Skinner arranged his face into a mixture of regret, shame and resolve and turned back to face him. 'Forgive me, Renato, but for a while, until I realized you were in the engine room, that it was impossible, the answer was … yes.'

Renato's eyes registered alarm and confusion. 'Captain …'

Keeping his voice and face as reassuring as he could, he put up a hand to stop Renato before he could protest an innocence both men knew to be true, but for very different reasons.

'They're persuasive, Renato. Chillingly, calculatingly believable. That's why I'm warning you. If they think you can do them harm they'll say anything to escape. They're so far gone it shouldn't be hard to disbelieve their lies. They're the lies of the mad. Humour them as much as you can without putting yourself at risk, and concentrate on removing their weapon.'

Renato looked out of the black windows to the hold deck. He nodded. *Mad. It was all mad. But it needed to end. He was a first officer now, and he was crucial to the whole thing.*

'Let's go.'

How could he describe the pain? There was no physical impairment, no fleshly agony or slow methodical torture that could come close to the sensation that scoured Matthew Cotton as he lay on his back on the cool metal deck of the *Lysicrates*. His chest threatened not to be able to contain its swollen searing heart for much longer, but the rest of his body felt nothing. Flesh, bone and blood had been distilled into torment.

'Molly.'

He groaned the name with a throat that was raw from wailing and wrapped his arms over his face.

Esther lay beside him, the gun clasped between them like a baby. Her sweat-soaked clothes stuck to her body as though she had been hosed down, and with closed eyes she spoke sporadically into the night, a garbled and senseless soliloquy that seemed to alternate between expressions of joy and pain.

Renato stood at some distance taking in this bizarre scene, his fists clenched and his heart beating in his throat. Any doubts he might have had about the captain's interpretations of events were put to rest. Esther Mulholland and Matthew Cotton looked utterly degenerate.

Renato glanced up the deck to the holds at the bow where Skinner had taken his circuitous route, but there was nothing to see yet. He was on his own, and he had little idea of what he was going to do or say. A groan from Esther kick-started his resolve again and Renato Lhoon walked forward. It seemed as he stood over the couple that the captain's plan was unnecessary. The evil-looking weapon that lay on the deck between their limp bodies was there simply to be picked up. Renato wiped a hand over his mouth, looked up quickly to the dark shadows of the holds, then bent down carefully and stretched over the softly groaning Esther Mulholland.

Matthew Cotton's hand shot out and gripped Renato by the wrist. He fell forward onto his knees beside Esther and let out a gasp of pain and surprise. Cotton's grip was particularly firm, making Renato wince, and the ferocious nature of his expression suggested that he had no immediate plans to release it.

'Leave it.' Cotton spat the words in Renato's face.

'Okay. Okay. Easy, Matthew.'

Esther opened her eyes and squinted up at them. She smiled the relaxed smile of a Californian surfer, and pointed at Renato's contorted face. 'You shouldn't have hit your wife that time in the kitchen. She doesn't love you any more. She's just scared of you now. And anyway, she was right about the money for your son's schooling. There was none missing. None at all. You just added it up wrong.' She closed her eyes again and laughed, not unpleasantly. 'Men. Fuckwits, all of them.'

Renato stared at her, the pain in his wrist forgotten.

Matthew picked up the AK47 with his free hand then hauled the kneeling Renato back into a standing position before pushing him roughly away. 'Stand back. Hands on your head.'

Renato Lhoon did not know whether to be more shocked by the fact that his shipmate was training a gun on him, or that a paying passenger had just related news of his private life to him that it was impossible for her to know. He tried to breathe normally, to regain his composure, and to start the process he placed his hands obediently on his head and looked back at Matthew.

Cotton was in bad shape. His puffed eyes were swollen from crying and his face was dirty and tearstained. When he spoke he had a catch in his voice. 'What the fuck are you doing, Renato?'

Cotton looked too mad, too unsteady with the gun in his hand for it to be sensible to upset him further. Despite wanting to run screaming from this loony duo, Renato tried to keep his voice calm. 'I just wanted to help out, Matthew. You know. See if you needed help.'

Matthew stared at him as though he had only just noticed it was Renato. 'What?'

He was clearly confused. Renato tried again. 'Are you okay, Matthew? Is anything wrong?'

Matthew took one hand off the gun and pressed his fingers to his brow. 'Where are the rest of the crew?'

'Safe, Matthew.'

'I said, where the fuck are they?' he shouted.

Renato took one hand off his head to make a patting motion in the air. 'Sorry. Sorry. They're still in the engine room. Everyone.'

'We have to get them up here. Keep everyone together. Skinner. Where's Skinner?'

Renato had been wondering the same thing, but before he could answer a shadow flitted between the derrick and the hold behind Cotton. He was there.

'I don't know, Matthew. I came to find you.'

Matthew Cotton looked at his prisoner properly for the first time. It was no monster. It was Renato Lhoon, the man who had been saving Matthew's skin for years. The man who picked him up out of his own vomit, who put him to bed, who covered his back when he fell asleep on watch or did any of the dozens of moronic, irresponsible, dangerous things he did when he was loaded. It was his friend. Why in God's name was he pointing a gun at his head? Matthew lowered the weapon and let it hang by his side. Slowly and with great caution, Renato did the same with his arms.

'I'm sorry, Renato. I'm all fucked up.'

'No problem, Matthew. We all are.'

'Pasqual and Libuano are dead.'

'I know.'

'It was Skinner.'

Renato stared at him. The accuracy of the captain's assessment was astonishing. He had been on the verge of believing that Matthew was coming to his senses, that he was no threat, and yet here were the crazy lies starting. What had the captain said? Humour him, pretend to believe him until Skinner could creep up and surprise him. Renato didn't need to feign horror. He was still reeling from Esther's piece of news, still seeing his wife's bloodied and broken face in the kitchen two years ago. He tried to keep his mind on Cotton. 'Skinner? Jesus, that can't be possible.'

Matthew got down on his haunches, gun over his knees. His head was bent forward in exhausted submission. 'This is his gun, Renato. Guess it comes in handy if anyone objects to going down with the ship. But know what? Our murdering captain isn't our worst problem. We've got more than one monster on board.' He laughed and looked up at Renato. 'You think I'm crazy. I reckon I might be, but we saw the fucker. Looked right in its eyes. The one that's been doing the slicing and dicing. I blasted it and ran. Didn't stick around to see what shape it was in.'

Without looking at her, he indicated Esther with an affectionate flip of the hand.

'Our oracle here is saying it's still out there, and know what? That's good enough for me.'

Skinner was only five feet behind him, low and dangerous, the handgun held up close to his shoulder. Renato tried very hard to keep his eyes on Matthew in case he should look up and follow the gaze that was fixed on what was behind him.

Cotton groaned and mashed at the back of his scalp again. Both hands were on top of his head, off the gun. 'I know. You think I've gone apeshit. The whole thing is fucking out of hand here. Help me, man. I can't see any of us getting out of this in one piece.'

The butt of the handgun swiped the back of Matthew Cotton's head with a force that sent a pink spray of burst blood vessels from his nose as he crumpled, unconscious.

Esther half-opened her eyes and looked impassively up at Skinner. She had, of course, been expecting him.

Lloyd Skinner snatched up the AK47 and despite the amount of new information that Renato's brain was being required to process, it nevertheless registered some subtleties about the process that made him uncomfortable. It bothered him that instead of throwing the handgun to Renato, the captain slipped it into his own shirt. But what bothered him more was the way in which Skinner was handling the semi-automatic. It was with a visible familiarity. Renato quickly reminded himself of Skinner's past in Vietnam and dismissed it.

But since the fluidity with such a specialist weapon as Skinner was displaying was not exactly an appropriate skill for a captain of an old tub that hauled iron ore from one dead-beat country to another, his subconscious mind did not dismiss it. Renato drew in a large breath of air through his nostrils and turned his attention back to Esther, who was looking at Skinner without interest.

'You threw the ring your mother left you into the sea. Just off the coast of Nigeria. Emerald surrounded by diamonds. That was the last thing of theirs that you owned. It's thirteen feet below silt now.'

Skinner pointed the gun at her. His face had lost its composure. 'Shut the fuck up, you freak.'

Esther laughed and closed her eyes. 'The combination on the aluminium case in which the mine detonators are hidden is contained in the dog-tag numbers round the handle. They're not your dog-tags. They belonged to Samuel Denton Mendez, the man you murdered. His family thought you tried to save him. They sent you the tags after the funeral. You keep them because you like to remind yourself about stupidity and hate. You reckoned that your positioning of the mines will sink this ship in less than ten minutes. Know what? You're better than you think. It'll take less than eight.'

She looked across at Renato as if he'd just joined them, her eyebrows arched in surprise.

'He's going to kill you.'

Skinner moved quickly across to her and pressed the barrel of the gun against her temple. 'I said, shut the fuck up!'

Renato took a step forward, his hands out. 'Lloyd, please.'

It was a name Lhoon never used, and it made the captain look up. Skinner took very little time to realize how he looked and he wrestled his facial contortions back into the calmer façade of a trustworthy human being.

'I've had enough of this drug-crazed shit to last me a lifetime.' With a glare at Esther that was shielded from his first officer's view, he lowered the gun and stepped back to Matthew Cotton's slumped form. 'We need to get this psycho secured down below with the men. The crew can take care of him. Take his arm.'

Renato bent and wrapped Cotton's arm over his neck. Big, well-fed American bones always weighed heavily on Renato's slighter Filipino frame, and although he was used to guiding the drunken Matthew along corridors to his cabin, the one thing he had never managed to achieve was to carry Cotton when he was completely unconscious. The difference in their builds was simply too great. When that happened Renato would either drag him somewhere safe or leave him until he could at least bear his own weight. Although he knew it, the situation here was pretty different from the simplicity of a passed-out drunk, and so Renato gave it his best shot, grunting to get the body upright. It had never worked before. It wasn't going to work now.

'I don't think I can manage him on my own, Captain.'

Skinner made an irritable noise between his teeth, transferred the gun to his other hip and grabbed Matthew's left arm.

She moved quicker than either man would have thought possible. Before Skinner could drop Cotton and point the gun, Esther was already well shielded by the row of holds leading to the accommodation block.

'Fuck.'

Skinner narrowed his eyes. She was gone. He took stock for a moment and then made the decision that Esther Mulholland was old news. He had both the guns. Cotton was out of the picture. She could go tell the world its fucking weird secrets for all he cared. It was time to wrap this thing up. He motioned to Renato, and together they dragged Matthew Cotton along the deck to join the others.

19

As its powerful jaws worked on the piece of Pasqual's upper arm it had chosen to consume, a finger poked lazily at the last two lesions in its own skin that were still to close. It was a finger that consisted mainly of bone, but the fleshy lumps that spiralled around the digit were growing on to it rather than peeling off, giving it the pallor of a wound that had been coated in yellowing, waxy fat. The thing that crouched over the half-eaten body of Pasqual Sanquiloa was almost ready, but its gratification in that state had been sullied. Hatred boiled in its borrowed veins as it ate. This was not how it had planned the moments before the final consecration. Scavenging to repair itself was not fit for a creature that was to become a god. The mix of magic. That was the weakness. It had been too tempting to use both the mastery of the powers of the Sun God priest that it had once been, and those more pungent ones bestowed upon a dark master of the soil that it would soon be again, to bring about the unholy glory of this living, breathing state. But soon the darker of the two would dominate. The toying finger moved down to the long penis which hung from a blood-encrusted, scabbed crotch. It stroked itself and closed its new eyelids as it stirred the organ. But not yet. Not yet.

The thing swallowed Pasqual's flesh and moved its face closer to the corpse to choose another morsel. A hand that was still partially constructed from the metal of an oil drum, ripped at the soft throat and deftly removed a piece of muscle the size of a small pigeon breast. It could feel her. It had called her and she was ready. But there were complications that fermented in the dark hollows of its soul. It bit into the red wet muscle. The food was also giving it little pleasure. This was scavenging.

To have any kind of piquancy, flesh consumed had to be from creatures that were still living, still suffering, aware of what was happening to them.

It chewed mechanically on the tasteless dead sustenance and ruminated on the irritations of ceremony. The handmaiden was no different from the other offerings. All sacrifices were granted a knowingness by the Sun God's magic that even it as a priest, as maker and bestower of the gift, could not be privy to, and barely understood. That had always torn at its soul when it was a man. How dare the prey be more aware than the hunter, even though in their innocence they could do nothing with it but sweat in an ecstasy in preparation to die, spouting their uncontrolled verbiage for anyone wise enough to know, to listen, and act on the morsels that fell from such a random and unpredictable table? His darker side would rectify that. It had other powers now, other gifts that were far in excess of the simple gift of knowing too much. Had it not foiled death itself? When had the Sun God performed such a miracle? Soon, not only would it possess that same gift of truth possessed by the sacrificed, but it would have a timeless, changeable, endlessly powerful and agile body that could sustain the physical demands that such knowledge laid on a mortal frame. But until then it must be wary. The man who was with her, the one who had dared to tear its flesh with the weapon that shot fire, he had already caused it harm. It was not to happen again.

It stopped chewing. The flesh on its back that had skin prickled with electricity, and the flesh that had not yet fused with skin oozed instead with lymph. It was the most primordial of warnings. It craned its neck round, an animal disturbed at the feed. She was there, standing in the doorway, hands at her side looking at it with longing and love as it crouched over the corpse. It gazed back, drool spilling from the corner of its gaping mouth. But its pleasure was undermined. She was here. It was time. But since it had not yet called her, it had not been searching for her clean, repugnant smell as it ate, not scanning with its senses to know where she was. His handmaiden was here, but there was a brooding and hungry rage in its soul that it had not felt her approach. Her smell always told it where she was, but how could she mask her thoughts so successfully as to approach unannounced? For that, amongst

many other things, there would have to be retribution. The grin
widened at the thought and the chewed remains of its hasty meal
fell to the floor with a soft slap.

His headache was worse than any hangover Matthew had ever
experienced. For several minutes he lay perfectly still, teeth bared
in agony, breathing hard as he fought back nausea and tried to
work out where he was. There were low voices all around him,
and as his vision returned he realized he was looking at the shiny
curve of a turbine.

Matthew took a breath and pushed himself into a sitting position. Sohn Haro was sitting on a bench next to him, and Cotton
rubbed the wound on the back of his head and looked at the
engineer.

'What's going on, Mattu?'

Matthew coughed, the reverberation shooting white-hot rods
into his skull, and then looked solemnly at the man. 'You tell me.'

'They say to keep you here prisoner. That you done bad things
up there.'

Matthew straightened up further and held his forehead, trying
desperately not to cough again. 'They're lying.'

Sohn nodded. 'So what going on?'

'Stuff that would make me sound crazy if I told you.'

Sohn shook his head. 'I know you ain't crazy. I think I going
crazy when Chelito tell me some things before he die. Things I
can't tell nobody. But I not crazy. You neither.'

Matthew looked at the little man's wizened face with relief and
affection. He looked round at the other men who were sitting in
groups around the room, at Felix Chadin trying to retain his men's
trust and calm. Some of them looked up at Cotton, but it was not
with hostility. They looked scared.

'Do they think I'm a killer?'

'No.'

'Why not? I'm sure Skinner did a good job of persuading them.'

Sohn looked out into the big room that was more his home
than anywhere else on earth. ''Cos you don't say to someone like
me to keep a man prisoner. Don't say, "Keep him here real careful
and no one leave the room." You don't say all that if you tell the
truth, and then lock the doors from the outside.'

'Shit. They've locked us in?'

Sohn nodded. 'I tell the men it's okay. Stop them panicking. But I reckon it ain't all right. Is that so?'

'That's so. We're fucked.'

Sohn sighed as though Matthew had said the soup on the lunch-time menu was finished. 'Something got Fen. Got him in the cofferdams. We hear it taking him.'

Sohn shook his head remembering the horror of those screams. 'Maybe it come for us next.'

Matthew closed his eyes as he thought about how Fen might have met his end at the hands of the thing he'd glimpsed so briefly. It had left its repulsive image forever adhered to his soul. And then he opened them again.

'When did that happen?'

'About an hour ago. Seem like a lifetime.'

Matthew looked across at the door that led to the cofferdams and then back out into the room. He was thinking hard. Thinking about the manhole cover to hold two that Esther had unbolted and left open. Thinking about how that escape route was clearly for the monster to leave the hold by. Thinking that if it could come and go only from the hold, then how could it cross the engine room to get into the cofferdams with the room full of crew members?

'There must be a hole in the hold.' He said it softly, as though to himself.

Sohn looked at him wearily. The blow to the head Matthew had received was not doing him any favours. Sohn's voice was gentle when he replied. No one was in good shape. It was the least he could do to humour him. 'What hold, Matthew?'

'Hold number two.'

'Yeah? Captain checked the cofferdams two days ago. Don't think there's no holes. Don't worry now.'

Sohn wasn't getting the point. And why should he? He knew something strange was up but he didn't know how bad it was. If the beast could make its way through the garbage in the hold down through a hole into the cofferdams, then maybe a man could do it in reverse. If the manhole cover was still off. If he could find enough air to breathe in forty square feet of stinking trash.

Matthew stood up.

'Sohn. You got fire-fighting equipment down here?'

'Sure.'

'Breathing apparatus?'

'Sure. You know we have.' Sohn pointed a finger at Cotton's chest. 'You responsible for checking it.'

A wave of hot shame broke over Matthew's face. Sure. He would have been responsible. And he would have been blind drunk when that check was supposed to have been done. 'I'm going to need it, Sohn. A flashlight too.'

Sohn looked at him. 'What for, Mattu?'

'I'm going to get us out.'

The engineer looked around the room at the remaining crew of the doomed *Lysicrates*, felt a stirring from his own death sentence deep in his belly and winced. Sohn thought about how much he wanted to see his squabbling daughters again, his hard-working wife and his untidy yard full of machines that needed fixing. How he wanted to die in his own bed and not gulping freezing water in a sealed metal room that was headed for the ocean floor. He nodded.

'Thank you, Mattu. That would be good.'

Being a man possessed of highly-tuned intuition and watchfulness, it would have been unlikely that Skinner could have missed the evidence of Renato's doubts. He watched him sizing up the situation, his anxiety as naked as a child's, and once again Skinner despised the stupidity that made Renato's mental processes so visible that an observer could practically see rusty wheels turning. The captain was going to make very sure that his newly-promoted first officer didn't leave his side until it was time for him to do his party trick of climbing aboard that fishing boat. He walked a step behind Lhoon as they made their way in silence to the bridge.

There was such comfort in having his own gun-strap over his shoulder and the barrel by his hip. Part of him wanted that thing to come again. It would feel good to blast it open with twenty rounds and see it get up after that. But there would be plenty of time to use up his ammunition. There was a whole boatload of ignorant peasant fishermen who needed to be removed quickly and without fuss. It was going to be a busy night.

They reached the bridge and Renato walked over to the long bank of windows, crossed his arms and looked out to the hold deck.

Skinner watched him carefully as he picked up the hand set of the VHF and hailed the fishing boat. He hadn't wanted to do this in Renato's hearing, but there was no way the man was parting from him. He would just have to be careful with what he said. They were being careful anyway. Just in case another unseen boat was picking up their transmissions. It might not look good at the wreck enquiry if some passing sailboat could quote a conversation about how the plans were coming along to sink a bulk carrier. No, he was sure no confidence would be breached.

'This is *Fishing Fancy*. Calling *Lucky Lad*.'

Renato stayed still, staring out at the tiny lights of the boat that was being hailed. There was a delay and then a reply.

'This is *Lucky Lad*. Go ahead *Fishing Fancy*. Channel 23.'

Skinner retuned. He glanced at Renato and cleared his throat. 'Fishing completed. Ready to launch and come aboard. Over.'

There was a longer delay than the first and then the crackle of the American voice. 'Looking forward to welcoming you, Captain. Over.'

Renato turned round and faced the captain. Skinner shot him a winning smile that was undermined a little by the grip he kept on the handle of the AK47. 'Nearly there, Renato.'

'Why are you not using the *Lysicrates* name, Captain?'

Skinner sighed, thinking fast, then using a tone of conspiracy held his new first officer with a stern look. 'Can I trust you, Renato?'

Lhoon nodded.

The captain nodded back. 'I didn't just come across the fishing boat. It has a company man on board. He has the orders from Hong Kong concerning why we're meeting another boat all in order and legal and I'm sure it will be explained, but it's company orders. I don't know why any more than you do. I guess the skipper will make everything clear when we get aboard.'

Renato looked doubtful. 'And the fishing you just completed?'

Skinner controlled the urge to pin Lhoon to the wall with bullets and instead sighed. 'Sonstar are sticklers for procedure, Renato. You know as well as I do that if the two senior officers leave the vessel we have to make sure there are officers on watch and in charge. The fishing code was to tell them that had been done without alerting any listeners to the fact.'

'But there's no one on watch.'

'I think, given the circumstances, that will be forgiven when we tell them what we've been through.'

'Is someone from Sonstar on that boat?'

'Yes,' replied Skinner truthfully, then added, 'We need to go now.'

Renato leant forward onto the instrument panel and bent his head. 'Captain. I'm having a really bad time with all this. Can you just give me a minute to get my head together?'

'We don't have a minute, Renato.'

Renato rubbed his eyebrows. 'Can I ask you a personal question?'

Skinner tightened. 'If it's relevant.'

Renato looked as deeply into Skinner's eyes as he could. 'Did you really take your mother's ring and drop it into the sea, just where the girl said?'

Skinner looked down at his feet and when he looked back up, he had softened his eyes. He gazed steadily back at the man with the kindest and most compassionate expression that was in his repertoire. It was a good one. It was full of sadness and stoicism. 'I never knew my mother, Renato. I was raised by Jesuits in an orphanage in New Jersey. Those gentlemen of the cloth took great delight in telling me that she was an alcoholic, abandoned single mother who choked to death on her vomit in a one-roomed apartment above a real-estate office in Queens. The only thing she left me was a desire to stamp out religion and save drunks.'

Renato swallowed. 'I'm sorry.'

'The girl is crazy. Don't let it get to you.'

Renato held his gaze. 'She was right, though. About me.'

Skinner was getting bored with this. 'So maybe she heard talk from the crew. Who knows?'

'There was no talk. No one knew.'

'Then I can't help you. I don't know how she could have guessed such a thing.'

Renato hesitated. 'Tell me, then, that she wasn't right about other stuff.'

Skinner kept his eyes soft though his heart was made of granite. 'She wasn't right. She's out of her head.'

Renato looked at him for a beat, then nodded and moved across the floor to join him. Skinner gestured for him to go first and Renato looked askingly at him again. The captain answered the unasked question. 'I need to cover us both. In case.'

Renato said nothing, but walked on. Skinner let him go then picked up the VHF radio and placed its carrying strap over his shoulder. Renato looked at him. 'Shouldn't we leave that here in case the crew need it?'

Skinner was stone. 'You think it's good seamanship to be at sea in the lifeboat without communication?'

Renato said nothing, but moved to the door.

Skinner watched the back of Renato's head as he exited, then followed him. The man who followed was a man who for the first time in years was thinking about his parents. Lloyd Skinner was remembering his mother's tight-lipped refusal to listen to him as she sat on her cheap brown sofa, the television remote in her hand, changing the channels all the time as he spoke, as he tried to find some words to describe his war to her, his face streaming with the last tears he ever shed. He remembered the round, grey face of his father poking from the kitchen doorway, hiding in there with a beer, hoping that the atmosphere would change sufficiently that he could come back in, sit down and get on with his bovine life in front of the TV. The TV that in the sixties never showed the pictures of what their son had been through. Of what he had become. Of what it had done to them all. And he remembered the ring.

The one she'd thrown weakly at him seven years later from her hospital bed, gasping from under her oxygen mask that if he wasn't some kind of a faggot why didn't he go out and marry a nice girl? The same ring he'd thrown to the strange, fat African fishes off the coast of Nigeria.

Like everything else on board the run-down, beat-up piece of scrap metal that was the *Lysicrates*, the fire-fighting apparatus was not exactly state-of-the-art. But as he moved slowly through the dark, dank tunnel of the cofferdams, Matthew Cotton could not stop himself touching the mask and cylinder that hung on his back on the webbing harness, as though they were an enchanted sword and shield.

The dripping, echoing vault was like a dreamscape in the beam of the flashlight. Darkness that seemed interminable stretched before him, but Matthew walked as quickly as the physical restrictions would allow. There was no time for fear, even when his journey took him over the hideous remains of Fen Sahg, a dark ugly mess that Cotton kept the flashlight off as he stepped over it with haste. He carried on quickly with a shudder. A sweep of the beam as he passed along the high sides of the hull revealed that each hold wall had its own neat steel cylinder attached to it. He had to admire the captain's thoroughness. It didn't take a genius to work out that a hole blown in every hold simultaneously would take this ship to the bottom in minutes. Particularly given the kind of cargo being carried. Matthew couldn't think of a better cargo to absorb water quickly than uncompacted trash. How could Matthew have thought that the captain's acceptance of such a volatile and illegal cargo had been misguided or haphazard? It had been meticulously planned.

There was no point in Matthew trying to remove or defuse these devices. He knew nothing about explosives. The best he could do was to get out of here and stop the person who did from detonating them. If anything, though, Skinner had done him a favour.

It made it easier to count the holds by their marker mines as he progressed towards the bow. If Matthew thought that it would be hard to find hold two and its split side, then he needn't have worried. Already by hold four the smell in the confined space was enough to tempt him to put on the foul-smelling rubber mask that would exclude it. But no. There was at most fifteen minutes of air in the cylinder, and God knew if he could get through what he had to face in that time. He took a breath through his mouth and closed off the breathing through his nose to stop himself being sick.

A few more yards and he was there. He swung the beam up the wall and there about nine feet above his head was what he'd been looking for. A ragged gash in the side of the hold wall caused by nothing more sinister than rust had been widened by God knew what into a roughly oval opening around two feet by four feet wide. On the floor beneath was a pile of stinking, putrescent trash that had fallen from the hold's wound, and as he looked up, smaller bits of unidentifiable matter were continuing to fall at random. It simply looked like a gash in a garbage bag. It looked impenetrable, disgusting, solid. But worse. It was nine feet up a smooth metal wall.

Matthew stood looking up at the hell-hole for a moment, then stepped back and stretched out his arms. He could easily touch both sides of the cofferdams at once. That meant that if he could wedge himself against one wall with his shoulders he could push himself up like a climber in a chimney. For a moment he shuddered at what he might encounter in that hole full of seeping mush, but there was no choice. Well, there was. But the Matthew Cotton that might have quietly welcomed death was gone. Esther had given him back Heather and Molly. He could think about them again. Most importantly, he could think of his darling Molly and not skewer himself on that spit of uncertainty as to whether the most beautiful girl in the world had died at her father's whispered agreement to a consultant, and a shaky signature on a consent form. If he was going to die now, it would be trying to save the woman who had given him back his past. He owed Esther that. It would be trying to save all those men back in that room who had no idea yet what Skinner had in mind for them. He looked up at the hole once more then, since he would have no hand free to do so once he had pulled himself into that hole, he tied the flashlight handle to his shoulder strap, slipped the mask over his head, tightened it and began to breathe sweet air.

The push up the wall was good in theory but an ordeal in practice. Legs that had once been strong and athletic had lost their tone an age ago when drinking replaced running as Matthew Cotton's favourite sport, and as he forced his body up, snagging his sweating back on shards of rough iron, part of him wondered if he would make it. He stopped, trying to keep his breathing shallow, not to use up too much air, and then with one more push, he was level with the bottom of the hole.

There was nothing about it that suggested an entry point. Matthew imagined the weight of several hundreds of tonnes of trash pressing down on this one point and his stomach flipped. But the monstrous thing had come and gone through here. He was sure of that. And even if that thing was more powerful and more agile, it was only slightly bigger than him. He had to trust that it could be done.

Cotton took a deep suck of air and with one swift movement, before he had any more time to think, grabbed the ragged metal edge of the hole and swung his legs up and into the mush of trash. A small avalanche of material tumbled over his head, slapping him wetly and adhering to his body as he tried to contain his panic and stay still until it subsided. It stopped and, with his arms aching with the strain, Cotton pushed and corkscrewed his feet deeper into the solid pile. He found enough purchase behind the lip of the opening to wedge his legs, let them take his weight and relieve the pressure on his arms, and he used the moment to stop and take stock. The task seemed ridiculous. How could a human being burrow its way through such an impossible obstacle? He was mad. He closed his eyes for a moment, a tangible fear threatening to choke him.

Death was everywhere on this ship. It was potentially and immediately ahead of him, a grotesque, ugly, crushing, choking death of the kind that had taken Thomas Inlatta. But it was also waiting back in the engine room, offering a choice between being mown down like trapped rats by Russian hardware, or being left to drown as the *Lysicrates* dived for the bottom. Matthew Cotton gritted his teeth and an anger started to burn in his breast. It was anger that had lain dormant for years and the release of it made him cry out with fury. He kicked at the garbage with a strength he didn't know he possessed and with a primal scream that came from the depth of his lungs his foot lashed out at the solid lump and broke through into a space.

Matthew stopped and panted. He moved the leg around, pushing it further into the hole. It still touched nothing. A frenzied scrabbling with one hand ripped at the garbage and within a minute he had exposed a hole big enough to get his shoulders through.

Matthew stopped and breathed normally, then, manipulating the flashlight on his shoulder with difficulty, he pointed the beam into the blackness of the hole. There seemed to be a tunnel off to the left, but it had an end. Whether that was because it merely stopped or because it then cornered and climbed again, Matthew couldn't be sure. But he had already made up his mind. He pulled his foot clear carefully to avoid any more falling debris and, wedging his knee against the metal edge of the gash in the hold, pushed himself up and into the macabre tunnel.

It was a surreal experience being inside the rubber mask. Two round circles of glass were his windows on the scene around him, and the sound of his own breathing in this confined space was almost deafening. The tunnel was of an irregular shape but it was big enough that his shoulders could fit in and allow him to move forward without rubbing the sides. It was a gradient that climbed in shallow incline and then steepened, but at the moment it was not too troublesome to crawl in. The main difficulty was keeping his head. The sides of this fragile and repulsive environment were crusted, oozing and pocked with things he recoiled from as his hand pressed on them. But the end he had picked out was approaching and he concentrated on navigating his way safely. It was taking all his force of will not to think of the weight and nature of the material that was piled above him, of what would happen if this frail ceiling loosened and collapsed. To give such a horror head-time would make him scream with claustrophobia. He had to think of this repugnant tunnel as a routine and secure way to the surface, keep that thought to the fore and try to save his air. Matthew shuffled forward a few more feet to where the light hit an end to the passage and stopped. It was not the end. He turned over to put the weight on one shoulder and shone the light up what was almost a vertical chimney.

His heart sank. Already he was completely disorientated. The tunnel had been climbing and he thought it was heading for the bow, but he couldn't be sure. Could he climb up this nightmare vent without falling and bringing the whole thing down? Where the fuck would it take him? He knew the manhole led from the Australian ladder on the starboard side of the hold. But what if it just led to the surface and he was trapped beneath the huge metal plate of the hatch covers, unable to find his way to the ladder at the edge that would lead to the manhole?

Matthew licked his dry lips and craned his head back the way he'd come. It had been solid enough to take his weight and the disturbance of his movements. He had to trust that the vertical ascent would be the same. For one horrible moment he let in the unthinkable. What if the creature that made this route decided to use it again? After all, he had no idea where it was. That was too much to bear: he closed his eyes, took another sweet breath, pulled himself up and started to climb.

The footholds were not hard to find. He could either gently move his foot from side to side until it pushed into the putrescence, or perch a toe on the edges and corners of the various hard objects that protruded from the wall, hoping that they would take his weight. The worst was the handholds. When he was in luck his hand would make contact with something relatively dry. But more often his fingers would close around something with the texture of soap left too long in water, a cold slime that oozed between his fingers and ran beneath his shirt and down his arm.

Matthew grunted with the effort but despite the desire to stop and rest, the only way to survive it was to keep going. Two pieces of metal, like the ends of copper pipes, stuck out prominently in the beam of light to his left and he pushed up towards them to see if they could be stood on. The pipes were jutting from an open cavity in the wall, exposed by having been dug around in the way a ribcage is explored by vultures. But from where he was perched a foot or two below the hole, Matthew thought it did not have quite the same quality as the passage he was ascending. It looked more ragged, as though something smaller had made the gap. He slowly pushed up, lifted his head level with it and turned the beam in. There was a beat while he registered what he was looking at, and then the moving black-brown shiny mound of fur swarmed at him, pouring over his head and shoulders before tumbling into the dark void below as the rats fled their nest in panic. Matthew screamed, the sound inside the mask being amplified a thousandfold, and let go his hold on the side of the wall. The other hand instinctively reached out and flailed for something to save him, coming to rest on something solid in the mouth of the hole. He turned to it with wild eyes. Matthew Cotton was holding the half-eaten remains of a human arm.

He threw the horror from him, gagged and retched and fought back the vomit back, scrambling wildly up the chimney of waste like an ape stabbed by a spear.

Matthew was gasping and gagging, and his hands, lacking all caution now, tore at the wall's surface, causing great falls of trash that battered on his head like hail. He could no longer see where he was going, but the encounter with that nightmare-creature's larder had nearly finished him off. A frenzy of horror, claustrophobia and terror had overtaken him, and when Matthew's hands made contact with the solid roof of trash, his wits were nearly gone. There was no connecting tunnel. He was at the top with nowhere to go.

Matthew panted like a dog, an involuntary whimpering coming from the back of his throat. He stopped his mental and physical thrashing, and tried to calm himself and work out what to do.

It would be folly to try to punch a hole in the ceiling. He had no idea how near the surface he was. If he was not near then there was still the very real possibility of bringing the whole thing down. Matthew's eyes darted from side to side in the half-moon beam of light that illuminated the foul, irregular shapes of his prison walls. Where was he? In the centre of the hold? To the port or starboard? He closed his eyes to think and took in a deep suck of air. His lungs failed to fill. There was no air left in the cylinder.

Matthew Cotton opened his eyes and faced the fact that he was about to die. It wasn't true, he decided in that split second that seemed to last for ever, that your life flashed before you. His childhood was not revisited, nor his high school years, his apprenticeship at sea, or any of the mess of the stuff that made Matthew Cotton who he was.

Instead, for one blissful, fleeting, honeyed moment, he was sitting quietly, propped up in bed at home on a Sunday morning. Heather was drinking tea beside him reading a paper and between them Molly lay in the crook of his arm watching cartoons on the TV at the foot of their bed, laughing at the antics of a pig that was driving a car too fast. The sun was slanting in through the bedroom window and striking Molly's hair. He gazed at its shine, smelling the woolly smell that hot, clean hair makes, and feeling the shuddering of her little body as she giggled and squirmed. Her chubby finger pointed at the screen.

'The pig's going to crash into the pumpkin stall!'

Matthew was laughing. He could keep on laughing, stay in bed with Heather and Molly if he just gave in. Why didn't he?

He breathed the smell of her hair again. It didn't smell like hair any more. It smelled bad. It smelled like rotten dead things, like excrement and maggot-riddled meat, like the effluent running from an abattoir. Matthew opened his eyes. He ripped off the suffocating mask and his lungs were suddenly full of burning, acrid gas. His hands scrambled in the trash to his right and he pulled frantically at the viscous mess. Skin tore from his fingers, his nails snapping back to the quick, and the sharp points of things he couldn't see ripped deep gashes up his arm. And then his fist hit hard metal. Lungs burning, tears streaming from his eyes, he pulled at the wall of trash with the last strength he had. It gave no more resistance. There was no more trash. His hand had reached a rung of the Australian ladder.

He gripped the round iron bar and pulled his body towards it. His leg snagged on something and he ripped it free, leaving a bit of his flesh with it. The madly-swinging flashlight beam revealed that enough room had been excavated to the side of the ladder to allow him to climb.

Almost passing out, Matthew Cotton gripped the ladder and climbed with the speed of an acrobat.

Five rungs later his hand hit the riveted edge of the manhole cover. His arm went out to the lip. It was open. With his vision going, his head swimming and his chest on fire, he made one last effort and jack-knifed his body up and through the hole.

Cotton's head burst from the top of the small round aperture in the deck. He pulled his upper body into the night air, his mouth gaping like a beached fish. Still half in the manhole, he slumped forward and spewed up the hot bile from his stomach.

His eyes were red and streaming, his flesh was torn and bleeding, and his body burned inside from his navel to his throat. He felt he was going to die. But Matthew Cotton was not going to die. Not yet. Matthew Cotton was alive.

Heather and Molly would have to wait.

20

It made sense now. Perfect sense. There had always been a part of Esther that wondered why she had never wanted to have a man become part of her, enter her, take her, consume her. There had been plenty who had wanted to. But she was not interested in the casual, squalid affairs the men of her trailer-park life offered. In her mind the sex act had become synonymous with entrapment. She had watched her few girlfriends fall pregnant, ending up tied to some deadbeat who gave them a couple more kids before leaving for something better. Sex in her young life had boiled down simply to that act of abandonment, and Esther Mulholland was never going to be abandoned. She was always in control. One day, she knew, the act of sex would be a joyously liberating and intoxicating experience and nothing about it would tie or bind her to the life she had struggled free from. In that sure and certain knowledge, her abstinence had felt like no more than a minor discipline; no more taxing than eating properly or exercising. If she felt like it, she masturbated when she was horny, and made sure she never fell in love. It wasn't nearly as hard as the combined forces of Hollywood and women's magazines might suggest. Esther was not screwed up about her body, her sexuality or her virginity in any way at all. It was simply no big deal.

Until now. Now, as she gazed on the naked form of the most beautiful man she had ever seen, she realized that it had been for this moment that she had been waiting. She had already forgotten his name, but his eyes glowed with a recognition that needed no such mortal formalities.

He stood around six feet tall, and his smooth, brown face was as angular as if sculpted from bronze. Dark eyes stared at her from beneath a wide, curving brow, and his long, thick, shining, black hair was tied back with a golden clasp at the base of his powerful neck.

He took a step forward and Esther let her hungry eyes roam over his body. She had looked at pictures of such bodies in her teens in a porn magazine a gay friend used to steal from a store downtown. But even if the physique of the man before her resembled those perfect, wide-shouldered, huge-cocked creatures, there was a purity, a delicate fluidity, to the lines of his body that made such comparisons almost blasphemous.

Esther could barely breathe. Her desire was overwhelming as she stepped towards him. He smelled of spices, incense, the thin, subtle, woody odour that wafts in a forest clearing after a camp-fire.

To give herself to this man was not entrapment. It was liberation. She was already part of him. She knew what he had been through, had seen his life, understood the triumph in his heart. Only one tiny voice in her own soul protested that she should not proceed. It told her to listen to the things she knew, the special things that this intoxicating state of grace was telling her. But the blessed silence that had descended on that racket of unwanted knowledge since she'd entered the cabin was like having pain relieved. That, and the combination of her desire, smothered and silenced the protest.

He spoke.

'These are the words you will pray as I take you. Say them.'

She watched his sensual mouth make shapes, his tongue move as he formed strange and alien sounds. Esther listened and repeated them. Her skin prickled and the sweat on her body dripped as she spoke. They were not words her human understanding could decipher. They were grunts and hisses, guttural rasps and whispers, and although their sound was ugly and disturbing, the passion they aroused in her made her almost unable to speak at all.

As he watched her mouth as she made the best approximation of the sounds she was able, she could see that his desire was as fierce as her own. As she spoke the last syllable, Esther removed her clothes and unbidden lay on the cold metal bench of the radio room, her knees open and hanging over the edge.

There should be ceremony, she thought as he came to her.

But there was none. There was just the act itself, and the grunted, delirious repetition of the words he'd taught her as he took Esther Mulholland without resistance.

'Get in.'

Renato had already pulled out the safety pins and undone the two cleats to release the lifeboat that sat on the starboard side of the accommodation block, but Skinner was glancing around anxiously as he waited to pull the lever that would let the davits fall down and swing the boat over the side. It was perhaps anxiety that had made the captain bark the order, but whatever the reason, it grated on his new first officer. There were already a number of things that were making him reluctant to follow any more orders before he had time to think. But the captain was pushing along this venture with a haste that did not seem logical to Renato. Even the choice of the starboard lifeboat was peculiar when the fishing boat was lying off the port side and the wind suggested to any seaman that the port lifeboat would be a more obvious choice. And the celerity of Skinner's actions was perplexing. After all, there seemed to Renato to be no immediate danger. Whoever had massacred Fen in the cofferdams was still locked in there. There was no way out. Now that Fen was cleared and the rest of the crew accounted for as either dead or alive, he felt a certain amount of relief that the culprit could only be a stowaway. Renato himself had made sure that door was sealed: the bastard could die in there for all he cared. Cotton was in the engine room under the protection of the crew, and only a drugged girl – who could do little harm without a weapon – was at large. So what was the hurry? What the hell had a Peruvian fishing boat to do with Sonstar's commercial plans for the *Lysicrates* and her cargo or in hailing help for her crew?

But the question that burned at the front of Renato's mind was what the girl had said about Skinner. Since her casual reference to the existence and purpose of some aluminium flight case, Renato could not get it out of his mind. What mines? Which ship to be sunk? He had tried everything he could think of to find a rational explanation for Esther's intimacy with his own domestic secrets, and he could find none. Why would her mind-reading party-trick be confined to him? Renato Lhoon was forced to make an admission to himself. He was afraid. Everything they were doing made no sense. He had no clear explanation at all about what was going on. He cleared his throat and avoided Skinner's eyes by looking casually out to the dark sea.

'I'm nervous leaving the *Lysicrates* with the girl still loose. Can't the skipper of the fishing boat board us instead?'

Skinner examined Renato carefully. He was already bored with this charade, longing to end it quickly, but now was no time to lose his cool. It was never time to lose your cool when there was still risk. History had taught him that. He sighed. 'I got my orders, Renato, and all I can think about is doing this quickly, finding out what the hell is going on, then getting back on board and getting my men home safely.' He paused for effect. 'Right now, they're all that matters.'

Renato turned back from his pretended interest in the ocean and looked at his captain. There had been such sad sincerity in Skinner's voice, such a note of lonely regret at his obvious disbelief that he felt a sudden hot stab of shame. He revered this man. He had admired him, had longed to be noticed by him for years. Now, because of an inexplicable incident involving a woman he didn't know, and the drunken exploits of a man he knew only too well, he was doubting his captain. Now was the time he should be trusting him. Now was the time when his career could really be in the balance. He had to bury those doubts and do as he was told.

Renato nodded in agreement then put his hands over the edge of the big fibreglass boat and pulled himself in. Skinner handed him the radio but not the gun, pulled the hydraulic handle and the davits shuddered into life, lifting the boat from the deck. All the time Skinner scanned the deck as though he expected company. Renato moved into the boat to make checks that were second nature to a man who'd been at sea most of his adult life. He lifted the panel in the middle of the boat to expose the small diesel engine, and made sure it was primed. He wiped a hand over his nose, moved across to where the first-aid and survival kit were stowed, crouched and busied himself with his silent inventory.

The davits clanked to a stop, fully extended, so that the boat hung out over the side of the *Lysicrates*.

Skinner was looking up at the chains supporting the boat, which was fortunate for Renato Lhoon. Because at that moment, the expression on the new first officer's face was no longer one of trust and obedience that was temporarily keeping him alive. It was a face that registered horror and despair, and most importantly, naked fear. But for now it was concealed and that was good. Renato would have to work hard to think before he stood up again and faced the man with the gun.

For now though, he stayed perfectly still and simply stared at what he had found tucked in neatly beside the first-aid box. An aluminium flight-case with a set of battered dog-tags clipped neatly around the handle.

The physical pain of the penetration was a sensation secondary to the white-hot explosion of the lock imprisoning Esther's mind. With her eyes closed in ecstasy, she felt him enter her, felt the bursting of that membrane more precious to him than it was to her, and the thin trickle of blood down her thigh. Her body arched back and she hissed in pleasure and release. The solid bank of insistent, feverish knowledge had gone. There was just her body, and the deep, satisfying ache of their act.

Since the moment she had entered the cabin there had been no Esther Mulholland. There had simply been desire, and the desire had grown darker as she had approached him and invited him to touch her. Before he had even penetrated her, she had been aching for pain as well as pleasure. She had wanted to feel what he had felt when he had been violated, and when his fingernail, sharp as a blade, had traced a teasing arc beneath her left breast, she'd longed to press it deeper, make it cut her, rip her.

But now, this second, her virginity was gone and with it the killing burden of her overloaded brain. She threw her head back even further and luxuriated in a long inhalation of air.

And then Esther Mulholland gagged.

Her body jerked as she gagged again and coughed. Her nose and mouth filled with a stench more foul than she had ever endured. Bile rose in her throat. She twisted under the flesh skewer that held her down in order to release the vomit that was filling her mouth.

Esther groaned as she retched. Her streaming eyes came open. Her head was twisted sideways, away from her lover. As she blinked away tears, her focus returned. She was looking at a deck cadet. Or more correctly, the corpse of a deck cadet. She had never been introduced to him but Esther accessed somewhere in a strange, dream-like part of her memory the fact that he was called Gaspar Libuano, that he was twenty-one years old, and that Skinner had shot him. But this truth was not the crammed, bulldozing fever of knowledge that she had been suffering before this release. It was a simple, uncluttered memory of a fact she had learned during that madness.

Everything had stopped moving, gone still. The man inside her was still. The stinking, fetid air in the room was still. And most importantly, Esther's heart had stopped as she struggled to figure out where she was and why she could remember something that she hadn't known in the first place. More urgently, what the hell was happening to her? Slowly, her head turned back to face the only other living creature in the room. The one that was inside her.

The noise that came from her was too deep to be a scream and too high to be a bellow. It was a vocal eruption of terror and revulsion that was beyond the control of the human being that emitted it.

The thing that was still joined to her towered over her body, its blistered, suppurating face wearing a leer like a slash in a carcass.

Esther thrashed, howling and screaming in a frenzy of primeval terror, bursting blood vessels in her throat. A stabbing in her chest held her firm. She looked down. A metal claw growing from a disfigured, half-fleshed hand was pressed against her heart.

The creature spoke, but this time even if her screams had allowed her to hear the words, Esther Mulholland would not have been able to understand them. They were no more than a series of rasping, phlegm-filled grunts, words that came from no language a human being ever could or should speak. But though the vocabulary was unknown, the meaning of the sounds was clear. The monstrous creation was mocking her.

Esther's eyes, crazed with terror, fell on the part of them that was still joined.

The pieces of flesh, skin and cartilage that hung together and had entered her body were so clearly not alive, so clearly harvested from dead men that at that moment Esther thought she would go mad.

The black, beady slits of hatred that were its eyes closed in pleasure as it pressed the shard of metal through her breast with a small and skilful twist.

The next moment was one of such confusion that she had no mental tool to understand it. All was insanity. All was death and terror. But as she watched, her mouth still open and expelling her screams, half of the creature's head was sliced away. She watched as a clean, rectangular blade arced over the top of the matted, fur-patched skull, and descended through it, removing everything from halfway through the left eye down to the collarbone. Even in her catatonic state of terror there was fascination in the revelation that the skull had contained more than one brain. Bits of the grey matter that had been assembled in the borrowed skull fell away as it reared back with a screech, pulling its metal and flesh weapons free of Esther. The slime of the liberated brains caught on the fur and hair protruding from its torso and slithered downwards as it clawed at its own body, and fell screaming to the floor.

Matthew Cotton had not aimed Becko's meat-cleaver as well as he might, but it would do. For now. Esther leapt up, adrenalin all but replacing her blood, her face deranged with animal fright. Cotton grabbed her wrist and hauled her from the bench, dragging her to the door as she gagged and vomited once more down her bloodied, half-naked body.

They were gone before it could raise its half-head, leaving it writhing in a black-brown fluid that pooled around it like an oil slick. And as it thrashed and floundered, its pain and fury was witnessed only by the dead eyes of two corpses, in the room where men came to make calls to shore and tell their wives they loved them.

Sohn Haro wondered how long it would be before the other men knew what he knew. None had tried to leave the engine room, but when they did he was wondering how he would be able to contain their panic. He glanced across at Felix Chadin and noticed that even the fearsome bosun had let his authoritarian demeanour slip. He looked as scared and confused as his men. It had been a long time since Cotton had disappeared through the door to the coffer-dams. Sohn knew how much time he would have with that air cylinder if he really had tried to find a way out through the holds. It was already way past that time. If Cotton was dead then what was to become of them?

He got up from the bench he'd been sitting on and walked to the open door of the cofferdams. What was in there? Fen Sahg lay in there, unattended, left like a fallen animal. *No man should be left like that*, he thought. He wondered what would become of his body and those of all the men in his care, when they lay in the deep, dark, cold ocean. Was Matthew Cotton incarcerated in some broken section of the holds? There was no answer to be had from the echoing tunnel of black before him. The answer was in his soul. Cotton had not found a way out. Why should he have? He was, after all, nothing much more than a pleasant but hopeless drunk. Sohn's short-lived belief in the man who had never showed the slightest hint of leadership in all their years of friendship, died in his heart.

The men in the engine room were still talking. Their voices reverberated around the huge room and the sound of their humanity plus the heartbeat of his idling engine soothed Sohn for a moment. He closed his eyes and leaned his head against the dark doorway to nowhere.

The noise changed gradually, before he noticed it. Men were talking more animatedly. There seemed to be a fuss of some kind. Wearily, Sohn straightened up and looked round. Standing at the top of the metal stairs, on this side of the open door to the outside world, was the hopeless drunk, the man with no leadership.

Matthew Cotton's face and body were cut and torn, his clothes splattered with dark blood. His eyes searched the men's shocked faces and found Sohn's. There was no reason to smile and neither man did, but the rebirth of hope was lighting the engineer's face even more effectively.

'We have to get out of here,' said Cotton. 'Right now.'

'Put it down.' The captain's voice was steady.

Renato's, when he replied, was not. 'What is this? What the fuck is going on?' He held up the flight-case as best he could. It was very heavy and the lifeboat was still swinging gently on the davits.

Even though Skinner was on deck and his officer was over the side on the boat, their faces were almost exactly level with one another. Skinner looked deep into Renato Lhoon's eyes.

'Just put it down. Carefully.'

Renato shook his head like a child. He was close to tears. 'No. I won't put it down, Captain. What's in it? Why should I be so fucking careful?'

Lloyd Skinner slowly raised the AK47 from his hip to his shoulder and pointed it at Lhoon. He flicked off the safety-catch with a considerable flourish. 'Because if you don't put it down, you'll die.'

Renato screwed up his face in misery and fear, but his grip remained tight on the case. 'I'm going to die anyway. You're going to kill me. Just like she said.'

Skinner said nothing. His gaze was unwavering.

Renato lowered the case and hugged it to his body. He sat down heavily on the raised fibreglass bench that ran athwart the boat, and a whimper escaped his throat. He wiped at his nose and glared at the captain, real fury jockeying for space in his eyes with fear. 'Why me? What have I done? Huh? Have I ever let you down? Ever fucking betrayed you?' He bent his head and shook it over his chest, the case held tighter to him than before as though it were a thing of comfort.

Skinner was doing some mental calculations. Renato was going to have to be executed now, there was no question of taking him to the fishing boat. But he had to get him to drop the case. One stray shot into that irreplaceable container and the last tattered remains of Skinner's plans were nothing more than straw in the wind. The smell from the holds was not helping matters, making him feel mildly nauseated as the night breeze carried the stench to him in warm, loathsome wafts. His patience was thinning. 'No, Renato. You've never betrayed me. That wouldn't be possible. That would require intelligence, analysis, a mental prowess capable of operating at a level slightly above helping you decide which underwear is clean.'

Renato looked up with hatred in his eyes. 'Why Cotton, then?'

Skinner's voice was flat and sarcastic. 'Because he's such a talented, sober, responsible, indispensable first officer.'

'You're an evil shit.'

'Just put the case down.'

Renato stared at Skinner with defiance, shuffled his bottom to the back of the boat and propped himself up on the edge of the stern. If he fell backwards now, he would fall into the sea and so would the case. 'Come and get it.'

Skinner sighed through his nose, his mouth closed in a tight line. He cocked his head to one side. 'I'm interested to know how you imagine you're going to stay alive, Renato.'

Renato held his gaze. 'By keeping hold of this, you bastard.'

'And when I simply come aboard, take the case and then shoot you through the head?'

'You come aboard and I'll drop it over the side.'

'After which, of course, I'm free to splatter what little brain you have over the lifeboat at my leisure.'

Renato blinked at him.

Skinner almost smiled. 'Oh dear, dear. The reasoning powers of the incurably stupid don't extend much past the present, do they?'

Renato's mouth twitched, turned down and he stifled a sob. He bent his head to the case, his forehead touching the handle, and began to pray loudly in Filipino.

Skinner was irritated. The position the fool had unwittingly adopted was just about the most effective he could have chosen to foil any chance of Skinner getting a clean shot. He waited, thinking. Clearly Renato would be doing the same, although whatever he came up with would doubtless be pathetic. The smell from the holds was strong enough now to bother Skinner. He stifled a cough.

Renato looked up suddenly. Skinner studied him. In less than a second it was clear that the best the terrified man could offer was to be no more than a feeble attempt at a vaudeville trick. It started with Renato's frantic eyes looking straight at him with the hatred it had last registered. Then, as Skinner watched with some amusement, Renato's eyes began tracking an imaginary moving object behind the captain, his face melting into an expression of dread that even Skinner had to admit was impressive. Renato's eyes were wide with terror and his mouth hung open, a thread of drool descending slowly from his lower lip to his chest. A deep, shaking sob made a groan creak from Renato's gaping mouth, as one trembling hand came slowly up to point at the imaginary foe at his back.

Skinner couldn't help himself. He shook his head and laughed. 'You dumb fuck.'

The imaginary thing that Renato had been tracking bit through the back of Skinner's skull, severing his spine and windpipe just below the jawline. The AK47, which had still been gripped hard in his fist, burst into life. Four of the wildly-sprayed bullets caught Renato in the shoulder, sending him and the precious case flying sideways into the boat and onto the floor.

Skinner's body twitched as the creature's powerful arms held it in place, the front of the captain's face still intact and twisted into a grotesque silent scream.

He Who Remakes The World fed hungrily on the man's living flesh, tearing at it and cramming it into the enormous mouth with the claw that was not busy tearing at the next morsel. Already the gash that Cotton had made had begun to close, but the damage was severe. It would feed well and quickly. And then it would hunt and kill. It needed more than just human flesh to heal its wounds. It needed to be whole, to be powerful, to be fully risen again. It needed that whore's heart.

The sweatshirt, pants and sandals were almost exactly the right size for her, which said a lot about Filipino men and American women. Cotton had grabbed them from the first cabin they had passed, and Esther had let herself be dressed meekly, offering up her arms like a child as he pulled the sweatshirt over her head, and holding her face up to his as he wiped a wet cloth across her hot, sweat-streaked cheeks. The clothes felt good. Warm, clean, soft and comforting. She hugged herself in the corridor outside the engine room where only a few yards away on the other side of the door, Cotton was gathering the men. Esther crouched down with her back against the wall, reluctant to enter the large room and face the crew.

Right now, she was simply trying to remember who she was. Not in the crazy sense, not in the way in which amnesia denies a person access to their own name. She was trying to remember who that girl was, the one who used to be strong, driven, morally assured and invincible. She had been damaged. She didn't feel the same any more. But this loss of identity was not a blanking-out process, not an attempt to forget the demented nightmare that she had just starred in. There should be no confusion concerning her role in that. She had been violated by hell itself, and she had escaped. The confusion was to do with shame, and it was a shame so profound that she was writhing in discomfort as she forced herself to articulate it internally. Esther Mulholland faced up to the truth that a deep, dirty, dark part of her still recalled and responded to a desire for the man that had been created in her mind. She was sane, she was bred tough, and she would recover from the horror of the thing that she had woken to face and broken free from. Recovering from the corruption of her own appetite would take longer.

She knew the truth. It had been an illusion, of course, but she knew for certain that the man she had ached for had really existed. That face, that body, that low animal lust had once been as real as she was now.

But what kind of buried sexuality did she possess that she found his lascivious evil and perverted hunger so attractive? That was not a part of the girl she knew as Esther Mulholland. But then again, maybe it was. She made a decision that it must be buried again, because remembering the sex was still too pleasurable, and the combination of that plus the horrific memory of what had been really happening, could lead only to insanity.

She lifted her head and breathed deeply. The ache between her legs was getting in the way of her thinking. It was stirring the wrong emotions. Because there were two things that she was focusing on, things that could temporarily blot out the nightmare and bring back the girl she was, and she didn't want them interrupted. The first was the student in her, her craving for knowledge. With a struggle she pulled herself back to her college studies. Esther had read with fascination and scepticism about the state of grace allegedly bestowed on sacrificial victims, pondering as she had plodded through translations of unreliable Spanish accounts of the victims' revelations on what primitive, hallucinatory drug the unfortunate youngsters must have been forced to take. But now she knew the truth. Incredibly she had been there, survived it, and more wondrous than anything else, she could remember if not all, then a great deal of what had been revealed to her. Some of it was useless. She had no wish to remember the childhood details of the *Lysicrates*' crew. But some of the other things ... it was nothing short of a miracle. It was hard not to wonder if such events had occurred before, if some victims in the same state had escaped the knife and lived to put their remembered knowledge to some use. She concentrated hard on this, the dark nightmare of what had just happened to her trying to win through and distract her. But with effort she dragged her tortured mind back to the shiny light of revelation. She closed her eyes and thought not of nightmares that could command flesh, but of the baffling line drawings at Nazca that only make sense when seen from several thousand feet in the air, the accuracy of the Inca astronomical interpretations, and their impossibly finely-masoned stones. It worked. She was excited. Thrilled. Even though what she had learned was going to be taken more seriously by a shrink than by a professor of anthropology, she knew truths that no other living human being shared. That would always be hers, and it was one of the most amazing things that had ever happened to her.

But the second thing that was keeping the night at bay was even stronger. It was an emotion that she always conquered, always denied, recognizing its destructive force as well as its temptations. It had been growing and gathering momentum as she sat and thought, and this time she was not blocking it.

It was hatred.

She opened her eyes and looked up as Matthew came back through the doorway. Matthew was not surprised to read the darkness in Esther's face, but what alarmed him was the urgent, predatory undertow of that expression. He would not care to be the one who had incited it. He put out a hand and offered it to her, and the softness of the fingers that wrapped so gently around his own was a million miles away from the black intent so visible in her eyes.

The noise. If he lived, although that seemed unlikely, he would never be able to get that noise out of his head. Renato lay as still as he could, almost blinded by the searing agony in his arm, and listened to the crunching and wet chewing noises that animals made when they fed. He had heard that noise before as a child. His uncle, who had kept pigs in an undersized pen in his yard, had once thrown them a dead cat. Despite his revulsion, the ten-year-old Renato had stood and watched the ugly, stinking beasts consume the mangled corpse, listened to the crunching of the cat's bones and the wet slurping the pigs made as they chewed. Now he was hearing the same noise. He clutched his ruined arm, concentrating hard on controlling the urge to vomit or pant for breath, and considered his options. The thing he had just seen, the thing that was still there, that he was listening to, should not exist. Such demons were impossible. But then since the *Lysicrates* had sailed from Callao everything in Renato Lhoon's world had changed. Nothing was as it should be, and now he was going to die. The question was, should he wait and die as Skinner had done, or take the opportunity and the very last of his strength to push himself overboard? He knew that in his condition, his shoulder torn apart with ragged bullet-holes, half his upper body paralysed with pain, and wounds bleeding profusely, the fall alone would probably kill him. And if not, the dark, cold currents of the ocean below would soon finish it.

Renato's eyes screwed up tight and tears squeezed from under the lids. He didn't want to die. He started to pray again, but the prayers died in his heart. The God he worshipped was not a god who created such abominations. His God was an ordered tool, conjured up and used to ease the burden of sin, or to fill the abyss of human ignorance with repetitive, meaningless chanting and liturgy. Such a god was of little use in the face of the inexplicable terror that chewed its way through human flesh on the other side of his flimsy fibreglass shield.

He tried to draw a full breath but a combination of the fear of discovery and the foulness of the air prevented him. Renato gulped a shallow mouthful of air and realized at that moment he would be unable to take his own life. Such a course was not open to him. Everything in him wanted to live and the only course of action on offer was to wait and see how long that would be allowed.

He pulled up his good arm, pressing the shoulder against one ear and curving the arm over the top of his head to cover the other ear with his hand. It blocked the sound. Like a frightened child, with eyes and ears closed to the world that was too real and too bizarre to deal with, Renato lay very still and waited for death in his home-made silence.

As the line of men and one woman filed up the stairs of the accommodation block, the silence was unnatural and unsettling. Matthew had cautioned them to keep quiet but without telling them why, and they walked behind him like frightened school-children, the only noise being the shuffle and clicking of their shoes on the sticky metal floor. At Cotton's request Sohn Haro and Felix Chadin, as the most senior crew members, walked at the rear, and as they climbed the stairs Sohn thought about his first officer and what he had just endured to get them this far. There was so much more to all this than Cotton was telling them. But something in Sohn had calmed since Cotton's return, and it was not simply the obvious relief of their escape. It was the feeling that someone he trusted utterly was back in charge.

He lifted his face to the stairwell where the stench of the trash was increasing as the men climbed, and decided that it was good to have a man like Cotton back again from wherever he'd been these last few years. It was good to have a man you would follow anywhere.

It seemed an age. The breeze rocked the boat as gently as a cradle as the blood oozed slowly from his wounds. Renato took in air in shallow snorts, the quietest he could manage, and listened to the blood rushing in his padded ears. The boat shuddered and swung with a new weight. Renato did not need to look up to know it had been boarded. There was little point in his silence now, and with eyes still closed Renato Lhoon let out a howl of terror, pain and abandonment that liquefied his heart. When the first touch to his arm came he jerked and scrambled as though electrocuted, and only the slow realization that the touch was like the grip of a human hand made him cease his struggling, open his eyes and face his fate.

Renato was staring into the face of Parren Sionosa, who was making cooing noises and patting a calming motion in the air with his free hand. Behind him were the stony, shocked faces of two

more crew members. Renato gulped and gasped for a moment
and then, open-mouthed and wild-eyed, he began to cry.

No one had touched the guns that lay amongst the bloody remains
of Captain Lloyd Daniel Skinner. Only Esther stood looking impassively at the gore that was spread around the deck, her gaze
unflinching as she took in the ragged body parts that still adhered
to clothing, and the shattered bones that had been snapped
unevenly like wet twigs. The handgun lay blood-soaked in the
middle of the mess where it had dropped from Skinner's pocket,
and the AK47 had spun off to the edge of the deck, still flecked
with the strips of skin that had been torn from Skinner's trigger
finger.

While men attended to Renato's wounds as best they could,
Cotton continued his hurried evacuation of the rest of the shocked
and terrified crew into the lifeboat. Apart from himself and Esther
there were eighteen souls left alive on the *Lysicrates*. Since the
lifeboat took thirty-six there was blessedly no need to launch the
other. But even a tub like the *Lysicrates* had more lifesaving space
than it could ever use. Apart from the portside lifeboat, there was
an emergency life-raft at the stern, a small capsule that could be
launched explosively in one movement and inflated on contact
with the water. In theory they were in good shape for getting off
this nightmare. In practice, Matthew Cotton wondered where in
the whole world they could go to be safe now that hell had opened
its gates.

Several of the younger crew were crying with fear and Sohn
and Chadin did their best in conquering their own terror in order
to calm them. Manuel, the third engineer, was the last to be herded
on board the swinging boat and Cotton turned to put a hand out
for Esther.

She was still staring into the mire.

'Come on. Let's go,' he said softly.

Esther looked up as if from a dream. 'Go where?'

'Just get in the boat, Esther.'

His voice was gentle, full of kindness and sympathy, but his
body language betrayed a frustration that was nearing breaking
point.

Esther looked at the men on the boat and then back to the

bloody mess on the deck. 'And you think you'll be safe from it just because you're on a different vessel?'

'Yes,' lied Cotton, moving closer to her so that the men couldn't hear their exchange.

She shook her head. 'It'll hunt us all down.'

Cotton glanced back at the boat. No one, thank God, was listening. The men were all in their private hells. 'How? We just leave this boat and then blow the fucking thing out the water.'

Esther smiled sardonically. 'Sure. It'll just stay right here while we do that.'

'You're saying this bastard can swim?'

'I'm telling you that not only can it swim, if it wanted to it could drop three miles to the ocean floor, walk along the fucking sea bed and meet us in Callao.'

Matthew scanned her to see if she was serious. She was.

'I've been in its head, Matthew.'

'We can get to shore. Get help.'

Esther looked at him and her eyes told him that the girl that had boarded this ship had aged a lifetime. 'You saw it, Matthew. You know I'm right.'

He nodded. 'I've no choice. I need to try and save these men.'

'I have a choice.'

Cotton put his hands on her upper arms. He felt the hardness of her muscles beneath his fingers. 'Esther. You need time to recover.'

Her eyes hardened. He removed his hands. Esther held his gaze though her own was softening a little. 'No. You need to listen to me now, Matthew, and you need to listen carefully.'

He said nothing and she nodded as she took his silence to be one of complicity.

'The combination on the flight-case that you'll find on the boat is 4014. It's on the dog-tags. It's part of Mendez's serial number. When you open the case you'll see two small metal panels and a key in a pocket between them. When you need to detonate you pull the aerial out to its full extent, put the key in the hole above the right-hand panel. Turn it clockwise until you hear a click, then press both black buttons on the panel simultaneously. A light will come on and start flashing red. It gives you thirty seconds to abort, which it does automatically unless you proceed.

Press both buttons again simultaneously any time within the thirty seconds to detonate. If you miss the chance within the thirty seconds you have to remove the key and start again.' She looked at his crumpled face. 'It's simple. It's not a particularly modern device. It's just what he was comfortable with. But you need to be no more than one mile away for the radio signal to be fully reliable.'

Matthew's mouth was dry. He croaked, a catch in his voice. 'You still know impossible things.'

She shook her head. 'No. I just remember some of the impossible things I knew.'

Matthew's gaze was hungry, and Esther knew exactly where that hunger lay. She looked down before he could ask her to tell him things she had no wish to know, no business to remember. Instinctively he understood her reaction, and clearing his throat he took a moment, fought back his tears and regained his composure. 'Why tell me this? You can detonate Skinner's mines as well as I can once we set sail.'

She looked back up. 'I'm not coming.'

'The fuck you're not.'

It was Esther's turn to take Matthew by the arms. But her grip was not for his comfort. It verged on the painful. 'Listen, Matthew. You just said it. You said you've got no choice. You have to try and save these men's lives. If I come with you, that thing is not going to stop until we're all dead. We can't kill it. We can't outrun it. You've seen that.'

'Then what can we do?'

'We can contain it.'

Cotton looked away, hand over his mouth, shaking his head as though his denial would make it all come good.

Esther spoke quietly, but there was fire beneath the calm. 'Right now, all it wants is me.'

Matthew turned back and looked at her with an emotion she hadn't seen before. 'It can't have you.'

She returned his gaze for a moment then let her hands fall to her side. She turned from him, walked across the deck and picked up the AK47. Pulling the strap over her neck, Esther bent down and fished the handgun from the gore and wiped it on her sweat-shirt, leaving a bloody smear. 'It's not going to.' She handed him the gun. 'You might need this. Just in case your company man on the fishing boat decides to take his chances.'

He looked down and took it. When he looked back up again she had tears in her eyes.

'You get these men three quarters of a mile away from this floating death-trap. You radio a constant SOS and don't let that fucking fishing boat near you. I reckon it'll disappear pretty sharp anyhow when it realizes that Bluebeard is out of the picture. You give me fifteen minutes' grace, and then no matter what, you blow this fucking thing out of the water.'

He started to shake his head again.

She put a hand up and touched his lips with a finger. 'You have no choice. I have no choice.'

'I do have a choice. I can stay.'

She shook her head. 'You've saved me once, Matthew. I can't tell you how badly I need to save myself.'

He looked at her, struggled with the urge to throw her in the boat, then gently took her in his arms and held her.

Esther's body was rigid, unresponsive, and her inability to return his embrace made it impossible not to think of the reasons why her declaration was so horribly true.

'Go,' she said in a small muffled voice into his chest. 'And start the clock from now.'

The heart. That was all it needed. She had performed well. Even as she had spoken the words it had taught her, it had felt that final surge of power so near it could almost taste the final journey back to whole flesh. The fury it was containing at the painful and damaging interruption was boiling in its blood, threatening to erupt into unplanned violence. But it was not a creature of unthinking reaction. It had not been so as a man, and neither would it be in this new and temporary identity. It hung in the shadow of the bridge wing, clinging to the underside of the metal lip, and sniffed the air through the holes in its face it used as nostrils. Her scent was so strong it was practically visible now. She smelled alive. It ruminated on the order of the actions it would enjoy after it had performed this last delicious task.

It tracked her easily and purred at the back of its throat at how that clean smell of living, self-repairing cells, of healthy growing hair and fingernails, would shortly be replaced by the nourishing, cloying and sensuous odour of her death.

She didn't even watch the boat depart. As soon as she had helped lower it to the water, Esther was gone from Matthew's sight. Ernesto started the engine and the boat chugged away from the towering cliff of rusting metal that had been their home for so many years. Already the bosun was busy on the VHF calling for help and Matthew watched the lights of the distant fishing boat and wondered how long it would be before they started to grow even more distant. He sat with the flight-case on his lap, fingering the battered dog-tags that were fastened around its handle. What in Christ's name had he agreed to do? What kind of man left a young girl alone to fight for the lives of nineteen strong, healthy men, even a girl with an AK47 and a rage in her heart that could tear down buildings? He knew she had a plan, but that flimsy hope didn't excuse his madness. The possibility of opening this doomsday box seemed very remote to Matthew Cotton. He looked up at the retreating ship and frowned. As the lifeboat turned to port and chugged around the stern a dark shape caught Cotton's eye. He watched it go and then quickly scanned the boat to see if any of the men had caught a glimpse, but they were engrossed in their own survival. It was as well. How, Cotton wondered, would they have dealt with the thing that must all along have been silently watching their evacuation only metres above them? Something very dark, very fast and very agile, its movements a cross between a rat and a lizard, that had just scuttled down the side of the accommodation block, onto the deck and out of sight.

She couldn't use what was left of Skinner. It had been watching them all the time. She knew it, had felt its eyes boring into her. They were joined now in a way that would not please it if it knew, but that in itself was only of minor use. The trick now was speed. Esther burst through the door of the accommodation block and ran down the corridor of B-deck, her heart already starting to pound with adrenalin. The radio room was on the next deck up and she slowed as she approached the stairwell, only too well aware of the variety of planes the bastard could come from. The safety-catch had been off the gun since she'd picked it up, and her finger stayed poised on the trigger. But there was no possibility of Esther firing in error. This is what she had trained for. Not just at camp, but her whole motherless, loveless, hard, uncompromising life. She kept low, glanced around and proceeded up the stairs as quickly as she could while covering her back. At the top of the landing the corridor ran both to the right and left.

The radio room was to the right, but the left-hand corridor afforded a view past rows of cabins that culminated in a large black window. She moved forward, then halted. Esther turned quickly. It was fleeting, but her reactions were sharper than they had ever been. She saw the dark, damaged, hacked-open face appear briefly at the edge of the glass, and before the foul torso could follow it on its course up the metal cliff outside, she let go a round of bullets that made the window explode.

'Fuck you!'

Esther was gone before the glass had settled, not waiting to see if her handiwork had yielded results. She ran on, the gun held at an angle that could shoot behind her, and burst into the radio room. There they were. The corpses of two innocent men, one intact, one half-eaten, lay sprawled on the floor of the cabin. Esther put a hand to her head, trying to block out the stuff she remembered about them from her brush with supernature. This was not a time to dwell on the personal details of these men and their families. Those men were gone. All that remained was this mess of skin and bone and flesh, the stuff that already had the sweet odour of decay, the way that bodies in heat always have. What she was about to do was not to defile them, but to avenge them. She took a deep shuddering breath, and with her shooting hand still reassuringly around the trigger and her face towards the door, she dipped her other hand into the slime that had once been Pasqual Sanquiloa's body. She would have liked to have closed her eyes in disgust as she smeared her face and body with the internal juices, feces and unclotted blood of the man who lay before her. But closing her eyes for even a second now would be suicide. Instead, Esther Mulholland kept her eyes open, and only the slight, down-turned tremble of her mouth would alert an onlooker to the fact that the girl inside this warrior, painting herself for battle, wanted to run screaming as far away as she could get from the stink of death in which she was bathing.

Hatred was life itself. But that truth was only part of the dark secrets it had learned in the timeless, indifferent, pumping heart of the jungle. It had been hatred that had kept it intact and brought it back from the brink of the abyss, but right now it was hatred distilled into revenge that was charging its stolen blood. The bitch had missed its torso with her weapon, but a bullet had torn away a piece of flesh from its newly-repaired neck.

It hung from the metal wall on one arm and fingered the wound. A memory came back from its days as a humble, mortal priest, and it chewed it over as it squirmed under the impossible healing process that was fuelled only by its dark prayers and ritual.

The man that it had been had found such variety, such fulfilment and pleasure in killing, when he slaughtered those base savages in the deep, green, diseased world of the forests. The best had involved a mother and her two-year-old child, and it cursed itself that no such pain could be inflicted on this childless whore. There was no pain abroad in the human world that could match the agony of a parent watching its child die slowly. What else would do? It could consume her as she watched or, more entertainingly, it could make her eat herself. It could do so many things. Hatred, far more than love, was the very core of invention.

It swung through the shattered window into the corridor and took a moment to let the flesh of its neck join once more. Then it lifted its head and followed the heady scent of her living flesh along the corridor to the cabin that had temporarily been its larder.

It was just a distant, indistinct crackle of a voice but it was enough to excite the quiet tension on the boat. Felix Chadin had taken his orders from Cotton seriously, despite their baffling nature, to ignore any hailing from the boat in sight called *Lucky Lad*. It hadn't been necessary. Not long after he had started to put out a distress call, the boat had not only remained silent but had moved off and was now almost out of line of sight.

This new transmission was from something they couldn't see yet. A container ship, Chadin thought from the garbled voice. But whatever it was, it was less than eight miles away. It meant safety.

Chadin looked up towards the *Lysicrates*, and despite the grim nature of their situation, felt the urge to smile. Sohn Haro, however, was not smiling. He stared down at the open case on his lap, the key to the detonator already inserted in one of the holes. The piece of paper that Cotton had torn from the log-book aboard the lifeboat was clutched in his hand. It was thorough of Matthew to leave it with Sohn before they turned back and dropped him on the *Lysicrates*, but he wondered if any insurance inquest would genuinely accept this scribbled note as evidence of the chief engineer's diminished responsibility. After all, Cotton, as acting captain now that Skinner was dead, was asking him to do a crazy thing, a murderous thing. What sane captain would ask his engineer to sink nearly twelve million pounds' worth of steel in a part of the ocean that could never be explored? What captain would ask him to sink it with that captain and the girl passenger still on board if they didn't get off in the next fifteen minutes? And all Sohn Haro had to prove to a tribunal why he would do such an insane thing was a torn piece of paper signed by Cotton reading, '*I, Matthew Cotton, acting captain of the MV* Lysicrates, *order Sohn Haro, chief engineer of the MV* Lysicrates *to detonate the mines planted by the late Captain Lloyd Daniel Skinner, thereby sinking our vessel, in order to preserve the lives of the remaining crew members.*'

Insane. Clearly. And yet Sohn Haro had every intention of following his orders. The ship contained evil and death on a scale that he neither understood nor cared to understand. The eighteen terrified men on board this lifeboat would testify to the madness that had overtaken the ship in the last forty-eight hours and Haro was not afraid of any tribunal. He was afraid of other things. He was afraid of what was on that ship with Cotton and the girl, and he was afraid that they would never get off before he turned the key and pressed the buttons as instructed. Because, make no mistake, in exactly fifteen minutes from now, that was exactly what he intended to do.

The dark power from having taken her was already burning in its veins. The neck wound had closed fully in a matter of minutes. It moved cautiously along the ceiling of the corridor, and as it moved it allowed itself the delicious savouring of the joy to come, when it would unite with its new disciples on the mainland that it could smell nearby. There was so much to teach, so much suffering to inflict that would build the momentum of the Dark

Sun's destiny. It would remake the world, and the world would be its to command.

It stopped above the door to the radio room. Her smell stopped in this room, and her last frantic thoughts had come from here only minutes before, garbled waves of panic and rage and revenge beating as loudly as a drum from the brain it would soon enjoy scooping from her skull. It had halted, however, because those thoughts had also stopped.

A blackened tongue darted from its over-wide mouth and licked at bared, pointed teeth as it thought. Her involuntary mental noise had been quieted once before. In this very place, when it had been feeding and she had approached unannounced. How had the bitch done that? It ruminated about that irritation, about how she must have learned that secretive cerebral control from the state of knowledge that it so jealously coveted but would have for itself so soon. And then it sniffed the air again. There was no doubt that she was in there. Her scent stopped. She could think herself invisible if she liked, but its visceral senses would always find her. It shuddered with the pleasure of what was about to come, then dropped lightly from the ceiling, and slithered through the cabin door.

Cotton had left the handgun with Sohn. What use would it be here? They had plenty problems of their own in the lifeboat. Renato needed help fast, and it sure wasn't going to come from the Peruvian fishing boat whose hull would not be painted, Cotton was quite certain, with the words *Lucky Lad*. He had watched the lifeboat chug away again, a hand held up to Sohn, every face in the boat turned upwards to him, and his heart had grown twenty pounds heavier. But there was no time for delay. He had to find her.

The boat had put him back on board near the bow, and he ran along the side of the holds, the deck pounding under his feet. Esther had given Matthew the greatest gift in the world. It was so precious, so unexpected, that the joy of it made him want to cry. As he ran, with the sea air blowing his hair, Matthew Cotton knew that for the first time since Heather and Molly had died, he wanted to live. He wanted to grieve properly, with dignity. He wanted to take full advantage of his new self-granted permission to remember them both. And he wanted to unfreeze his heart and mind, those organs that had atrophied almost beyond recognition.

Now all he needed was the chance. Living meant not dying. That might be hard. But he was going to try.

'*Come to me. Come to me, you sick fucking trash-bag. You nothing. You nobody. You worthless, powerless shit. Come and try to get what you need.*'

Esther was not saying this. Esther was thinking this. Thinking it as hard as she could, in that place in her head she had discovered that joined them together. The place that also told her so many things about her violator, things it would rather she didn't know now that she was still alive to use them. As she thought it, her eyes never left the door of the location in which she had now installed herself.

She was crouched for the moment, her right hand tight on the gun, her left hand digging around inside Salvo Acambra's corpse for anything liquid she could find. It was fully thawed and smelled almost sweet, in the peculiar way that human and chicken flesh share in their decomposition. The dripping of the blood and water from the hanging meat behind her in the warmed walk-in freezer was an appropriate accompaniment to her grotesque task. Esther Mulholland was unrecognizable. Her hair was a matted helmet of blood and gore, her face obscured by a red-brown mask of dried, muddy goo, and her entire naked body was covered with a mixture of fluid and matter that was unspeakable in its repugnance. The result made a figure that was barely human. Only the whites of her eyes blinked clear from the dark, putrid skin she had created over her own, as she continued to concentrate on her thoughts and not what her hand was doing.

'*Come to me, He Who Remakes Nothing. He Who Cannot even Remake Himself. Come, you low animal, you failure, you fucking joke.*'

And if the slight frown on her brow that was folding the crust of feces on her head and threatening to flake it was an indication of worry that these thoughts were not sufficiently focused, then Esther need not have worried. Her thought process was working fine. It had heard. It was coming. In fact it was very nearly there.

*   *   *

'*Vulcan, Vulcan, Vulcan*, this is the MV *Vulcan* calling *Lysicrates*. Do you read?' Several men cheered, but the sound was half-hearted, empty of any real joy. There was still too much fear, too acute a memory of the horror they had left behind.

Felix Chadin, the bosun, blinked at the VHF and looked across to his superior officer. Sohn Haro held up a stalling finger.

The *Vulcan* was closer now, but what to do? It would be as well not to reply until the deed had been done. The ship would come for them. It could probably already see the *Lysicrates*, lit as it was under the glare of its two dozen halogen floods. How would the captain of the *Vulcan* react when he watched that long strip of light extinguish as the ship up-ended and slipped beneath the ocean's surface?

Sohn shook his head to the bosun, and licked his lips. Their reply would have to wait a few minutes. He looked down at his watch once more, and then at the detonator on his lap. He crossed himself to a god he no longer believed in, then slowly held the tip of the aerial between his finger and thumb, and pulled it out to its full extent.

To be still, completely still, in both mind and body, was a skill that was beyond most humans, even the greatest martial arts teachers in the world. But to be still in the face of the horror that had entered the storeroom beyond the open freezer door was to call on a strength that transcended mere ability. Esther stopped breathing. Only half of its deformed, unholy body was visible from where she waited, but it was enough to skin her soul. It was on the ceiling. She could see the long tendrils of fluid and drool falling from its body like syrup as it moved silently across the top of the door-frame. The stench was overpowering, but Esther's nostrils were already assaulted to the point of insensitivity by the violence of her own adopted odour. She watched it as it moved with the cautious reptilian gait that hinted at abnormal speed and power, and kept her breathing for later.

Keeping that part of her mind that was the unwanted conduit blank was taking its toll on her reserves. Everything in her body and soul wanted to scream, wanted to run. But she knew it was working. She could feel it when it probed for her. But the best evidence that it was working was that she was still alive. For now.

She screwed her eyes shut for a moment, trying to keep her concentration, trying not to let her fear, her hatred, her humanity, leak from this protective shell she had created. She opened her eyes. The blackened shapes of its limbs were no longer visible. She allowed herself a tiny sharp inward breath, as silent as the movement of grass. But even as she took it she knew it had not been silent enough.

The freezer door frame filled with the bulk of a million nightmares, the darkness of its form blotting out the white strip-lit room beyond. There was no light in the freezer since Cotton had cut the power all those hours ago. It was dark, wet, dripping and foul. It moved a step into the huge metal box, and then Esther's heart moved into her throat. A sound came from it that was the very belch of hell. It sounded like ancient gas escaping from a burst and rotten carcass. It was laughing. Triumphant. The human figure that huddled against the very back of the freezer had tried to make itself tiny, wedged as it was behind two huge sides of beef that had been taken from the row hanging down the centre of the freezer. The arms, wrapped in a sweatshirt, covered its head like an illustration for the brace position on an airline safety card, and it was staying very still. The creature that laughed could smell the death-smell from the huddled figure, and it understood immediately what she had done to conceal herself so expertly, to mask her scent. It lowered its body, maggots falling from the furred portion of its back as it crouched, and moved slowly towards the object of its desire, towards the last beating heart that would fuel its black ambition.

Its massive misshapen shoulders brushed the hanks of rotting meat as it moved, sending them swinging gently on their hooks like the chimes of a glockenspiel.

It would remake the world. It would remake it as it wished, calling to its bosom all the legions of darkness it knew were waiting for its dominance. It pulled itself up to its full height, flexed its claw fingers and widened its gaping jaws into a crescent of slavering hatred.

'Fucking whore bitch,' it gurgled through phlegm and bile in a guttural language that its subject would never understand, although the meaning could not easily be misinterpreted.

There may be seconds, or fractions of seconds, between apparently seamless events that can never be calculated, although their presence is not just important but crucial. In this instance, although the next minute seemed to Esther to contain one single event, it was in fact subject to a number of things that parted into just such tiny, immeasurable divisions.

The first thud of the mines exploding in sequence from hold number one rocked the entire interior of the freezer, and as it shook and trembled, Matthew Cotton called out in alarm from the doorway to the storeroom.

'Esther!'

As the creature turned, Matthew's call was returned by Esther with a wail of despair and anger. But not from the back of the freezer. There could be no human reply from there because there was no human to utter it. Only the body of Salvo Acambra lay huddled behind two sides of meat, dressed in a sweatshirt and pants. The cry came from considerably further back, near the open door of the freezer.

'Noooooo!'

Esther dropped down from the meat-hook that had concealed her, the one that had been going to be her saviour, that was now no longer of any use since Matthew had blown her plan. And then she let go of everything the AK47 had to offer. She aimed first for its genitals before bringing the gun up to its head, watching wide-eyed, her teeth gritted, as its penis splattered into mush as the bullets burst its body apart. As it juddered maniacally under the hail of lead, screeching like a hundred stuck pigs, the ship heaved and lurched, tipping the floor beneath her.

Esther turned and scrambled for the door, the gun still firing behind her. It moved faster than a snake striking. Esther screamed in agony as the claws tore at the naked flesh of her leg, the gun firing directly into its skull. Cotton's hands grabbed her wrist and pulled, hauling her through the door as she left behind a strip of leg flesh the size and length of a neck tie.

She fell across the threshold of the freezer, firing randomly into the freezer and as she collapsed onto the rapidly-sloping floor, the creature's upper body, torn beyond recognition, dervished through it after her, screaming and bellowing in pain.

She had nothing left. Her hand loosened on the gun. Cotton pulled her to her feet, and with his hand around hers squeezed the last life out of the Russian automatic. The force of the bullets made the monster jerk back in an explosion of blood, and with the only thing they had left, the combined weight of their two bodies, they swung the huge metal door back and slammed the lock in place. The door dented into a hideous relief as the nightmare on the inside beat against it.

Matthew grabbed Esther. She was bleeding profusely, the bone on her leg visible where the flesh had been torn from it. Already the floor in the storeroom was at an angle that made running a challenge, but he dragged her out and into the galley corridor as the *Lysicrates* creaked and groaned in its death throes.

Getting the door open to the deck was almost more than Cotton could manage, but he wedged it with a fire extinguisher and dragged the barely-conscious girl through like a rag doll.

The fear that hit Matthew Cotton as they gained the main deck was different from the nauseating terror he had been conquering below. This was the real and palpable fear of every seaman. It caught his throat and made him heady with a whole new injection of adrenalin. The entire bow of the ship was already underwater, the white foam of waves breaking over the top of the hatch covers.

He fastened his arm under Esther's and stumbled for the stern. The life-raft was there. Her head was floppy on her chest but she was taking her weight, staggering along beside him. Even so, their progress along a tilting deck towards their only escape was an Everest expedition to a man out of condition. His feet slipped constantly, making them both stumble, and the lurching and creaking of the breaking ship made his guts churn. A sudden judder made them fall heavily against the rail and Esther gasped in pain as her leg-wound made contact with the metal.

'Shhh,' he calmed her without conviction as he scooped her up. 'We can make it. We're there. We really are.'

Twelve more metres of tortuous, angled clambering and Matthew arrived at the inner rail of the stern that separated them from the life-raft capsule. He laid Esther gently against the rail, her body wedged against the metal supports to stop her rolling down the slope of the deck, then leapt over and got busy. It took a man who had once been a captain only seconds to launch it, and as he watched it catapult out from the deck and onto the ocean below that was further away than it should ever be, he found himself making one last internal prayer. Its rubber roof bobbed about fifty feet below. It was a long way down.

Matthew wiped his hand across his face then turned, climbed over the rail and lifted Esther gently over to the very edge of the ship.

Esther looked up, her eyes opaque with pain. 'We fucking got it, didn't we?'

He nodded. He looked at this revolting spectacle, this woman encrusted in filth and excrement, caked with the juices of the dead, and he bent his head and held her face to his shoulder.

'Yeah.'

He closed his eyes for a moment, then looking up with a resolve that shone behind tears, moved them both to the gap in the rail, held her in front of him, his arms beneath her armpits, his hands locked around the front of her chest. Then, with a huge intake of breath, Captain Matthew Cotton jumped.

The darkness that swallowed up the sea when the last halogens of the *Lysicrates* dipped and died beneath the foam of the Pacific was useful in some ways. It concealed the tears that were running down Sohn Haro's face, and the wide-eyed terror in the eyes of the men, who had now focused their attention on the pin-prick lights of the container ship *Vulcan* that was sailing full power ahead towards them.

It also hid the face of the man who lay on the roof of the tiny rubber life-raft, a naked, bleeding, filth-encrusted girl held tightly beneath him to conserve her failing warmth, as he stared up at the cold white stars and willed her to live.

The dark could be healing. It could hide and soothe and soften the edges of truths too abrasive to stand in the cold white light of day.

But three and a half miles below the two tiny vessels that carried the last surviving crew of the MV *Lysicrates*, was a darkness that neither soothed nor comforted.

It was a darkness in which the very notion of light was crushed before it ever reached such depths, in which the cold was a solid entity, apart and different from ice, and in which nothing that ever fell there could ever hope to return.

But enveloped now in its crushing embrace was a darkness and a cold that was even deeper than the sea could conjure. And it would wait.

It had, after all, forever.

9 780008 158262